The Merrythought

FireCrest Fiction

Shelagh Meyer

Shelagh Meyer was born in Hampshire but, in the company of two sisters, a brother, and assorted cats, dogs, rabbits, chickens and the occasional pig, was brought up in at least six counties of England—ranging from Lancashire to Dorset—and was also educated somewhat peripatetically, at as many schools, of varying quality. She now lives mainly in Westminster, London, with her husband, an artist; they also spend stretches of each year in Suffolk and Greece.

Her novel *No End to Yesterday* won a Whitbread prize in 1977. The story was based on her mother's extraordinary upbringing and early adulthood in the 1920s and '30s. Written under the name Shelagh Macdonald, it is now being republished by FireCrest as a companion volume to *The Merrythought*.

The Merrythought

SHELAGH MEYER

FIRECREST
FICTION

The Merrythought
An Original Publication of FireCrest Fiction
An imprint of FireCrest International Limited

First published in 2008 by FireCrest International Ltd
62 Stone Street Llandovery Carmarthenshire

FireCrest
Fiction

Copyright © Shelagh Meyer 2008

Shelagh Meyer has asserted her moral right to be identified as the author of this book

Cover image: Courtesy of Shelagh Meyer
Cover design: Mick Cathcart
Typography and typesetting by Peter Brookesmith and Lesley Riley

A CIP catalogue record for this book is available from the British Library

ISBN
978-1-906174-05-7

Printed and bound in the UK by Lightning Source UK Ltd, Milton Keynes,
and in the USA by Lightning Source Inc, LaVergne, Tennessee

CONDITIONS OF SALE

All rights reserved. No part of this publication may be reproduced, stored in a retrieval system, or transmitted in any form or by any means, electronic, mechanical, photocopying, recording or otherwise, without the prior permission of the publisher. This book is sold subject to the condition that it shall not, by way of trade or otherwise, be lent, re-sold, hired out or otherwise circulated without the publisher's prior consent in any form of binding or cover other than the one in which it is published and without a similar condition being imposed on the subsequent purchaser.

This is for Phil,
with more love and thanks
than can be expressed in sixteen words
and
in affectionate memory of dear old Aunt Hilda.

And the end of all our exploring
Will be to arrive where we started
And know the place for the first time.

T.S. Eliot, *Four Quartets*, 'Little Gidding'

Prologue

LYING ON WHAT WAS shortly to be her death-bed, Grandma McIvor spoke privately to her eldest daughter Jemima.

"For almost all the time I've lived in New Zealand, this house has been my beloved home. I want you to know it will be yours, my dear. You'll be glad of the space. I know you always liked the idea of converting the loft, but promise me you won't bother. I looked into it long ago, but the floor's unsound and it would be dangerous—and far too expensive for you and Frederick to fix up." She almost smiled. "Besides, you don't like spiders. The only things up there are spiders, and my old trunk. Nothing to interest you." Her voice fell, and she murmured to herself—or so it seemed, for Jemima was unable to hear the words distinctly. What Grandma McIvor said, however, was: "Somebody will be interested, some day. Not yet. The one who—"

She fell asleep, but these were not her last words.

Jemima never did bother with the loft or the trunk, not only because she had always heeded her mother's advice, but because she had no room in her mind for expensive ideas, being married to an artist and with some of her four grown offspring still dependants. And the thought of spiders quashed any fleeting curiosity about her mother's old luggage.

Grandma McIvor's very last words, on a resigned sort of sigh as Jemima held her hand, were: "Poor Margaret, poor Margaret."

This was far stranger than anything that might be in the loft, for she herself was Margaret, and nobody had ever before known her to indulge in self-pity.

Chapter One

GEE WAS TWELVE YEARS OLD when she first wished her father dead. This desire had lain inarticulate for some time, she realised, for she hadn't been shocked when along came the wish, ready-made in solid, though silent, words. She made it on the Christmas turkey wishbone. Her father pulled the other end. As ever, he tried to cheat. But she was ready for that, and snapped off the larger share, triumphant.

"You cheated," he said.

"I did not!"

He snickered at her indignation.

"You should see your face, Georgina!" he pointed. "Shades of my self-righteous old Grandma McIvor."

This was his habitual insult for his daughters whenever they protested at his injustice.

She later wished, as she considered the pros and cons of wearing the winning piece of wishbone around her neck as an amulet—eventually settling on her private shoe-box of beads, bracelets, diaries and mementoes—that she had had the courage to speak her contempt. But she never did have that courage, ever; she was, she knew, quite despicable.

That her father failed to drop dead within a week didn't cure Gee of superstition, and she continued to make her wish at every pagan opportunity. During the years of early adolescence, when she still accepted that there must be a listening Omnipotence out there somewhere, she added regular prayers for her father's demise, as soon as possible please. Her reasonable view was that if the Omnipotence was really all-knowing, all-seeing and all-loving, *and* as vengeful as the Old Testament surely showed, he'd be sympathetic. Gee had absorbed this idea of a benign yet fierce Almighty at the Sunday school to which she and her sister had been firmly sent each week during childhood. Years later, she had realised, this was not for their spiritual welfare but to give their parents the opportunity for undisturbed sex. Once this really rather distasteful truth had struck her, the notion of a Deity no longer convinced.

After that there was nothing for it but plain superstitious wishing. Actual murder did briefly occur to her, but she recoiled from that in fright at herself. What she wanted was merely his *vanishing*. Ideally, he would fall suddenly, terribly, ill; or be the victim of a swift accident, dying instantly somewhere out of sight. Her feelings weren't straightforward, and defied her attempts to understand them. She would not have said she hated him, exactly. But there were aspects of him she hated. It would have been fine if she had never known, never seen, never realised; if there were not that look on her mother's face.

And so she wished. On the forked bones of countless fowls, on the heavy stir of Christmas puddings, on the first bite of every birthday cake, on one dank woodland place that her sister Jo (quite ignorant of her ambitions) persuaded her was a wishing-well, on stars, rainbows, tossed coins, lucky numbers, cracks in pavements, on absolutely anything that just might grant her yearning. For the rest of his life. Once in a while her wish was more benign, in the hope of persuading the Fates: he could go back and visit his homeland, New Zealand, and decide to stay.

Her father never even guessed at her disillusion. As far as he was concerned they were still pals, with much in common: and she brought home the kind of school reports that swell a fatherly ego; then, she became an artist, like his own father—and her paintings sold; she gained a reputation. He could only approve.

HER FATHER DID at last die, proving that wishes work if you are patient. That had been six months ago. He was ninety-one, the year was 1980, and Gee had waited over thirty-seven years since that first turkey-wishbone wish.

"HAVE YOU THOUGHT about the possibility that you might be repressing your grief, Georgina?" Jo had ventured, when several evidently sorrowless weeks had passed since Gee's dry-eyed appearance at the funeral. The use of Gee's full name gave away Jo's determination, but she was clearly wary too. Slowly, she pushed a mug of coffee across the table to nudge Gee's forearm. Her looming face, combined with the warmth of the afternoon sunshine penetrating Jo's living-room and flooding Gee's vision, bore down upon her. The room felt too hot and crowded.

The question had made her blink. Jo would always make her blink.

"That's *your* opinion, is it?" she replied dangerously, and was gratified to see her sister flinch. "Spare me."

She could declare she was glad he was dead, but of course she wouldn't. Jo breathed to speak, but closed her mouth.

Nonetheless, Gee had been sufficiently unsettled afterwards to keep watch in case a huge black parcel of loss, remorse and regret fell like a second cadaver out of some concealed mental cupboard. But by now she was certain it wouldn't. She had mourned him decades ago.

There was just one area of regret about his demise: the questions she should have asked. If only there were a phone box in heaven, or even mobile phones in hell, on which she might pester him.

SINCE THEIR TEENS both Gee and Jo had been corresponding with an aunt in New Zealand, 'dear old' Aunt Mildred, their father's only surviving sister, whom they'd never met. Their mother Miriam also wrote to the old lady occasionally with family news, the most recent being the death of Gee and Jo's father. Warm-hearted

Mildred, her first thought being of the bereaved children, had immediately sent notes of profound sympathy to Gee and Jo.

After replying with dutiful sadness, Gee had recognised Mildred as probably her last chance of climbing around in the family tree. Questions had followed; answers had come, some interesting, none particularly revealing. But one day, a paragraph from Aunt Mildred's wavering pen had seized and shaken Gee's memory and imagination.

Perched on a branch of the tree was a barely-remembered name, McIvor. Margaret Esther McIvor, *née* Moore—her father's maternal grandmother, Gee's and Jo's great-grandmother, she whose self-righteousness was her only heirloom handed down the generations. Yet here, roused to reminiscence by Gee's curiosity, was Aunt Mildred referring to her Grandma McIvor affectionately. What was more, Aunt Mildred revealed that Margaret Esther had travelled alone and very young from Britain to New Zealand, sometime in the middle of the nineteenth century. Now why hadn't Gee's father reported *that*?

Gee read and re-read Mildred's revelations. "My dear Grandma McIvor—your great-Grandma—was, as I remember her, kindly, but often appeared stern, but I was only fourteen or fifteen when she died so though I adored her I couldn't claim to know her properly. There were things in her background we were *never told*. If we asked too much we were hushed up. Her father (he was Charles Maximilian Moore) died when she was nineteen and she came all alone to the colonies to be a governess."

Infuriated with her father and all of an itch, Gee decided to search for Margaret Esther Moore.

TURNING THE HEAVY, crackling, black-inked registers of nineteenth-century births, Gee reflected that there were those who, had they known her history of wicked wishes, would be nonplussed to see her now, scouring these pages for her father's mother's mother. They'd be doubly perplexed to learn that she was also weighing up the pros and cons of Aunt Mildred's invitation to visit New Zealand. They might deduce that remorse and grief had caught up on her, and she was seeking out her paternal roots for reconciliation.

Not that she would put them straight with the truth.

A woman nearby whispered: "All these people, all these newly-borns, and they're all dead." She spoke with awe, possibly relish.

Gee, glancing at the pensive woman, caught the strangeness of it. Yet they were oddly romantic, these hundreds of names on thick sensuous paper, the just-born names of the long-dead, written with a dipped nib in large loops, more than a hundred years ago. And then it was not romantic in the least. Marks on dusty pages spelling out transience, decay.

Gee rattled crowded pages in vain. Margaret Esther's beginnings were not to be found. She must have been born before these records began, before 1837. Frustrated, Gee smacked together the last weighty covers. Too little to go on. A name, a father's name, an old aunt's vague memory of a watercolour of Rugby, some Scottish connections, and her own guess at the decade containing the birthdate. And Margaret was a common name: many Margarets mocked her, none fitted. Too often, in answer to questions Gee had fired back at her aunt about Grandma McIvor, Mildred had scribbled "don't know" or "can't remember". Now Gee would have to fling a wider net.

"You could," the young man at Enquiries suggested, "write to New Zealand's Department of Internal Affairs." He smiled and looked in a book, scribbling the address for her. "If you know roughly when she died, the death certificate would state her age. Might even say where she was born. It would give you a starting point." He added apologetically: "Of course, it could take weeks for them to answer."

Gee stamped out exasperated.

WHAT, ACTUALLY, had her father ever revealed about his past? What did she and Jo know? There had been occasional, nostalgic bursts, tales of hunting and shooting with his father Frederick the artist, a romance of two strong men foraging together in a rough and early world. And sometimes he casually dropped in his father's blood connections with British aristocracy. It could easily have been fantasy. Memories being, deliberately or innocently, creative: lives repackaged, misdeeds rewritten. She should know.

Once, in her teens, realising she knew little more of his mother than her name Jemima, she had asked: "What was your mother like?"

"She was a sweet woman." Sentimental wetness in his eyes had alarmed Gee. "Kind and gentle." He droned on about home-made jam and bread, chutney bubbling on the stove. Leaving home at twenty for a job in a distant town, he'd turned to see his mother, sad in the doorway—and was wretched.

But Gee's mother refused to tolerate that. "Come off it." Stepping briskly out of the kitchen, Miriam had clearly relished the way he jumped and flushed as he realised she'd been listening unseen. "You told *me* you never gave a backward glance, couldn't wait to get off to the big city and your own life."

He was on his feet, glaring, stalking out. Miriam had snorted scornfully.

"What was she like?" Gee asked her. "His mother. D'you know?"

"God knows. How would *I* know?" Miriam had spun and left, scathing.

Jo had felt similar curiosity one later day, and also questioned their father, mournfully reporting the result to her sister.

"She was a bit of a school-marm in some ways," he had astonishingly told Jo. "Cold, rather reserved." Jo described his posture: just the way he looked when in pain. She had melted with pity for him, understanding his suffering. She too yearned for a warmer mother. He had added stoically: "She didn't want me. I was an unwanted child."

Jo hadn't asked more. "I couldn't, I just couldn't," she protested, "it was too sad." Gee was disgusted at her sister's feebleness and lugubrious face—while glimpsing, dimly, that the answers were perhaps tailored to the questioners.

But now she saw, as she addressed a letter to an Antipodean office, that the chief occupant of her thoughts was great-grandmother Margaret Esther McIvor. It might be enjoyable trying to put Margaret Esther Moore into paint, perhaps as a very young woman, mid-nineteenth century. She would probably be wearing a bonnet and gloves and a decorously-buttoned dress, velvet, with a lace collar. It might help to draw her closer, out of that century and into this, for a conversation with Gee, comparing lives. Gee could indulge the feeling that great-grandmama McIvor was standing not far away, waiting, breathing, looking at her. And with an expression that was not even remotely self-righteous.

Chapter Two

ONE THING WAS CLEAR in the stultifying, moist weight of this summer afternoon. There was no such thing as the right time to tell Sebastian, if she really was planning to go to New Zealand.

Now or later, accusations were inevitable. Sebastian and everyone's, once the truth—which was never quite the truth—was out. Prancing off on this selfish trip on her own, leaving him to fend for himself, letting down this wonderful man. Sebastian was universally acknowledged to be admirable. All would say—with words, looks or silences—that she was abandoning him. (Well, not quite all. Her friend Caro wouldn't. But Caro was different, intuitively sniffing out the facts before she was told. Besides, she understood about staying or leaving.)

As if she were hauling herself up a steep hill, Gee's feet dragged along the tree-shadowed square. The air steamed, the heavy portfolio of sketches slithered under her arm, a plastic carrier bag in the other slippery hand thumped at her legs. Flying ants were lumbering creepily out of cracks in the pavement, roses fainted over the square's railings, dusty shrubs drooped their shoulders. She felt quite old. Everything was too late. Christ, she'd be fifty at the end of next year. Not, people said, that she looked it. As if that was the point.

A relief: Sebastian wasn't home yet. A message on the machine from the charity's breathy secretary let her know the AGM was running late. *The President should be home by seven-thirty.*

For godsake, did she have to make it sound as if Sebastian ran the bloody United States?

The house was quiet and cool, but this evening its atmosphere of neglect accused her. Dust, unwashed paint, a stained mat. You'd never imagine she had a regular cleaner. She should fire Marie, should speak to her firmly at least. She had cherished this house, had made it beautiful, but she'd abandoned it to an incompetent hand, like a bad mother hiring a sluttish nanny.

In a temper she dumped her portfolio and threw groceries into the refrigerator and cupboards, opened the back door to let in the scent of roses and slammed it shut as winged ants lurched brainlessly in. With relish, she stamped them dead. And wouldn't sweep them up, either, damn them. She wanted a shower, clean clothes, a drink.

"You're drinking more," Sebastian had said a few weeks ago.

"You can talk," she answered evenly. "You drink a damn sight more than I do."

"I'm doing my best for you."

He waited, but she had refused to ask what he meant.

As she zipped her cotton skirt and scooped sandals over her toes, she heard Sebastian arrive. Metal clunk of car door, voice of driver: *Can you manage sir? I'll get the front door.* Assorted thuds and knocks of entry, the driver's solicitous farewell, controlled click of latch. Gee combed out her damp hair and wound it up loosely, and thought about escaping quietly to her studio at the top of the house.

That was his briefcase slapping on to the hall chair. He was waiting, listening. He would see her portfolio and know she was in. The car drove away. She heard Sebastian moving towards the stairs.

"Hello? Georgina?"

Just after they'd met, he had said he rather agreed with her father about nicknames. It had been one of many signals she had ignored.

AFTER DINNER THEY SETTLED in the sitting-room, he with a newspaper, she with a book she had no intention of opening.

She spoke in a rush: "Seb—I've decided to go to New Zealand, maybe in the autumn, six to eight weeks. To visit old Aunt Mildred. She's invited me so often and she's the only one left of Dad's family, nearly ninety now—I'd regret it if I never met her. The college will let me take a sabbatical."

Sebastian opened his paper, folded it back on itself, and rested it on his lap. Then he looked at her without expression. "You're not inviting me, I notice."

Gee marvelled. How much pretence did he demand? She said: "No." Loathing herself, she added, "As if you would take that much time off."

He said: "And that's it, isn't it? You're leaving me."

The words sounded appalling.

"Aren't you? Or are you too much of a coward to admit it?"

"This trip," she compromised, "will give me time to think."

"Think. You think too much as it is."

As he advanced on the drinks table and hurled ice cubes into a tumbler, she wondered how often he'd said that in the years since they were married. As many times as she had voiced a thought that made him want to close his ears.

"You're going with *him*, aren't you?"

She answered miserably: "I'm going alone."

"You expect me to believe that?" Sebastian's mouth quivered.

Gee was swamped by pity, and sorrow for the people they'd believed they were.

"I'm going alone, Seb."

She floated, dislocated, hardly recognising the furniture, forgetting the sequence of rooms and stairs in the house spreading around and above her.

And there he sat, holding his whisky tumbler at chin level, looking at her coldly, sceptically. This man opposite was the one she had married in her twenties. Young-looking for his age, everyone said so: *Sebastian's worn well!* Usually she replied: *You make him sound like an old pair of wellies.* But, true enough, he'd kept his straight back: even seated you could see he was tall. A little heavier but lean enough, thick brown hair with just the slightest grey edging that people labelled distinguished. A widowed neighbour, over-wined at a party, once murmured to Gee: "He's *so* attractive, isn't he?"

The libidinous look she cast on Sebastian took Gee unawares, and she said, before she could suppress the lift of surprise: "*Is he?*"

"New Zealand, of all places," said Sebastian. "You couldn't get much further away. How can you treat me like this? You have become such a—such a *bitch*."

"Thanks." She too would have a drink.

"If you wait six months you'll be free anyway. Then you can go to him with a clear conscience."

"What makes you think he's still waiting?"

She hadn't intended to say that. What did he mean, *six months?*

"I'd wait for ever for you. You're a wonderful person." There were tears in his eyes.

Confounded, she said: "You just called me a bitch."

"I suppose you've forgotten it's our anniversary in a fortnight. Have you accepted the Robinsons' invitation?"

"No."

"You're not going to. Not even that little courtesy for my sake."

"I just can't stand the charade any more. It's so bloody hypocritical."

"Hypocritical? Not to me."

"It is to me."

"If you leave me now you'll feel much worse later on. You don't believe me, do you?"

"What, that you'd rather be dead than face facts?"

"The fact is you don't care about me facing public humiliation."

"Look. I'm going to New Zealand to see my ancient aunt before she dies. Which, at coming up ninety, she could do rather earlier than you're likely to. I want to look into some family history, and I'll be painting where my grandfather painted before me. There, that's the press release. I'm sure your public will understand."

"You should hear your voice. And what about me while you're away? Who'll look after me?"

"I'll arrange everything."

"Ah. It's all planned."

"No, it *will* be planned. For Christ's sake, Seb."

He swung his chair to face her directly; there was violence in his stare. For a second she thought he would threaten her physically. But she knew he couldn't. He was in a trap, and he had made it. And she hadn't stopped him.

That evening about two years ago, Sebastian in a fury had yelled a question at her; her answer had enraged him further. He had stamped out of the door, driven away. But for her, she knew, he wouldn't have been drinking, wouldn't have had the accident. And he'd put himself in a wheelchair for life. Too ironic for words. His most prominent public role, City directorships aside, was heading a huge disablement charity. His status improved no end. He never, not even implicitly, complained. How brave he is, they said, how stoical.

If anything, Sebastian seemed happier. He said to Gee: *You mustn't blame yourself.*

I can't leave now, she told Caro.

Caro shocked her, saying: *Sebastian is a satisfied man.*

PEOPLE LOOKED speculatively, pruriently, at her and Sebastian after that. Could he still do it? Sebastian could. His physiotherapist had tested which parts still worked. Gee had returned early one day, passing the small room that had been set aside for his treatments, hearing sounds that might well accompany exercise. The part-open door revealed the woman impaled on his lap, her great breasts hanging from her nurse's bodice. Both were too busy to realise they had an audience.

She made a painting of it, which had never left her studio, to make herself laugh. Even so, she remained trapped by his chair and her guilt.

SEBASTIAN FINISHED his drink. "And what do I say when you don't come back?"

"I don't think I want to settle in New Zealand."

"You know damn well you won't come back to me."

"I don't know *any*thing damn well. I wish I did."

"You can wrap it up any way you like to justify yourself. But everyone will know you're heartless, and you left me for another man."

"Anyone who knows me would know there must be more to it than that."

"Your parents had problems but they stayed together."

"Problems? That's a pretty mild little word for what happened. And you think that was right, do you? You think they were happier like that?"

"I'm not talking about being happy."

"No. You wouldn't, would you."

"You wouldn't have done this if your father had still been alive."

She stared at him as if he had struck her. Wouldn't she?

Sebastian said: "I'm going to tell people the truth about you."

"Please do. If you know it."

"Different from the stories you'll tell."

"I don't go in for stories about our marriage."

"Not even to *him*? Don't make me laugh."

"Not even to him."

His whisky tumbler hit the wall behind her ear with a crash that brought her out of her chair, bespattered. What must have been a tiny shard was stinging her cheek, but her hands were frozen. He had turned his chair and left the room before she found herself able to move.

Chapter Three

A DIGNIFIED PAGE within a creamy vellum envelope, addressed to Gee in a fountain-pen script reminiscent of the age when children were force-fed calligraphy, flew in from New Zealand.

Dear Madam,
    We have searched for the death of Margaret Esther McIvor (*née* Moore) in the General Registration Records of New Zealand. As you believe her to have died *circa* 1905 (basing this on your aunt's information to you as to her age at the time) we searched the years 1903-1907 to be certain of covering the period.
    Unfortunately there is no trace of such a person recorded in our death indexes for these years. We extended the research to encompass the years 1902-1909, as it is often the case that human memory, especially in the elderly, can be unreliable as to dates.
    But despite this, once again, no trace of a death could be found. In the circumstances, if you wish us to pursue the matter, we request assistance in our moving forward a generation in order to confirm the starting information. If you are able to supply a birth or death date of one of Margaret Esther McIvor's children, we might then be able to locate the relevant certificate, which should provide parental details that might well be useful.

For a moment, Gee imagined her great-grandmother, having beckoned invitingly down the years and teased her with the possibility of befriending her, was now deliberately eluding her, peeking out of the nineteenth century, mocking her. Margaret Esther had supernaturally destroyed all traces of herself, making herself more dead than dead.
    Watch out, great-Grandma, I'm coming after you.
    Aunt Mildred had been at High School, she'd said, was fourteen or fifteen, had gone to the funeral with her mother and two aunts—and Mildred had had to make their three black silk blouses. You remembered things like that, deaths and funerals, how old you were, what people said and what they wore.
    And hadn't Mildred written something about when her mother—Jemima—had died? Wasn't it just after Mildred's wedding? Now that was a combination of events you weren't likely to forget.
    You remembered deaths. Where you were, who told you. Gee was ten years old when Sam had died. Gee had never seen her mother weep before, and rarely

would again. But she knew that this was an aching held-in weeping, like her own, and the real grief would come later in some quiet place. How much better to be like Jo, able to burst into immediate sobs. Yet it was Jo who had resented Sam.

Odd memories stuck like scraps of pictures. After the tears, Jo's important, grown-up tone: *There will have to be a funeral, won't there?* Hearing her contained satisfaction, Gee had wanted to hit her. Their mother seemed not to notice. She nodded, looking down at her tea, hands at the sides of her face, like little walls.

Soon after that their father had started to do what he did.

That had been Gee's second experience of human death—though few would judge the first as significant as she did. That earlier death had become more poignant after Sam, haunting her anew, in a scene that could be relied on to leap forth fully lit in dreams or with the smallest nudge of memory. She and Jo and their mother: they'd been toasting crumpets on the fire; the smell and taste lingered. Their mother was darning socks leisurely, rounded with the surprise Sam-pregnancy, the fire splashing gold on her nose and cheeks. Wallpaper in beige and rose, frayed dark red armchairs, fire-heat on Gee's shins, a book on her knees. Jo was arranging balls of wool, their mother's needle was held up, threaded, and put to its rhythmic weaving. She was relaxed, the danger period was well past, there would be no miscarriage this time. And perhaps intuition told her that this baby would be the longed-for boy at last.

"Suppose it's twins," Jo had said, ever wanting to talk about the new baby in the months before it became the enemy. Jo liked babies; always, she'd been more motherly than Gee, more ready to hug and kiss the small and helpless. She would be hoping the new child would be an improvement on Gee. She was knitting a tiny coat; its exquisite laciness touched Gee and underlined her guilt, for she disliked the slow monotony of knitting and had not offered to try. Jo was, all in all, a better person than herself.

"Heaven forbid," their mother laughed. "Mind you, twins do run in the family."

One of Miriam's aunts had had twin boys, it turned out, and she herself had miscarried twins about three years after Gee was born. And then, so casually, the truth was spoken: "You were a twin, as a matter of fact." She had nodded towards Gee.

Nobody would have understood the physical shock shooting through her, the scramble in her mind. "Was I? How was I? How could I've been? You're joking!" She only half-saw Jo's open mouth and paralysed knitting needles.

"One baby was still-born, the other was you, that was how it was. It happens sometimes. One develops fully, the other doesn't."

"You mean," Jo threw a look at Gee, "*she* grew faster and took up all the room?"

"In a way," said their mother, quite blind.

Gee was sinking. But she saw no reflected sorrow on her mother's face for the dead baby. Perhaps they had been relieved—one more mouth to feed instead of two. They had been poor then: their father would sometimes remind them of his sacrifices.

"You killed it!" Jo accused Gee.

"Don't be silly," said their mother mildly.

"Was it a boy or a girl?" Jo continued.

"The doctor and midwife said it was impossible to say. It hadn't developed sufficiently."

Gee saw at once, it could have been a boy. They wouldn't have wanted to reveal that she had lost a son and gained a daughter.

"If it had been a girl," Gee asked carefully, "what would you have called her?"

"Charlotte, probably. Always liked that name." And, her mother didn't need to say, Charles if a boy.

The mysterious cavity she had always felt in herself. That sense of something missing, of a chair standing vacant. And of being inwardly, oddly solitary, even within the family or the jostle of school; somewhere, there was a hand that might grasp hers in understanding. There were many friends, but never the one she sought. Sometimes, she found herself standing in a street or classroom, suspended, as if she were the only person there, not knowing the time or her purpose. Her strongest sensation was of waiting. But for what or whom? Only now could she begin to understand. And the missing person had a name. Charlotte.

"*You* murdered your twin!" Jo could always win the moral high ground with those four crushing words. Once, their father had heard her and remonstrated—but with a smile. "That's a bit steep, isn't it?"

Nobody denied it, so it was true. Like a young cuckoo she had eaten all the nourishment and pushed the weakling aside. Her loneliness was explained: it was her punishment. The hollow place, the waiting chair, the absent hand. But she hadn't meant to do it.

Or maybe she had. Maybe sin was built in, long before consciousness.

Then, later, she discovered a destructive bent in herself—a chilly curiosity about death. She had drowned two green caterpillars in the bird bath, just to see if she could. It had taken a long time: the caterpillars were unwilling to die. Finally, sick with self-disgust, she had given their limp and swollen bodies a funeral in the orchard, muttering a guilty prayer. Another time, imitating the school bully's habits as if this were the only way to stop fearing him, she had hurled a stone at a singing robin and struck it. She must have struck it: it was gone, she hadn't seen it fly. Her hands tore on dense brambles, trying to find its wrecked body, but it was impossible. Sobbing with remorse, deep within her she had a formless understanding of the ability to murder. Of how a mindless idea, impulse or rage might defy control.

She'd seen no significance in the timing of these events, but she grew to realise they'd happened in the period after Sam's death, around the time her father had corroded her illusions. But none of that was in her conscious mind on the day she encountered a little boy around Sam's age, playing outside a cottage gate down the lane from their house. A new family had moved in. The unknown child, absorbed in making engine noises over a wooden truck, had hair like Sam's, wore a blue-checked shirt like Sam's. Some serpent stirred. She stood watching him, hating his healthy existence. Yet, she was not there really. Colours faded, hedges sank out of sight. Nevertheless, she spoke. *Let's walk over there to the woods, she said, I'll show you some birds' nests, I'll be your special friend.* What exactly she would do she didn't know; what she knew, if incoherently, was that she meant him harm. His mother came out in search of him.

"Jimmy? Come inside the gate, you know you're not to play out there." She smiled at Gee kindly. "Hello. What's your name, do you live near here?"

Gee's body and mind thumped back together. The hedges became green again, the sky blue. She'd answered politely and gone away ashamed and bewildered. When, decades later, the papers filled with the story of another girl of ten or eleven who had murdered smaller children, some little piece of her was unsurprised. More surprising was the intensity of others' disbelief.

Chapter Four

GEE SHUDDERED TO REMEMBER that long-ago day in her studio. Ten years ago, probably, and she had never let Jo in this room since. And wouldn't today.

It had started so ordinarily, that day, with Gee working, preparing for a new show, and Jo turning up unannounced for coffee. But Jo promised she wouldn't stay long, she just needed to talk a while—about Eric, of course. Gee had allowed the interruption. There had been bruises on Jo's neck.

They drank coffee, they talked. Jo was comforted and had been on the point of leaving when the front doorbell rang. Gee went downstairs, leaving Jo in the studio, and was stuck for a few minutes with a neighbour who'd lost her cat. When she panted back up, expecting to find Jo tugging on her coat, she could see at once that Jo had been turning some of the canvases previously propped facing the wall. Jo knew very well how Gee disliked that: it was akin to reading someone else's letters. But Gee's protest caught in her throat as she realised which canvas her sister was ostentatiously displaying—standing behind it, gripping its top edge where it leaned on her thighs, presenting the picture to the doorway for Gee's return. Jo's enraged mouth waited, ready to scream.

"How dare you? How *dare* you?"

Gee almost gave in to an old, unkind urge to laugh at Jo's penchant for melodrama.

"What are you doing, poking about in my paintings?"

Nobody, almost, had seen that painting. Only Sebastian had seen it, briefly, and that didn't count since he'd missed the point, not recognising the people painted there. She'd kept the picture in the same way she'd kept her portion of the wishbone, a secret talisman. Its inadequacies as art, which she knew full well, were irrelevant.

A family occupied the canvas, a pastiche of a nineteenth-century family group portrait. Formally dressed and posed, seated and standing. Ten people were depicted, most of them gazing out at the artist, against a pastoral background sweeping off into the Dorset hills and including the house where Gee and Jo had grown up. Their four grandparents sat there stiffly, included for Victorian respectability. The others were her father, mother, and Jo and herself in their teens, Sam at three, and Gee's twin shown as a baby asleep, or dead, on her lap. Jo was seated looking straight ahead, beautiful but blank-eyed. Their father stood between Jo and Miriam. His face was a leering smirk. His hand was inside his elder daughter's low-cut blouse. Gee herself was beyond her mother, staring at her father as if challenging him to realise he was being observed. Miriam was seeing none of this. Her gaze rested only on Sam. She clasped his hand in both of hers, as if she knew she was soon to lose him.

"How *dare* you put me in your disgusting picture without my permission?"

"I don't need anyone's *permission*, for godsake."

"I suppose you think it's funny. Do you? A *joke*?"

"It's none of your business what I paint," Gee had said quietly.

"It's my bloody business if you put *me* in it!" Jo shouted.

"*I'm* the only person, Jo, who was ever meant to see that painting."

"Nobody else has seen it?" Jo's eyes accused.

"That's right."

"I don't believe you."

"Tough."

Gee took and turned the picture, replacing it against the wall. There was a movement in Jo's arm, as if she would hit her, and Gee just managed not to flinch. But Jo flung her hands at her own face and sobbed, falling on to the couch.

"How could you *do* that to me?"

"I didn't *do it to* you. I did it for *me*. Isn't that what artists do? They paint, write, compose music, for themselves, and bugger everybody else. At the time—ages ago—it was cathartic. And if you hadn't started nosing about where you shouldn't, you'd never have seen it."

"It's *my* fault then, is it? Your dirty picture is *my* fault?"

Gee considered her sister.

"*I* painted the picture," she said eventually. "Nothing is your fault."

Jo was on her feet and shrieking.

"It's all right for you. You're the one with the bloody power in this family—"

"Power?"

"I've thought about this a *lot*. You've got power, and you make damn sure you hang on to it."

"What? Would you mind translating?"

"Don't you talk to me in that superior tone. You've got an *image* in this family and you *foster* it. It's you that Mum and Dad take notice of, it's you my own bloody *children* listen to. You've always had your own way. Top dog! The one with the money, the successful marriage, the great *career*. I'm just the bloody poor relation."

Gee's heart began to thump. How long had this been stewing, she wondered.

"*You're* the one that gives Mum and Dad the expensive presents. Don't you *dare* smile. *You* listen to *me* for once. You polish your image, you cling to your power. I'm not saying you haven't been good to me, and to my children, materially as well, I'll always appreciate that, you've supported me through my problems, and that's been good solid sibling stuff—"

Gee began dumbly to sort her brushes, and stopped abruptly when her hands started to shake. She wouldn't give Jo that satisfaction.

"—I've turned to you and I've depended on you, but that's what you *like*—isn't it? That's been the way you've *kept* it—admit it!" Jo was beside herself, yelling.

"You're younger than me but you act like a parent. You enjoy being in control. You *like* me weaker, you like me to be *seen* as weaker by everyone else, as emotionally *ill* even, because then *you're* the healthy one everyone admires. You're so bloody *rational*—clever with words and clever with your brushes, and you use them to keep me inferior. Look at that bloody painting—it's cruel. *You're* cruel! You've used your skill and *relished* an idea that you're better than me and wanted everyone to know it. I bet you've done other paintings of me that you wouldn't have the guts to tell me about. I'm creative too, you know! *I* want to write, I've told you often enough, but do you care? No! You're the one that *creates*, that *produces*. I'll *never* write, *I'm* the one who'll *never* do it."

Jo was beating her fists on the couch, beyond sobbing.

"Because of me, you mean." Gee spoke faintly. Her skull felt swollen. Her face was cold. Maybe her lips were blue, they were icy enough.

"Yes! No! That's not what I mean. I don't know what I mean. I just want you to *know* that."

Gee had seized and rejected possible replies. Was she actually so loathsome?

I don't know what you mean by power, she did not say. *I wanted safety. All I did was build a defence—a carapace.*

Jo cried: "I need to regain some power. I need you to lose something!"

"I don't know what you mean."

"You refuse to. You aren't going to give up anything to me, are you?"

"I don't understand——"

What do you want? she did not ask. *What have I done? I've just been.*

Her silence had enraged Jo the more: who'd slammed out, leaving Gee to sit unnerved and tattered until nightfall.

A long letter, densely-written in angry strokes, had repeated the charges and enlarged on Gee's "cold arrogance". She demanded "equal honesty" from Gee, and *please telephone.*

Building and demolishing likely phrases through wakeful hours, Gee had no idea what direction to take. It was days before she managed to pick up the phone.

She had barely said Hello.

"You've kept me waiting deliberately. Haven't you?" Surprise was a punch in the stomach. "You are *so* calculating."

"Calculating."

"And cruel. You knew I would be suffering."

"I didn't answer at once because I didn't have the words——"

"*You?* The *know-all?* You didn't have the *words?*"

Any restrained phrases Gee had rehearsed became a surge of acid in her stomach.

"Look, Jo. I don't understand. I don't recognise this person you think I am. I don't think you know me at *all*. What the hell have I done other than just *be* whoever I am? Whatever that is. And please don't lay it at *my* door that you haven't started writing, because if you really wanted to you'd do it. I'm not responsible for that. So

just stop being so fucking pathetic and get off my back." She stopped, appalled. Jo's voice cracked in sobs.
"How can you say such cruel things to me, when you know I can't handle it?"
Gee gasped: "You wanted *honesty*, Jo. *I* didn't know you couldn't handle it."
"I didn't know *myself* then!"
Gee couldn't handle it either.
"I'm not going on with this. Enough."
"You're slamming the door in my face!"
"Sorry. I can't deal with this—*hate*."
"I don't want to lose you as a sister," Jo had wailed, but Gee's sympathy had been burned away.
"Sorry," she said once more. And put down the phone.

She wasn't proud to remember that. But the door had stayed closed for some years before she and Jo communicated again beyond the mundane obligations of family life.

Eventually Jo had taken the initiative, opining that "certain things that happened are no longer important", and "we are on a better footing". A truce was declared. Gee could have disturbed the minefield, but she stood back, hiding her wounds, ignoring the smouldering underground. And the harshest wound, she now saw, had never fully healed. Her sister hated her.

GEE HAD LEFT the newly-reprimanded Marie sulking and muttering over a mop in the larder.

"I'll be in the studio," Gee told her. "Would you give me a shout when my sister arrives? Show her into the sitting-room, and I'll come down straightaway. OK? We're going out for lunch."

Marie barely nodded, and Gee realised that the morning's overdue lecture to her cleaner, laced with hints of replacement, had guaranteed an insolent greeting for Jo (*Oh it's you, the* artist *is messing about in her studio, wait here, she doesn't want you up there*) followed by an unusually raucous announcement up the stairwell. Jo could be annoyed: no frame of mind in which to hear Gee's news. *But dammit*. It was worth a little passing annoyance to keep Jo out of here.

Her studio had always been her retreat. A wide window framed the outdoor scene of tree tops and tiles. This personal landscape—her own section of London that she could dream towards at will, watching the changes of light and season—this would be hard to lose. A massed mixture of shape and colour, dirt and brilliance, concrete and spires, the glare of new glass, the soft green of mellowed domes. It didn't matter that some of it was ugly; those ungainly lumps, flats near Victoria, nevertheless belonged to her. Even the tower of Westminster Cathedral, that one hint of a broader hideousness, could provoke an irritated sort of affection, as for some ill-dressed old relative.

She had decorated the room in wild colours. *Talk about chaos*, Sebastian had said. But there was a certain design to the chaos if you knew how to look. Anyway, it was all hers, every brush-stroke: nobody else need understand. The same with the crowds of pictures, hanging, leaning, or waiting unfinished, the smells and textures of paints, rolls of canvas, blocks of blank, enticing paper, stretchers, brushes, charcoal, the whole damn mess. Hers. It calmed her. And now calm was needed, to get her brain in order before Jo arrived, to decide on her words. She knew only that afterwards it would be easier to tell her mother.

"And my damned father."

Swinging towards the canvas on her easel, she snatched up tubes of acrylic. Her brushes worked fast; she even felt laughter under her ribs as the thought arose: Suppose, just suppose, he made it to the celestial payphone.

"HELLO?"

Hello, darling. Georgina? I got it on the ether that you wanted to ask me something.

How does it feel to be dead?

Goodness. Is that your question?

No. I want to ask about your being a bad Daddy.

Bad? How could you, Georgina? We had such happy times. We were pals. Remember the kingfisher by the bend in the river, early on summer mornings? We went on our bikes. I painted that bike for you. Red spokes, rather original. We'd cycle out and explore places, and you'd collect dandelion leaves for the rabbits. Remember the tree full of willow warblers? The green woodpecker digging up ants? One day we saw an otter. Well? Weren't those happy days?

That was when you were still a good Daddy.

We sailed in the harbour. Nice little ketch, dark red sails, Mashouka. You used to like coiling the ropes on deck at the end of the day. You'd say: Look Daddy, I've made it all shipshape. They were good times.

It was you that fucked up the good times.

Must you use such coarse language?

Disgusting deeds require disgusting words. Why did you do those things to Jo?

What things?

I was in the next bed, Dad. You'd come in to wake her early for school. Every bloody morning you'd stick your paw inside her nightie. I *saw* you.

[But why *didn't* Jo stop him? How often have I asked myself that but never dared ask Jo? Why didn't she lie on her front? Why did she move like that, under his hand? Why didn't she shove him off? She told me she was pretending to be asleep.]

Nonsense darling. Your imagination. A dream. You thought you were awake.

Y'know, you're bloody insulting. The same dream, every morning? I saw. You thought I was asleep, you were meant to. And I still feel guilty because I didn't sit up and yell at you.

[Why *didn't* I stop him? Because I didn't want to believe it of the Daddy who loved me best and showed me the kingfisher and the otter, gleaming

in the morning light. If I'd yelled, that might've been the end of love. That's why Jo couldn't stop him. That's why she's furious with me and herself. No wonder she hates me.]
I think I'd like a bit more respect from you.
Now that's a shame. I don't seem to have any with me.
I think we should drop this subject. Do you have any idea what this call is costing?
Don't you *dare* hang up. I *saw* you, and *she told me.*
I was merely responding to beauty. If something's beautiful, I want to touch it. It was like stroking a kitten. She liked it. [I hear his leery little laugh.]
That's exactly what you said to Mum after Jo told her. I was on the landing outside your bedroom door, there you were, lying smugly on your marriage bed, smoking a cigarette, Mum standing by the dressing table, looking so old. You actually *laughed,* like just now. Fuss about nothing, *stroking a kitten.* She wasn't a bloody *cat.* She was your *daughter.* She was afraid you'd stop loving her.
It was completely innocent.
It was *sex,* Dad. What about *her?* Her feelings. You went on doing it, even after she'd told Mum—which *might* have hinted she was just a titchy bit bothered, what? *And* you did it in the car with her, getting inside her bra *and* up her skirt, don't you deny it, until she left home for college, and—odd, this—hardly came home again. *She told me.* She didn't tell Mum again—she was afraid Mum'd blame her. And *you* said: "We won't say anything, it's our little secret." How's that for innocence? It's a wonder you didn't go further. I suppose you'd stroke her, get a hard on, and then go and stick it into Mum or wank in the bathroom.
How dare you speak to me like that. Behave yourself. I'll ring off.
Behave myself? That's a good one. Piss off then.
You never spoke to me like this when I was there.
No, sadly. We all pussy-footed round you. Even Mum, in the years before acid corroded her spirit and you couldn't do a thing right in her eyes. You had no sympathy for her feelings or ours, but you certainly fooled us kids for years that you were soft, and Mum was hard.
I was kind to you!
Kindness got dirtied, Daddy. You were big, strong and adored, and you took advantage. Result—Jo never felt worth anything. Doing it to Jo, you did it to me too.
I never touched you!
You knew I would've stopped you. And as for Mum—she told me once she couldn't stand the sight of your hands after she knew. And she'd loved you so much. Do you know the state Mum's mind is in now?
Your mother's ill. Don't you dare blame me for that.
O silly me. As if you could possibly have anything to do with it.
Georgina. Please. I didn't realise.

Bollocks. You wanted, you took. And don't start blubbing.
I'm sorry, I'm so sorry.
Don't snivel, it won't help.
You despise me. Is that why you wanted to speak to me?
I want to ask about your sister Alice.

DAMN, SOMEONE'S at the door. *Knock knock knock.*
"Who's that?"
"Can I come in? Gee?"
The studio door moving. *He's going. He's gone. Oh God: Jo.*
"Gee? Is it OK to come in?" Jo was on the threshold, staring. "Who were you talking to? Gee—are you crying?"
"Heavens no, I just had a sneezing fit. I was talking to myself." She laughed, wiped her face and blew her nose. "What are you doing here?"
"We're having lunch, aren't we? Your daily—Marie—told me you were up here. She was pretty rude, practically *ordered* me to sit down. I wasn't having that, so I came right up." Jo sniffed.
"I wanted to finish some work. Never mind. I'll just clean up a bit. Won't be a mo."
"Can I see?" Before Gee could waylay her, Jo was around the easel.
"Is that *Dad*? Good heavens, he looks gruesome."
"Recognisable then."
"Is that you? Is that me? Are those babies dead?"
"You know I never explain. I can't. And, you know," Gee was carefully mild, "I don't usually show anyone things I'm in the middle of. That's why I generally don't let anyone in here." She smiled ruefully as she added: "It can be too disruptive."
"I *am* your sister." Evidently licence enough. But Jo did slowly move away, looking around the walls, beyond Gee's control. "That's not supposed to be *Sebastian*, is it?"
The physiotherapist's breasts hid his face, but the wheelchair was a giveaway. "Oh, how *could* you, Gee?"
Gee looked from the painting to her sister with a small laugh. She should be nicer to Jo. Gee knew, now, that she was the guilty one, the one who had let her sister down.
"Are you *laughing* at me?" Jo was already bristling.
"No. Really. Honest. That painting makes me laugh. Caro said it was Beryl Cook after Francis Bacon. There's a story to it. I'll tell you over lunch."

Chapter Five

THE NEXT LETTER FROM Aunt Mildred brought a dash of blackmail and a touch of intrigue. Aunt Mildred was in hospital, going home soon, after a hip replacement. But she sounded as spry as ever.

"I'm tottering about a bit more each day. Tough old thing, they call me. The physio-terrorist comes and beats me up regularly for my own good. I tell you, I'll be a New Woman with my hippy new hip!"

It seemed that Gee's cousin Pamela had been all for Mildred living in a home, being looked after "properly".

"No thanks, I said. I can afford the help I need. Besides, I don't fancy spending my last days with ga-ga old folk smelling of pee! Oh my, life's a cheat and just whizzes by...."

And then began the persuasion.

The hip adventure had made Mildred contemplate how little time she might have left on Earth. Now, instead of just thinking how wonderful it would be if Georgina could visit, she was "*hoping* and *wishing* all the time" that she'd come. Soon.

"I know—long journey, expense, and you so busy. I'll totally understand if you can't. But I just *know* it would be fun. And I'm sure I'll get better faster with you around because you make me laugh. Best medicine. Yes, this is shameless blackmail!"

She suggested September, springtime in New Zealand. Mildred would be settled back at home then, with her helpers in place.

"Come for as long as you like! Only one condition: you must call me Millie, not Mildred (too stuffy). I'm a modern old baggage. William always called me Millie."

Her next weapon was more vague, but irresistible. Mildred was delighted in Gee's interest in the family's history—particularly, that of Grandma McIvor's history—especially because she "just *might* have something very exciting *indeed* to report (and with any luck, to show you!) in the very near future. But I won't say more, in case I'm wrong and it's a dead end. Fingers crossed!"

Mildred ended prosaically with the information that Gee's cousin Pamela and her husband Daniel would be very happy to meet her at Auckland airport, hugs and kisses, write soon.

She wrote by return. *Perfect. I've booked a ticket.*

SEPTEMBER AND SPRINGTIME. Exactly what Gee had hoped for, the bright season of new beginnings. That's what she was telling herself. Look ahead. It was that or sink. And Gee was impressed by Mildred. Nearly ninety, alone, and evidently without a scrap of self-pity. She'd had her sorrows and disappointments—Gee recalled being told that Millie's beloved William had died young—yet had never allowed her losses to crush the daylight out of her. Being ninety-something and alone had never crossed Gee's thoughts of her own future, but now, with a qualm, she pictured the potential bleakness of her old age. At once she shoved the image away.

DEAR GEORGINA (or Gee, as Auntie Mildred tells me you prefer),
I'm your cousin Pamela, daughter of Alice. You might not know my surname, Forbes, my husband being Daniel Forbes. Auntie Mildred tells me it's definite, you're coming to visit N.Z.—she's thrilled and longing to see you. I admit I'm rather excited myself at the thought of meeting one of my (geographically) distant cousins at long last.

Auntie's asked me to post you a parcel on her behalf. She said it's to read on your journey, something to do with her Grandmother McIvor (our great-grandmother). She said to tell you this as further 'bait'—so you won't change your mind about coming!

The reason she can't post it herself is, I'm sorry to say, she's not too well at the moment. Within days of getting home after the hip operation she caught a bad cold, which went to her chest and she got a nasty bout of bronchitis. But don't worry—she's on the mend now.

There is absolutely no problem with meeting you at the airport when you arrive. I'm enclosing a recent photo of me and Daniel so you have a chance of recognising us at the barrier. I've already seen one of you in Auntie's album!

With best regards, Pamela.
P.S. Do please let me know when you get the parcel so Auntie doesn't fret.

DARLING GEE
(And fancy your not telling me that before. I bet your father didn't approve!)

Forgive me being such a hopeless old bag of bones, but you know by now from Pammy that I got a horrid cold and bronchitis. Left me fair worn out. Some mornings I've wondered if I'll ever get out of bed again. Much better now. Mind over matter! And I am so *thrilled* you are really coming to see me.

I've been wanting to tell you something *really exciting* darling. The story begins over ten years ago, before my eldest sister Rose died. She told me, out of the blue one day, she'd got an old trunk that used to belong to Grandma McIvor—Mother had had it tucked away somewhere, and Rose found it when Mother died. Rose said she'd meant to burn the contents (horrors!) and keep the trunk, or even sell it, but if I'd like it and was prepared to pay for carriage then I could have it. So I said yes, of course. But this silly old fruitcake had it put in the attic and what with my joints getting creaky I never did look inside it properly—spirit willing, flesh weak! Well, guess what. Your questions inspired me to have that old trunk brought down, and (pre-bronchitis) I started rummaging. Aside from clothes and other odds, there are books. Several seem to be diaries, many literally falling apart. The nameplates inside the covers are all left blank but I'm positive they are Grandma McIvor's journals, you can tell. I started reading the very first she wrote, as a child—and from the things she says it can't be anyone else's. Isn't that exciting?

It's that first journal that's in the parcel I asked Pammy to post to you. I thought it might be a good read for you while you're flying half way round the world!

And when you're here, we can sort out the rest of the trunk together. Darling Gee, I also want you to know I added a bit to my Will to make sure you get the trunk and contents. I love it that you want to know about the family. And the trunk's a beauty, all real leather, needs a good clean-up but it's a proper antique (like me!).

Lots of love, write soon, Millie.

P.S. The first journal, the one I'm sending, was begun on Grandma McIvor's twelfth birthday. The date is 10th December! What a coincidence. Also of interest for our searches—the year was 1843. So *now* we know she was born in 1831.

Gee stared at these sentences for some time. At first, momentarily, she felt giddy, while hairs stood up briefly on her arms. This was the date, this was the month, of her own birthday. Margaret Esther Moore had been born a century before her, to the very day.

Chapter Six

Her mother would be waiting for Gee now. An unpleasant tremor jittered in Gee's stomach as she drove into the centre of the market town.

"Would you have had the courage to do this, if Daddy were still alive?" Jo had asked over lunch, startling her in its echo of Sebastian. Before Gee could reply, Jo went on: "Daddy would have been *terribly* upset. I mean, you couldn't do a thing wrong in his eyes."

Saying this, she did not look at Gee.

No point in answering. Or in starting something, and ruining her own relief at Jo's reactions to her news. Gee's editing of the facts had achieved its end: there had been no reproach, no *Oh-how-could-you-Gee*, no *Poor Sebastian*. Jo had wept at the revelation that Gee's brilliant marriage was a sham, shored up by lies—although she claimed to have had her doubts sometimes. But she had wept more, possibly, for her own demolished dreams and mess of a marriage.

Gee's shiver of trepidation about her mother returned as Miriam's front door came into sight. She parked her car outside the pub at the end of the road, went in and ordered a large whisky. Home-made Bacon Sandwiches, said a sign on the bar. She could smell their saltiness on the smoky air, an aroma that always teased her appetite and, latterly, her memory. His voice, his laugh, came back to her: "You Brits have *no idea* how to cook bacon. I will now demonstrate how the real thing is done. Take notes."

If Miriam were to come to her front window and look down the road she would see Gee's car. But she would be fiddling in the kitchen, fixing details that required no fixing, preparing dinner for them both as best she could, using too many pans, forgetting what she was going to do next. She wouldn't forget the important thing, that Gee was coming; although she might have forgotten the time of arrival and Gee's vague explanation for being here, unexpectedly, in the West Country.

It still felt strange that her mother lived in a small house. But Miriam had never had the same affection as her daughters for the old family home on the edge of the town. Once their father's ashes had been thrown into the sea, Miriam hadn't been able to move out fast enough.

"I've always liked small houses, as a matter of fact," she had stated, declaring that for years she had coveted these elegantly-terraced Georgian town houses. "And you might recall that I've said for years how much I'd like to get out of that place. Far too much space and such a pig to keep clean. But your father refused to budge." Miriam's eyes had flashed accusation: "And you kept talking me out of it too."

None of them had been fair to her, and Miriam must have felt it, for she hadn't consulted them. She'd called an estate agent, thrown out furniture, and done all she could to demolish the past, before rushing to the town's cosy, hearth-like centre. After that, she should have been all right. But then, as she herself put it, she felt the stuffing go out of her. It seemed their father's death had robbed their mother of whatever had glued her together. While he'd lived, her unarticulated wounds, resentments and regrets had emerged as acid, cold disgust. Now there was no such release.

"She's depressed," Jo had said, "because she's got nobody to hate. She fed off her hatred, that's what I think. Heavens, Gee, you look quite shocked."

"I am. That's altogether too simplistic."

But she hadn't elaborated or argued. Jo's conviction was too great.

Such a short time ago, Miriam had darted everywhere like some little pebble-probing bird, always busy, quick, bright-eyed—except when looking at *him* of course. Now she stood still, perhaps unable to escape from all she had fended off. Her senses had fragmented, memory and reason seemed to have lost their way. She could still be lucid and sharp-tongued, but Gee had come to realise not only that Miriam couldn't have continued in the big house, she might not be able to cope in a small one.

The doctor had been vague, his sigh bored. Gee had asked, couldn't it be depression? He shrugged, disdaining a lay diagnosis. *Maybe, we'll wait and see.* But soon anti-depressants were prescribed. Miriam forgot to take them.

Now, Gee wondered, would breaking her news put more strain on her mother's fragile mind? To Miriam, Sebastian was a paragon. If asked for an opinion, she would have come up with the epithet 'ideal' for Gee's marriage. The way people did.

ANYONE WHO KNEW MIRIAM would know that this must be her house. A bright red door, shiny knocker, gleaming doorknob. Curtains draped, just so. An exuberantly healthy, glowing geranium on the dustless sill. The paint might have been applied yesterday; the window-panes held not so much as a fly-speck. Such glossiness was still important to Miriam. Would it be, if she were really depressed? Perhaps the tiny details were what kept her sane, were the last remaining bits of glue.

Miriam had been pleased when Gee had phoned. "Lovely, of course stay over. Not Sebastian? Never mind, it'll be nice just the two of us. *You* know what I mean."

Gee knew. Sebastian might be a saint, but men had to be tended.

Her mother looked worn, and Gee saw a new tremor in her hands. Once it would have been a few brisk strides to the kitchen, but now she went haltingly, saying *Thank you darling, lovely flowers*, and occasionally putting a steadying hand on the wall. Still, her spine and shoulders were as straight as ever, and her small frame as wiry.

"I know you like the yellow ones," Gee said. Her mother's white hair was pinned up clumsily, not her usual precise coil.

"Hope you like chicken," said Miriam, as if she hadn't known her younger daughter for nearly half a century. "I did a casserole." She put the flowers down on the kitchen table and looked at them. "Did you give me those?"

"Who else? Here, let me do them for you. Which jug?"

"Cup of tea? Coffee?"

"No thanks Mum. Wouldn't mind a snifter before dinner though."

"Ah." Miriam didn't approve, but she wouldn't say so. "Gin and tonic?"

"I hate gin."

"*Do* you? I thought I was the one that hated gin."

"You do."

"Can't remember what else I've got." Miriam sat, watching Gee arrange the flowers. Gee saw her frown, as if squeezing at her memory just behind her forehead. "I'll go and look."

"Don't worry. I'll go. No rush, I'm not actually desperate." She laughed, and her mother smiled. "There. They look nice don't they? Where d'you want them?"

"He never bought me flowers. Not once, in all the years. Said they were a waste of money, because they died. You could say that about people."

"Mean old sod," said Gee. "Here, if I put them on the sill they'll catch the sun in the morning. They'll look pretty in the sun."

"Oh, the *sun*. I thought you meant son. You know—s, o, n. I had a son."

"Yes Mum, I remember."

"Do you darling?"

The love and sadness on her mother's face. Neither Gee nor her sister had earned such warmth. Had she hugged Sam, kissed him, spoken the word *love*? Perhaps not, for Miriam had given love in other ways, without speech or too much touching. Perhaps as a beautiful birthday cake or an immaculately knitted jumper. She would say *darling*, and you would hear some gentleness; she'd wipe your forehead in a fever or your tears after a nightmare. But Gee had never known her, even when she and Jo were little, open her arms and enclose her children. Did it matter? It had mattered to Jo, starved of the right kind of touch, and she'd consciously made up the lack with her own children. It had mattered less to herself; she hadn't expected, so wasn't disappointed.

"As if I could forget Sam," Gee said.

"That's right. Yes." Miriam spoke as if acknowledging a widely known fact. She got up and went to the cooker. "Now. What was I doing here?"

"I'll give you a hand."

"It was my punishment," Miriam said into a saucepan of string beans.

Gee was halted *en route* for the dining-room drinks. "What was?"

Miriam turned towards her, her face older and more wrinkled than it should be in her early seventies, the hollowed cheeks magnifying the already large green eyes. Nobody looking at her now would have believed her twenty years younger than her late husband. A tragic face.

"What was what?"

"Your punishment?"

"Punishment. Really? What did I do? I haven't got anything on my conscience."

"I'll drink to that," Gee said feebly. "I see you have whisky. Fancy one?"

Miriam surprised her. "I'll have a small one. Then I'll set the table."

Gee returned with their glasses, and said: "Why don't we eat in the kitchen? Less bother for you than the dining-room. And more comfy." And she would feel more at ease, telling her news. "You sit down and enjoy your drink and I'll finish off the cooking."

But Miriam insisted on setting the kitchen table. Every familiar item involved a struggle of memory. Where for the napkin? The knife and fork were placed thoughtfully on the wrong sides, the pepper-mill was moved from cupboard to table and back again several times, with a look of surprise as if at an alien object.

Gee asked: "Have you salted these spuds?"

"Can't remember. Better taste them." Miriam sighed. "Memory's terrible. You'd be amazed. I couldn't find a cucumber yesterday. I knew I'd bought one. Then I found it in the duster drawer."

"As long as you didn't chop a duster for your salad."

Miriam giggled: suddenly her old self.

"Speaking of memory," Gee said, "on my way here I took a detour, went to see the old house. Last chance, I reckoned, before it falls into strangers' hands."

"Ah, memory *lane*."

"It sounds daft, but it was quite a shock to see the For Sale notice, bold as brass."

In fact, it had struck her as an affront.

Miriam almost scoffed. "Well, of *course* it's got a sign on it, what d'you expect?"

"Don't know, quite. Wonder who'll live there?"

"Doesn't matter much, as long as they pay the price." Miriam looked at Gee shrewdly: "Did you go in the gate?"

"Mm. It still squeaks. I felt like a burglar! The goldfish pond looks a bit weedy. D'you remember when Dad spent a whole weekend doing that crazy paving at the front and building the pond because he was sick of mowing the lawn?"

"And he dropped a paving stone on his hand and swore, and you danced about with glee."

Gee laughed. He had used filthy, forbidden words—and she'd thrilled at his transgression. "You said *shit*! You said *fucking hell*!" No speck of sympathy for his pain.

"Obnoxious kid," she admitted. "No wonder Jo used to call me hard-hearted."

"Sam fell into that fish-pond when he was two," Miriam said softly.

"With his best coat on."

"Pooh, who cared about the damn coat."

That was when Gee first learned that you could drown in mere inches of water, a puddle, if you couldn't help yourself. But Sam was fine, only startled. He splashed and yelled, giving the goldfish hell. He wasn't due for death just yet.

"So," Miriam said briskly, as if to rush past that memory. "What else did you do?"

"Oh, peeked in windows, looked around." Gee put serving dishes on the table.

"Ah, fond farewells."

"I suppose I loved that old place at first sight."

"I know," Miriam said as they sat down. "But there it is. Sorry, darling—I *had* to leave. And you see, with *this* house, it just felt like *mine* as soon as I stepped inside."

Gee nodded. "That's good then. It's funny about houses. You can go into one and just feel comfortable there: like meeting a person you immediately know you'll hit it off with."

"I reckon," Miriam teased her, sounding far more herself, "you lived more in your sycamore tree than indoors."

"In the summer, anyway. If I could've, I would've slept in it." Gee laughed. "I always reckoned I could think more clearly up there."

High in her eyrie, away from everyone.

"Maybe I should take up tree-climbing," Miriam said. "Might improve my state of mind." She smiled slightly. "But I feel better now you're here."

"Oh good." This seemed to be the time to take the plunge. "Because I want to tell you something—er, unexpected."

Miriam looked at her calmly, waiting.

Gee felt a little out of breath. "Seb and I have been, well, going in different directions. For some time. This trip to New Zealand, it's my way of making a new start. If you see what I mean."

"New Zealand?" Miriam had not blinked. "Ah yes, you said you might go. *His* family. They disapproved of me, those sisters." She put a tiny piece of chicken on her fork and arranged vegetables on it, saying: "Of course, I'm very sorry, darling."

"I knew you would be. So am I."

"Have some more wine," Miriam encouraged, for the first time in Gee's life. Perhaps she'd dropped her sniffiness about drink now she didn't have to see its contemptible effects on her husband.

"Everyone'll be horrified, I know. Everyone thinks Sebastian is wonderful, so I'll be the shit."

"Didn't mean that," Miriam said. "Fond of Sebastian, of course, but if things are wrong, that's not the point, is it?" She was far from shocked.

"We've had problems for years." To her mother's raised eyebrows, she added: "Since long before the accident. We hid them. From ourselves too. It isn't as sudden as it seems."

"Never is," said her mother, looking directly at Gee. "I did wonder at one point. You were hardly ever in when I phoned."

"It's complicated. We promised each other we wouldn't gab about details."

"Ah." Miriam never pried.

"I'm glad you know at last." Gee refilled their glasses with a relieved and celebratory flourish. "And thanks for not assuming it's all my fault."

Suddenly she knew Jo had thought it was, but hadn't dared say.

"Who said anything about fault?" Miriam peered into her glass as if into a crystal ball. "What matters is if you're happy. No point going on with something that makes you miserable."

Gee was astounded. What on earth had this woman done, if not that?

"If you have a choice," Miriam added, as if she had heard.

"Doesn't everyone? It's just you get bogged down and afraid. Think there's no way out."

"In...a...bog," Miriam pronounced weightily. "No, *not* a choice. Not always." She looked angrily at her plate.

Gee said: "It took me a long time to work out."

"Once, I met someone. I nearly then. I nearly."

Gee was afraid to speak, in case open curiosity chased away this fragment.

"Pah. Silly of me. He was married too. Frying pan, fire. You know."

"When?" Gee asked.

"When what?"

"When did you meet someone else?"

"Oh, long time. You were at school. After Sam. After——" Miriam's lips closed and locked. Then she looked up and asked an uncharacteristically direct question. "Is there? Someone else?"

"No," Gee said, and received a distant, unconvinced look. "Well. I won't speak for Seb. There *was* someone for me. But I found it so stupidly hard to... extract myself. Bloody fool." She wobbled a smile. "Funny, hm? You and Dad unmarried all those years when the world called it sin, and Jo and I both have this hang-up about the marital vows. Could there be a connection?"

Miriam frowned. "I don't see why. Your lives are your own." But at once her face was clear again.

"Shame," she declared.

"It is a shame, but——"

"No. *Being* ashamed. That's what bogs you down. And fear."

"Yes." Gee waited.

"So, did he get tired of waiting?"

Gee nodded. "And I let him go."

"Yes," Miriam said, as if she knew. "Was he angry?"

"No. He didn't reproach me at all. Made me hate myself even more."

"It would, yes. I did the same thing. Only I *really* made it tough on myself—and him. Went and saw him off."

Gee stared at her. Her own memories were too similar to bear.

"At the bus station, of all places," Miriam admitted with a wry, matter-of-fact grin. Gee found herself pushed to the edge of tears.

"Did Sebastian find out?" Miriam asked, neutral as ever.

"I told him. Early on."

"Ah. That explains."

"He doesn't know he *left*, though. At any rate, I haven't said so. Seb doesn't seem to have noticed that he's been living with someone half out of her mind."

"No, he wouldn't," Miriam said. Very briefly, Miriam reached across and laid her hand softly, just for a second or two, on Gee's forearm. "This other bloke, though, he's not *dead*. And where there's life— You never know."

Brightly, bemusingly, she switched the mood: "How's Sebastian doing?"

"He's fine. All in all." What else to say? "He'll be well looked-after."

"Does Jo know? She'll be upset."

"She was a bit. She cried. But—" No, she wouldn't talk about Jo.

"She likes Sebastian."

"A far finer man than her own dear Eric, was how she put it."

"Your father would have been sorry."

"If sorry's the word."

"*He* wouldn't have believed it," she almost sneered, "not of his own special little girl. He used to say, At least Georgina's got a stable marriage. Not like Josephine, he meant."

"That's all that would've upset him. That *I'd* done something wrong. Bloody hypocrite."

"He always liked Sebastian."

Gee was incredulous. "He didn't like *any* of my boyfriends. Or Jo's. Never good enough. You said so yourself."

"After you were married he liked him."

"He liked his success. His money. Someone else's filthy lucre always brought a gleam of approval to the old man's eye."

"Greedy pig," Miriam said vehemently.

"He didn't actually *warm* to Sebastian until he was safely crippled."

"What a thing to *say!*" Miriam laughed with pure delight. Gee laughed with her, partly enjoying her own spite: but mainly because her mother's laughter so changed her face, chasing out the years of pursed bitterness that had erased her prettiness and doused the light in her eyes. Her smile brought back the girl.

"Send me a card from New Zealand," Miriam switched tack again, "about those sisters."

"There's only one left. Mildred. Or Millie, as she prefers."

"Where'd the others go?"

"They died. Quite a while before Dad. Remember?"

Miriam was drifting again. "Like the flowers. On the coffin. Waste of money."

"They were pretty old. Millie's eighty-nine. I got interested in her grandmother— on their mother's side. McIvor. Millie's got some of her stuff, diaries and things, in a trunk."

"*They* said I was a floozy."

"What?"

"Those sisters. When his wife wrote to tell them I'd stolen her husband, thrown myself at him. Ha. No mention of the fact she'd tried to knife him a couple of times, well before I was around. *That Miriam, she's just some little floozy,* they said, *she'll leave him when she's tired of him.*"

"I hope he told them otherwise."

"So I couldn't, could I? Leave. They would have said, *Told you so.*"

Gee squeaked. "What did *they* matter?"

"Mildred might've been different. She wrote a nice letter when your father and I got married. When wifey upped and died at last. Remember?"

"You don't forget your own parents' wedding in a hurry."

But the marriage had been too late, the happiness had gone. Why marry? Because of what ought to have been? Her father said it was so Miriam would get the widow's pension. *So* romantic.

"So. You're off to New Zealand. Never fancied it myself. Tough as an old boot."

"What?"

"He was always on about it. *Why don't you buy New Zealand lamb?* And I said, tough as an old boot. To him, anything from New Zealand must be wonderful. Sentimental old fool."

"One of his sisters," Gee tried to drag her back, "looked like Jo, didn't she?"

"Alice, that was. *Sweet Little Alice Blue Gown.* Remember that silly song? Not that there was much sweet about *her.*"

"Alice, yes."

"Hated me, Alice did. She hated her, too."

"Her?"

"Your father's first wife." Miriam rubbed her forehead as if it ached. "Jealous. Green with jealousy."

She made as if to clear away their plates.

"Let me," Gee said, "You sit there. I'll get the pud."

"Treacle tart. Your favourite when you were little."

"You said you'd made apple charlotte."

"Did I? Well then, I must've. Memory! *Tart.* That was the other thing they called me."

When Gee came back, Miriam said: "You should've had kids."

"Just didn't happen, Mum."

"They would have been handsome. You and Sebastian."

"That's as good a reason as any for having kids. Sit them on the mantle piece as ornaments."

"You might have had twins. Probably would've."

Gee was jolted in a way she had almost forgotten.

Miriam smiled. "Two for the price of one."

Gee spooned out the pudding and pushed the cream jug towards her mother. Apple charlotte, little twin Charlotte.

"Was it true, Mum? About me having a twin? Did it really die?"

Only now did she realise: that she'd always wondered if they had given the child away, because there were too many babies. Too many girls.

Miriam put down her spoon and fork and, very slowly, placed her hands on either side of her face like little walls. Her elbows rested on the table and she gazed at the cloth, while tears flooded down her face.

"Poor little thing, poor little thing." Miriam's voice was a soft stream of pain. "Oh how could that be, why was it, that poor little baby, and then poor Sam, my poor little Sam, poor little thing. Poor Gee, poor Jo. Nobody could help it. Poor everybody. Even your father. Poor stupid, stupid bastard."

Chapter Seven

WHEN FRANK FIRST SAW MIRIAM, she was walking briskly towards him along the linoleum corridor between rows of office doors. He had first stared, then pulled up short, looking as if he wanted to speak. Politely, she stopped.

"Yes? Can I help you?"

"You're new here, aren't you?" he said.

She noted his short, dark brown beard and thick hair. "Fairly. I've been here a month or so."

"Ah. That's why we haven't met. I've been off for six weeks. Broke my leg playing football. Greenstick fracture." He looked quite proud of that. "My name's Frank." He stuck out his hand. "Engineering section."

In all her nineteen years, she had never learned so much about a person in so few seconds. She shook the hand, bemused. "I'm Miriam." She pointed along the corridor. "Admin."

"Welcome to Eldridge and Eldridge," he grinned. He was quite good-looking really, she observed.

"Thanks." She hurried on her way, smiling.

Behind her, he called: "You're beautiful!" She had stunning legs, too, he noted.

He was thirty-nine, and married. He had met his wife Anita when he had landed in London after six years before the mast. Romantically, fulfilling a boyhood dream, he had abandoned his safe banking job in New Zealand for life aboard one of the last square-rigged ships flying the red ensign. Unromantically, he saw what the pox and the clap did to some of his shipmates, and bedded no women in foreign ports.

By the time he met Miriam in Eldridge and Eldridge, he had been Anita's husband for seven years. He had started off liking her well enough. She was in her early twenties then, fair-haired, reasonably pretty, and a good cook. Many years later, he admitted: "I only married her because I couldn't wait to get inside a woman."

But Anita had married him for love—or at any rate, out of a fierce infatuation. And she wanted children. He got his sex, but she did not get her children. She became obsessed with temperature charts, and rationed sexual intercourse to selected days of the month. Spontaneity vanished along with frequency. He sulked, they quarrelled, he spent less time at home. After a while she became depressed, not washing her hair, not cleaning the house. He spent even less time at home.

Girls tended to flirt with good-looking Frank, and, seeing his flattered responses, Anita gradually became convinced he was being unfaithful. The more her suspicions grew, the more erratic her behaviour became. Twice, still in her nightdress, she pursued him down the street with a knife, screeching accusations. Another time she stood on a chair behind the door and beat him over the head with a heavy tea-tray when he came home late, shouting he smelled of sex. In her diary she listed the assaults she still had in store for him. He hadn't, in fact, been unfaithful yet.

After a few weeks of contrived coincidences and snatched conversations in the works canteen, Frank asked nineteen-year-old Miriam out to the cinema. And, a few days later, to dinner. On the third date they kissed. On the fourth he declared he had never been so much in love. He wrote her love-letters. And then one evening he confessed his situation. "The marriage is a mess," he said. "A mistake."

In a way, Miriam wasn't surprised: one of the office girls had dropped hints. But by then, she was mad about him, and reckless. They were both made a little crazy by desire and the excitement of the illicit. Believing they loved as nobody before had loved, they were sure they would somehow find a way to be together. Secretly, almost without realising it himself, Frank hoped Anita would say she'd had enough—and walk out.

Meanwhile, Anita stalked him. In due course she saw him holding hands with a beautiful black-haired girl who smiled into his eyes. Anita took advice from a friend. One evening shortly afterwards, seductively dressed, perfumed and voluptuous, she caressed him, aroused him, vowed her adoration, and took him. More than once.

Next morning—perhaps from shame, or merely exhaustion—he barely spoke. But at work he borrowed money from a pal and bought a gold ring. He asked Miriam to meet him at the back of the office block one lunchtime, where he slipped the ring on Miriam's finger, saying: *With this ring I thee wed, with my body I thee worship.*

A couple of weekends later they took a bus to Epsom Forest, walked in the autumnal woods, and consummated their homemade marriage. He would leave his wife, he promised. Their marriage was dead, she was crazy, she made life impossible, unbearable. He would tell her everything and do the decent thing, allowing her to divorce him.

"If you were to divorce me, or try to," said Anita one day, as if she had read his intentions, "I would go to your boss and tell him about your philandering. And you'd be sacked."

Divorce, back then, was scandalous, a stigma. People did lose their jobs because of it. He told Miriam: "I'm waiting for the right moment. I don't want her causing trouble at work."

Miriam, a couple of months later, pale with nerves, told Frank she was pregnant. "I missed two. But I didn't want to say until I was sure. My friend Beryl said she knows a woman who—you know—gets rid of— But you hear horrible stories…"

"And it's expensive," Frank said. "What about a very hot bath and half a bottle of gin? I've heard that does it."

It didn't work. Miriam was unspeakably, unforgettably sick, and never drank gin again. The baby hung on. "What are we going to do?" she asked him. "If my father finds out—"

"I'll tell her. What the hell. She'll have to see sense, for the sake of the child. She'll divorce me."

Anita said: "*Pregnant?*" He braced himself for some violence. "Well Frankie boy. Bad luck. So...am...I." She smiled, extraordinarily calm. "You can't leave me now."

Miriam wept: "How *could* you?" It was a betrayal she would never entirely forgive.

"She engineered it. Practically bloody raped me. *I* didn't want to."

But, Miriam thought, how can I believe that? Couldn't he just say No?

"Look," Frank said. "I want to do the honourable thing. We'll sort it all out after she's had the kid. But now, we'll go together to tell your father what's happened, and that I love you and want to marry you, and he'll take you in, until we can be together properly."

Her father swore at Frank and said Miriam was no better than a whore. He threw her out. Miriam refused to go to an institution for unmarried mothers, where she would be lectured on her sins and be made to give her baby away.

Despairing, Frank told Anita, who astoundingly said: "She can't live on the streets. It's your responsibility. She must come to us." She added: "We'll tell the neighbours she's my cousin, and her husband's a soldier somewhere abroad." It was as if she'd already thought of it.

Frank was overwhelmed. "She was an absolute brick," he told Miriam. "Really magnanimous."

Miriam saw there must be a secret agenda. But she agreed to the plan. What else could she do?

Miriam spent her pregnancy in a fog, dazed by the bizarre nature of the household, examining nothing. She would come to look back on her time there with disbelief. She and Anita shared the cooking and shopping. They were strangely courteous, even amicable. The three of them slept in separate rooms. Frank sneaked into Miriam's room at night. Anita knew.

Anita gave birth to a boy, James, three weeks before Miriam's child was due. The birth was difficult: Anita fought nature, struggling to keep the baby inside her, sensing that, once born, it might no longer be a weapon. The midwife and doctor called Miriam into the bedroom to help hold Anita still while forceps dragged the infant out. The doctor murmured: *It's done for*, turning to tend the mother. Instinct made Miriam pick up the limp little body and slap some breath into it.

The secret agenda emerged a few weeks after Josephine's comparatively uneventful birth.

After the births, Anita was openly hostile, barking orders at Miriam as if she were a skivvy. All courtesy vanished. One Sunday afternoon she called a meeting and announced her agenda.

"Miriam's had her share of our hospitality. Now she can *get out*—and leave her daughter to be brought up as our own child."

"No! No!" Miriam shouted, leaping to her feet.

"Give your little bastard up for adoption, then," Anita spat. "*You* can't support her. Either way, you go."

Miriam heard herself yelling: "*Nobody* is taking my baby!" And then she passed out.

She never knew, because she never asked, what—if anything—Frank had said in protest or support. She never knew, either, whether he had been aware of Anita's plan. But next morning Anita had departed, taking the infant James with her.

"She's taken my son!" Frank said angrily.

Miriam looked at him, incredulous, but was silent.

Anita found a clever lawyer who, as Miriam put it later, took him to the cleaner's. And she refused to divorce him. If they wanted to marry, Anita would have to die first.

Chapter Eight

AFTER TWENTY-FOUR HOURS with her mother, Gee stepped exhausted into her own front hallway at midnight. She didn't immediately recognise the smell that seized her throat. Nor, in the dimmed light, did she register the haziness of the air. Sniffing, she tracked the odour to the kitchen and pressed the light switch. For a second she thought she had entered the wrong house.

This wide back room had been converted to a more-accessible kitchen after Sebastian's accident. In a mood she hadn't chosen to analyse, she'd had it equipped and painted in virginal white. Tonight it was clothed in funereal greys and blacks. The source of the smell, now stinging her eyes as well as her lungs, was on the darkly spattered hob—a jet-black pan. Partly covering it was a rug from the hall evidently used to smother the pan's fire. The wall and ceiling above the cooker were blackened, the entire room was layered in greasy soot with wheelchair tyre-marks crossing the once-snowy floor. Every surface was smeared. Gee stood rigid.

Sebastian had decided to cook a late supper. He did sometimes. Especially after sex. He must have put a pan on, then got distracted. Probably had a drink too many. He might be hurt. Burned. He might have been rushed to hospital. Like before.

Gee ran upstairs, her hand collecting soot from the banister. Its dark veil spread across walls, ceilings and mouldings. A thousand cobwebs were revealed. The begrimed chair-lift was halted at the landing.

She heard Sebastian snoring before she got to his room. Turning on a small lamp, she braced herself for bandages or worse. He was on his back, mouth open, neat in his silk pyjamas, not so much as a blister on his hand. The wheelchair as usual within reach, his spectacles resting on his bedside book. He looked wonderfully unconcerned. Smug. And she knew again how easily murder is done.

Teeth clenched, Gee climbed on through the house. The soot was thinner on the top floor, but even so it speckled her studio door—which she always locked, so with luck her work was untouched. But the door alone stoked her anger. The top floor had been tacitly agreed to be hers alone, containing only her studio and a room that had evolved into her bedroom. But now he'd invaded and left his mark, to remind her of her failure as a wife, and to keep his hold on her.

Sebastian had done this to her, trying to make himself helpless. Made an accident. Sent the new housekeeper home, though she'd been supposed to cook and clear up on both the evenings Gee was away. You could bet he'd had his bloody physio woman here to screw. Decided he could manage alone if he wanted to eat. And he could. He followed directions on a packet well enough, understood the microwave, and had never spilled so much as a jug of milk. Or if he had, he'd always cleaned up. Not this time. This was an exhibition.

Descending past the sounds of the unharmed Sebastian, she marvelled that he could remain asleep despite the smell and her own stamping feet. Perhaps the exhaustion of triumph. He hadn't even closed his door. Nor the kitchen door. Had done nothing to contain the pervading, bitter air. The paintwork near the cooker was actually blistered, she saw; the ceiling charred. Sebastian had been incredibly fortunate not to be burned. It was a miracle the house hadn't burned down. For a second, she allowed the wish that both he and it had ended as cinders.

In the morning she would dig into Yellow Pages for one of those companies that sent in a team of workers to clean up a whole house. Every bloody carpet, every stinking ceiling, wall, door, window, blind, curtain, every last filthy cobwebby corner. She picked up the black pan and hurled it into the bin. It stuck there, its handle poking out like an impudent tongue, and she kicked at it, sickened by her helpless tears.

Beyond fatigue now, she cleaned the work surfaces, the worst encrustations on the cooker, and the sink area; she washed the kettle, coffee-maker and teapot and crammed the dishwasher with blackened crockery. At least she could get breakfast in the morning without ending up like a chimney-sweep.

"IS THAT ALL you can think about?" Sebastian said. "The house being a bit dirty?"

"A *bit*? I suppose I should consider myself lucky I didn't find a heap of smoking rubble. What on earth were you doing?"

He spread butter on his toast with precision. "How sad that your first thought was the state of the house." His mouth trembled with injury. "Didn't it occur to you I might just—*just*—be hurt? Even seriously burned?"

Gee looked at him and considered silence.

Bugger that martyred stuff.

"As it happens," she said deliberately, "the *immediate* thing I did after finding the disaster zone was run upstairs to see you were all right. You were. Snoringly so." She resisted telling him he had looked pleased with himself.

He was taken aback, but only for seconds. "I expect you would have preferred to find me dead. Or carried off to hospital with ninety per cent burns."

"Oh for Christ's sake."

"It was an *accident*, Georgina. Anyone would think I did it deliberately. I don't know why you're so bad-tempered. Wouldn't *relief* be more appropriate? I was on the phone, and I just forgot." Sebastian actually smiled, passing his cup for her to top up his coffee as if they were Darby and Joan. "You *could* congratulate me on my quick action, putting out the fire with great efficiency. Not everybody in my condition would be able to do that."

"Congratulations. No wonder you were sleeping the sleep of the righteous."

"You really should listen to your own voice sometimes." His lips tightened, he sighed. Gee unexpectedly thought of her father. "I might say that it was an extremely alarming experience. And I was exhausted."

"I'm sure it was." And yes, it must have been. "Why wasn't Mrs Parker here cooking for you?"

"I told her not to bother. Obviously." He seemed appeased by her milder tone. "I had a visitor, as a matter of fact."

"I'd guessed that."

Sebastian moved his chair back, apparently to survey Gee better. He nursed his coffee cup and retained a slight smile, as if she were an odd specimen. She knew in that moment with great clarity that she would never fully understand their life together.

"As a matter of fact," he repeated, "your sister came to see me."

"Jo?"

"Josephine, yes. She very sweetly came to see how I was. Frankly, she was quite upset by what you had told her, out of the blue. *You*, leaving *Sebastian*."

Gee had not used that word. Not exactly. "I never said I was *leaving* you."

His stare was icy. "I suggested she stay for dinner. And Josephine kindly said she would prepare it." He paused. "You could learn from your sister. She's a very warm, caring person."

"Maybe," Gee rejoined, as nastily as possible, "you should marry her. I'm sure you, of all people, could persuade her to leave the lunatic Eric."

"What a spiteful thing to say," Sebastian said coolly. "Where was I? Yes, so I sent Mrs Thing—Parker—home early. She was grateful. Did you know her husband is extremely unwell? Diabetic. Severe case." Sebastian had always adopted a lugubrious air of relishing others' illnesses and tragedies. "Mrs Parker seems devoted to him."

"Ah, another good wife. Let's not exaggerate. Her husband's a perfectly *ordinary* diabetic. He's quite fit. Works hard as a gardener—even offered his services for this garden while I'm away. It's small, he'd manage easily. And that reminds me of something I have to talk to you about."

As if she hadn't spoken, Sebastian continued: "Josephine cooked excellent steaks and made a delicious salad. We split a bottle of claret. It was very pleasant, quite a treat. We talked. As a matter of fact, I found Josephine *most* sympathetic." He wore his smuggest face. "She certainly doesn't approve of what you're doing."

"My, that makes a change. And if you had such a delicious dinner, what the hell were you doing frying up God knows what for supper?"

"We ate early, she had to get back. I got peckish later and thought I'd fry some eggs. I must have put the oil on a bit high. The phone rang—I got into a discussion, and—" Sebastian actually laughed. "Oh well. Could've been worse."

Discarding several corrosive replies, Gee left her chair and directed her violence at the dishwasher. Sebastian remained at table, picking up a banana and peeling it. Gee leaned against the sink, looking out of the window at a blackbird stretching a worm out of the grass until it snapped.

"What do you think of this idea?" she began, trying for a reasonable tone but hearing a bossy prattle. "I spoke to Mrs Parker about arrangements while I'm in New Zealand. She would be very happy, if you agree, to live in—with her husband, of course. The basement is as good as a self-contained flat—or it will be, once I've sorted it out. It's not as if we use it nowadays. Mr Parker could look after the garden while she continues in charge of the housekeeping as well as doing all the cooking and supervising Marie's cleaning. Mrs Parker's efficient, and trustworthy too. What do you think? They wouldn't intrude on your privacy—they'd have their own front door. There'd have to be some sort of inter-communication, obviously—another phone line probably. The point is that they'd be on hand, day and night, and you'd be well looked-after." She paused, eyes on the grey ceiling. "I think I'll organise some smoke alarms."

Sebastian said nothing, and his face was unreadable.

Talk of smoke alarms reminded her of Miriam: she still smoked in bed. She ought to have an alarm too.

"Oh, I forgot to say," she went on. "My mother sent you her love and best wishes."

He looked a little bemused. "Thank you. I hope she's well."

"Yes and no."

"*She* certainly stood by her man, as they say."

"I think we've had that conversation."

"I imagine she was shocked and upset when you told her."

"Told her what?"

"You know perfectly well. Told her you're leaving me."

"I didn't."

"Whatever words you skilfully selected. Do you think I'm stupid? Did you tell her you're leaving me for *another man*?" He made a contemptuous noise. "I *bet* you did."

Gee went out of the kitchen and returned with Yellow Pages. She slapped the book on the table, poured herself more coffee and noisily turned pages. "I'm hiring a bloody great army to clean the place from top to bottom. Carpets, the lot. Basement too. You might want to be out for a day or two."

"Georgina."

She was unsure of his tone, but wouldn't look up. She stabbed her pencil against numbers in the book.

"Georgina. Please. Don't—leave. Let's——"

He stopped short, she looked up.

"Let's what?"

Sebastian shrugged. "Let's put it this way." That hadn't been what he was going to say. "If you leave me, it'll be worse later. I tried to tell you. It'll be better if you wait."

"You did all this to stop me, didn't you?"

He drew himself up in his chair angrily. "Don't be ridiculous."

"You sound just like my father."

"And you sound hard and bitchy, just like your mother."

"Thank you," she said. "Look. I'm going to New Zealand. Everything's fixed, and I just heard that Aunt Mildred's been quite ill, and she's really old. She's convinced she'll get well faster if I come and see her, and I can't let her down now."

"But you can let me down."

"Oh, *Seb*."

"Don't call me Seb. You know I hate it."

"I don't know anything of the kind! I've always—I never thought you minded." Gee was breathless.

Possibly he was on the edge of tears, swivelling his chair towards the door. "Damn well go to New Zealand then," he hurled back. "But afterwards—if you don't come back— You'll wish you had. In a few months. It's you I'm thinking about. Your *happiness*. And I'll tell you something else. You'll never do another decent painting. You haven't got the *depth*."

She stood stunned, watching him. He stopped in the doorway, and his shoulders rose and fell with a deep breath as he turned his chair to face her again. Then he sat looking at her stiff-faced for perhaps half a minute, in silence, as if steeling himself for his own words.

"What?" she asked, afraid.

"It's cancer," he said.

IT DIDN'T MATTER whether or not he had actually spoken the truth, Gee at last saw.

Rising and swooning in a dawn sleep that still blanketed her brain, there visited an hallucination, the kind that encourages sane people to believe in ghouls, ghosts and incubi.

He was in the room: she knew the clean, delicious smell of him. She actually felt his hand on her upper arm, its warm, enticing pressure.

"Gee," he said, and she laughed into her pillow again at his soft transatlantic voice turning her name into an exclamation. But he sounded serious. "That isn't fair. It just isn't fair."

Her eyes popped open, the inside of her skull lit electrically as she sat up, looking for him, *Oh where are you*, and saying aloud: "You're right, it's *not* fair."

The fog dispersed. And the last of her respect for Sebastian collapsed into rubble, burying and smothering her guilt.

Taking the photograph from her bedside drawer she stared at a beautiful, humorous face. If only she could feel his embrace right now, the way it cast a wave of exhilaration and desire through her. She wished she could have told him, this very minute, that her indecision—her *cowardice*—had ended, and that his patience shamed her.

"I'm leaving him, I am, really," she said aloud.

Chapter Nine

GEE HAD MANAGED AT LAST to face packing up her studio, getting started by preparing a compact package for her trip: sketch-blocks, paints, pencils, brushes. That piece of luggage arranged and committed, she saw her way more clearly. For godsake, this was only a bloody room. There was another one somewhere. A new studio might help her start painting again. Another horizon. Somewhere back there she'd mislaid her purpose. Looking at her old paintings, she marvelled that they'd come off her brushes. Caro called it Painter's Block, and pointedly did not point out when it had begun.

The phone rang.

Jo said: "*You've* been quiet!" She laughed lightly. "Still, so've I. Madly busy."

Two weeks had passed since Jo's dinner with Sebastian, the kitchen fire, the clean-up, Gee's reinvention of the basement with paint and fabric.

"Me too. Still am." But she had not, actually, wanted to see Jo. A lingering sense of annoyance had got in the way. And injury; betrayal, even—ever since Sebastian had revealed Jo's disapproval.

"You're off next Thursday. Fancy a lunch?"

"Terribly sorry Jo. Not a chance." But she could hardly leave the country without seeing her sister. Thinking fast, she suggested Jo come for a farewell drink at the airport. "Caro's driving me. We can all go together."

"Oh. Okay. That'd be nice." Clearly she hated the idea. "You're going so far *off*! Whatever are you going to do out there?"

"See Aunt Mildred. Paint."

"What about that old granny you were on about? The po-faced one?"

Gee felt driven to needle her sister.

"According to Dad, she was. From what I've heard, you'd have expected him to *brag* about her."

"Brag?" Jo asked mildly.

"*You* know. Aristocratic connections. The way he'd hold forth about his posh ancestors."

"You're exaggerating as usual." Jo sighed where she should have snapped.

"Ha! I can just see his superior smirk. Transparent old fool."

Disconcertingly, Jo replied in the weighty, probing tones of a therapist. Could Gee be hoping to justify her inability to mourn her father? Possibly even to dig up some dirt?

The combination of hostile words and tolerant tone was unsettling. Gee rudely jeered.

"I don't have to dig very far to find *dirt*, do I? Yeah, I *am* curious about his nastier side. But I'm not going on some breast-beating voyage round my father, much as you might like that. Sentimental crap." She added meanly: "I have a similar curiosity about serial killers and psychopaths."

Jo sounded like a disappointed parent. "You are *such* a child. *Such* a know-all." With which, she briskly took her leave. "Never mind! Must be off. See you next Thursday—let me know what time to turn up. 'Bye!"

Gee was left gasping. *What the hell was that about?*

EVERY MEMBER of Gee's family was in a car, and she was driving. Not a car suddenly, but a sled, on ice. She knew she had never been in, let alone driven, a sled. But she wasn't driving, not exactly. She was the one *pulling* the sled. On her feet were some kind of sliding shoes, not snow-shoes, not skis. Something like boats. Rowing dinghies. She set off, sliding over icy rocky rubbly ground. Sometimes she was, after all, driving a car and the things on her feet were like accelerator and clutch. The ground got rockier. She knew her enormous responsibility for the safety and wellbeing of her family. Sam was there too as a toddler, next to their mother, while in her arms was a tiny baby. Her father was very old. Jo was wearing her lace-edged nightdress. A huge rock appeared ahead, a great rock hill with crevasses and chasms. Two small cars crossed her path at different, sudden angles. They slithered dangerously, but negotiated the rock's chasms like toy cars might, wobbling from side to side as if they were bound to overturn, but they didn't. They went on their way. She saw one of them actually leap across a chasm, a canyon even. Then she realised that the things on her feet were themselves rocks, and it became achingly difficult to make the sliding motion forward. These rock-shoes were crumbling, flaking away like shale. She stopped and unstrapped them, picked them up, examined them. They were disintegrating fast. It would be impossible to continue pulling the sled. Even so she put them back on her feet, hoping they might somehow last until the end of the journey. But she soon saw it was useless. The rock-shoes were relentlessly crumbling, collapsing under her feet. Now they were as small as tea-plates. She knew she had failed. Behind her in the car or sled, she heard Jo's voice: "The word you are looking for, Georgina, is *clay*."

IN THE POST, thirty-six hours before Gee was due to fly to Auckland, Jo's dark, sharp-cornered writing stood out from blander envelopes. She thrust it in her bag for the stronger end of the day.

An hour later, the doorbell announced a brown and battered package with flowery New Zealand stamps, postmarks illegible, delay unexplained. It weighed thrillingly in her hands as she ran upstairs to the safety of her studio. Demolishing its outer wrappings, she found Aunt Mildred's blue notepaper tucked into the end of a cardboard box.

Listen darling Gee, forgive scribble, as you'll know by the time this arrives I'm

not awfully well but Pammy will post it for me. You will have had my letter telling you about it being Grandma McIvor's very first journal. Part of it tells of her long journey to Edinburgh and early weeks at school. It's an appetiser!
Bon voyage! Heaps of love, Millie.

Slightly lightheaded, her hands unsteady, Gee sat down and slid the cardboard box towards her, removed sticky tape and unfolded flaps. Then, as if handling delicate crystal, she pulled out a solid journal with faded red marbled covers and scuffed leather spine and corners.

Cautiously she lifted the front cover. There it was, as Millie had said, on the first discoloured page: *The 10th day of December in the year of Our Lord, 1843.* Written in Margaret Esther's own neat hand, on her twelfth birthday. For a while Gee sat holding the treasure in both hands, fearful that the pages might fall to dust like relics from a thousand-year-old tomb. The smell of their long-enclosed secrecy and erosion lifted and spread, altering the air of the room. And then, gently, she closed the book again. To begin reading now would be cheating: Millie had intended this for her journey. She re-wrapped it and placed it beside her flight-bag.

Only in the early evening, when Gee had finished packing her suitcases, did she remember Jo's letter—and then only because it confronted her as she tipped out her handbag. She would read it while waiting for Sebastian, who had insisted he take her out for dinner on this final night, having declared some days earlier that he was obliged to be in Brussels on the day of her departure. In return for this tact she had not resisted. At least there should be no animosity: Sebastian's manner nowadays was coolly amicable—but, unnervingly, gave the impression that he believed she would come back to him, that his final word in the kitchen doorway had secured his case. Yet he knew she'd been packing up her studio. It was beyond her to guess at his thoughts and feelings.

After pouring herself a drink, she unfolded Jo's letter.

My dear Gee,

I've been thinking day and night since we spoke, and on balance I've decided it would be best if I didn't come with you and Caro to Heathrow. The atmosphere with the three of us might be rather forced and artificial, and while I feel sad about my decision, I also feel that our conversation revealed how much remains unresolved between you and me, and this goes back, I believe, to that time approximately ten years ago when you effectively 'stopped' me when I tried to express my feelings of (justifiable) anger about your role in the family dynamics. This was after I had come across your (I'm sorry, but this is what it was) *offensive* 'family portrait', as I expect you recall. You closed a door on me, and possibly you are still not prepared to acknowledge my feelings here, but I hope that at a future time we might talk and *examine our relationship* in more depth and with honesty on both sides.

Heaven forbid. Gee groaned into her drink. *What was this letter really about?*

> I say this because the other day it seemed to me that one minute we were talking normally about this great-grandmother person, and the next you were making one of your *attacks* on Daddy. It upsets me when you do this because you do it *knowing* it upsets me. So your attack is on *me*, and I don't know what I've done to earn it. Except that I feel instinctively that our disharmony dates *right back* to that old confrontation.
>
> That notwithstanding, it's true to say I would come to the airport if Caro wasn't to be with you. This is not to criticise your best friend, who has admirable qualities, but to emphasise that given our circumstances the atmosphere would be even more difficult for me. Caro and I don't exactly gel, do we? I'm sure your send-off will be all the more fun without me there. You and Caro always seem to have plenty to laugh about.

Gee had to hand it to Jo: she knew exactly how to stick the knife in.

> There are some things in my own life I've allowed myself to realise for the first time—but I'm not yet ready to talk to you about that. For once I have to work out something important by *myself*, without *your* guidance. Meantime I want you to know I've always valued your objectivity and, yes, wisdom, and that no matter what else I love and respect you.
>
> I do wish you a wonderful trip, and hope you'll think of me kindly.
>
> With very fondest love as always, Jo.

At various times in her life, Gee had wondered if she and Jo were actually related. To this sensation was now added an uneasy perplexity. Even after a second reading, she was still left feeling that something was eluding her.

Chapter Ten

SLEEP WAS OUT OF THE QUESTION. Gee's brain was lit up, alert, and she was feeling weird, slightly outside herself. *Disembodied.* And this wasn't solely the result of a couple of drinks with Caro in the airport bar or the headiness of having been inexplicably upgraded to Business Class, with generous wine from a real glass accompanying a halfway-decent dinner, not to mention the unfamiliar luxury of extra limb-space. Such treats had added to her comfort and even a fleeting sense of adventure. But now, with most of the passengers asleep after food and a Hollywood romance, nobody within earshot snoring, and few reading lights interrupting the darkness, Gee felt vividly unreal, swept up by what might just as well have been silence around her—a roaring kind of silence, the steady rush of aircraft engines, the unceasing hiss of air-conditioning absorbed into the same numb cushion of soundless sound on the edge of her skull, like traffic heard from the top of an insulated skyscraper in Manhattan, present but absent. And she was high above the earth, in the middle of what felt like nowhere. Going where?

Maybe Margaret Esther Moore, leaving her homeland, had felt a similar disembodiment, stepping aboard a wooden sailing ship at some British port with a horde of strangers, probably crowded into conditions of unimaginable discomfort. Standing on deck, she would have watched the moorings loosened and the shore receding as the ship headed into the utterly unknown in a huge world. Was she incredulous, appalled, even afraid? Her dangerous journey might last five or six months, or her ship might never arrive at all, like so many emigrant vessels that were lost to ferocious oceans, terrifying storms, icebergs or even reckless seamanship. Gee's journey to the Antipodes was luxury in comparison, namby-pamby. Aircraft did, occasionally, fall out of the sky, but the odds against continuing comfort and safe arrival did not compare with the risks of being under sail on an unpredictable ocean. But then, pure novelty might have blunted Margaret Esther's fears. Probably she'd never been on the sea before. Surely she was lonely?

Abruptly, Gee was herself cruelly lonely, feeling the magnetic pull of her country's shores as the plane drew relentlessly further and further away, making her still more aware of her mental island. It would be easy to be seized by panic now. She had untied and cast off her own mooring ropes, allowing herself to soar aloft into nothing but air. Everything was in the air. Her head, her life, her decisions, her painting.

Everything she'd painted lately was uninspired, the effort and plodding were obvious. The only canvas with any of her old spirit was the unfinished painting of her father that had sprung into being that day of his fantasy phone call. Nothing since then. Even the idea of Margaret Esther as a child hadn't got as far as a pencil.

Caro, in Gee's studio helping to sort sketches, had said: "Call it a kind of depression. You're entitled. Like grief, it takes time. Maybe this trip to New Zealand will help. Cast off from the past, *et cetera*."

Caro leaning against the wall with that typically smooth movement, one wrist pushing back the straight fall of red-lit hair from the Botticelli features that made men stare, vacuous and helpless. A true beauty, yet Caro seemed always so unconscious of her power. She had looked up at Gee almost shyly; they had always understood each other well, but shared a reluctance to be confessional. "The past is a tenacious thing, Gee old pal. I say that to myself as well as to you. Fly away from it."

It was the first time Gee had heard her hint at personal wounds. But at once Caro laughed, switching subjects with a wisecrack to make Gee laugh too. (Jo had referred to Caro as Gee's best friend. Was she? She had never awarded anyone that label.)

Fly away from it. But towards what? Margaret Esther might well have asked the same question. Or was that girl, barely a woman, too strong a character to be daunted, instead feeling relief to be on her way to a new life? She might be full of excitement. Adventure. Equally she might simply have accepted her lot, her decision made. People believed in God's Will then, and how your choices turned out would be as the great One ordained, as He moved in mostly mysterious ways. Great-grandmother McIvor wouldn't have wondered *why* she was as she was. People were good, bad or in between, with badness the result of heredity, or not battling sufficiently with the Devil.

Nevertheless. Feeble modern wretch that she felt, in her cocoon of roaring silence, Gee's solitude struck her, mean and bruising. The void was what she feared. Singleness was at the centre of her dread. It stretched beyond all horizons. She had never considered how it might feel once she had actually cast off. That's what she had done: untied the knot. She'd said the words. Out loud.

SITTING IN THE RESTAURANT at the end of dinner, only last night, Seb had been pleasant enough, almost formal, as if it were a first date, asking interestedly about her plans once in New Zealand. They drank coffee, discussing a few domestic practicalities, and suddenly she knew this was the moment she had to tell him. It was only fair.

"When I come back, Seb," she said. "Sebastian."

He'd smiled slightly, looking at her as if he knew what she would say.

"When I come back——" Her voice was shaking, damn it. "Well. I'll start looking for somewhere else to live. A studio flat. More studio than flat." He was unreadable. "I'm sorry."

"No need to say sorry." He seemed extraordinarily calm. "I think I saw it coming."

"I'd like us to stay friends."

There was something glittering in his look then, and his voice sharpened. "Forget *that*."

"But—"

"Nothing more to say about it. Apart from have a good time." He finished his coffee and put down his cup. "Let's go."

He called for the bill.

GOODBYE, SEB.

What was he feeling? *Don't think about it. Don't think about him at home by himself. Don't think about what Jo had said.*

It had been a mistake to ring her. But a few friendly parting words had seemed essential. She might even uncover whatever had eluded her.

"I keep thinking about Sebastian going home to that empty house," Jo had murmured.

Damn the woman.

"Thanks, that's just what I needed to hear," she had answered, not thinking to say he was bloody unlikely to be on his own, was probably merrily screwing at that very moment.

With that thought Gee was instantly furious at her own self-pity, her lack of spine. You could bet that Margaret Esther didn't swoon trembling upon the decks. There was no turning back for her—and she was a mere teenager, not a mature woman who ought to know better. She bloody got on with it—without any of the comforts here on offer, least of all a flushing lavatory and a toilet-roll.

"DON'T BE SURPRISED," Caro had said in the airport bar, "if you feel a bit lost to start with. Just keep in mind that you're not really alone. And just to prove it, you've got your ancient great-grandmama stuffed in your luggage."

Dear, clever Caro, reminding her of her companion and her purpose on this journey to the underside of the planet.

Echoes sounded: herself, shortly after her twelfth birthday, with wishbone in hand and ill-will in her heart. (*You should see your face, Georgina! Shades of my self-righteous old Grandma...*) Her great-grandmother, taking up her pen on her twelfth birthday almost a hundred and forty years earlier—to write, Gee supposed and hoped, of what lay in her heart. And right here, right now, Gee could pluck her from that century into this, and start getting to know her.

Chapter Eleven

*My Private Journal, Volume One,
beginning on the 10th day of December
in the year of Our Lord, 1843.*

MY GOVERNESS, MISS HARRIET AVERY, gave me this journal for my birthday today. When I saw its beautiful thick blank pages, waiting, smelling so clean, I felt I could never bring myself to defile them with my handwriting, which is less than perfect. Miss Avery said: "It is for your own thoughts, my dear, for I know it pleases you to write." This causes her satisfaction, for she herself taught me reading and writing when I was four years old. She said I had an "aptitude". It is she, I believe, who has an aptitude—for teaching.

Miss Avery added that she would give me a new journal every year if that would bring me pleasure. How kind she is. At once I resolved to do justice to this fine book and any others that may follow it, by making strenuous efforts to write with honesty of my observations, and furthermore to allow no trivial musings. My journal will contain only true things. Since the truth is to be the most important aspect of my writings, I must ensure that nobody but myself shall see my journals until I am dead. I shall not write my name in my journal, for it is my belief that as a result I shall find it easier to express matters truly.

I am twelve years of age today. When I was born my Mama died, and ever since that day my Papa has hated me. As far as I am able to tell his only emotion towards me has been that of hatred. Therefore my Papa has hated me for twelve whole years. If I spoke these words aloud in the presence of others, everyone would be shocked and agitated and say it is not so. This does not mean it is not the *truth*.

My Mama was nineteen years old when she died. Miss Avery, who although not ten years her senior, was my Mama's governess from the time when Mama was my own age, and then was her maid after she married Papa. Miss Avery says Mama was a true lady, beautiful and graceful, and my Papa worshipped her and she him. Elizabeth Sarah was her name. I am certain I too would have loved her greatly. There are no portraits of her, which I much regret, but Miss Avery (who is the only person who does not hush me if I wish to speak of my Mama) says I have her eyes. But the truth is I have a silly face. My eyes bulge and are an ugly mixed colour, neither brown nor green nor yellow but all three, my mouth is big and fleshy, and I detest both my nose that turns up and my chin that points down. I am a frog with a sharp chin and thick sand-coloured hair. Frogs are neither graceful nor ladylike. I cannot blame my Papa for hating me.

I do not know why my being born made my Mama die. Miss Avery looked saddened when I asked, saying no explanation was given to her, but my Mama had been attended by an excellent midwife and her family's doctor. Miss Avery explained that such sad occurrences were not uncommon; she had known two other young women, in her own village, who had died in childbirth. I reflect that if childbearing is so dangerous a business, it is surprising that so many women undertake it.

I now know a certain amount about the matter of birth. A long time ago one of the doe rabbits, tended by our stable-boy Tommy, had seven babies and he showed them to me. They had no fur and their eyes were fixed shut as if glued. They wriggled together like little soft pink sausages inside the nest that their mother had made out of hay and with her own fur pulled from her undersides.

I said to Tommy: "Where did they come from?" He laughed and showed me a hole at the back end of the Mama rabbit. I tried to conceal my astonishment.

He said: "They came out here after growing inside her. You saw how big and fat her belly was." Indeed I had, and now it looked quite flat and empty. Tommy showed me her teats and said the babies would drink milk from them until they were old enough to eat food. I reflected that God was very clever to arrange matters so well, and I asked Tommy if God had put the babies inside her and he said that the Papa rabbit put seeds in her and the babies grew from them. I felt sure he was telling the truth for he is an honest boy and would not mislead me just to tease. Later I grew to understand from things I overheard in the kitchen when Mavis and Elsie were whispering and giggling, that human beings must be similar and that the part polite people do not talk about is how a Papa puts seeds in a Mama.

Since the birth of the rabbits I have often seen newly-born foals and calves, and the hole they came from. The hole does not look large enough for such big babies, but Tommy says it stretches with ease—as, I observe, does his grin.

Recently one of the mares died when her foal was born, and the foal also died. Tommy was weeping. I had not known that men wept—and he is nearly a man, at fifteen. (Miss Avery has explained to me that gentlemen prefer not to show their feelings, and this is probably for the best as they are obliged to run the country and the world. I was unable to read her expression as she uttered these words.)

Tommy said he blamed himself for going to his bed, which is at the far end of the stables, instead of waiting with the mare, for he knew she was near her time. The men declared it was not Tommy's fault, nobody could have foretold, the mare had foaled previously without mishap, and besides what could he have done when the foal turned the wrong way and something broke and all the mare's blood came out.

I wondered then, and still wonder, if that is what I did to my Mama. I am certain I killed her and that this is the explanation for my Papa's bitter face on the rare occasions he speaks to me. He cannot forgive me. I am sure I did not intend it, even though the Vicar said one Sunday that Mankind is born in Sin, and as he pronounced this he was looking at me directly. I found courage to say to Miss

Avery that he knew I was to blame for killing my Mama, but she turned pale and said, "Hush my dear child, you did no such thing. The Lord may sometimes take a mother in childbirth and we do not know why. We are in God's hands." She said this in the same way she says I have my Mama's eyes, not because she truly believes it but because she wants *me* to do so. It is kind of her, but the truth is in my Papa's face.

My Papa's name is Charles. I therefore suppose that had I been a boy I too would have been Charles, as is the custom. Charles Maximilian. Perhaps Papa would have forgiven a son, for girls are not as important as boys. My aunt Clarissa has explained:

"A lady's first obligation is to be content to be inferior to men. As a girl, you have inferior mental powers, in proportion to the inferiority of your body's strength. What matters, my dear, is to be good."

I am not good, although I pray to be made good. I have been praying since I was very little, but if everyone in the world prays at bedtime many millions of prayers must be prayed at the same time. How can God listen to everyone? We must all take our turn, so I may have to wait a very long time to be good.

This is all I shall write on my twelfth birthday. Today my thirteenth year begins.

11th December, the second day of my thirteenth year.

A resolution! I shall not write every single day in my journal, or it will be filled with dullness. I shall write of what is most important to me, perhaps those matters that I may wish specially to examine or remember. Further, I know that when I have a difficulty, writing about it can sometimes relieve me. I also hope that writing in my journal may help create greater order and discipline in my mind, defeating its oddities—occasions when I find myself not where I expect to be, unable to recall events, and afterwards am in difficulties trying to explain myself. Of this I have told nobody.

25th December.

Christmas Day has drawn to a close. My Uncle and Aunt, Sir John and Lady Talbot, are visiting for a fortnight. Their home is far away in Edinburgh, Scotland. We went to Church in the morning and afterwards ate roast goose and Papa complimented Mrs Williams, our Cook. My Aunt Clarissa, Papa's sister, is good-natured enough, but I do not care for my Uncle John, whose lips are wet and his hands plump, with a big and rather tight ring. My Aunt speaks to me kindly and has no objection if I address her first as long as I am careful not to interrupt. Papa usually commands, "Speak when you are spoken to, child," but today, perhaps because it is Christmas and he and my Uncle drank wine, and my hateful birthday had passed, he did not look so angry.

I noticed when my Aunt reclined on the sofa that, although her form is much concealed by the bulk of many petticoats, she is considerably broader at the waist than I remember, with a hint of a round belly. ('Belly' would be considered an impolite word for a lady, but I permit myself forbidden words if I consider them accurate, in my journal of truth.) I thought of the doe rabbit's belly and of seeds and Aunt Clarissa's plumpness—then looked at Uncle John's fat soft fingers; and I was uncomfortable in a way I am unable to describe.

4th January 1844.

Today after lessons I said to Miss Avery, without intending seriousness, "What will happen when you have taught me everything that you know?"

She replied soberly, "I have considered this question myself, my dear."

I was most alarmed. Did she mean that she would go away one day? Miss Avery can be strict, but she is kind and has been with me my whole life. Even though she must be now nearing forty, which is old, she is my friend and nurse and governess, and I would miss her miserably. I said fearfully, "Surely you still know many things that I can learn?"

"Oh yes," she said, and smiled to see me so concerned. "We have not run out of subjects."

Miss Avery comes from a poor but respectable family; her late father was a parson. Her two married sisters and elderly mother live in the village of which our house is the Manor, known locally as The Hall. Miss Avery and her sisters attended the village day school, where they learned Reading, Writing, Arithmetic, Sewing of Samplers, Mending, the Kings and Queens of England, the Countries and Seas of the World, and The Bible. The last, naturally, was also studied at home. Her only brother was sent away to a big school, where he learned many more things as boys do, including Classical Languages. "But," she has told me often in a triumphant way, "I made my brother teach me the Greek and Latin verbs in the holidays, and Euclid and algebra also."

Once, thinking about opinions expressed by my Aunt Clarissa, I asked Miss Avery, "Is it true that ladies do not strictly need to learn those subjects?"

Miss Avery drew a stern breath and replied, "I am not of the prevailing opinion that education is wasted upon a lady. The female brain is perfectly able, so pray look sceptically upon those who would tell you otherwise. I fear that too many brains are wasted, through lack of exercise. There is no reason, once a young lady has learned to read, why she should not learn everything in the world that she wishes to learn."

This must be true, for as a result of her having taught herself so many things, she is able to teach me Geography, History, Botany and Mathematics, and has just begun to teach me the ancient languages of Greek and Latin. She herself can read whole books in these! I have not told her that Aunt Clarissa says the Classics are a Godless, immoral influence on the female mind. Miss Avery is now also teaching herself French. I enquired why, and she said, "So that I can read the literature in this beautiful language—and indeed I shall be able to teach you as I learn more myself. Besides, I like to expand my mind."

Miss Avery is the person I most admire in the whole world. Not only is she clever, but she is also different from every other member of the female sex of my acquaintance. She looks at gentlemen directly and fearlessly, without lowering her lashes or patting her hair or bonnet. O, to be like her! I, alas, am rather afraid of Papa and of most members of the male sex that I have met—excepting Tommy. They are so certain of things, so commanding, making all decisions on our behalf.

I would, further, like to look like Miss Avery, but of this I have no hope. She is almost as tall as Papa, with a back slim and straight. It is to encourage my deportment to be equally upright that she insists that I lie strapped to the backboard in the schoolroom for an hour a day while learning my lessons. It is not comfortable, especially when combined with Historical Dates, but I persevere, to achieve the end she promises. But however straight I learn to stand, I can never possess Miss Avery's shining, dark brown hair, noble brow or elegant features. She is most handsome, and her smile makes her doubly so.

I am not sure if Papa knows how clever Miss Avery is. He never asks me about my lessons, but I hope very much that he discusses them with her. It is my regretful belief, from the manner in which Aunt Clarissa speaks to Miss Avery, that she thinks people from poor families must have dull brains. This, however, is not my own observation. Miss Avery can converse on many topics, and even Tommy, and his and my new friend Dottie who works in our dairy, who have had almost *no* education, could not be described as stupid or dull. I have resolved to tell Aunt Clarissa about how exceedingly knowledgeable Miss Avery is, in the hope that she will be impressed and in turn tell Papa.

I enjoy my lessons at home, but I have wondered what it must be like in a school. One day, perhaps three or four years ago, Miss Avery and I passed by the village school just as the children came running out. Many had ragged clothes and only a few wore shoes. The little girls must have worn only one or two petticoats, unlike my six or seven, for their skirts lay almost flat instead of standing stiffly out like my own. Two boys were shouting and hitting each other most cruelly, but most children were taking part in a game, holding hands and running in a line, laughing and chanting—behaviour which made me smile but which my Aunt would describe as vulgar, and typical of the lower orders. I stopped, watching the children's play, and saw two little girls—perhaps sisters—rush towards each other and embrace with great affection. A strange feeling I did not understand came upon me—like sadness, and a yearning, but for what I could not tell. I stood until Miss Avery urged me on. In a little while I asked her why I did not go to the village school.

"Oh, my dear!" she cried, with unusually pink cheeks. "That is not considered suitable for a young lady of your standing. Your Papa would not want you to mix with—" Here she stopped.

Surprised in turn, I said, "But Miss Avery, you went to the village school, and I spend almost every day with you."

She smiled, unmerrily. "That is different, my dear. I am an employee, a servant."

I was greatly taken-aback and confused. "A *servant?*" I cried. I had never thought of Miss Avery as such. But she shrugged, saying nothing, and all I could find to say was, "It isn't fair!"

8th January 1844.
Having resolved to persuade Aunt Clarissa of Miss Avery's great intelligence, I have been awaiting my chance to speak to her alone. Today it came. My Aunt was sitting on the drawing-room chaise, sewing with beads and velvet. I asked if I would disturb her if I sat at a small side-table to work on my Mathematics. She smiled and welcomed me.

After a period of silent industry, my Aunt asked—just as I had hoped—to see the subject I was studying, and was most startled by a page of algebra, utterly foreign to her. "Of what use is that to you?" she enquired.

I declared with some bravado that it helped to solve many puzzles and problems—although in truth I am not sure of algebra's usefulness, much as I like it. My Aunt then obliged me by enquiring what else Miss Avery taught me, and I eagerly described my governess' cleverness, listing Euclid and Arithmetic as well as History, Geography, Latin and Greek verbs (and soon we would begin French), Drawing, Painting, Literature, the parsing of sentences in English Grammar, Writing, Poetry, Botany and—

Here she interrupted me, her voice quivering. "Botany! Is that not Science? Does Miss Avery not know that Science is the foe of Godliness?"

This so astonished me that I stared, impolitely I am sure, at my Aunt for some seconds before I could find a reply. At last I said that Miss Avery was very godly, knowing nearly all the Bible by heart, her Papa having been a parson, and as a result of her godliness I myself could recite several psalms. Aunt Clarissa here gave a loud and, I would say, unladylike sniff. I made so bold as to add, "Besides, dear Aunt, did not God create Science? Surely God created plants and flowers and birds?"

My Aunt snapped, "That is quite enough impertinence, child!"

Alas, the conversation had not turned out at all as I had intended and, fearful of how she might relate it to Papa, I quickly apologised to my Aunt and mollified her, though in my heart I was far from sincere. I was not impertinent. I had told the truth.

My Aunt and Uncle leave us tomorrow and, as I have vowed to tell the truth in these pages, I confess that I am pleased.

10th January 1844.
I am in bed before supper-time and feeling sick, the result of forcing myself to stop weeping. Miss Avery asked Elsie to light a fire in my room. My eyes bulge more than ever and I am the ugliest and most detestable girl in the world.

It is my own fault. I heard Miss Avery and Papa talking and paused to listen. It is wrong to listen to other people's conversations, but I had heard my name and could not help myself stopping outside the library. The door being slightly open,

I saw Papa at his desk. Miss Avery was not visible but it was her voice that had caught my attention. Cigar-smoke floated delicately around Papa's head, and his black curly hair shone in the afternoon sunbeams. He is very handsome. His dark green serge frock-coat was most comely against the white frill of his shirt. Papers on the desk were bright in the sun, and diamond shapes shone like mirrors on a decanter. As I looked at him I thought of how I would like to draw and paint him sitting thus at his desk in the golden light. But that was before he became angry. At first he was looking merely thoughtful, pulling his moustache.

"Sir," Miss Avery now said, with greater firmness than I would dare. "Pray do not misunderstand me. You must know that I do not believe education is wasted on a lady."

"Oh, do you not, Harriet?" said Papa in a smiling way, but he did not smile; he sighed.

"And your daughter has a good brain. She deserves the best education possible. But sir, this place you speak of is far away."

Papa sat up sharply and frowned. "What does that matter?"

"Sir, you will forgive me if I speak my mind," said Miss Avery in a tone that made her intention clear. "We have been acquainted for many years and I do not believe you have a harsh nature. Pray consider this, sir. This establishment is far from all she knows best. And—far from you, her father." I could imagine Miss Avery's boots planted solidly on the library carpet, her chin determinedly up.

"Bah." Papa stood abruptly, and kicked his chair away from his desk, like Tommy kicking the fence in a temper. He turned his back and I could not hear him well. He mentioned my Uncle and Aunt. "A most thoughtful suggestion…" he said. Then I heard the words, "fortunate child", "guardians", "a fine academic reputation", "discipline", "character". My heart had begun to make a loud noise and I pressed my hands over its horrid leaping.

"But sir——" I heard Miss Avery, "——there must be other fine establishments, nearer to home. Forgive me sir, but the child has lost one parent. Can it be right to deprive her of both?"

My Papa spun about, startling me greatly. Now, alas, I could hear him clearly. "Harriet! You——" His voice shook. "You of all people must know how I cannot bear to look at the child."

My entire body was quivering. Backing away from the door, I almost fell. I wanted to run away but I could not. There was silence in the room for a long time. I could hear my petticoats rustling as my legs wobbled.

At last Papa spoke and was calmer. "And she is growing up. My sister is right. How can you complete her proper education here? Pray do not protest further. I agree with Lady Talbot about my duty, at least, to ensure the child develops as a lady and makes a good marriage. My daughter cannot be left to run wild with the servant boys and girls."

Miss Avery's reply trembled with my skin. "I believe, sir, I have made certain your daughter has not run wild. Nor, indeed, is that in her character. I do not disagree in principle that she would benefit from a better education than I can provide, but I am concerned for her inner wellbeing—her happiness. I merely sugest that it is so very far away, and—"

"Let it be! The further, the better," my Papa cried, his face white. "I do my duty by her, and that is all I can do."

Now I found strength to run away, not heeding the clatter of my boots. I rushed along the hall and down the back stairs to the water-closet by the sculleries and I was sick over and again until I ached all through.

Miss Avery may have heard me running and guessed that I had been listening, for she showed no surprise in finding me ill from weeping and unable to eat. However, she neither scolded me nor asked questions. Indeed, she appeared subdued. Possibly she too had been weeping, although I have never seen her weep, so I cannot be sure.

Chapter Twelve

14th April 1844. Edinburgh, Scotland.

   O, far longer than a mere five days does it seem since Miss Avery and I boarded the train at Rugby Railway Station. We are in Edinburgh three days, and this is my first opportunity to sit with my journal. Today being Sunday, we Young Ladies are permitted one hour and a half for our own reading or writing. This follows a half-hour in which we are obliged to write our weekly letter home. I wrote to Papa with great difficulty, for I have never written to him before and surely he does not wish to know my thoughts; even if he did so, I could not possibly express to him my true feelings. I briefly outlined the journey, and told him I was well. I revealed no impressions of the Academy, for it is the rule that our letters remain unsealed in order to be checked by the Headmistress. This injustice (or perhaps shrewdness) surely means that any girl is most unwise to express to her parents any adverse opinion of the Academy—or indeed any personal emotion that she would prefer kept private.

   Scotland is the country where I was born. My Mama was born and bred in Scotland, and (Miss Avery told me) returned to her parental home for her confinement because her own Mama wished her to have the services of a skilled local midwife. Papa travelled with her, but returned home within days of my birth—and her death. I was under six months of age when, in the care of a wet-nurse, Fate—or God's Will—removed me from Scotland to my Papa's family home near Rugby. It had been decided, when my Mama died, that her Mama would have care of me. That was my Grandmama's wish, and no doubt Papa agreed readily. But my Grandmama's health failed, through grief at the loss of her daughter, and I was taken away. My Grandmama died before I was a year old. I now see that I caused the deaths of two people while yet an infant. Are these, in God's eyes, wicked sins, even if committed unknowingly? Perhaps it would have been best if I too had died, like the little foal with the mare. What is God's purpose in allowing my beautiful mother and blameless grandmother to die, while I, with a face like a frog and evil in my heart, am permitted to live?

   Edinburgh, as we entered its streets in a stagecoach, seemed crowded with frowning grey buildings. I allow that I was fatigued after long travel, and it had been raining, so all was colourless under the heavy sky. The space between street and castle was hung with lead-coloured cloud and I thought desolately of battlefields and death. Trying to cheer myself by picturing Tommy's impudent grin, I merely succeeded in wondering wistfully if he missed me.

   We would be arriving at the Academy twenty-four hours earlier than originally planned. It had been intended that we spend a night at the home of my Uncle and

Aunt, but news had come that Aunt Clarissa had been delivered of a baby boy and was too fatigued to receive us. (I was satisfied to be proved correct concerning her belly at Christmas, and pleased to have a baby cousin—almost the same as a brother. He is to be named Lachlan Humphrey! Spoken aloud, the names remind me of my Uncle clearing his throat.)

Fear seized my heart when our coach drew up at the Academy. Sheer despair would have made me leap down and flee, had Miss Avery not accompanied me here. How bravely she had risked Papa's wrath in applying for a teaching post at the Academy. He learned of it only when he summoned us both to the library to tell me my fate. His news was not entirely a surprise, but nevertheless tears tried to escape my eyes while I gazed rigidly at my blue kid slippers so that Papa would not have the misfortune of looking upon my face while he told me of my expulsion. In the weeks since my eavesdropping—when indeed the saying proved true, and I heard nought but ill of myself—I had learned nothing further and had been praying that Miss Avery had succeeded in changing Papa's mind. This, alas, was one of many unanswered prayers. Now Papa announced my good fortune in that I would be attending an Academy in Edinburgh, for which he would be paying a considerable sum—forty-five guineas a year. Further, my Aunt and Uncle, who had recommended it, would act as my guardians during my years at the school, and I should be grateful for their kindness—and also to Miss Avery, who would be accompanying me on the long journey north.

Here Miss Avery astounded him with her own announcement. "Sir, I am obliged to tell you that I have been offered employment by the Academy to which your dear daughter is going, and have accepted."

I too was astounded.

"You are to stay there? Whatever next? Why did you not tell me before?"

"Sir, I wished to say nothing before my post was confirmed. I assure you that our own agreement remains as regards your employing me to supervise the child during Academy holidays, either here or with Sir John and Lady Talbot in Scotland. You understand, sir, it would not be possible for me to live solely on a part-time income, and it made good sense to apply to the Academy. Thus I could reassure myself—and you, sir—of your daughter's continued wellbeing."

My tears slid back behind my eyes and I lifted my head to stare at Miss Avery, more relieved than I can possibly express.

"I see. I see." Papa was displeased. "You will teach there? Are you sufficiently qualified? I understood that the teachers are gentlemen."

"It is true that many are, but several are female. The Headmistress knows my subjects and experience but naturally requires to see my abilities demonstrated to her satisfaction and that of the Governors." Miss Avery spoke as if she had carefully rehearsed her reply.

Papa said in irritation: "How did you arrange all this?"

Miss Avery smiled. "By the Penny Post, sir. In the weeks since you revealed your plans for the child's education, I have sent and received several letters."

"I see," said Papa again, glaring at us both. Miss Avery looked fearlessly straight back at him, but I returned to the scrutiny of my slippers and sadly reflected that Papa's annoyance at this defiance was greater than any concern for our happiness. This was a disrespectful thought, which I attempted to banish, but I fear it is true.

Thus this great change in my life has come about. Weeks of preparation included the purchase of much clothing for me as listed by the Academy. My first impressions of my new wardrobe were less than joyful, but I now feel fortunate in this cold climate to possess long-sleeved, fleecy and exceedingly ugly under-bodices as well as calico and flannel "garments" (the polite name for what in reality are drawers), articles I have never before worn. The calico is worn beneath the flannel and both are buttoned to the bodice. They are most strange. I also own heavy flannel petticoats, stockings of black wool which cause itching, a thick coat with attached cape, a felt and a velvet hat, dresses, mittens, boots and much else—not forgetting, alas, two corsets which Aunt Clarissa insisted in a letter are essential for keeping my waist very slender, as befits a fashionable young lady. Miss Avery pursed her lips at these, and so far I have not worn one, being sure of her sympathy. Tedious days were spent inking my name on lengths of tape and stitching these into every item. Then my handsome new leather trunk was packed—and at last we were ready for our journey.

I had never before been on a railway train nor indeed been very close to one, so—despite the sadness I had felt in the chaise as I waved to Cook and the butler and maids, and to dear Tommy who waved and waved, shouting "Good luck Miss!" in a wobbly voice—despite all this, as we stepped on to the station I was amazed and excited at the engine's hugeness and noise, the steam and smoke and smells, and the words MIDLAND COUNTIES in high shining letters. A porter stowed our trunks and led us to our First Class carriage, settling us courteously in our seats. Miss Avery discreetly slipped some coins into his open palm, at the same time suggesting that if it were at all possible, we should like to be left undisturbed. He touched his cap and said: "Certainly ma'am," with the utmost respect, and afterwards took care to direct other passengers to different compartments.

I was full of awe and some alarm when the train began to move: such enormous power had the engine, drawing its great burden out of the station like a gigantic living creature with a breathing, steaming head, little by little gathering speed with triumphant growls. I said to myself firmly: This is an adventure, one should not be sad or fearful. I put a smile on my lips and Miss Avery smiled in return.

At times we travelled very fast; we enquired of the guard as to our speed when, during our pause at Leicester, he approached to check tickets. He informed us proudly, as if it were his own doing, that the average speed was above thirty miles an hour, but on occasion it reached sixty miles an hour. I could not help wondering if this is faster than mankind was ever intended to travel!

From Leicester we continued to Derby. I saw church spires, high walls, important buildings with columns, streets, shops, dirty lanes, market stalls, ragged people bent against the wind, unkempt little beggar-children—thin, barefoot and surely frozen—women in fur-edged cloaks being assisted to and from their carriages by gentlemen in tall hats. How strange it all was!

At Derby, nearly two hours after leaving Rugby, we were obliged to change to another train with GREAT NORTHERN painted upon it, bound for York and Newcastle. Miss Avery confirmed the safe transfer of our luggage and then, since we had an hour before departure and were in need of private facilities (there being no such provision at the railway station) we went to an hotel nearby. Here, the miserable facilities for our relief—a bucket and plank, in a small and stinking wooden hut—are best forgotten. O, the ordeal managing my petticoats and skirt! What contrast with our water-closets at home! (But I know from Tommy that few people have such luxuries, and we are fortunate. Not that he cares. How simple such matters are for men! When Tommy wants to relieve himself, he simply turns his back next to a tree—while I politely turn away—and does so with little inconvenience to himself or his clothing. This is because of a difference between male and female anatomy, as I have seen in Miss Avery's books of Art. This difference may be seen in animals also.)

As we left Derby Miss Avery drew a damp cloth perfumed with lavender from the sponge-bag in her reticule. We cleaned our hands and opened our hamper of food prepared by dear Mrs Williams, generally addressed plainly as Cook. Had I then known the kind of food we would be given at the Academy I should have attentively relished every mouthful—from Cook's home-cured ham to her fluffy apple-cake. We were careful to drink little of the delicious lemonade, not knowing when next we would find facilities for relief. We then lay down on the seats to rest, first removing our boots. I slept a little with a dream of Papa very angry at some wrong he was convinced I had done, despite my desperate protests, and from this I was glad to awake.

Our train stopped briefly at a few different places—Sheffield and York are names I remember—and again I glimpsed the contrast of wealth and poverty in the cities. I wondered why God ordered the world with rich and poor instead of with everyone fortunate. Is it to teach us to look after one another?

At seven o'clock in the evening we arrived at York, having left Rugby at noon. Here our guard discreetly informed us of a twelve-minute wait and indicated a Ladies' Waiting Room, where our good fortune was to find a closet with a reasonably clean commode. Our train stopped a few more times but I remember only Thirsk, because it made me think of thirst. At last, at half past ten o'clock, we came to Newcastle, and were exceedingly fatigued and—it seemed to me—covered from bonnet to boots with soot and grit. Here was the end of our journey by rail. As yet no trains travel across the border to Scotland and one is obliged to continue by stagecoach. Should anyone wish to go to Glasgow, Miss Avery explained, there is an even greater challenge. One must take a train to a distant place on the west coast and complete the journey by sea, in a steamer!

Miss Avery had information about a Newcastle inn, and a hackney-carriage took us there. The inn was clean, with smooth sheets on our beds, and the luxury of a water-closet close by! Its clankings were terrible, but we willingly forgave it. Each of our beds had its own wash-stand with bowl and ewer, while a curtain modestly divided the room. (Here I reflected on the puzzle of human nakedness being deemed acceptable in paintings and sculptures, yet not in reality. However, Aunt Clarissa might also declare the art improper, so nothing is straightforward.)

Miss Avery insisted upon water being brought in order to wash away the grime of our journey. I would have happily fallen unwashed into bed but when the maid brought copious warm water, it was a joy to wash from head to foot and don a clean nightgown.

Next morning more warm water arrived and, after my toilet, Miss Avery brushed, dampened and neatened my loathsome hair. As she laced my boots she said: "Well my dear child, I cannot say how many more times I will be permitted to do this for you." She sounded wistful, as if she were saying goodbye.

My own sadness of the previous night returned, when I had lain awake thinking of Papa as I last saw him—standing on the driveway beneath my bedroom window, waiting for his carriage. I had experienced one of my strange episodes—interruptions in my mind—and afterwards been overcome by dark thoughts that told me of evil in my heart. I wept in my strange bed in a faraway town—quietly, lest Miss Avery was also wakeful. Now, as she finished my boots and I looked at her dark head, my eyes filled with tears at how much had changed, for both of us, but I knew I must be strong and independent. I held back my tears—for I had made a private vow before leaving home that I would henceforth conceal my weaknesses behind an imaginary shell, thus protecting myself from this hostile world. I must often remind myself of that vow.

Breakfast revived me and, when our stagecoach drew in front of the inn with four horses tossing their heads as if eager to transport us, I was in better spirits and Miss Avery's smile had returned. We travelled the entire day with much bustling of many strangers, some of whom carried odious smells. It is a long road from Newcastle to Edinburgh, and although we passed through beautiful scenery, I am too weary to write everything. Many stops were made for passengers to alight and depart, and for refreshment and relief (frequently in conditions that I can hardly bear to think of), as well as for changes of horses.

It was dusk again when we arrived at the Scottish Academy for Young Ladies, and now relief at the ending of our travels was obscured by the dread I have already noted. Never have I been so weary and afraid, and never shall I understand how I succeeded in concealing my terrors, forcing myself to climb with steady gait, and straight back, up the glistening stone steps towards the lofty pillars and huge door. Here stood a large mansion built of exceedingly grey slabs, cold and hard, quite unlike the dark red brick and worn beams of our own dear house left behind. But I was determined to overcome my despair, and lifted my chin. Seeing this, Miss Avery sent me an approving glance and gave me a gentle push so that I should proceed ahead of her.

As we reached the topmost step, the looming door startled us by yawning wide.

A white-capped maid stood smiling on the threshold, her cheeks the only rosy things in the gloom. She could not be more than two or three years older than myself, yet her manner was as assured as that of an adult.

"Good evening, Miss! Good evening Ma'am!" said she. "Miss Moore? And the governess, Miss Avery? Welcome to the Scottish Academy for Young Ladies." With these words, spoken with Scottish inflections, she bobbed a curtsey to each of us, adding: "Our Headmistress awaits you both in her sitting-room. I shall escort you. Please enter."

As soon as we had done so, the maid confidently issued orders to the porters as to where they should place our trunks. How strange and frightened I felt in this foreign place! We stood at the edge of a vast hall; its high ceiling, lofty arching windows and stone-flagged floors were strongly reminiscent of a church. Astride the centre of the hall was an enormous table, and beyond it I dimly glimpsed a broad staircase. The twilight of the street had become darkness within, and little more could be seen in the glow from wall-mounted oil-lamps and one globular lamp upon the table. It was just possible to discern heavy panelling, closed doors, the gleam of oil paintings and gilt frames. I could feel no welcome in the atmosphere, and I trembled with apprehension. The chill, moist air smelled of lamp-oil, beeswax, candles, and some other, lurking and less appealing odour that caused me to wrinkle up my nose.

"You are most fortunate," now remarked the maid approvingly, "in arriving a day ahead of the rest, for you are privileged to have a leisured conversation with the Headmistress before more demands are placed upon her valued time. Pray follow me."

Plucking a candle from a side-table she conducted us along a corridor with frugally lengthy spaces between its lamps. Observing the maid's prideful swagger I was suddenly possessed by an urge to break into laughter—but one backward glance at my governess' sober features made me control my own. Fatigue and fear, I am certain, caused this contrary mirthfulness—but I had made my resolution and would abide by it. By the time we stopped before a dark-polished door, I had forced my features to be inscrutable. The maid knocked and announced with some drama: "The Misses Avery and Moore have arrived!"

A Scottish voice sounding as deep as a gentleman's commanded us to enter. It was a voice, I reflected, accustomed to obedience. Enter we did, and now my heart quailed anew at my first sight of the gaunt, imposing Headmistress who was to be in charge of my life henceforth. Miss Amelia MacIntosh rose like a tower unfolding from her armchair, filling the small room. Dismissing the maid, she turned towards us and addressed us pleasantly yet without a suggestion of a smile. The room held three armchairs, two of them as angular as their owner, and three or four upright wooden chairs of dubious comfort; Miss Avery was directed to one of the former and I to the latter. The Headmistress of the Academy then resumed her own armchair, a softer creation of dusky pink velvet much at odds with her own spare, dark-clad appearance.

The next thing I observed was that Miss MacIntosh had a moustache—at which I feared to stare, lest it resurrect my laughter. I stared instead at my own trembling fingers. My throat was now so dry I could not swallow, while my eyes burned, and a surge of misery rose throughout me. I held my back straight against the cruelly carved chair, and felt quite alone in the world. I was now fully an orphan. Miss Avery was with me but I knew that she would be kept more distant from this day on. I told myself sternly that I did not need the indulgence of her assistance with dressing or boot-lacing. Nevertheless I would miss its comfort. I would miss our discussions and our walks and meals together—simply, our friendship. Most of all I would miss her ready understanding whenever I wished to talk about my Mama. In those moments it seemed that I had lost everything, and the Headmistress' moustache seemed after all a depressing thing.

"Tomorrow," boomed this lady, "when all pupils arrive, I give my welcoming speech. Suffice it for me to say now that I do indeed welcome you here, my child, to this leading Academy for Young Ladies, an Academy where it is a privilege both to teach and to learn. The curriculum is far ahead of any other such institution, either in Scotland or England, as regards standards for women."

She stated this plainly and with only the smallest intonation of a boast, and I saw Miss Avery take interest.

"I do not believe," continued Miss MacIntosh, "that because a woman's career may be to marry, run a household and bring up children, she does not benefit from as good an education as may be given to a boy. Here at the Academy, by example and instruction, superior teaching, and with emphasis on discipline—that of mind and body—you are intended to develop into a truly broadly-educated woman, able to take part in discussion upon all manner of subjects. A Young Lady's only expected career need not be marriage and motherhood—but, should these prove to be her destiny, she will surely be the very root of a much improved education for her entire family."

Miss MacIntosh paused, and I sensed that she was looking at me. I continued to stare at my hands, and was grateful when Miss Avery's words rescued me.

"We are of like mind," she declared. "And Miss Moore has been well versed in such attitudes, despite some familial dissent. You will find that she has reached a respectable level of education, and has a willing intelligence and well-formed curiosity. She will work hard at the Academy."

"I am gratified to hear your words," replied the Headmistress, "for I was unsure if Lady Talbot, Miss Moore's aunt, was convinced of my educational aims, her greater concern being a lady's gentle accomplishments."

"Ah," said Miss Avery, and here I found myself able to raise my head to look at my new Headmistress with the slightest of smiles.

"I was able to assure her," Miss MacIntosh continued, rising from her chair, "that we paint, we embroider, we play the pianoforte. And so forth." Here she sighed and strode to the window, now continuing to speak as if to capture the attention of a listening crowd beyond the dark panes. She held her right hand in a fist and smacked it several times into her left palm. "My greatest wish," she declared, "is to send my Young Ladies to Universities. To see them gain the same degrees that are awarded to men. Why not?" She spun and glared at us as if challenging us to disagree. "Why not?"

"Why not?" cried Miss Avery, clearly impressed. She turned to me. "Perhaps you, my dear, might be such a pioneer!"

"I?" Amazement restored my voice, for such an extraordinary notion had never been presented to me. It could never have occurred to Papa, nor indeed to my Uncle and Aunt. But it struck me with exciting force, with the result that my apprehension about the future, while not falling entirely away, was greatly lessened. I replied: "Why, I had not believed it possible. I did not think it would ever be permitted—But it would be wonderful! I should be able to read every single book in the world and learn every language!" I stopped, fearful that I had sounded foolish.

Miss Avery, however, appeared delighted. Miss MacIntosh did not smile, but her expression softened. She nodded, slowly. "Indeed," she agreed, "that would be wonderful."

21st April, 1844.

My second Sunday at the Academy. My hopes have soon faded and I have felt sorely alone, as well as uncomfortably chilly almost all the time. Scotland is cold and windy—indoors and out, for our dormitory windows are opened wide each night, for "copious fresh air" (as our Housemistress expresses it) is deemed essential to health. As I am nearest to the windows in our dormitory, I ruefully surmise that I shall be the healthiest in our group! A girl of my own age with a cheerful demeanour occupies the bed next to mine and has informed me that the windows remain open all year, even through frost and snow. In January, the girls were obliged to break the ice on the water for their morning wash! Warm water is provided only on Sunday, for a hip-bath: it is an oasis in an icy desert.

At the beginning I was very fearful and bewildered; the latter has somewhat lessened as I have understood my surroundings a little better. At first it seemed that everywhere about me was the sound of hurrying feet, and so many rooms and corridors that I was soon lost. I simply followed others and hoped to remember, but I remained muddled for days. There were so many faces, strange girls who looked curious or mocking—and all the mistresses so stern-eyed! Never before had I seen so many females all together, and alas they alarmed me and continue to do so, being so knowing, industrious and purposeful while I still frequently feel foolish and timid. In addition they did not and do not speak. The Headmistress, Miss MacIntosh (who has yet to smile in my presence), informed me at the outset that general speech among the Young Ladies is forbidden during school hours, unless one is addressed by a teacher or in an emergency. The reason for the rule was not explained. I am accustomed to solitude and silence, but my difficulty has been that I could ask no questions when perplexed. An older girl severely informed me (in a whisper) that I must work things out for myself.

Sunday, 28th April 1844.

I am very unhappy. There are many hateful things and silly rules here.

It is almost impossible to be alone. Edinburgh has been my home for over a fortnight, but only on my first Sunday have I been able to write at length in my journal—perhaps because my being a newcomer encouraged others to leave me unmolested. My entry last Sunday was exceedingly brief despite having ample Personal Writing Time in the Common Room—my letter to Papa being written in a few minutes. However, I soon abandoned all attempt because the curiosity of others became greatly troublesome. We are obliged to work clustered about a table, and the moment I first opened my journal—shielding it with one arm—and dipped my pen, I was surrounded by nudging and inquisitive whispers. (This despite the prohibition on speech—a rule which, for the first time, I would have preferred obeyed.) It was soon clear that girls on all sides were craning impolite necks to see what I might write. I therefore closed my journal and took out an exceedingly dull history of Scotland by Sir Walter Scott. Reading this had put me into an ill temper by the end of the period.

Whispers became plain-spoken questions when we returned to the dormitory to put away our books. "O! Little Miss Mystery! Is it a very private book? Does it tell all your secrets?" Here followed giggling and teasing attempts to seize my journal. I affected a careless air, saying, "It is just a silly book my governess gave me to do writing exercises, but I was not in the right frame of mind." No girl quite believed me, but pestering had to cease or all risked being punished for lateness at tea. I succeeded in concealing my journal in my trunk beneath my bed where it remained until today.

Today, therefore, I have abandoned the Common Room on the pretext of an urgent need to visit a water-closet. Here I write this small entry, seated upon polished mahogany in reasonable comfort. The reward for my little escape will certainly be a laxative medicine from Matron, since I shall be obliged to tell an untruth as to why I was so long away.

Friday 3rd May.

It is not Sunday, and yet I can write my journal! This the result of excellent news this rainy morning. My Music Master has been stricken with illness, and my pianoforte lesson is cancelled. I do not rejoice at another's misfortune and wish the gentleman no great harm even if his attitude to music is somewhat lifeless, but his absence gives me an opportunity to write, although I am breaking an Academy Rule to do so. The Rule: No Young Lady may enter the dormitories before bedtime, unless to change clothing or books, and never without permission.

"You will find something useful to do," my House Mistress instructed me, doubtless intending that I should practise Scales or Rudiments, but I took the decision to interpret her words differently. I stole out of the Music Room and up the back stairs to the dormitory. I am seated on the boards between my bed and that of the person whom in these pages I shall name Emmie, and am ready to hide quickly if necessary.

If only we had curtains about our beds! Then I could easily conceal myself. We are not given curtains until we reach the age of fifteen. This is one of many Rules with which I disagree. We are exhorted morning and evening by our House Mistress—Miss P., a lady whom I shall include in my proposed list of Detestations—to remove and don our garments with the utmost modesty lest we sinfully look upon our own bodies or allow others to see us. If modesty is so important, why do we not have curtains? I am uncertain whether Miss P.'s demand for modesty is an Academy Rule. Emmie says it is merely her "Puritanical whim", adding that if it is such a sin to look at nakedness, why does our House Mistress spend so much time with her darting eyes spying on the least exposure of flesh?

As to privacy for my journal, I try to cheer myself with the thought that matters may improve as the season advances, for during the light summer evenings I may be able to write secretly in my bed when the other girls have fallen asleep. There are eight girls, including myself, in our dormitory. My luck will depend on how swiftly they slumber.

Sunday, 2nd June.

O, this has been a miserable month. Were it not for Emmie (who has asked me if I will be her special friend) and an occasional word with Miss Avery, I should have despaired.

I have endured the horrors of the Punishment Cupboard, the result of my being discovered in the dormitory. Miss P., finding me absent from the Music Room, had guessed my mischief—my deceit, as it was called. Suddenly there she stood, her ugly neck purple with anger, eyes starting from her face. Thanks to God I was able to push my journal under the bed before she saw it. My excuse for being there was that I had dropped a music sheet, an untruth she could not believe, since I had left no possessions in the Music Room to indicate my return. "Were you reading Forbidden Books?" she demanded, to my astonishment. "Were you indulging in Bad Habits?" Her neck veins throbbed as if she would suffer a seizure. I was seized roughly and marched to the Punishment Cupboard under the back stairs; she fiercely thrust me into its pitch-black cavity. The door banged, the bolt grated, and her voice followed me: "You will be reported to Miss MacIntosh straight away. You shall remain here for two hours, and be deprived of luncheon, tea and supper."

The Punishment Cupboard is a dungeon that all dread. It is exceedingly dark with a damp stone floor—the only place to sit—and deathly cold. Soon I was shivering all over, and my teeth were knocking together. Sometimes I heard scuttlings and was in a terror lest a rat ran to bite me. I leapt to my feet and remained thus, unable to lean upon the wet walls. Worse, a horrid odour suffocated me, a heavier version of that which wafts at the front of the Academy. Soon convinced I was breathing poison, I was assailed by nausea. Two hours passed like as many months in this fearsome gaol. Had I committed so great an evil as to deserve such a punishment? But this was not to be the end of it.

After everyone else had eaten luncheon, I was led by Miss P. (burning with righteous triumph, as Emmie later described it) into the Great Hall. To my consternation, all the Young Ladies and Staff were here gathered. Miss MacIntosh, with stony features, commanded me to stand upon a chair to be seen by all. Hungry and afraid, I believed I might faint and fall. Miss MacIntosh stood apart from me—perhaps lest she be contaminated by my evil nature, which she then declaimed. Mistresses covered their faces in horror at my DECEIT, my FLAUNTING OF RULES, FAILURE TO SEEK PERMISSION, UNLADYLIKE BEHAVIOUR and UNTRUTHFULNESS. I was fortunate not to have been BIRCHED. All Young Ladies were forbidden to speak to me for a week.

It was most disagreeable to be faced by a mass of disapproving expressions—save two. Miss Avery's eyes were lowered, and I could not tell if she felt pity or shame. But Emmie looked boldly straight at me, giving a most Unladylike wink! Had she been seen, she too would have been punished. My courage rose. I had surely not deserved a dungeon *and* this melodrama! My spirits thus bolstered I was able, without a tear, to obey Miss MacIntosh's command to apologise to the whole school—uttering words of false remorse, with downcast eyes. However, my heart thudded when Miss MacIntosh informed me that she would be writing to Papa.

The week of silence was most unpleasant. Certain girls, not satisfied with merely ignoring me, shunned me exaggeratedly, spitefully and with the disgust afforded to a leper—although they knew almost nothing of my character. This led me to reflect that when people are enclosed together in one place, small and often pointless rules appear to have huge importance, and these people may become unable to think for themselves. Only Emmie helped to make this period less hateful, for she and I exchanged short whispers in the darkened dormitory while others slept, or so we hoped. Some surely heard us, but were kind enough to pretend otherwise.

As that week ended I was surprised when a few girls privately congratulated me upon the fact that no-one before me had succeeded in not being brought to sobbing during a Miss MacIntosh reprimand, such is the weight of disapproval cast upon the culprit! The truth is, however, that I was not especially brave, and had I felt myself genuinely to be in the wrong, I would probably have wept out of remorse and shame. But "deceit", "sin" and "evil" are extreme words for the mischief of breaking one small rule.

Soon I received a stern, cold letter from Papa. "Ungrateful", "dishonest", "shame" and "family honour" all appeared. This, the only letter I have ever received from Papa, succeeded—unlike Miss MacIntosh—in making me weep miserably.

At the first opportunity I showed Miss Avery the letter. I had not spoken to her since my punishment, she having been visiting her ailing mother. She sighed and said: "Do not let this make you unhappy, my dear. Your Papa knows only what he has been told." She smiled kindly, looking around to be sure we were unobserved, and whispered: "You were not so very wicked." Foolishly, I burst into tears once again.

In future, I have resolved, I should take greater care not to be discovered. That is the important thing. I have no wish to experience the Punishment Cupboard again. The rest I can endure, even if I were to be birched on both hands with all Miss MacIntosh's strength.

Today, at last, the outlook is brighter. For not only is the weather fine (for the first Sunday since my arrival) but this very day I have discovered a place where I can write undisturbed. Hence I have written more today than for weeks. But now I hear the striking of the stable clock and must make haste to return indoors—or risk another Terrible Chastisement!

Chapter Thirteen

Sunday, 9th June.

I have returned to my secret place. (Only Emmie knows its whereabouts and she has sworn to tell no-one, not even if she is condemned to the Punishment Cupboard for one whole week.)

Until the rains ended last week, I had scarcely set foot in the Academy's gardens, which extend some three acres, part-wooded, all surrounded by high walls.

Fresh air and regular exercise are insisted upon, no matter the weather—but our obligatory daily walks have been conducted in the town, it being too muddy in the grounds. Cloaked and bent under umbrellas, two by two in a long line, it is a dreary way of taking the air! Therefore, when last weekend the sun shone, everyone was greatly cheered and I learned that in good weather our Sunday reading and writing time may be spent in the Academy grounds. This news delighted me, for I have missed my freedom to rove the woods and fields with Tommy and had come to believe that life in Scotland must be forever within grey walls or on grey pavements.

One may go anywhere in the grounds as long as one is within earshot of the stable clock announcing tea-time. My first aim being to avoid the eyes of the House Mistress on duty, I stayed close to the wall bordering the vegetable garden, it being somewhat shielded by shrubs; here I hoped to find a seat out of sight of the Academy's windows. By happy chance I glimpsed a small cat—whom I followed, hoping to befriend it. It ran behind a gardener's hut and thence to a narrow pathway—leading through further shrubs to a patch of rough grassland. Here the path ended; the cat, too, had disappeared. But a little spinney was before me, leafy and brambly: I ran across the grass and plunged within, my skirts catching upon thorns. This was reckless indeed, for if I tear my clothes I shall be obliged to explain myself, *and* to mend them.

How wonderful to be in woodland again, with its delightful twitterings and rustlings and smells of leaf-mould and ferns. I soon came upon a large tree fallen against another, creating a niche that at once became my chair. Saplings and thick bushes crowd upon this part of the spinney, and I am quite safely concealed. There being quantities of twigs upon the ground, I would hear any approach long in advance. I sat listening to a mavis singing its varied song, delighting in my solitude. I believe I am most contented when not surrounded by the bustle of others. Human beings are said to be happiest among their fellows, like herding animals or flocking birds. But I wonder if this is *presumed* simply because of the difficulties of *avoiding* one's fellow humans? *I* should not regret never being in another crowd, or never again entering a room with more than two or three other persons in it.

The *truth* is that there are not many people for whom I have affection. The *truth* also, I fear, is that I myself am not likeable, being a discontented person with many detestations and lacking Emmie's stoical forbearance.

Here I begin my List of DISLIKES *and* DETESTATIONS *at the Academy.*

1. *I Dislike seeing very little of Miss Avery.* Although expected this still saddens me. Now and again she is able to speak to me personally. Yesterday we coincided on the stairs with no-one near. She enquired if I had heard again from Papa, and I said I had not, adding calmly: "It is not important, for I well understand that I am of no interest to him." Alas, my words caused Miss Avery to look upset, but unhappily I could not make amends for a group of Young Ladies appeared and we could not continue.

I see her for longest periods when she teaches our class English Grammar and Geography, but on these occasions Miss Avery is obliged to address me as just one of several pupils for it would be improper for her to show me greater attention. Occasionally, however, on a Sunday morning when she has no teaching duties, she visits our dormitory and—"for old times' sake"—she laces my boots before we leave for Church. She helps the other girls too, if they wish it. I am happy to see how well they like her. These are precious moments, and I must remind myself that had fortune not smiled upon us a little, she would not be here with me at all.

2. *I Detest: Too Little Privacy—Too Much Curiosity!* We Young Ladies are under constant supervision, not trusted to perform any activity alone—excepting sleeping, and relieving oneself in the closet! And even *that* is a matter for enquiry! "Bowel movements" are of some significance to Matron. She commands a large wheeled wooden chest of many compartments and drawers of *Remedies*, and she trundles this about the dormitories every Sunday morning after bed-making. (Few maids are on duty on Sundays and we are obliged to make our own beds; this I had never done before, and was at first so inept that all in the dormitory laughed at my efforts.)

Matron's voice, shouting out for our symptoms, enters the dormitory before her person; then in she comes, with her assisting maid. If a girl has a head-cold, she will give her nitre. If a sore throat, she must gargle with powdered alum. If her head aches (or back, stomach, or any other part) she will receive Gregory Powder. But the most important items are *Senna Pods*, which Matron enthusiastically dispenses. Every girl is asked when her bowels last moved; if more than four and twenty hours have elapsed, Senna Pods are compulsory. Matron is wont to spank a girl who has taken Senna Pods and still reports no bowel movement.

In short, very few of our actions go unremarked. If I were to write all intrusions down, I should have no other subject in my journal! The general watchfulness and inquisitiveness of the teachers make it seem that anything we might undertake without supervision carries with it some hint of unhealthiness.

Sunday, 16th June.
  My List continues.
  3. *I* DETEST *the Detestable Miss P.* Thus shall I refer to her henceforth, for since my Punishment Week my distaste for every aspect of her being is greatly increased. When she is on duty on a Sunday—and, I fear, even as I write in my secret place she is roaming the grounds and would be overjoyed to discover me—she shows a particular (and offensive) intrusiveness, constantly pouncing on different girls and demanding to know what we are reading or writing—and, if writing, on what subject and to whom. She does this in so fierce a manner, quite often snatching up a girl's book to discover if she deems it "suitable reading" for a Young Lady, that it is exceedingly difficult for her victim not to be intimidated. Detestable indeed, and yet I believe she detests me even more than I detest her.
  During History lessons—a subject she succeeds in making duller than can be believed—I sometimes look up to find her staring at me, and her expression discomfits me greatly. When my eyes meet hers her stare becomes a glare of loathing—and my heart falters. Perhaps she simply detests my silly face! Emmie says: "She is just a horrid old woman who smells nasty and she is jealous because you are clever. Pray ignore her."
  On the matter of smell I do agree. Often, at letter-writing time, I have been suddenly aware of her immediately behind my shoulder—a position gained inaudibly, but smell has given her away. A most malodorous person is she, emitting an effluence of sweat, fishiness and camphor, with breath like rotting cheese. At such times she openly and improperly peers down at my page. I do not care if she sees what I write to Papa, but her behaviour confirms the impossibility of writing in my journal, lest she seize it. I cannot imagine what scenes might ensue!

  4. *A Severe Dislike: The Academy smell!* I refer to the sickening air of the Punishment Cupboard that appears in milder form in various parts of the building. I believe it to be caused by drains, for I am reminded of the time one of Papa's gardeners was obliged to clear a bad-smelling drain. Soon afterwards he and his family fell dreadfully ill and the youngest boy died. Papa paid the Doctor to attend them and also for their medicines. I can say nothing, for nobody is interested in a child's view. We are told we may discuss any problems, personal or academic, with our House Mistress; once a week each girl may request a short meeting. In the days before I had fully realised the Detestability of Miss P., I took the opportunity of mentioning this Academy Smell to her, explaining my concerns about drains. The Detestable replied, sarcastically, that I must be possessed of an unusually sensitive nose along with childish ignorance, and that it was normal for all drains to have a "slight odour". It was clear that she regarded my query as an affront to Authority.
  One day our walk took us by the river. We saw all manner of disgusting things

floating there and I realised that drains must flow directly into our rivers. Emmie, who has visited London, remarked that matters there are even worse; in the summer the stench of the River Thames is so repellent that people vomit or faint.

5. *I greatly Dislike: Our Food.* Exceedingly dull and flavourless. I think longingly of Mrs Williams' roasted meats and potatoes, rabbit pies and mutton stews, fresh beans and peas, fresh-baked bread, fruit *compôtes* and apple puddings. *Our* fare is watery rice, heavy bread, potatoes and suet pastry. Meat and fish are scarce. Fresh eggs are rarities, yet there is a pen with ducks and hens; vegetables and fruits are few, yet there is a kitchen garden and a little orchard. It is said these good things are reserved for the Headmistress and Teaching Staff. We *never* set eyes on sweetmeats, these being signs of "indulgence". We are obliged to sit at table and finish everything, no matter how vile. I could not have guessed that I would look upon a plate of food with dread!

6. *I Dislike: Unnecessary Discomfort.* Discomfort is good for us. To quote Miss MacIntosh: "Stoical acceptance of life's discomforts has a character-forming effect." Her sitting-room has fire-place, carpet and soft armchair. I conclude that *her* character must be fully formed for she has no further need of discomfort. The Staff Room also boasts carpet and fire-place.

No such luxuries exist elsewhere. To quote Matron: "Hard beds and pillows are good for the spirit. Soft beds lead to impure thoughts." Also: "Young Ladies must be hardened early. Those who loll in cushions are doomed to a sickly life." Hence cold baths, wide-flung windows and one thin blanket upon our beds. Hence also agonising chilblains in winter. No "weakness" is indulged. Girls who faint in Church are harshly treated. One poor pale person, whose mother insists on her being tightly laced in her corset (even at night!), swooned during a sermon and was told that repetition would be punished. Another girl was punished for coughing in Church. For "insufficient self-discipline" she received two blows of the birch upon her hand and spent half an hour in the Punishment Cupboard. Next day she had a severe fever.

7. *I utterly* DETEST: *Kissing.* This item should, strictly, be included with my Detestation of Miss P.—but I understand that some other House Mistresses behave similarly.

Every Saturday night when all are in bed, our malodorous House Mistress visits the dormitories in her charge, and kisses every girl. At other times she indicates no affection for us. Emmie finds Miss P.'s habit laughable—if undesirable—while my own feeling is of deep revulsion. Her glassy blue eyes gaze down. She then bends and presses her wet lips on top of mine. I close my eyes tightly and cannot help but shudder, but when it ends and I look, she is smiling down at me in a strange and distant way. It is not a smile that warms my heart.

Other girls whisper and giggle about her dreadful "kissing hour". I cannot laugh.

I try to dismiss Miss P. from my mind by conjuring my Mama into my imagination, thinking what my life might have been had she survived. Miss A. has said she was loving and kind. I see her clearly. Her large eyes are set in a sweet oval face, and hers is the prettiest of smiles. That smile is for me alone as she bends to adjust the bedclothes for my comfort. Flower perfumes drift over me—roses, honeysuckle—and I hear the rustle of her petticoats and elegant taffeta dress. Her hands softly stroke my face as she asks if I have said my prayers, and if I am sleepy, and if I have any troubles to tell her. When quite sure of my happiness, she kisses my forehead or cheek, a kiss truly welcome and truly meant, and says goodnight. Perhaps she says goodnight darling, or dearest child. Daughter.

O, but what is my Mama, but my dream? And, alas, the outcome of my dreaming is that I fall asleep weeping secret tears, for I miss my Mama.

Sunday, 30th June 1844. Talbot Castle.

As this day ends, I sit in the damp chill of my room at Talbot Castle and am most peculiarly agitated, so much so that I have pushed a heavy bench against my door—there being no key in the lock. This has been the strangest day I could have imagined. It dawned without a hint of unpleasantness, yet it ends with discomfort, confusion and shame. In writing of today's events I hope to unravel my turmoil.

First, however, the pleasant things. The morning began with some excitement, when a carriage arrived from Talbot Castle, the residence of my Uncle and Aunt, to transport me and Miss Avery to visit the Talbots for one day and night. (The Young Ladies are occasionally permitted Sunday visits to the homes of nearby relatives. It was impressed upon me by Miss MacIntosh that I should take care at the Castle to deport myself in a manner befitting a Young Lady of the Academy, giving me to understand that the entire reputation of the Academy rested with me. I received her words with the gravity she expected.)

I was charmed to meet my new baby cousin Lachlan, whom his doting Mama has nicknamed 'Lossie'. He is a dear child, just over two months of age and with a lively gaze and sunny nature. I begged my Aunt to allow me to hold him; she did so, but hovered over me with flapping hands, fearful that I might drop him. "Please do not worry, Aunt," said I, "for this is very little different from cradling a rabbit or kitten, and I have never dropped nor harmed either!" Aunt Clarissa at once took back her baby, looking most affronted. She has eyes only for her appealing little infant, and I observed Uncle John sulky at the attention given to his son and heir. Now she has her own child she is also less concerned with my own affairs, asking me nothing about the Academy or whether I am happy—but, I reflect, one is not asked about one's happiness.

Further pleasures of the day were our food, and Miss Avery's company. The Sunday luncheon was wonderful after the dreary Academy dishes. I was exceedingly greedy, eating quantities of roast beef and sweet apple dumplings. (I am not at all ashamed to have told an untruth to Aunt Clarissa when she asked me, in a whisper, if I was wearing my corset!)

After luncheon Miss Avery and I strolled in the grounds and enjoyed leisurely discussion of the books I am reading. I was much encouraged to be told I was doing well at my lessons. (No praise or encouragement is given at the Academy, lest we develop unhealthy conceit.) Miss Avery suggested, also, when I had complained of some of the Academy Rules, that I should not be downhearted at the "petty oddities" of life in an "institution", and continued: "It is what you know to be right in your own conscience that matters, dear child, no matter what others may declare. It will be hard at times to keep your own counsel in the face of the disagreeable, but it will be worth the effort. And if you are ever troubled, pray do not hesitate to come to me." These friendly words are of even greater comfort now than they were when she spoke them.

When we returned indoors Miss Avery wished to read, but I was restless, perhaps because I felt free for the first time in weeks, and asked Aunt Clarissa if I might explore the castle. She was perfectly willing, merely warning me not to get lost or to trip on the spiral stairs of the towers. I enjoyed half an hour or so discovering strange rooms, towers and staircases, and several exceedingly old-fashioned dirt-closets, into which the maids throw ashes to absorb the waste and its odours! There is one such closet adjoining the cold bathroom shared by Miss Avery and myself. I do not believe there are such modern inventions as water-closets in the Castle.

Then, I was in the stone-flagged main hall, finding my way back to the drawing-room, when I saw a previously-unnoticed door; it stood ajar, revealing a large bookcase. Attracted by what I thought to be the library, I cautiously pushed the door. Nobody was within. I saw a desk, a leather armchair, a table with playing cards and decanter of wine, and countless bookcases. Then a voice behind me startled me so much that my heart leapt to my throat and my feet left the floor. It was my Uncle John, saying jovially: "Well! What a pleasure to receive a young lady visitor in my den!"

His hand on my shoulder urged me forward. "Come in my dear," he said, his voice sounding thicker than usual, "let me entertain you." He laughed, and his breath smelled of wine. "You like books, don't you?"

"O, yes sir," I said, but I did not like the sensation of his hand, whose damp heat sank through the velvet of my dress, while his lips were wet and bulging.

Uncle John said: "Then look around, my dear. You may borrow whatever volume attracts you. How d'you like that?"

"Thank you, sir," I exclaimed, breaking away from his grasp. "I would like that very much."

I rushed to a bookcase but was so agitated I hardly understood its contents. In seconds he was beside me, leaning his head across my shoulder to look at the books; the odious heat of him was next to my cheek, and now both heavy hands were on my shoulders.

"Goodness me," he declared, "I cannot imagine these dry old tomes will interest you. Come over here—we have stories of romance and adventure."

Squeezing my shoulders he pulled me from the bookcase, and in the next moment his hands slid downwards over my chest (it cannot yet be called a bosom), where they paused and pressed as if to explore me before landing alarmingly at my waist. Here he seized me with some power and propelled me to another bookcase.

How was I to escape his grasp without being impolite? Confusion overcame me. I feared his strength. I pretended to scrutinise books but he was murmuring in my ear—what a pretty little thing, such a tiny waist—and next was pulling me backwards against his body, while breathing as if he had been running. His two hands had multiplied to four or five, rubbing my chest, pulling at buttons, squeezing my hips, while begging me to kiss him. "A kiss is all I want, just a kiss"—and suddenly I knew that whatever he wanted, it was more than a girlish kiss. Filled with revulsion and in a fearful panic, all fear of offending him vanished, I twisted about, hurled myself away and cried out: "No! I do not want to kiss you! Do not touch me so!" I ran past his staring eyes, hearing him say, "Shh!" At the door, I said, "Pray excuse my haste, Miss Avery is calling me." I did not know why I told this courteous untruth, but now I believe it was out of fear that he would be angry and report ill of me to Papa.

I was not yet fully composed when I entered the drawing-room, for Miss Avery remarked that I was flushed. I replied brightly that I had merely been running upstairs and down. I added to Aunt Clarissa: "It is a most appealing castle!" My voice was high and shaky, and I knew Miss Avery was observing me. I took up my book and tried to read, praying that Uncle John would not join us. This prayer was answered. A maid came to report, with the kind of expression that battles with a smirk, that the Master was working and would take his supper at his desk.

I had hoped that in writing of this repulsive event I might discover what brought it about. Did I myself do or say something? Had I, contrary to Miss MacIntosh's instruction, deported myself unbefittingly? I cannot think so. Yet, were my Uncle to stand before me and declare none of it had happened, I would be in doubt—even though my shuddering body *knows* it happened, and my hand trembles to write of my Uncle's loathsome actions.

At the end of this account, I am able to see one thing clearly: I can tell no-one, not even Miss Avery. If she were to complain to my Uncle, he could have her removed from the Academy—and from my life. Should she tell my Papa, he would not believe her; especially, he would not believe *me*, and the result would be the same. It would be cruel and equally pointless to tell my Aunt. If word also reached Miss MacIntosh, I too would be ejected from the Academy. Where then? To another, perhaps worse, institution—and without Miss Avery! I would be in disgrace—wicked, malicious, and full of sinful thoughts. My Uncle is Sir John Talbot, a gentleman of standing in Edinburgh. I have no choice but to remain silent.

I pray that I do not see my Uncle in the morning. I pray also that we might go back to Rugby in the summer and not to Talbot Castle. I am in some embarrassment as to how, henceforth, I am to behave in my Uncle's presence, for I cannot avoid him for ever. I conclude that I must behave as if nothing happened, and perhaps in this way I shall manage to convince myself.

5th July 1844. About Emmie.
Emmie is my best friend in all the world. Had I a sister, I would wish her to be like Emmie. We could be mistaken for sisters because we are of similar height and colouring, but she is *far* prettier than I. Her hair is *smooth*, unlike my horrid thicket, and she has a small neat mouth and short straight nose. *Nobody* could liken Emmie to a frog! However, she is indifferent to appearances, declaring that "looks are of no consequence", and adding teasingly: "O, but you are very *interesting*-looking."

I did not say so, but this was the very word that Miss Avery had once chosen to describe my ill-matched features. We had been for a walk and I complained to her that people often looked at me in the street, and looked again, and sometimes then glanced at one another and smiled. "Am I so comical to behold?" I asked her. She said: "My dear child, it because you are *interesting*, and I would dare surmise that those who look at you and smile are pleased with what they see, and furthermore reflect that you will grow to be a most striking-looking woman. Beauty is not necessarily confined to those whose features are classically regular." "*Beauty!*" said I, and laughed. For I believed her kind words to be her affectionate way of avoiding stating that I have a Very Odd Appearance! I believe Emmie's words were intended in the same way.

This may be improper of me, but I still consider Miss P. to be ugly, and my Uncle also, and cannot help but dislike them for it. Emmie says I am muddling their natures with their faces. "Would you dislike me if overnight I suddenly looked like a pig?" she asks. I declare I would not, so Emmie must be right, and I must be a shallow-minded person. She is far too kind to agree.

Emmie and I tell each other our secrets. Not quite *all*. I have not told her about Uncle John. I am uncertain why. *She* would not disbelieve me. Perhaps I fear that I was at fault, and I do not want her to have the same thought.

Emmie and I have sworn to be friends all our lives.

16th July, 1844.
Miss Avery has just told me that we are to return to Rugby for the long vacation. I am so happy to hear this. Emmie will go to her home town in the West of Scotland—to *two* parents *and* two brothers.

I told Emmie about my Mama dying when I was born, and she wept. She asked: "But why did she die? *How* did she die?"

Explaining that I was uncertain, I told her what had befallen the mare with all its blood coming out.

Emmie was silent and thoughtful for some while, then at last said: "Please tell me. What happens when babies are born?"

Evidently she knew nothing of the things I know.

"I asked my Mama once," she said, "and Mama told me that God starts it and then the doctor completes the work." I smiled and she laughed wryly. "It sounded silly, but Mama was uncomfortable so I asked no more."

I told her what I knew, although failing to explain how the seeds get into the mother's stomach. I described what I had seen dogs and sheep do, and what Tommy had told me about rabbits, adding: "Humans must do something like it." As I said this, thinking about the differences between male and female anatomies, I suddenly understood better. But I added nothing, for Emmie already looked most shocked and incredulous.

"It is very hard to believe," she said at last.

Agreeing that it was, I then changed the subject—the thought of Uncle John having come disquietingly to mind. O! I shall *not* think of him. I shall think *only* of going home!

Chapter Fourteen

20th July, 1844.

How happy I am to be at home. My only sorrow is that I miss Emmie. Papa is not present: he is in London attending to business. In truth I do not mind his being away for I do not need to fear his disapproval. I have not heard further from him since his angry letter after my Punishment, and I am afraid that his opinion of me will not, meanwhile, have improved.

Mrs Williams had tears in her eyes when she greeted me, and pressed newly-baked ginger biscuits into my hands. Our maids Elsie and Mavis are the same, full of fun and laughter, mischief and questions. They danced about me saying I had grown tall, and how skinny I was, did they not feed me at the Academy? (At this, Cook placed more biscuits in my hand.) Elsie has her hair done in the latest style, looped down her cheeks with a neat bun at her neck. It is most becoming to her little face, and her muslin cap adds the finishing touch. How I wish *I* could look as charming.

When I asked if Tommy might be here, they teased me saying: "O, listen to Miss! She wants only to know about her Young Man! A fine thing! Barely has she set eyes upon us and she cannot wait to see Master Thomas. O my, we are *most* offended!" Kindly Mrs Williams rescued me from my own blushes by sending them back to work and then proceeding to ask me every detail of what we ate at the Academy. When she had heard my account she said disapprovingly: "I believe they do not want the Young Ladies to grow up. They want to keep you as children." At this she embarrassingly prodded at my chest, adding: "You should have a bit of a bosom by now!"

I write now about an important thing that has occurred, and I have my dear friends here to thank for it.

After leaving Cook and the maids I went in search of Tommy and, if she were working today, Dottie the dairymaid. Looking for a sign of a human being but finding not a soul in the dairy and nought but horses and cats elsewhere, I walked through the stables until I reached the far end, below the hay-loft. Here sounds above my head made me pause. I heard shuffling and bumping, followed by a giggle that surely was a girl's, and a murmured reply from a young man—indeed, I believed it to be Tommy's voice. Then came more laughter from both female and male, and further rustlings. Deducing that some game was in progress, one that I might perhaps join if they would let me, I climbed the ladder stealthily, intending to surprise Tommy and friends. At the top I gradually raised my head through the trap-doorway.

Tommy was indeed there, amid the hay, but so was a young woman whose face I could not see. Both were panting and laughing, rolling over together as one, pausing every now and then to kiss! The girl's bodice was unbuttoned; she wore no cap and her golden hair was all long curls and clinging hay. Suddenly she took Tommy's hand and placed it, without shyness, right over her naked breast. He kissed her yet more, on her mouth and on her throat, and then, indeed, upon that very breast! In that moment she turned her head, and I recognised my other friend, Dottie, who was murmuring Tommy's name and begging him to continue! And indeed, I am sure he would have done so had I not given my presence away. Such was the strange heat and excitement running through me, my foot slipped and I clutched the edge of the trap-door—alas, also loudly gasping. Tommy sat bolt upright, white-faced, and saw my own burning face staring back at him. His friend, with a cry that was part laughter, hastily closed her bodice, straightened her skirts and said cheerfully: "O, Miss Moore! You *did* startle us! Just look at you Tom—you would think 'twas a ghost, and it is just the young Mistress home for the holidays."

Now I felt a little foolish and found myself saying formally: "Good day, Dottie. And Tommy. Pray accept my apologies for disturbing you. I was looking for Tommy and did not realise he had company." With these surely unsuitable words, I part-slid, part-clambered downwards and ran out of the stables. I heard Dottie's lively, unembarrassed laughter, and felt yet more foolish. How childish and ill-mannered I must have seemed!

Uncertain as to what I should properly do now, I retreated to the seat at the edge of the rose garden; from here I could see the stable door but could not immediately be seen myself except as the result of careful scrutiny. Soon I saw Tommy emerge, alone, his shirt and jerkin now neat. He stood in the stable doorway tidying his hair and slowly looking about. How handsome he was, grown taller and broader in these last months. I wondered what it would be like if he were to kiss *me*. This Unladylike thought shocked me and I felt my face grow hot again—but still I could not help picturing Dottie enjoying Tommy's kisses. Before I could understand my emotions, Tommy spied me and came straightaway to where I was sitting, speaking immediately.

"Miss—I do beg your pardon, Miss. I should like you to know we had an hour or two free—we were not shirking our duties."

I replied: "Why Tommy, I did not suppose otherwise." I invited him to sit next to me. He did so, and I could feel the heat of his arm near mine, through the fabric of his shirt and my dress, and I confess to these pages that I *longed* to kiss him!

I am thankful, however, that I did not act upon this impulse, for Dottie, her lovely locks now concealed beneath her cap, appeared in the stable doorway; she caught sight of us at once and walked smiling towards us. Realising from their expectant expressions that both had something to say, I invited her to be seated. She thanked me, electing to sit on my other side. They then looked at each other across me, and Dottie nodded at Tommy with a little smile.

Tommy said: "We would, Miss, like you to know that Dottie and myself will be wed one day, I being now sixteen and she but a year behind. Perhaps next spring, if we save money enough." He added: "Sooner, if she find herself with child."

I stared at him, startled. "With *child?*" I said, and heard Dottie's stifled giggle.

Here Tommy looked a little shy, saying: "That is how it happens, Miss. When a he and a she do couple together."

Truly I was becoming confused. I asked: "Like the rabbits?"

Then I was *most* embarrassed, for both Tommy and Dottie were trying not to laugh. "Somewhat," said he, "except that Dottie and me, we love each other, and rabbits do not fall in love exactly."

At this moment Dottie came to the rescue of Tommy (who was looking increasingly bashful) and of me (who was feeling exceedingly foolish). Dottie had impressed me on previous occasions with her forthright, unaffected manner and natural wisdom. She is but three years older than I, yet she seems far more grown-up and worldly.

"Tommy," said she, with a nod towards the stable clock, "should you not be helping in the tack-room now?" She smiled at him most winningly.

Tommy's relief was plain. He rose, taking his leave politely. Dottie sprang to her feet to kiss his cheek and then push him playfully on his way, before seating herself beside me, gently patting my hand and saying: "Ask me anything you wish."

I swallowed, and did as she bade. "So did Tommy mean that doing that—mating?—is not *only* for making babies?" How ignorant I felt!

"Not only," she replied pleasantly. "For most boys and girls—or gentlemen and ladies—who love each other, it is the natural way to show their love, by giving great pleasure one to the other. It is the closest a couple can be. Babies come later—usually much later, but that is in God's hands. Some people make babies easily. Some do not." With a smile she added: "But anyone can have fun if they want!"

I was silent for a few moments, absorbing this new information. In a strange way I understood, despite my ignorance, recalling how my body had felt when observing Tommy and Dottie in the hay-loft, and afterwards imagining him kissing me.

"But Dottie," I said, "I believed babies were made only by *married* people—and are not you and Tommy very young to be Mama and Papa?"

"In some opinions, yes," Dottie nodded. "But the law says a lass may say yes at twelve and marry at thirteen—and a lad may do likewise a year older. My own Mam and Pa, may the good Lord rest their souls, were wed at those ages."

Now I was truly astonished. "Then *I* am almost old enough to marry?"

Dottie laughed to see my incredulity.

"But 'tis different," she explained, "with your kind of folk. There's different rules for rich and poor, though the *law* be the same. Rich folks feel it proper to fix the wedding first. But with us village folk, 'tis quite usual to wait until an infant's on the way. Nobody frowns upon it. 'Tis natural, and we don't speak of virtue, or whether or no a maid be a virgin."

"A Virgin?" I cried. "You mean holy, like Jesus' mother?"

"O no, not *that* sort of Virgin," Dottie said with amusement. "A virgin is a maid who has not made love with a lad."

I reflected: So *I* am a virgin—and indeed no-one would call *me* holy. *Made love.* These two words sounded so gentle to my ears. And again I thought of Tommy and Dottie laughing in the hay. My clumsy arrival had interrupted their intentions to *make love.* I weighed the remarkable news that I, too, could say "yes" if I wished! In that instant, and utterly against my wishes, my Uncle's pink face and damp hands sprang into my mind.

"O!" I said aloud, before I could prevent it.

Observing my consternation Dottie said: "If something troubles you, pray do speak."

With some disquiet I said, "Dear Dottie, I would like you to tell me the truth about a matter that has indeed troubled me." She at once replied that she trusted she would always be truthful no matter what I asked. I went on: "Do people do this thing *without* love?"

"Yes, they do," she answered plainly, "simply for the excitement of it. Two people may be drawn to each other without true love—although they might mistake their desires for love. That is how my own Mam explained it to me, and since her demise I have passed this good advice to my sisters. It's *wanting* somebody, see. Wanting your bodies as near together as they can be, being pulled to them like they was a magnet. There's plenty of folks do it without love, if the feelings be strong. But," she continued with a knowing smile, "these feelings are stronger still if there's true love."

But I did not smile in return. I whispered: "What if it should happen, Dottie, that one person—a man—wants to do it and the maid does not?"

"Why, she would say No," Dottie replied, with a small frown. "And he must heed that."

"But what if the gentleman were strong and refused to heed her?"

Dottie was now most serious. "You mean, if he should *force* himself upon her?"

"I suppose that *is* what I mean," said I.

Dottie's cheeks, always rosy, were now flushed. "Well, Miss, then he would be *no* gentleman! He would be a man without honour. My father, my dear Pa, taught my brothers that a lady is to be respected and cared for, and a gentleman's strength ought to be used to that end."

I was certain then that I could trust Dottie completely. And there rushed out of me words that I do not recall in detail, but I related the story of what my Uncle did and said, my alarm and disgust, and my continuing fear that I might have been at fault.

When I stopped there were tears in Dottie's eyes as well as my own. She spoke quietly, but I could hear her anger. "You will forgive me speaking ill of your family, but I am bound to say your Uncle Sir John was at fault and you were innocent." Her face looked hot. "You are his *niece*, he is your *Uncle*, and married! What would Lady Talbot think? Or the Master?"

I begged Dottie not to upset herself—but in truth her vehemence reassured me. I explained my certainty that should my Aunt or Papa be told, they would not believe me, and everything would go awry.

"*I* believe you!" she cried. "Why should not *they?*"

"O, Dottie," I said sadly, "you are my friend, and you—and Tommy—have greater sense than they."

"Greater sense?" Dottie regained her smile. "I? I'm but a poor village girl. I am able to read and write a little, I can do my sums and I know enough to run a household, but that is all."

"The sort of good sense I speak of has nought to do with school learning," I replied, sounding more like Miss Avery than myself.

After a thoughtful pause, Dottie asked: "May I tell Tommy what you have told me?"

"Indeed you may. But do pray impress upon him that it would be worse for me, and possibly Miss Avery, if others were to be told." Gratefully, I added: "And thank you Dottie. You have reassured me that I did nothing to warrant self-reproach."

"Nothing whatso*ever*," she emphasised.

As we parted I kissed her cheek. How fortunate I am in my friends, I reflected. This thought returned later in the day when I went to find Tommy, knowing that he would be feeding the rabbits.

As I approached I called his name. He closed a hutch door swiftly and turned. "O, Miss! Good evening. I did hope you might appear." He was pale, his eyes exceedingly bright, and he said without further ado: "Dottie has told me about your Uncle. Were you my sister, I would kill him."

"Tommy!" I laid a hand on his forearm. "Pray do not say such things. Do not distress yourself on my behalf. I cannot describe to you how much relieved I am now that you and Dottie know and understand."

I drew him towards the low brick wall beside the hutches so that we might sit for a few minutes. "That is all that matters to me."

Tommy solemnly said: "If that be the case, then may I offer you advice as to your Uncle?"

"Pray do, Tommy. In truth, I dread being alone with him."

Tommy spoke with care: "Your Uncle cannot be *sure* you would not be believed. In this you are stronger. Should he make such an attempt again, say forcefully that you will report it to his wife."

"O!" I cried. "But he would tell my Papa that I have been wicked, and telling lies! And my Papa would believe *him!*"

"Ha," Tommy said with contempt, "Such a man is a *coward.*" He then whispered, as if fearing to be overheard: "There *is* something else you can do, Miss, to let him know his manners are wanting. You can deal him a blow with, beg pardon, your knee. In *this* quarter." Tommy pointed at his breeches. "Forgive me if I speak improper, but that is a man's tenderest part, and if you strike fierce enough, you remove all his strength."

I almost laughed—because of Tommy's sweet seriousness and loyalty. O, how very much I love dear Tommy. But all I said was: "Thank you Tommy. I will certainly remember this."

As I spoke, Miss Avery's voice called me for supper, and I was obliged to bid him good evening. At the last moment I remembered to say that I hoped he and Dottie would be very happy.

5th September 1844.

We travel back to Edinburgh in two days' time. My journal has been much neglected these weeks, for I have been too occupied with our life here at the Hall, and have enjoyed more reading and drawing than writing. Miss Avery and I have read and discussed books together, taking long sunny walks in the process, and I am glad to say that she also talks to me of current affairs in the world and explains much I do not understand. Not one other grown-up that I know talks to me as if I have a brain of my own! I have also enjoyed many happy hours with Tommy and Dottie when they were not working, and visited their family homes in the village.

I now understand far better what a contrast there is between their lives and my own, and I have been greatly humbled by their good cheer and lack of complaint or resentment. Both of Dottie's parents were taken last winter by low fever. In one night, she became an orphan. As the eldest child, she was left in charge of her five brothers and sisters; all live together in a one-roomed cottage on Papa's estate (as indeed do Tommy, two brothers, and his parents). Dottie's family could barely have survived without village charity and payment in kind from Papa's dairy. When I visited her house, little more than a hovel, I was much moved to see how courageously even very young people overcome—or bear with good spirits—the worst conditions. How easy it had always been for me, I reflected, to take my material good fortune for granted. Only a few days previously, for example, I had taken a trip into Rugby with Miss Avery, our errand being to purchase lace trimmings for collars and heavy woollen stuff for my winter cape. Without particular thought, we were able to take one of the carriages and spend a whole day in that town, rummaging through luxuries that do not even enter Tommy's or Dottie's imaginations. For the first time I felt a twinge of some discomfort to be so privileged. When I said as much to Miss Avery, she merely said: "That, my dear, is a very good sign."

I shall have many things to tell Emmie—one being that I am developing a bosom. At the start of the vacation I possessed two barely-visible swellings. Now, after some weeks of feeding by Cook, my dresses are tighter around my waist and chest and I see signs that I may yet become a woman. I wonder if Emmie has begun to grow a bosom. Perhaps bosoms grow more readily in the warmth of summer.

One afternoon when Miss Avery and I were in the garden, I confided in her about my bosom. She smiled, saying that if I was impatient for womanhood I might be pleased to learn that when I reach the age of thirteen in December I shall be regarded as a young lady and no longer a child. At this I related Dottie's information that thirteen was the age at which a girl may marry. Miss A. was amused, commenting that Society behaved differently no matter what the law said, and I would be expected to attend finishing school at seventeen and Come Out into Society at nineteen. "Your Papa," she said, "or your Uncle and Aunt, will arrange everything." Observing my alarm, she added: "It is years hence, and will not seem so strange when the time comes. Besides, I hope to be present to guide and support you."

My Aunt Clarissa has told me that when I marry I shall make a "good match", as a woman of property. Families of her acquaintance, she declared, include sons who may prove suitable. I think of Tommy and Dottie, planning to marry because of love and pleasure, and wonder about Aunt Clarissa's "suitable": a most chilly word. Tommy has told me that when a marriage takes place, all the bride's property becomes the groom's, so that she possesses nothing of her own and it is the husband's responsibility to take charge of all her affairs. When I expressed indignation at this, he laughed at me and said: "But it is an agreeable arrangement, Miss, for a wife never has to pay her own debts!" I asked Miss Avery if this was so, and her expression was wry as she nodded.

A silence fell as I gathered courage to ask Miss Avery a question. "Have you ever wished to marry?" I asked at last, immediately adding: "I do apologise if I am impolite!"

She appeared unoffended. "Yes, my dear, I have. But I loved a man who did not love me. I would not have been a suitable bride for him in any case, for I had nothing to offer—no fortune, no property." She sighed. "In certain circles, these things are important."

"But not if he had loved you!" I cried.

"Perhaps," she said.

I waited for renewed courage. "Miss Avery," I whispered. "Do you love Papa?"

Her face turned pink and then pale, and she did not speak.

"Please forgive me!" I cried, wretched at my own selfishness.

Miss Avery laid down her embroidery and, taking my hand, said: "There is nothing for me to forgive, dear child. I did love your Papa, yes. And I loved your Mama, as you know. When you were a small child and I had care of you, I did wish your Papa might recover sufficiently from his loss to ask me to be his wife—if only because he respected and liked me, and I would cherish his daughter. But he never saw me, nor any other woman after your Mama, in that light. There was another gentleman who asked to marry me, but I could not countenance marriage without affection." Miss Avery smiled at me frankly, "I preferred to stay as I was, a friend to your Papa and with you as my charge. Marriage for its own sake never appealed to me."

Many different emotions ran through me, but I did not dare intrude further. I believe she read my thoughts, for she continued:

"No, my dear, I do not love your Papa in that way any longer. As years passed, he changed, and my feelings also changed. I regard him highly, and pity him for the way life has embittered him, but I fear I cannot——" Here she stopped abruptly. "No, I do not love him, not now." She added brightly, once more taking up her embroidery: "There. Now you know the whole story."

Then I knew that Miss Avery had stopped loving Papa because of me and the way my Papa behaves towards me. Without my wishing it, tears began to run down my face, and even if I had found words to speak I could not have spoken them.

6th September.

For the first time during our entire vacation I set eyes on my Papa and he set eyes on me.

One day last week, I had been astonished to overhear one of the stablemen remark upon the Master's late arrival the previous night. Another man laughed, and I caught the words, "a little the worse for——", but he was swiftly silenced by a coachman who had seen my approach. Later, Tommy confirmed that Papa had indeed returned home at midnight but had left at dawn. From this it was made clear to me that my Papa does not wish to see me, and therefore visits his home when he can best avoid doing so. That, I believe, is the *truth*, and it was confirmed by the events of today.

We were occupied with preparations for our journey tomorrow. Elsie starched and ironed my petticoats and helped me to pack my bags. Cook bade me tell her all my favourites among her dishes, declaring she would fit as many as possible into our journey-basket. Miss A. said she would help me wash my hair, but I delayed this ordeal by going with Tommy and Dottie on a ride about the grounds in a new pony-trap.

Lost in thoughts both happy and sad, I returned to the house to prepare for the torture of hair-washing. I had placed one foot on the stairs when my Papa emerged suddenly from the drawing-room. Judging by his expression he had no more expected my presence than I had his. I remained motionless—indeed, unable to move.

"Good afternoon, child," he said at last. My Papa did not smile. He took his timepiece from his pocket and frowned irritatedly at it.

"Good afternoon Papa," I answered, in a silly whisper. "I trust you are well," I dared to add.

He ignored my courtesy. "You are behaving properly at that school nowadays?" he barked.

"Yes, Papa," I answered.

"Good," he said. "Let it remain so. You are fortunate to be in such a reputable institution, for which I pay handsomely, and you will not forget it. I want no more disgrace or shame. You understand?"

"Yes, Papa," said I weakly, with downcast head. But all at once I was overcome by feelings of injustice and I spoke out in a stronger voice—though without raising my head.

"Sir," I said, barely able to believe my boldness, "I *do* appreciate your goodness, and I should like you to know that I work hard and am doing well at my lessons."

Silence followed and I dared not look up. The next moment my Papa's rapid footsteps came towards me—and I shrank back, clutching the banister in fear. He gripped my chin and roughly raised my head, to scowl darkly into my face. My heart jumped, but I recalled Miss A. saying I had not been so *very* wicked—and I forced myself to look directly back at him. But O, after a mere second or two I could not maintain this, for I could not bear what I saw. He made a loud noise—part groan, part cry of disgust—and thrust me away with such force that I would have fallen had I not been holding the banister. I heard him turn and walk away.

I ran upstairs gasping, my throat hot and tight. In my bed-chamber I wrenched at the fastenings of my dress, throwing it on the floor, all the time making horrid dry noises that I could not prevent. Pulling on a robe I snatched up my hairbrushes and ran out, calling Miss Avery. She rushed from her bed-chamber crying: "What has happened?" as if she thought the house must be on fire. Falling against her I sobbed, "My Papa hates me, my Papa hates me——" over and again, until at last she soothed me, kneeling to hold me and stroke my back.

She bade me tell her plainly what had occurred. I did my best to describe the incident truthfully while she wiped my tears. "He hates me," I said again, more steadily.

"No, no," she said softly, "it is not that——"

"Yes," I said. "It is the truth. And I—and I—" I could not complete the sentence.

Miss A. stood and took my hand. "And you," she said, "will come with me and we shall wash your hair. I shall use some of my special perfumed oil, to make your hair smooth and glossy." She showed me a little blue bottle. "And if you should get soap in your eyes, nobody will know you have been weeping."

I wept no more, and—with regard to Papa—I shall never do so again.

Chapter Fifteen

Sunday, 22nd September. The Academy.

The school year is but six days old, yet much that is extraordinary has occurred. I shall here record the events, but I must first write of my conversations with Miss Avery on our return journey together. How different a journey from our first! I was no longer fearful of my destination, and I greatly looked forward to seeing Emmie again. It is true that I felt some underlying melancholy, resulting from my now *utterly unshakeable* certainty of Papa's lack of affection for me, but I had strenuously lectured myself that I must face this robustly and live my life without unrealistic hope of change. Never could I have believed that I would so willingly leave my dear home!

Now that I know more of her story, I feel a special affection for Miss Avery. And she, too, seemed on our journey to be warmer in my company; not that she has ever been cold or remote, but in some subtle way we have drawn closer, perhaps because she is no longer quite in the same *in loco parentis* role, and also because she has confided some of her past feelings to me. In addition, it now appears to me that we have an important thing in common, having both been disillusioned by my Papa.

My thoughts led me to another person who loathes me, the detestable Miss P., and I decided to speak to Miss Avery of this. "What is it about me that she hates so very much?"

Miss Avery laughed. "You are not an obvious object for loathing," she replied, "so pray do not imagine so. You present yourself, by and large, as a self-contained and thoughtful person, well-mannered, friendly, blessed with a quick mind and far from unpleasant to look upon." Here, as ever, I could not help but pull a face. "Furthermore," she continued, "since your one early lapse, you have wisely abided by even the most trivial Academy rules—which is no mean achievement."

Here I expressed agreement, for it is not always easy to remember which minor infringements are punishable. Merely walking in the grounds while wearing indoor shoes, or returning a book to an incorrect shelf, are two examples of many transgressions that can be transformed into major sins. I have frequently felt that many regulations are not only trivial, but quite unnecessary—yet they must be obeyed, as if they possessed a power of their own. Digressing somewhat from my original question about Miss P., I voiced this thought to Miss Avery.

Nodding, she said: "Indeed, that is often so in closed communities. So little of the outside world is permitted to enter, and this results in the routine of life within becoming 'life' itself—all-important, all-prevailing. Inevitably it can, with time, come to constitute the only *known* way of life." I pondered this, and realised how fortunate I have been to have had Miss Harriet Avery by my side thus far in my life, for she has taught me much of the outside world, showing me newspapers and keeping me informed of political events. Only then did I realise that I had never seen a newspaper within the Academy. This, surely, is because of their possibly corrupting influence upon the Young Ladies!

Echoing my musings, Miss Avery added with a hint of acerbity: "And do not forget, that although no word is spoken on the matter, the consensus among those in charge is that if such rules did not exist there would be no security for the Young Ladies, no orderliness, no routine—and in their place would reign *chaos and anarchy.*" These last words she uttered with a mocking flourish and a smile.

"But," said I to Miss Avery, "To return to Miss P.—I *have* been obedient, so why does she so disapprove of me?"

"Such illogical feelings occur," she answered, "in our kind of cloistered life. People may become obsessed and go to extremes in hatred or affection. And once a fierce detestation is in place, there is no aspect of the detested person that is acceptable to the detester."

I remarked that this was most unjust, and Miss Avery agreed: "Yes, *and* unreasonable. But at least it indicates that the failing is not yours. Therefore I suggest that you ignore her manner as best you can. If you continue to abide by the rules, she cannot harm you."

These were words of wisdom with which Emmie would agree. I also understood, suddenly, that it is Miss P.'s spiteful character that makes her ugly. It is there in her eyes and the set of her lips. Were she a kindlier woman, those features would be plain yet pleasant. How fearful that one's true nature might be on display to the world through one's face! I should beware.

ON OUR FIRST evening here at the Academy, there was a sudden and unseasonal frost. It had been a beautiful bright but cold autumn day, and when darkness fell the air became exceedingly icy. As we reluctantly undressed for bed in the dormitory, the rule of silence was broken by muted cries of "ooh!" and "ah!", the mention of chilblains to be suffered ere long, and shivering whispers of yearning for our bed-chambers at home where little fires were lit in the grates, and one might have as many blankets as needed.

Our *sotto voce* commotion was interrupted by the abrupt appearance in the doorway of the Detestable Miss P., who cast upon us a glare of pure anger, scolded us for lack of discipline, and ordered all candles extinguished and that we enter our beds and cease our shallow babblings forthwith. We obeyed, each huddling beneath one sparse cover upon a clammy mattress, but I suspect all were feeling some relief that Miss P. was clearly not in a frame of mind to press welcoming kisses upon our lips!

I lay with little hope of my limbs warming, peering through darkness towards my dear friend Emmie in the neighbouring bed. There had been barely two minutes in which to greet each other in the busy time since our return. Across the room I heard another girl's tentative whisper to a friend, and an immediate reply. Before I could follow suit, Emmie's soft question came: "Are you awake?"

"I am—and shivering."

"I also. My feet are ice. I have wrapped my nightgown around them but I declare they are making each other colder. Ice on ice!"

"Winter is coming. Ice on everything, and cold porridge at breakfast."

"O, you are full of cheerful thoughts."

"Some cheerful, some not," replied I. "O, I have so much to tell you!"

"Come into my bed——" whispered Emmie, "——and let us hide under our two blankets and try to warm one another, and we can tell some of our news."

"Supposing The Detestable——"

"Bah—we shall be very quiet. Quickly, bring your blanket and join me—before we freeze to death!"

Our beds being narrow, not more than two feet across, we were obliged to lie straight, on our sides and face to face with our arms bent and tucked upon our chests. We arranged ourselves with considerable shuffling and smothered giggling, provoking an amused enquiry from Emmie's other neighbour, Dora, as to our mischief.

"No mischief!" hissed Emmie. "We have joined forces to keep each other warm."

This reply was relayed by mirthful whispers, bed to bed—and there followed soft sounds of approval, widespread rustling, and furtive padding of bare feet indicating a migration of girls from one bed to another. Within minutes half the beds in the dormitory were empty, each stripped of its meagre blanket, and the other half crammed with two girls each, two blankets over them and eight limbs growing warmer.

Emmie and I pulled our blankets above our heads to muffle our exchange of news. The recent memory of a meagre supper of bread, soup and potatoes made us speak first of food, comparing dishes we had savoured so avidly at home. This led to my describing a new delicacy that I had discovered at Tommy's home: the combination of bacon and bread.

"Bacon!" hissed Emmie. "My Mama says it is the food of the very poor!"

"So it is," I agreed, "and a pig is one of the few benefits of being poor, for one may make many delicious dishes from all parts of it!"

This led to further muffled giggling, increased by Emmie's question: "Does not eating pig make you pink and fat, with a curly tail?"

Here reminded, I confessed that I was growing a *bosom*, and our Cook had declared that it was high time. "What of you?" I asked. "Do you have a bosom to tell me of?"

This question was not to be answered, for even as Emmie and I smothered our laughter the rudest of shocks occurred. Cold air struck our newly-warmed limbs as our covers vanished, whisked away by a hostile hand, and there sounded Miss P.'s triumphant cry. She stood over us, panting, her lamp lighting her horrid features.

"What disgusting talk is this? What vile behaviour have I discovered?"

A general flurry in the dormitory indicated that every horrified girl present had been shocked into a sitting position. It was clear to all that Miss P. had been in the room sufficiently long to observe the scene of crowded beds and had eavesdropped upon us. Not one among us could escape severe punishment. Everyone waited, rigid with fright and cold.

But Miss P. gazed only at Emmie and me, her selected culprits, while crying out to the room at large: "Every girl not in her own bed, excepting these two, return this instant and be silent."

When the ensuing disruption had ceased, she commanded us: "*You* will follow *me.*" She turned, lamp held high. "*Now!*"

Later, Emmie was to tell me that for a moment she thought she was in a nightmare, and Miss P. was leading them to the gallows. I replied: "*That* would have been preferable."

Miss P. led us to her own nearby bed-chamber and pushed us inside. We saw a bed, a table, two wooden chairs and a small armchair beside a desk. Though far from warm the room smelled closed and stuffy, the rancid smell of its resident being pervasive.

Miss P. then set down her lamp and propelled us to the centre of the bed-chamber before closing and locking her door and bringing forward the two wooden chairs, placing them face to face. "Sit," she commanded, pushing us again.

Both of us were, I believe, in a daze. We obeyed. There was barely sufficient space between the seats for our two pairs of trembling knees. Unexpectedly (and somewhat grotesquely), Miss P. smiled, speaking in honeyed tones. "There, my dears. You like to be near, do you not? Is this sufficiently close?"

We were silent, eyes lowered, our hands clasped on shivering laps.

"Look at me!" Miss P. then barked, startling us. Again we obeyed. "You are *disgusting* girls. You are not *fit* to be Young Ladies of this Academy. In bed together! Pressing your *bodies* together! Talking of *bosoms*. Had I not interrupted you, I know *very well* what would have ensued."

Emmie said with admirable daring: "Our only wish was to be warm, Miss Pottinger."

Miss P. responded with a savage slap upon Emmie's cheek—and for good measure, donated a similar blow upon my own.

"*You,*" she said venomously into my face, "Tell me what would have ensued."

I was unable to grasp her meaning. "I do not know," I honestly (but shakily) replied. "We were speaking of our vacations. I swear that is all." For this I received a second slap.

"You are a liar. You would have *looked* at each other."

Later we agreed that at this moment we both considered, despite our fear and amazement, replying that it had been dark in the dormitory; but we did not wish to provoke further blows.

"You will look at each other *now!*" Here she forcibly turned our heads so that we were face to face, and commanded: "Now you will tell me. Have you ever kissed?"

Involuntarily, our heads swung back in her direction. "*Kissed?*" cried Emmie.

"*No!*" cried I.

"*Look* at each other!"

Our crimson faces exchanged uneasy gazes.

"You *shall* look," Miss P. ordered. "Remove your nightgowns."

Emmie gasped. Neither of us moved.

"Do as I say or I shall report to your parents your unhealthy conduct and conversations on obscene subjects. There will follow disgrace and expulsion, whereafter no respectable establishment will let you darken its doors. Remove your nightgowns."

The vision of my Papa's wrath rose before me. As, in Emmie's imagination, did that of her parents' sorrow and shame—and both of us were too exhausted and confused to doubt Miss P.'s prophecy of our doom, for where existed the parent who would accept the protests of a child over the word of a teacher? Therefore, shaking with cold and embarrassment, we drew our nightgowns over our heads.

With our crumpled nightgowns held upon our laps, we sat trembling, trapped upon her chairs. Miss P., now more Detestable than even I could have imagined, began slowly to walk around us, round and round, all the time staring at us. "Look closely," said she, "look at the *bosoms* in which you expressed such perverted interest. Are you not full of self-disgust?"

I, who had quite lost interest in any person's bosom, stole a perplexed glance at our tormentor. The strangest of expressions was in the gaze fixed upon our bodies, while on the lips there played a dreamy smile; she reminded me of a jungle predator relishing the prospect of a delectable meal.

At this odious sight my fear was swiftly replaced by overwhelming contempt and revulsion, so strong that they cast out dread of Papa's wrath and Miss P.'s threats. I now stared deliberately at our enemy, attempting to display on my face all the fury, scorn and loathing in my heart. Clearly I met with success, for in outrage Miss P. delivered a vigorous blow to my face and turned to do the same to Emmie—but I shouted out: "Do not touch her!"

Miss P. halted, hand in air. Neither she nor I could believe the authority that emerged from my mouth. I continued: "If you do not allow us to return to our beds this moment, I shall scream as long and loudly as I am able. No amount of violence will stop me. You, Miss Pottinger, shall be obliged to explain the circumstances of our nakedness and our bruises when the Headmistress hastens to this scene. And furthermore," (here I told an untruth without hesitation) "our parents would not for one instant believe your stories. Release us immediately or they shall certainly learn the truth."

As I spoke, Miss P.'s face changed colour many times and she began to gasp for breath. At the end her hands were clenched against her heaving chest as if to still her heart—or to prevent herself from pummelling us both insensible.

"Get out!" she then shrieked, as if half-strangled. "Out!" Miss P. backed away as if she had seen some demon in me, and leaned panting on her desk. Briefly I wondered what would be our explanation should she suffer an apoplexy. But Miss P. managed to utter a few more words in the form of a threat. "You will pay for this insolence, *and* for your decadence, as God is my witness——"

We were shaking from head to foot with more than mere cold as we lurched from our chairs and dragged on our nightgowns. Without a further glance at our defeated assailant, we dashed to the door, turned the key and fled.

Neither of us spoke again until morning, and neither slept. Our first lesson on the first day of term was Geography—taken, as it happened, by Miss Avery. The room in which the class is held was once the mansion's Great Hall. It is extremely large and some six classes were, as usual, assembling here, each allotted a long table seating a dozen to a score of girls and one teacher. (The Academy has yet to adopt the more modern schools' practice of smaller rooms, each holding just one class; in some cases such schools enjoy the luxury of *individual desks!*) The combined sounds of hurrying feet, scraping chairs, forbidden whispers, teachers' commands and dropped books and slates together create a true cacophony, under cover of which Emmie and I chose positions as far as possible from our teacher so that she might not observe our pallor or our bruises. Inevitably, I realised too late—for we normally choose to sit as near to her as possible in order not to miss a word in the conflicting noise of other classes—this unusual behaviour merely attracted her attention, as did the frequency of other girls' glances, whispers and nudges.

So it was not until Miss Avery was walking round the table, supervising the drawing of maps, that she observed the dark red bruises on my cheekbone. Although I dipped my head to conceal it, my right hand was employed in my work and I was unable to cover my face in time. Miss Avery stood in silence for a moment or two and then addressed Emmie, who looked up at her, keeping her hand in place over her left jaw and thus adopting a most unnatural pose. Miss Avery gently removed this hand and observed what it had concealed. The entire table waited with bated breath. Then she bent forward to lean between us and spoke quietly. "You will come and see me in the small music-room during the morning break."

The whispered consensus in the dormitory that morning had been that Emmie and I would be ill-advised to tell any teacher of our experiences, for it would be the worse for us. Miss P.'s versions of events would be taken as the truth, and any child's version as wicked invention and malice. There had emerged stories of earlier victims who had found courage to tell a parent; most had been rebuked for lies or exaggeration, or of somehow provoking the teacher's wrath by failing to work hard enough at their lessons or forgetting to conduct themselves like Young Ladies. Even if any grown-up had suspected there might be some truth in the stories, he or she rarely regarded the matter as so serious that one need do more than shrug at it; eccentric and even unsavoury people existed in the world, and learning to deal with them was improving to the character.

We knew the difficulties of convincing an adult of our bizarre tale—we could barely believe it ourselves! Would even the kind Miss Avery believe it? But despite this doubt, I felt some relief at hearing Miss Avery's words: the decision as to whether or not to tell had been taken for us. I was bound to tell her the truth, regardless of the spectres of Miss P.'s savage face, my Papa, my Uncle and Aunt all scowling in my mind's eye. At the same time I said to myself: We are two. What could be the reason for *two* inventing such a story?

Emmie and I found ourselves faced by an adult who indulged in no finger-waggings but who companionably seated us upon pianoforte stools and suggested with a gentle smile that we tell her simply how we had come by our bruises, since she could not assume that we had been indulging in fisticuffs.

We obeyed. By the time our story ended Miss Avery's smile had quite vanished. She walked silently up and down the music-room, angrier than I have ever seen her. At last she said: "Return to your lessons now. I shall seek a meeting with Miss MacIntosh. Our Headmistress is strict, but she is just."

We left Miss Avery with lighter hearts—a mood soon enhanced by Miss P.'s absence from the Academy classrooms all day, she having reported herself unwell.

Miss Avery, we learned in the late afternoon, succeeded in convincing Miss MacIntosh of the truth of our story, and in shocking her severely with the other pupils' knowledge of similar occurrences over some years, but she did not attain that which she had confidently expected—Miss Pottinger's dismissal.

"I am not at liberty," Miss Avery explained to us, "to reveal our discussion in detail; that would not be fitting. Let me simply say that, unbeknown to me, Miss Pottinger is the only God-daughter of the Head of Governors—and, furthermore, she is Miss MacIntosh's Deputy Headmistress. In other words she has more power and influence than I had suspected. As Miss MacIntosh has experienced in the past, any severe conflict with Miss Pottinger could too easily endanger our Headmistress' own position." With a regretful sigh, Miss Avery added: "And the outcome could be far worse. Were our Headmistress to be dismissed from the Academy, Miss Pottinger would be instated as Headmistress. I was bound to agree that this would be disastrous."

Emmie and I looked at each other in horror.

Miss Avery continued: "I will reveal to you that I briefly considered approaching the Governors myself, but at once realised the result could be my own dismissal and no change in Miss Pottinger's position."

"O!" cried I at this moment. "I should run away from here if you were dismissed!"

Miss Avery smiled a little. "It should not come to that. For all is not lost. Miss MacIntosh has agreed to warn her, making it plain that both she and I believe your account. And the threat of revealing her behaviour to her Godfather and Governors, should any further episodes arise, will curb her activities."

Emmie asked: "Miss Avery, will not Miss P. be exceedingly angry with us, and—"

"—and be vengeful?" Miss Avery shook her head. "I believe you will be pleased to learn that from tomorrow, *I* shall be instated as your House Mistress. Miss

Pottinger will have teaching duties only, and these will be discreetly supervised." She paused, looking at us seriously. "You will please remember that all these details are strictly confidential."

"O yes!" we promised in unison and, by some remarkable feat of self-control, neither of us leapt from our seats and cheered aloud. But our spirits had been raised a thousandfold and there were not sufficient thanks in this world for dear Miss Avery.

On our way to supper, we agreed that our affection for and gratitude towards Miss Avery is now boundless, and our loathing for Miss P. equally vast.

10th December 1844.

Today, I am thirteen years of age. Alas, I have written nothing further about this year since the unpleasant events with Miss P. Part of the reason for this is that I was severely afflicted—along with several others—with influenza, which left me greatly fatigued and subsequently strangely downhearted for some weeks. This set-back was followed by two months of the coldest, wettest, dreariest weather that might be imagined. (Indeed, it has not yet relented; rather it has grown worse with frequent sleet and snow.) As a result, we have not once been able to enjoy Sundays in the grounds and I have not visited my secret place since September. Nowhere else can I find sufficient privacy to write at length. However, I intend to indulge myself on the remaining pages in making some drawings, telling myself that this is an activity that can, for the most part, be pursued without undue secrecy. The subjects of my drawings will be pupils and teachers at the Academy, some of the more pleasing aspects of the grounds, and I shall attempt to draw both Tommy and Dottie from memory. One thing is certain: there will be no self-portrait!

Chapter Sixteen

THE UPGRADE FAILED to transfer with Gee to the plane from Sydney, but she reckoned she was fortunate enough, finding an empty place beside her new, narrower seat next to a window. Besides, this was the last leg, as someone behind her said with a brave laugh: "Nearly there, then. Only another thousand or so miles to go."

That was nothing to a time-traveller like herself, lately returned from the middle of the nineteenth century. Her skull felt weirdly full and hot. It seemed that her great-grandmother had taken up residence in Gee's sleep-deprived and possibly swollen cerebrum. It was barely believable that she'd been reading Margaret Esther's very own words in her very own Victorian ink. She had had to pause at times, to examine the neat penmanship and touch the discoloured pages, holding treasure in her hands.

How else could she describe it: *she felt Margaret Esther's feelings*. It wasn't that the same *things* had happened to her. Gee hadn't been sent motherless away to school by an indifferent father and virtually orphaned. But Gee had sensed the tremors in her twelve-year-old fingers and had absorbed her sadness: looking at her father in grief and confusion, wishing, not daring to think of what she wished, her mind flying away so that she was nobody, nowhere; the weight of loss, betrayal, longing, fear, the knowledge of having always been odd and isolated. Even so, she'd had strength, determination: Gee could feel that too in Margaret Esther's guiding hand.

Gee herself had been walking behind them—the girl and her governess—following the jaunty maid along the Academy's corridors. Margaret Esther had turned her head to smile at Gee, and she'd known it was to encourage her and to hearten herself. That wonderfully wild, vigorous hair tried to escape the prim bonnet, defying the day's fashion for straight partings and smooth sides. Her crescent-moon smile lit up her off-beat face, and Gee had recognised her thoughts: *I must live my new life with courage, do what I can, not be crushed.* Margaret Esther, the girl, straightened her back and lifted her sharp little chin. It could break your heart, Gee thought—but it didn't. For the first time in her life Gee didn't feel alone.

AN APOLOGETIC AUSTRALIAN VOICE introduced itself from the flight deck. A small delay, a technical problem. *We have every hope of being ready for take-off in approximately twenty minutes.* On airliners, Gee always wondered about a 'technical problem'. Having come this far, it would be a shame if a wing fell off now.

She sat back and closed her eyes, thinking she might doze. Behind her lids crept an image of her own departure for boarding school. In its own way, it had been a turning point.

Gee would be at this private establishment for girls for less than a school year. The family had briefly lived in East Anglia: her father's job, a six-month project of some sort. The local Grammar was bursting its seams: they would valiantly squeeze Jo in—she was at a crucial stage with exams. Gee's choice was a crummy secondary mod or a private Girls' Boarding, where the authorities would foot the bill. No contest.

Jo said: "Won't you miss me?" Her pretty face, pink and anxious.

Gee said of course she would. But she hadn't thought of it, being too excitedly preoccupied with Enid Blyton-inspired school fantasies confused with terrors of the new, and she had turned away, mean and ashamed, preventing Jo from saying more. Jo would be alone, except for during holidays, in their shared bedroom in the temporary, rented house. Gee didn't want to think about her there. She had meant to tell her to lock the door, but didn't. She'd let her down, always. Poor Jo, whom Gee wouldn't miss.

More interesting was her dark green velour hat and dashing blazer with gold cord trim and proud badge with school motto—something preachy about manners, in Latin, which her father trotted out at her frequently. Less thrilling were the mandatory Liberty bodices, hideous and old-fashioned, with buttoned-on elastic suspenders. Margaret Esther *would not have had elastic*. What was life like without elastic? It's like asking what it was like before clingfilm or, come to that, the wheel.

It will be posh, Jo had warned, *so don't act your usual common self.* Jo in adolescence was taking good manners seriously, regularly reading—and quoting from 'Your Etiquette Questions Answered'—a column in a teenage magazine. She instructed Gee, who was altogether too tomboyish for Jo's taste, in the use of cutlery and which way to tip a soup bowl, how to sit up straight like a *lady*, legs just so, hands in lap. *These things matter,* she said, *everyone will be watching the new girl.* Gee had believed her, and knew that being sneered at would make her shyness yet more agonising. Jo said: *We don't want you letting down the family name.* At the time, it hadn't occurred to Gee to laugh.

THERE SHE WAS, on the eve of departure, staring in fright at her newly-acquired trunk. She too had had a trunk! But not classy leather: it was dark blue canvas-covered board with pale wooden bands and shiny rivets; it had a label showing Gee's name and the school's address—her home from tomorrow. The trunk was packed solid with new clothes and books. Plus hockey stick. Packed with a new life upon whose brink Gee vertiginously hung, feeling sick.

Obviously, she had to change herself. And she, too, had resolved that somehow she must develop a protective shell as solid as a tortoise's. Henceforth, she had instructed herself, she would act a part—with all possible energy and deceit—in a manner so bold that everyone would admire her confidence. This day would mark the demise of the *gauche* mute.

But what, she wondered, about her height, long arms, bony angular face, and beaky nose? At least she wasn't actually ugly. Her eyes weren't bad. One of her father's colleagues had remarked on her being *interesting*-looking and—like Margaret Esther—she had taken this to mean *peculiar*. With a little effort she convinced herself: he really *had* meant interesting—or else why choose the word?

GEE'S ARRIVAL at her new school was quite unlike Margaret Esther's. It was brightly autumnal, yellow trees shining like lanterns. Their car swept too fast through a wide white gate, spraying gravel. A sign said NORTHFIELDS PRIVATE SCHOOL FOR GIRLS. A vast Victorian brick house, once somebody's country pile, stood in lawns with flowers and shrubs, with a Virginia creeper turning colour on the west wall. Gee had been wooed and calmed. It looked all right. She would *make* it all right.

Her father swished the car round in a curve on the drive, laughing like a schoolkid playing bicycle wheelies as more gravel went flying. Her mother muttered *Oh for godsake*. They stopped near classroom windows, and Gee saw several moons of faces rise and stare. She climbed out of the car, swallowing a qualm and striving to arrange the spindly angles of her legs elegantly as Jo had demonstrated. Standing tall and elaborately unconcerned, leisurely taking in her surroundings, she adopted the cool, confident smile she had practised in the mirror. Inside, she said: *I can do it!*

After a week, an older girl took Gee kindly aside. "People do *like* you, but they're saying you're a bit too cocky for a new girl." The carapace was modified accordingly: the first of many times. The truth was, Gee grew to know, that the fear is never entirely lost. You merely get more expert at pretence.

THE BEST THING about Northfields had been her friend Anne. Anne had asked, very politely, if Gee would mind being her *best* friend. OK, Gee said, but failed to return the compliment. Theirs wasn't an intense girl-friendship with hand-holding, secrets and confidences. They laughed together and were companionable, with common interests in tennis, netball, bird-watching, swimming, reading, art (mostly Gee), music (mostly Anne). They won the tennis doubles tournament for their House, likewise the swimming relay. Everyone said they were "good sports".

There was an unforgettable memory. They'd been sitting together on a fallen tree in a copse in the school grounds. They kept very still, for Anne had explained: if you don't move or speak, you become invisible; you wait, the birds arrive; move nothing but your eyes. And suddenly, up the bole of a tree next to them had climbed a dainty tree-creeper in little jerks, picking out insecty things. Anne's head, Gee could see from the corner of her eye, was turned the wrong way. She moved her hand a snailish inch or two and pinched Anne's arm. Her head didn't turn, so Gee pinched her harder, harder, cruelly hard. Still no reaction. Very slowly, Gee had turned her own head a fraction to be able to see Anne. She was smiling, her head motionless: only her eyes had followed the tree-creeper. She'd suffered Gee's torture without flinching. Astonished, Gee had laughed. So did Anne, and the bird flew. Gee's respect for Anne had doubled. After that, she had felt special admiration for those who suffered and survived, without drawing attention to their own courage.

As perfect friends, Anne cackled at Gee's jokes and admired her ability to draw; Gee admired hers at the piano. Neither invaded the other's privacy. Probably they both believed, if they ever thought of the future at all, they'd be friends for ever. Gee knew almost nothing about Anne's life beyond school, and she rarely spoke of her own. They stayed in touch beyond schooldays for a while. Then all at once Anne was a born-again Christian, and would bring Jesus into every sentence, with urgings that Gee let him into her heart. Their correspondence dwindled after her proselytising failed to woo. Nevertheless, Gee reckoned Anne had been a good person, certainly admirable. Sometimes she wondered what Anne might be doing, and where. But she was just one of the loose ends of life.

Margaret Esther had certainly found a best friend. And an enemy! Now that was a coincidence: *The Two Miss Pees.*

There was a detestable Miss P. at Northfields. P-for-Pullinger in this woman's case, who unquestionably hated Gee. It showed in every moment she set eyes on Gee's face or heard her speak. Miss P. was ecstatic, crowing, sarcastic beyond measure if Gee gave an incorrect answer in class. In her report Miss P. wrote: "Georgina should learn to curb her tongue and be less opinionated if she is to progress and become a respected member of society."

Gee detested her in turn.

While she knew she was no beauty herself, Gee was at that age when actual ugliness was unforgiveable, especially when combined with ugly habits. Miss P. was ginger, whiskery, pale-eyed, not even *interesting*—and she ate repulsively. Both Gee and Anne dreaded the days when the dining rota put her at the head of their table. Miss P. would pack chewed food into her cheeks like a hamster, never swallowing, mesmerising everyone. Anne's theory was that she hated the food but mustn't set a bad example by leaving any—so she stored it and spat it out later. This made Gee dread Miss P. overdoing it and choking, splattering the whole masticated mess on to the table. The thought was so revolting that Gee couldn't swallow either.

And this Miss P. was weird, almost as weird as Margaret Esther's.

Gee's Miss P. used to peer in the gym windows like a glutton outside a cake shop, licking her lips, watching the pubescent girls and their developing bouncy bosoms jumping about. One girl claimed she had seen Miss P. rubbing her 'private parts' while spying. Most of them had no idea what that signified, except it was obviously dirty. Miss P. would be encountered hovering in the entrance to the showers, chatting on some pretext to the gym teacher, eyes a-pop as the girls went naked to and fro. Gee's father often came to mind, and Jo alone in the bedroom, and Gee took out her discomfort on Miss P., glaring at her pointedly. Didn't the gym teacher think the woman odd? Didn't other teachers notice anything? Nobody appeared to.

Once, before Gee was at the school, Anne had been on a Girl Guides' camping week, with Miss P-for-Pullinger as one of the supervising teachers. She prowled round the tents when the girls were undressing for bed. It was giggled about; you made sure your tent flap was closed. One night Anne awoke to find Miss P. inside her tiny little bivouac—and then the woman was unzipping her sleeping bag and squeezing in beside her, murmuring *Come now dear, I'll keep you warm*, and then thrust a bony hand up Anne's nightie and tried to fondle her. Anne had screamed as much with astonishment as alarm, and her molester scrambled into the night. It became an anecdote to entertain Anne's friends. Everyone shrieked with laughter, but nobody complained. It didn't occur to her or any of them.

Margaret Esther had tried to convince herself her uncle's groping hadn't happened. But she knew too well that it had. Gee knew too well also, knew and couldn't get away from it. She'd seen her father with his hands on Jo and her moving like that and you hated them both. But on your own with him, it was as if nothing had happened. He would never guess you had seen. When Gee's friends at school talked about their Daddies, she used to wonder what they'd say if she told them about her own. They would probably say: *You made that up! You're horrible! You ought to be ashamed of yourself.*

She was ashamed all right.

ANOTHER MEMORY. About twelve years old, she had not long learned to swim. Mad-keen on getting good enough to win sports-day races, on summer mornings early she would bike alone to the beach. Nobody else would be about. The sun was up but the sand was still night-cold, while in contrast the waves were warm and soft, bouncing against her as she ran in. It was one of those memories of pure happiness. She would swim, towel dry, and change out of her swimsuit without fear of being seen, then bike back through empty streets for breakfast. But one morning, far along the beach, there had been another figure, and she had hidden under her towel to change—just in case it was a man, one with unusually good eyesight. For by then, she was viewing Daddies differently. After that she used to examine the beach carefully to make sure she was alone.

One morning Jo had come with her, lured by Gee's enthusiasm. That summer had been hot, and the sun was warm early. Jo had wanted to stay a while after their swim, and they'd lain down on the sand. Gee was lying on her front, fingers plunging into drifts of gold and silver. Jo had said: *This is the best time of day to get a suntan, did you know?* Jo was lying on her back in her bright blue swimsuit; at fourteen she had a woman's figure, real breasts and hips, and that lovely caramel-tanned skin with little bleached hairs on the arms.

They hadn't known that the man was there until his shadow fell. He was standing barely two yards away, wearing swimming shorts and a purple short-sleeved shirt, unbuttoned, a striped towel over one shoulder. About the same age as their father. He said: *Hello.* And smiled in a particular way. It was that look: speculative, furtive.

Taken by surprise, they had sat up. *Hello.* Gee had copied Jo's polite smile.

Have a nice swim?

Yes, they had both said. Jo added: *Very nice.*

In the normal way he would have walked on, but this man was chatty. *Lovely in the early morning, isn't it? My favourite time of day. Only time I'm not busy, you see.*

They had said nothing, not knowing what he meant.

I'm a doctor, he explained.

Gee had known he wasn't a doctor. She had jumped up and pulled her dress over her swimsuit, even though it was still damp. Jo was staring at her.

He said: *If you like, I can give you a free examination.*

He was looking at Jo.

We're going now, Gee had almost shouted. *We have to be home for breakfast otherwise my mother worries and calls the police.*

Jo was astonished. The man laughed.

Come on! Gee had thrown Jo's sandals, and Jo had read her glare.

Oh well, said the man with a false smile. *If you've got to rush.*

He walked away, rapidly.

Years later, Gee reminded Jo of that day, and the look, and Jo said thoughtfully: "You know, I didn't notice. It was only when you slung my shoes at me I realised. I really did think he must be a doctor. Talk about gullible."

In fantasies, Gee would reconstruct the scene, but without Jo, and the man looked more and more like their father. He would approach and say: *I'm a doctor. I specialise in women's development. I can examine you and see if your body is progressing as it should.* Gee would reply: *All right, there are one or two things I'm concerned about.* And when she had deliberately allowed him to pull her swimsuit down from her shoulders, she would take from her beach bag a sharp knife, and stab him to death.

Dreams and fantasies. Only in rare dreams had Gee's mother ever kissed her or Jo goodnight. Just a few nights ago Miriam had appeared in a dream, with Gee a small child again. Her mother was as she used to be—before Sam. She had moved quickly and lightly, smile and spirit bright, and Gee had woken up missing her. Just a dream, gone away.

Chapter Seventeen

Beside an Auckland airport luggage carousel soon after dawn, waiting in a throng of arrivals in various stages of coma or derangement, Gee was so tired she felt sick. Her skin was like paper and her interior hollow. Moving to the edge of the crowd, she closed her eyes and leaned against a wall; it was impossible to look for a moment longer at her fellow-travellers. At last Gee managed to push her wagon-load through Immigration and Customs without serious injury, through faces searching, arms waving, all the time looking about her in the hope of recognising Pamela. A hand touched her shoulder, a New Zealand voice laughed in her ear: "Hello, cousin!" Pamela's handshake was strong. She was taller than Gee, with a cap of tight-curled dark hair, long and muscular limbs.

Daniel materialised large and smiling through the crowd behind his wife, to seize Gee's hand in both his: "If it isn't Georgina herself, welcome to New Zealand, bet you're dying for breakfast, that'll perk you up. You and Pam don't look a bit alike, do you? Follow me, car park's this way."

Then they were heading roughly south, she realised, once she'd been reminded the sun was in a different place in this half of the world. It was a reddish rising sun. White scarves of mist were dispersing across the waters of Manukau Harbour, floating off towards the hills. The suburbs looked clean and damp as if newly-hosed, hardly a soul about, just an occasional jogger. Low-level wooden houses glowed in soft pinks, greens, blues, like chalk drawings, among mossy stone walls, and magnolia trees in lavish flower. Beyond everything was the sea, the harbour, mile on mile of sky, pampas grass, pines reminiscent of monkey puzzles.

Daniel pointed towards blue inlets where he and Pamela went sailing, and at extraordinary steep hills, forming soft wrinkles and peaks like green meringue.

"Just look at it all," Gee said, drunk on colour and light. "Putting some of this into paint might be quite a challenge."

"Just you wait," Pamela said, "until you see where Auntie Mildred lives, and the beaches, they are out of this world—and where our farm is, about an hour further south, that's knock-out too."

Pohutukawa Farm. Aunt Mildred's house and myriad outbuildings crouched at the bottom of a deep green valley. The hills rose steep and undulating, their slopes thick with the lush trees that had given the farm its name and, on the grassier sides, cows munching breakfast. The house lay snug as a sleeping cat: white clapboard, reminding Gee somewhat of New England; slender pillars with curly tops along the verandah, doors and window-frames in blue-grey picked out in white, a conservatory, a mature garden of unknown flowers around a sloping lawn. The names of the trees rattled off by Pamela were quite foreign, but she supposed she would learn.

Millie's night-nurse, coming downstairs to greet them in the dim and shuttered hall, told them pleasantly that Mildred had only just woken.

"But I'll let you know the moment she's ready for company. That'll be roughly when the day-nurse takes over." She smiled at Pamela. "Your aunt's had a good night's rest, Mrs Forbes, but I don't like to rush her."

Daniel said with relish: "That's OK, we were thinking of breakfast ourselves anyway." He led the way along a shadowy corridor of panelling and closed doors of dark wood: framed paintings crowded the deep ochre wallpaper, surely the work of Grandpa Frederick, Gee thought, by the look of those skies.

The big kitchen was almost as ill-lit as the hall and corridor. Window-blinds were pulled two-thirds down, even though the sunlight was already cut off by the overhang of verandah roof and thickly clambering plants. Paintwork and floorboards were a deep brown, the table too. Gee longed to yank at the blinds and let in the day.

"How d'you fancy some corn fritters? With fruit and sour cream. One of my specialities," Pamela smiled.

"May as well forewarn you," Daniel said, "Pam does everything well. Cooking, baking bread, pottery, painting, you name it. You should see the stuff she does for the grandchildren's birthdays."

"Do stop, Daniel. You're embarrassing me." Pamela didn't look in the least embarrassed, and they exchanged grins.

Gee looked at them, conspiratorial and comfortable, married forty years, and was alone again, envious.

THEY WERE LEANING BACK, dopily replete, when Jean, the day-nurse, appeared: Mildred was ready.

At the top of a wide curving staircase (more dark, polished wood), Jean opened the door to Mildred's room and stood aside with a smile. This room was brighter, the morning sunshine slanting through two unimpeded windows. Mildred—*Millie!*—was sitting up in bed, hands neatly folded in her lap. A daintily-boned face with a ballerina's neatness, a cat's green gaze taking in her visitors, and white hair against blue linen pillows. Unexpected prettiness.

She *couldn't* be eighty-nine, thought Gee. As a girl she must have been enchanting. Mildred smiled and held out a hand towards Gee.

"Come and say hello." There was nothing light or tremulous about her voice.

"Hey," said Gee, walking towards her swiftly, "so *you're* Millie!"

Mildred laughed. Without hesitation, Gee bent to kiss her cheek. Never had she seen such smooth skin on anyone this age; she looked younger than Gee's mother. But more than any physical attributes, gentleness rose from her like a soft perfume. And there was absolutely no visible likeness to Gee's father. Illogically and obscurely, she was glad.

"And this is Gee," said Millie, "at long last." She clasped Gee's hand. "And don't you imagine I'm lying in bed all day. I'll be up soon. Once the physio-terrorist has done her worst."

"You'll get up when I say so," said Jean, and laughed when Mildred stuck out her tongue. "I'll be right next door if you want anything."

"Aren't you lovely and tall!" Millie said to Gee, the moment all the greetings were ended. "I didn't realise from the photos. Lucky you. I always longed to be tall and elegant like you and Pammy, but I was always a shrimp."

"Tough little shrimp, though," Pamela grinned. "Don't let her fool you."

Pamela stayed for only a few minutes of general chat. "OK then," she said, "I'll leave you two together to catch up. The physio lady's due in about an hour. My bet is you'll be more than ready for a snooze by then, Gee. Daniel will put your bags in your room—other end of the landing, roses on the wallpaper."

GEE WAS LEFT ALONE with Mildred, her father's sister, and she felt as if she were taking part in a dream, her eyes and brain curiously dislocated, watching herself from the outside. Mildred was smiling, sitting up straight and spruce in her bed, a cotton patchwork quilt part-covering her, clearly overjoyed—and perhaps equally disbelieving—to see her here.

Mildred patted the armchair close beside the bed. "Make yourself comfortable. Let me look at you. Tell me things."

Obeying, Gee took a deep breath and said: "Right. But I don't suppose you want to hear about my trip. The best things about it were getting upgraded, not having to talk to anyone else and reading Grandma McIvor's first journal. And getting here."

"That sounds good," Mildred said, and added inconsequentially: "You must have inherited your great big eyes from Miriam's side. None of our lot had eyes like that. And you've got what Daddy used to call good bones. He would've wanted to paint you. *Very* interesting face." Without waiting for a response, she went on: "Tell me about yourself. I know you want to talk about Grandma McIvor, but indulge this old baggage. First things first."

Unlike most people Millie looked right into one's eyes, appearing to weigh each word spoken. Very likely, Gee suspected, she could read every flicker of her expression.

Gee stalled with a laugh. "Not from the day I was born?" A shiver of her childhood shyness went through her: she wasn't ready for full confidences yet.

Millie leaned towards her and laid the palm of her hand gently against Gee's cheek, and for an instant looked sad. Gee couldn't tell what had caused the sadness. The touch had been exactly judged, intimate, not intrusive.

Millie said: "I'd *really* like you to start before that—fill in the gaps about my brother Frankie and your Mum Miriam. He told us so little! But not today—you must be flaked out."

Gee was grateful. "Just a touch. What's your next choice?"

"Tell me the story of how you changed your name to Gee." Millie giggled. "I bet Frankie didn't like *that*."

Relief made Gee giggle with her. "I was about seven. It had just clicked with me that Jo's name and mine had *really* been intended for boys—George and Joseph—but they could be instantly adapted if girls rather disappointingly popped out."

"People always wanted a boy, didn't they?"

"Never any secret about it. And we didn't question it. Just *absorbed* the opinion that girls were second-rate. Amazing really. One day, I can't remember what caused the revelation, I suddenly thought: Cheek! That's not fair! Immediately hated my name. And after a bit of thought, I decided what to do."

"Ooh-hoo! What a serious little girl!"

"This was no laughing matter. In no time I'd splurged my entire week's pocket-money on chocolate—to bribe Jo to call me Gee from that day on, and to agree that she'd be known as Jo. The idea was that we'd sound *more* like boys, making the point as annoyingly as possible. Mind you, I'm not sure that's logical."

"It's very *sophisticated* for a seven-year-old," Mildred approved. "And Jo agreed?"

"A bit dubiously, but she loved chocolate."

"And Frankie?"

"It was great. He was even more pissed off than I'd hoped. Even stopped my pocket money for a fortnight, would you believe. But I refused to cave in. So, he *insisted* on calling us by our full names, loudly and pointedly. And he would make fun of my 'silly new name' in front of my friends—as if they cared."

"And your mother?"

"Mum just shrugged and said, call yourself what you like. She had other things on her mind—she was expecting Sam in a matter of weeks. Ah, I remember now, it was *Sam's* name that made me realise about *our* names. Mum'd just told us that the new baby would be Samuel if a boy, Samantha if a girl. And Dad commanded: 'And he or she will *not* be called Sam.' So naturally, when the desirable commodity of a boy arrived—"

"—you disobeyed!" cried Millie with relish.

"—Too right. I at once amputated Samuel's extra syllables in the interests of rebellion. Pretty feeble rebellion, but it was *something*."

Millie clapped her hands, but Gee felt suddenly saddened. Sam, her little brother.

Mildred looked at her, and spoke softly.

"Was Frankie a good father? I do hope he was." But perhaps immediately regretting the question, she added: "Still, I don't suppose you'd tell me if he wasn't. Why should you? None of my business." She put her hand over Gee's. "Sorry." And then: "Will you tell me about Sam?"

Gee nodded. She rarely spoke of Sam, but with Millie she could.

"I loved Sam. I often wonder what he would have been like if he'd grown up. He'd be forty-one now."

She could remember the day he was born as clearly as the day he died. Her mother was lying there exhausted—she'd had the baby at home—but she smiled slightly when Gee's face sneaked round the door.

"You can look," Miriam said, and Gee tiptoed to the Moses basket. She smelled Dettol and Johnson's baby talc. Little Samuel had black curls, navy-blue eyes, and a smooth fragile skin—no sign of the usual wrinkles and creases. He really was beautiful.

"And Miriam adored him," Mildred said.

"Oh yes. Too much really. Dad was jealous. So was Jo."

And when Sam died only three years later, Gee decided not to add, he carried off Mum's love with him. There was only a small, dutiful ration of affection left for anyone else.

"And you weren't jealous?" Mildred asked.

"I wasn't, no."

Jo had bitterly resented Sam for being born and taking their mother's love. Recalling it as an adult, Jo had said: *It was like a light going out.* But it wasn't Sam's fault, Gee had answered. Gee and Jo had never seen it the same way. Probably because Gee herself hadn't felt there was so very much love to steal.

"But," Gee added with a wry grin, "not because of virtue or anything. I think it was because I loved him too, and so I minded less."

But poor Jo. What a ready victim for their jealous father.

Mildred gently asked: "Were things never the same after that?"

"Never."

"And how——? No. Don't go on if you don't want."

Gee shook her head. "It's okay." Another deep breath. "It was summer, school holidays. At breakfast-time, Sam was feverish and Mum was worried enough to talk about calling the doctor. Dad said, 'Good Lord, woman, it's only the sniffles, you fuss too much over the kid.' And went off, cross, to work. Mum hesitated, doubting her instinct I suppose, and maybe not wanting to bother the doctor about a trifle. She never forgave herself, or Dad, for that hour's delay—never believed it probably made no difference."

But Gee remembered the doctor's serious expression, and the urgency behind his reassurance. *Probably just a 'flu thing,* he'd said, *but there are some funny things about, so best have him in hospital.* What Gee recalled next was Sam's blotchy face, lying against her mother's shoulder as they got into the taxi. How weak he looked. Her mother looked at her and Gee caught the fear in her eyes. Gee felt she'd been punched in the stomach by pure dread. As they drove off she glanced at her sister, and Jo was standing there, waving, almost excited by this new adventure.

"Of course," Gee acknowledged, "she wasn't to know the truth any more than I was, but I couldn't stand her being so cheerful. I ran off to my sycamore tree. My own special sanctuary. Climbed to the top, and stayed there, all day, till Mum came home."

Her father called her at some point in the afternoon; he was home early. Gee ignored him. Soon Jo shouted it was tea-time. *I've got tea ready, Mummy's not back yet, come on, Daddy's waiting!* To Gee, she just sounded pleased with herself. Gee kept quiet. They couldn't be sure she was in the tree, not when she was so high up. She just waited, thinking about what she might normally have been doing that day—a summer-holiday, hot day. She would have spent hours with Sam at the beach, probably, coming home at tea-time. And after his bath she would have read him his bedtime story. She always did that.

"Anyway, by the time Mum came home, I was exhausted and stiff, blinding myself by watching the sun going down in what seemed like flames, all orange and glorious on the horizon, and I told myself that was a lucky sign."

"So you showed your face only when Miriam called you?"

"Not at once."

Gee could see her mother waiting, absolutely motionless, on the path to the back door. She had on a blue cotton dress scattered with white daisies, and she was standing among the overgrown lavender and the roses. She waited. And Gee had climbed down slowly. As she walked towards her mother it was as if everything was flowers, the colours and their perfume, and Miriam didn't say anything, just stood aside—formally, almost—and indicated that Gee should go indoors. Jo was already there. Miriam asked them to sit down at the kitchen table. Her face: Gee would never forget. It was set in stone, as grey as rain. She poured tea and put biscuits on a plate in the centre of the table. It seemed like some kind of ceremony. Gee was shaking with fear.

"Mum pulled out a chair at the end of the table, quite slowly, and sat down. Jo and I were on each side; she didn't look at us or touch her tea cup."

And then it had seemed to Gee there was a stream of words, words she couldn't remember afterwards as real sentences. They were too terrible to believe but too ugly not to believe, filling the air between them: *Inflammation, brain, virus, meningitis, incurable, they did all they could, he died, he died.*

"At the end, Mum said: 'It was very quick, they said Sam suffered very little.'"

Millie whispered, wiping her face: "O dear, poor little Sam, poor Miriam. Poor all of you."

GEE'S EXHAUSTION RETURNED, nearly swamping her. She leaned back in her armchair, her own tears threatening.

"I'm sorry," she said. "Upsetting you."

"That's all right," Millie said firmly. "Can't tell life's stories without some sadness." She sighed: managed a small smile. "No more sadness for now. We'll talk a little about Grandma McIvor, and then you absolutely *must* have some sleep and we'll meet again at supper."

Gee was grateful, and snatched at her chance: "Tell me a bit about her now? How do you remember her?"

"Let's see. As you know, I was just a girl—in my teens—when she died, and she must have been well past seventy. Is that amazing or what? Years younger than I am now, yet to me she'd been old all my life—too old to be pretty, or so it seemed to my young eyes, and too old to tell if she had been. But she had the softest skin. Mother used to say, give Grandma a kiss, and her cheek was fine and silky. Then she would smile, such a slight and thoughtful smile, and I used to think it was as if she was holding it in. I don't believe I *ever* saw her laugh, though from what Mother said there'd been lots of laughter before Grandpa McIvor died, when Mother was small."

"Was she affectionate?" Gee wondered.

Millie nodded. "She was, but not in a demonstrative way. You could hear it in her tone of voice, or the way she looked at you. And she seemed to me to be never, *ever* idle. Always beavering away at something—never sitting down except to eat, unless she was sewing or embroidering—even after she'd retired from teaching."

"You mean, as a governess?"

"More than that. She was quite a pioneer. But that's a story for another day. Too long for now."

"And what do you remember best about her?" Gee asked, fascinated. "Is there one particular characteristic? I mean, to sum her up? If one can."

"I'd say this. *She spoke only when necessary.* No, really. And when she did, you sat up and took notice. Once, when Alice and I were invited to a party, I was begging Mother—being a proper little pest!—for black velvet for a dress. Grandma McIvor said: 'Oh *no*, Mildred my dear, you're *far* too young for black.'

"And Mother nodded meaningfully at me! I'd been given the Ultimate Answer. No question of argument. Presence, that's what she had."

Gee said: "That's a good picture you painted." But she couldn't prevent a huge yawn. "Excuse *me*. When shall we start on her trunk?"

"Tomorrow, when you've had a good long sleep and are raring to go! Today's settling-in day. Sleep a bit. And we'll dine at a civilised hour, so you get an early night. Jean's got it all organised. And tomorrow after breakfast and physio or doctor or whatever's on the agenda, don't ask *me*, we'll park our bottoms in the Blue Room, have a proper delve in the trunk, and make a Plan. I'd started to put things in some kind of order when the bronchitis got me, and left stuff all over the table. Pammie quite rightly gathered it up and put it all back in the trunk, not knowing how long I'd be out of action. So we'll have to start from scratch."

Mildred leaned her head back on her pillows and sighed and smiled at the same time.

"You're tired too," said Gee, feeling too dizzy and disembodied to state anything beyond the obvious.

"It's worth it. Dear Gee. It's so wonderful you're here. I feel as if we've known each other for years."

Chapter Eighteen

GEE LEFT MILLIE AND WENT to her own rose-papered room, closed the door, sat on her bed, and burst into tears. She hardly ever cried. Her brain was wonky, or so it felt. She was upside-down on this planet, excited, jet-lagged, battered by emotions.

She knew, however, that she wouldn't yet sleep. She repaired the damage to her face with cold water and some staring out of her open window, catching the breeze. Between the hills she could see the sea, a glittering triangle, a reminder of the view from her sycamore retreat. Taking a walk might be a good idea, she thought. Revive the system. She unpacked, took a shower, put on clean clothes. Not quite a new woman, but an improvement.

Pamela said: "Good idea. Shall I come along? See the sea? There's no rush for lunch—we've got plenty of time." Daniel, preferring to remain bent under the bonnet of Mildred's car, waved them goodbye.

Walking with Pamela was demanding, especially uphill. They strode up and down for perhaps two miles in the spring sunshine, through endless acres of the farm's bright green hills—Pamela pointing out Pohutukawa Farm's distant boundaries on the way—a route that led in dips and crags to skies unlimited and the broadest and longest beach possible, stretching and curving right out of sight, with the surf coming in, sunlit and gentle, bringing row after row of what looked like fine lace edging. Pamela laughed when Gee described it like that.

"Wait until there's a storm. It's the wildest beast you've ever seen."

Gee could hardly wait.

The beauty of the place knocked her sideways. All the photographs she'd ever seen of this country had given the impression of crisp, clear sunshiny scenes in which even the mountains and exotic flowers looked posed, a little too sharp and orderly. The reality here was huge, wild, thrilling.

Gee found herself thinking: *How Margaret Esther must have revelled in it.*

Once back at the farm they ate crusty bread with salad and cheddar-like cheese made from the milk of Mildred's own cows, presented by Jean, the more-than-nurse.

Jean told them Mildred had eaten her own lunch and was napping.

"But she'll be down in the evening for dinner. Oh yes," she answered Gee's unspoken question, "she can manage the stairs very well." Jean clearly adored her. "She's amazing."

"That amazing old lady," Gee said, "is younger than any of us."

It was, she thought, impossible not to love Millie: for her kindness; her perception; her spirit. She, Gee reckoned, had certainly got her fair share of the good genes in the family pool.

"DON'T YOU DARE help me!" Mildred commanded as she descended the stairs in the early evening. "I've got the banister and I've got my stick."

Mildred's stick was more a pointer or general gesticulator than a prop. "Better for my hip," she explained. "I don't want it believing it can take things easy. The stick's just in case. The physio tells me 'Use The Leg!' so I do."

Mildred walked with only the slightest hint of a limp. Not exactly fast, but not a snail either. She held herself straighter than any other elderly lady Gee had ever seen; her voice was clear and untremulous. Heard but not seen, she could be taken for a woman half her years. Gee told her as much at dinner.

"Oh," said Mildred, "it's so beastly getting ancient, turning into an old crone, falling apart, bones getting feeble. Life's very unfairly arranged, isn't it?" But she laughed, and entertained Gee with tales of her girlhood. "I might be ancient on the outside but inside I'm just the same—one of the Brookes girls. People always said, 'must invite the Brookes girls, they're so jolly!' Alice and Millie, they meant. Rose being much older, thirteen years older than me, wouldn't be seen out and about with us flibbertigibbets. Alice and I would be off to every ball we could when we were teenagers. We were good pals once I'd stopped being a little girl. There I'd be, all done up in my blue velvet, and Alice looking gorgeous in red. We weren't a bad catch, I can tell you. The boys used to come running. We never sat out a single dance. But how innocent it all was in those days."

When they said goodnight, they agreed to meet at ten in the morning in the Blue Room. There, two doors along from Gee's bedroom, Grandma McIvor's trunk awaited them. Gee would take Margaret Esther's first journal with her.

"That'll be our starting point," Mildred said. "We'll use those yellow stick-on note things, and write down dates. We'll be organised in no time!"

IT HAD SOUNDED brisk and efficient, but it was with a nervy mixture of disbelief and reverence that Gee found herself seated next day with Mildred at a pitted oak table, looking at the beautiful, scarred and dirty trunk that once belonged to that child, girl, woman, that Margaret Esther McIvor, née Moore. A lady. You didn't have a weighty leather trunk like this if you expected to carry your own luggage.

Mildred said: "You know, my William was born ninety years ago in this house. It was his parents' farm. And by the time he brought me home as his bride it was his own." After a pause, she went on: "Imagine, it's forty-six years since he died. We had so little time together, only five years of marriage. I must've told you in one of my letters."

"You did, yes. Another of life's unfair arrangements."

"Especially as I'd married late, for those days. I wasn't going to settle for any old body. And then—well. Even now I can still feel the shock of it. He was so well one minute, and sick with that horrible cancer the next. Gone within three months.

And I never met another man I wanted to marry. But in spite of that, I know I was lucky." She glanced round the room and smiled at Gee. "This room has always been blue—William liked it like that. It was his bedroom when he was a boy. And I've always loved it because I can imagine him here."

Gee looked in turn around the blue-painted walls, the slanted ceiling with its uneven beams, the sloping, shiny floorboards. It was like a ship lurching. She could imagine a boy delighting in such a higgledy place. "I can almost see him myself," she answered.

Millie smiled. "But now," she said, nodding at the trunk, "we can go even further back." She nudged Gee's arm. "*You* can open it."

She spoke as if offering a privilege, but it was some moments before Gee dared to lift the lid, and she jumped slightly when the hinges softly groaned. A mild mustiness arose, a cloudy perfume. And here indeed was disorder. Millie had said that they would have to start from scratch, but the first decision would be where exactly scratch was.

A collapsed heap of what could be journals was at one side, some spilling pages from damaged spines; nearby, a few bundles of letters tied with ribbon or tape; manilla envelopes large and small; assorted magazines; scattered exercise books; smaller books, perhaps notebooks. An oval watercolour painting of blue flowers in a plain wide mahogany frame was jammed at an angle in a corner. A broad border of lace attached to a partly-buried something—a petticoat or tablecloth? A china-headed doll, with painted black hair and a face more womanly than childlike, stared unsmiling from under a tattered newspaper. Small leather-bound volumes, probably novels. Bizarrely, a pair of men's riding boots, sticking out from a loosely-wrapped plaid shawl. Clothes, dresses perhaps—an edge of blue silk, folds of dusty white muslin—rolled in crumpled tissue.

At first she felt like an intruder. But Mildred nudged her again: "Go on, start taking things out." She smiled. "I'm quite sure Grandma McIvor wouldn't mind one bit."

As Gee obeyed, her excitement rose. This must surely be how archaeologists felt when they loosed and lifted from the earth some rare fragment of ceramic or an ancient necklace, something that had been created and used by strangers long dead. Those strangers' very breath was upon such discoveries. Seeing a journal that had already been given a stick-on note by Mildred, she lifted it out of the trunk.

The label said: *Begins 1847. NB: 1843–4 sent to Gee.*

"It makes sense to start with the journals," said Gee. "That's the easiest way to sort out the chronology, and anyway they're what we want to read."

Mildred was already writing *1843–1844* on a label and sticking it on the first journal, before handing it to Gee. With some delicacy Gee placed it on the far left corner of the table. "The beginning! Now, let's leave a gap for interim years, and then—" She positioned the 1847 volume. "Now what?"

An envelope of thick, cream, ochre-edged paper lay revealed. Written upon it in Margaret Esther's writing, in ink brown with age: *My letters to Harriet.* (Others, *incl. her last letter to me, are in my journals where relevant.)* Gee read this out to Millie, and said: "Anyone would think she was expecting someone to come looking, one of these days." She placed the envelope on the table near Millie. "We'll sort them another time."

Choosing another journal at random from the jumble, she held it for a little while without opening it. Margaret Esther, who had drawn so much nearer in the last two days, was close up now, taking shape—almost whispering in her ear. If Gee let herself, she could imagine the pages of these volumes still warm from her hands and could believe that she and Mildred had been granted special permission to read them. Holding the journal loosely, she let it fall open naturally. She saw a leap in years; and the words grabbed her.

> 30th June, 1850. The Academy.
>
> I know too well that the majority of mankind, even those with exceptionally tolerant and forgiving natures, if they could observe the interior workings of my mind, would be bound to say that its store of wickedness is frightful. At one time the thought of such a judgement would have filled me with guilt. No longer.
>
> Now–I look into the future with hope, and have but one wish. It is time I wrote out the truth of it.
>
> I was twelve years old when I first acknowledged the feelings that were the source of my subsequent secret wish.

The emotion was visible on the page, pressing into the surface, denting the thick paper. Here was an accumulation, pain by pain, of whatever had happened to her.

One pain too many, and you have to acknowledge what is true. If not with a wishbone and a murderous prayer, then in a private journal, in silent passion.

"What've you found?" Mildred was watching her face.

"Eighteen-fifty. She would have been nineteen in December that year." Looking further into the journal, she added: "To 1851, by the look of it. And there's a letter tucked in here, Grandma McIvor's writing. It's to Harriet. She's written on it, *This gives account of events not found in this journal.* How intriguing."

Gee knew she must resist. Step by step and logically must she go, or be carried off. Besides, she and Millie had agreed to read everything together.

"Mustn't be tempted to jump ahead," she told herself aloud.

The journal was carefully labelled and given a suitable position on the table. But after considerable searching, they realised there were no more complete journals.

"There seem to be three lost years," Gee lamented. "Can't find anything dated 1845 or '46. And this one that you labelled 1847 doesn't begin until December of that year, shortly before her sixteenth birthday. But look, she must have kept on writing her journals in the gap, because it begins: *I have perforce to begin a new volume of my journal before the New Year–the result of too enthusiastically filling page after page with accounts of my summer vacation at Mudstone and my happy times in Miss Avery's company and also with Tommy and Dottie—and almost no sight of my Papa.* What can have happened to it?"

"Perhaps we'll find out as we go along. Unless Rose got rid of some papers from the trunk and didn't say. But I can't believe even *she* would do that."

The rest of the morning was spent putting letters and stray papers in heaps, in date order where possible, and tucked into journals where appropriate. Notebooks made further piles. Letters in envelopes, variously dated, were given a *To be sorted* sticker. They pulled out watercolours and drawings: landscapes, flowers, portraits. None signed, none titled. Occasionally a date appeared on their backs, in Margaret Esther's hand. She was rather gifted, Gee noted with pleasure. The pictures were tidied back into the trunk along with the doll, some embroidered sheets and tablecloths, a blue silk shawl, a lace blouse, two hats and a box of jewellery.

"Let's look at that," Mildred pointed at once-white muslin poking out from tissue.

Gee shook out a dress, and held it up to show her aunt.

"Suits you," Mildred smiled. "Look in the mirror. Try it on."

Gee held it against herself, and looked. Her reflection was a shock. Her own wedding-dress had been much in this style, though in lawn rather than muslin: high-necked, full-skirted, piped from shoulder to waist; it was a Victorian look that had always pleased her, so she had seized her one chance to wear it. And this was surely Grandma McIvor's own bridal gown—why else keep it?

She merged in the glass with Margaret Esther and was giddy.

"No, I don't think so," she decided. "It wouldn't seem right, somehow." With some reverence she returned it to its tissue and the trunk. "We can decide about all these things later, when we've done the reading."

The riding boots, polished like new and stuffed with paper to keep their shape, were left undisturbed, apart from wrapping their tartan covering more closely.

"I suppose——" Gee began.

"Of course," cried Mildred, "they were Grandpa McIvor's!" They both stared, on the edge of laughter. There was something sad but comical about keeping a dead man's boots. "I wonder if he was wearing them when he died. My mother told me there was a riding accident."

But she didn't know details. "Mother was only eight or nine, her sisters and brother younger still. Poor little mites, losing their daddy so young. Though of course, they had each other—and their loving mummy. If Grandma McIvor put it all in a diary maybe we'll come to it. It *is* tempting, to search ahead. But no. No cheating."

"That reminds me," said Gee. "I want to write to the Department of Internal Affairs. They think they might track down records of Grandma McIvor if they can first trace the death of one of her children. Didn't your mother—Jemima—die soon after you were married?"

"I was on my honeymoon," Millie said. "I'll never forget that."

"New Zealand? How on Earth did you get there?" said Miriam on the telephone. Her memory seeped back after some reminders. She asked after "that Mildred", and what she was saying about her.

"All kinds of nice things," Gee decided to say. "How are you?"

"Hmph. I'm fine. Fine." A thinking pause, then: "Does Sebastian like it over there?"

Gee said: "Sebastian's at home, Mum. Remember? The idea was to come here alone."

"Oh yes, yes." Undoubtedly Miriam was rubbing her forehead. "Of course darling."

"How's Jo?" Gee asked. "Seen her lately?"

"She came last week. Josephine is a funny woman."

"Funny how?"

"Not funny-ha-ha. *You* know. Acts like she's got something to say then doesn't come out with it. As if she's waiting for you to introduce the subject she wants to talk about. Told her to stop beating about the bush and she got all huffy, so that didn't help. Just the same, there's a funny look in her eye. If I didn't know her better I'd say she's got a secret she's dying to tell. I asked how Eric was, and she just stared straight at me and said nothing. You'd have thought I was prying, or accusing her of something."

"Maybe she murdered him and buried him in the cellar." *Not before time*, she managed not to add.

"Jo hasn't got a cellar, has she?"

"Er, no, Mum. But under the patio would do."

"Do be serious darling. As if she would. Honestly, *I* think she's gone a bit doolally."

The words pot and kettle jiggled in Gee's mind. "I expect she and Eric had a tiff or something."

As if Jo and Eric ever had anything as mild.

After she'd put down the phone, Gee wondered why she had made the call. Perhaps she should call Jo direct and find out for herself how she sounded. But she knew she wouldn't.

Chapter Nineteen

Sunday, 5th December 1847.

I have perforce to begin a new volume of my journal before the New Year—the result of too enthusiastically filling page after page with accounts of my summer vacation at Mudstone and my happy times in Miss Avery's company and also with Tommy and Dottie—and almost no sight of my Papa! Summer seems so very long ago now.

Alas, once again, I shall not be returning home for our Christmas vacation. My Uncle and Aunt, the widely-respected Sir John and Lady Talbot, officially my *guardians*, have once again invited me and Miss Avery to Talbot Castle for the Christmas vacation—as has been their hospitable habit for almost every long vacation over the last two or three years. The stated reason—that is, stated by my Aunt Clarissa—for my not going home as often as I would choose is that my Papa was too frequently away on business to "enjoy his child's company", and besides it was an exhausting journey that we should not be obliged to make so frequently. This parental selflessness was applauded by the Talbots, who declared themselves most happy to "welcome the child as our own". Aunt Clarissa, her son now beyond fragile infancy, has been glad of the willing, unpaid assistance of a young nursemaid in the person of his cousin, to wit, myself. I note but do not resent this, for he is a dear little boy. I also believe that my affection for him and my usefulness to her encouraged my aunt to concur when I first announced to her that I wished Miss Avery *always* to accompany me on my visits to the castle, with a room next-door to my own. Whether Aunt Clarissa considered her niece to be immature, or overly charitable to a mere servant, one who had no sense of her proper station, I cannot say, but she submitted to my demand when she realised that if Miss Avery remained uninvited then I myself would not come.

I do not anticipate our stay at the Castle with any other prospect of pleasure, but this year I am looking forward to one part of our vacation with great excitement and emotion! Miss Avery and I are taking a special trip for the first week or so—the result of my confession to her of a long-held wish.

Approximately one month ago, I broached the matter: "There is something I would very much like to do, but I have said nothing of it in all the time we have been in Scotland."

Harriet (for thus am I permitted to address her, now that I am near to sixteen, when we are alone together) was clearly struck by my solemnity. "Is this something I may help with?"

"I know of no other who might help me," I replied. And thus it emerged that I strongly desired to visit my Scottish birth-place—my Mama's home-town.

"Why," exclaimed Harriet, "I would dearly love to take you there, a place I understand to be charming. But would not such a visit make you melancholy?"

I had considered this possibility. "It may, but I should nevertheless like to see where my dear Mama spent her girlhood. I feel it may bring her nearer to me."

Permission and expenses had to be sought from Papa for this small tour. Harriet cleverly avoided the danger of refusal by presenting the trip as an educational tour of historical Scotland without giving the precise itinerary or mentioning my birthplace. Permission was granted, and the funds arrived via my Uncle John.

I count the days! We leave in eight days: three days after my sixteenth birthday. Then our plan is to return to the Academy for fresh clothes and spend a night or so here before repairing to Talbot Castle for Christmas itself.

15th December 1847. Blairloch.

When we entered this little town this afternoon it was already twilight. How excited I was! As our stagecoach rattled along the main street I looked about with great eagerness. Lamps were being lit and I saw little stone cottages, a dark granite church, gleaming shop windows, rutted lanes. I was unable to see everything quickly enough, and Harriet feared I would leap from the coach in order to step upon the very cobble-stones that my Mama had trodden. "O do look!" I cried, "how delightful! How shall we find her house? What shall we do first?"

Harriet laughed at me, but kindly. "Do be calm, my dear. We cannot explore until daylight, so you must be patient a little longer. I am hopeful that the family house still stands. Your Mama's family was far from poor so everyone will know of it."

Perforce, I must be patient—and Harriet's calm demeanour calmed me also.

Our inn is the charming Blairloch Arms, a quaint building more than two hundred years old. A maid carried our portmanteaux up the snaking staircase to two small adjacent rooms under the eaves, and dropped the bags without ceremony inside each door.

She spoke with an accent far stronger than that which we hear in Edinburgh. I attempt to reproduce it here, nevertheless! "Ye'll find water within, should ye need to wash awa' the dairt o' yeer jairney. An' yeer chamber-pottie is beneath yeer beds. Awa' doon the passage theer" (here she pointed) "ye'll find the airth-closet itsel'. Aye."

And away she marched. We could not help smiling—with amusement and with gratitude for her practical good sense.

I write this after a companionable and nourishing dinner with Harriet (mutton pie and potatoes). The landlord of the inn has promised to furnish us with directions to my Mama's family house in the morning. Harriet has told me to get a good night's sleep. I will try!

16th December 1847.

Barely can I believe this day. It is almost twenty-four hours since my last entry and my life has utterly changed.

Immediately after breakfast, I returned to my room to collect my cloak and gloves, and Harriet did likewise. As I closed the door of my room I was startled to find another person within. There was little light, for the room has but one small window under the roof, but through the gloom I could see a woman bent over the oak chest in the corner, lifting a blanket. In doing so she did not fully straighten her back, and I observed that she was rather old, sixty years or more, with white hair showing beneath her bonnet. The woman made no apology for her presence, nor remarked upon my exclamation at seeing her.

"Guid day, lassie," said she politely, although in an accent even more marked than that of the chambermaid, and I will make scant attempt to transcribe it. She barely glanced at me. "I shall be giving ye a warm cover for your bed, for 'twill be a hoar-frost the nicht." With this she took the blanket to the bed and threw it across with surprising vigour for one so bent and sinewy.

I thanked her and crossed to the little window. Outside I saw clustered angles of rooftops and, if I craned, charming cottages and wrought-iron lamps in the street below; I heard the clatter of wheels and hooves and the shouted promises of vendors; and I could not help but smile to myself at the thought of being at last here in the embrace of my Mama's own town.

"Aye, lassie," said the woman, disconcerting me by appearing alongside me at the sill and seeming to read my thoughts. "'Tis a nice wee town."

I turned with a smile towards her—only to be startled anew by her clapping a bony hand to her mouth and crying out: "Upon my soul, I dinna believe it!"

Dumbfounded, I stared back at the old lady's now bulging eyes. Whatever had prompted this outburst? My appearance may be odd, but nobody thus far has been moved to cry out at the sight of it.

"What is it?" I asked, rather fearfully.

"Ye must be wee Lizzie's girl! Och, 'tis amazing. So many years past, but I see her bonnie wee face! Are ye not? Are ye not wee Lizzie Eddington's lassie?"

I felt I would surely faint, and clung to the window-sill.

"Aye," the woman went on, "ye have her bonnie eyes, there canna be a doubt! Ye have her bonnie smile!" Tears now filled her eyes and she clutched my arm. "I knew her since she were a bairn, the kindest bonniest lassie ye could wish to meet. I saw her wed, I was among the womenfolk there when she gave birth, aye, fifteen or sixteen years past it is. Poor wee Lizzie, taken away to our Lord with my arms about her and her own arms about her bairn. Tell me your name, lassie, tell me—"

I whispered: "It is Moore, but my mother's maiden name was indeed Eddington..." And then I did irresistibly sink to the floor, my legs failing to support me a moment longer. The woman was at once agitated, fetching a chair and helping me be seated. She dipped a cloth into the pitcher of water and dabbed my face. Through my dizziness I heard her: "Och, forgive me lassie, but I could not help myself, ye have such a kenspeckle wee face!"

('Kenspeckle', I later learned, means 'worthy of note'—or even 'conspicuous'!)

When she was assured I had recovered myself, the old lady's story emerged. Her name was Mary Macgregor. She had worked in the Eddington family's kitchens as a scullery maid while still a child. Mary's mother was famed for her skill with herbs and midwifery; from girlhood, Mary had assisted at many confinements and seen countless births; thus she had first-class training and had followed in her mother's footsteps. It was not uncommon, explained Mary Macgregor (just as, previously, had Harriet), for women to die in childbirth and she had seen many taken to their Maker. But Elizabeth Eddington's death, to her, had been the saddest of all—for 'wee Lizzie' had been one of those persons whom everyone loves, beautiful both within and without. All were delighted to see dear Lizzie happily married to her handsome gentleman Mr Moore—and later awaiting the birth of her first child. Lizzie had specially returned here for the birth so that Mary would attend her confinement.

Scarcely able to absorb this new knowledge, that this very woman had been present at my birth, I was silent for some moments. But then I knew that here was my one chance of asking the question whose answer I had awaited all my life. "But why," I began, trembling, "why, then, with so many caring for her, did she die?"

Mary Macgregor read my face. "Och, lassie, it wasna your fault. Ye were but an innocent bairn. It was naebody's *fault*."

"Then why—?"

Mary went to sit on the edge of the bed, and sighed deeply. "It was the other wee unhappy bairn, lassie. And not its fault, either: the poor wee thing was dead. Nobody guessed, ye ken, until after ye were in your mother's arms, that there was another bairn yet to be brought into the world. Dear Lizzie was in such difficulty, for the second wee bairn couldn't help itself come out, 'twas that did the harm, and nobody could save her."

"Another baby? There were two babies?" Faintness almost overtook me again.

"Aye, two wee girls. Ye had a wee twin, lassie."

A sister, I should have had a sister! "Why was she dead, the other baby?"

"Och, she was a poor wee thing, a puny wee bairn, she hadn't grown right. And the good Lord chose to keep her for Hisself. And the Lord took Lizzie too, to care for the bairn in Heaven, so I suppose. I canna explain it."

Neither of us spoke for a while. I thought of my poor Mama dying in pain because a baby was dead and could not help itself to come out. I felt that whatever else might happen to me in my life, I could surely never feel sadder than this.

"Did something break, and all the blood run out?" I whispered at last.

Mary Macgregor did not reply, but gazed at me with a troubled face. Perhaps she feared she had revealed too much to so young a girl—one who had seen far less of worldly matters than she herself at such an age.

"Did it?" I insisted. "Please tell me."

"Aye, lassie," Mary told me at last. "That was the case. And nought to be done."

An hour later I stood with Harriet under a small huddle of wintry trees beside the driveway of what had been my Mama's family home. We gazed in silence at the square, solid house, its lawns and shrubbery, pillared portico, and blank windows. It was vacant, we had learned, awaiting its new owner's arrival.

"This, then, is where it happened, as Mary Mcgregor told me," I said to Harriet. "In one of those rooms, I was born and my Mama lost her life and went to join the soul of her other baby whose life had been already taken."

I turned to look at Harriet, who was pale and dark-eyed. "I never knew about a second child," she said.

"No," I answered. "Mrs McGregor said they kept the truth from Papa, out of pity. O, it is a tragic story. And yet, I feel more complete for learning it. And now something makes sense to me. I have always felt alone in a way I cannot define. I have said to myself that it was because I had no Mama, and my Papa never wanted me—but it may be that deep in my soul I knew I had lost my sister." I took Harriet's arm. "Thank you for bringing me here. Now I understand a little better who I am."

Harriet did not speak—I think she could not—but put an arm around my shoulders and quietly drew me closer to her side; and I could feel the strength of her love and sorrow.

After a while I made a confession to her, saying: "Sometimes, in strange moments that I cannot describe but which I have, secretly, called my 'absences', I see—no, I *feel*, I sense the *presence*, of a woman, on the utmost edge of my perception, and it seems that she is waiting for me. It sounds so foolish. Anyone but yourself would call me mad. I wondered if she was my Mama, yet I knew inside that she was not. And now——" I was embarrassed, glancing up at Harriet. "Do you think me absurd and fanciful?" I asked.

Harriet shook her head. "No, my dear."

"It might be—*she*, might it not?"

And then, within a second and greatly to my own surprise, I had burst into long-delayed tears of mourning, sobbing on Harriet's breast.

It was impossible for Gee to read on.

"What is it, Gee?" Mildred asked.

"I simply can't believe this," Gee said at last. "Millie—it is *so* strange, so extraordinary. *I* was a twin—a surviving twin. Reading this about Margaret Esther—it's uncovering shards of my own memory, like hearing echoes."

"*Really?* When did *you* find out?"

"When I was around seven. Mum was pregnant with Sam and we were talking about babies. Just as with Margaret Esther, I lived and my twin died. Fortunately my mother didn't."

"Was your twin a girl, too?"

"They told Mum it had died too early on to be able to tell. If a girl, she would've been called Charlotte. The thing is, I just *know* how Margaret Esther felt. As if someone was always missing. Lost. I can't describe it. I always felt solitary, even with a gang of friends—and I never had one I could believe was a *best* friend. Feeling isolated made me appallingly shy, though I learned how to hide it. But what Margaret Esther wrote about someone *waiting*–that's *exactly* what I used to feel I was doing. Really. I was waiting, but I had no idea what for. I felt suspended, a bit unreal. Is this weird, or what?"

"It's more than that," Mildred said. "I'm not sure I have a word for it, but it's giving me goose-pimples. There seems to be a—well, a *thread* that links you to Grandma McIvor. But don't ask me what I mean by that."

A thread, thought Gee. *My own word precisely.*

Then Millie asked, tentatively: "Didn't marriage to Sebastian help fill the gap?"

Gee merely shook her head.

22nd December 1847. We return to The Academy.

O, such a change of scene and fortune.

A most inhospitable chill drizzle greeted us as we returned to Edinburgh this noon. A gloom hung over the town—a dreariness soon to prove in keeping with the situation awaiting us.

Harriet remarked, as we stepped into the Academy's back corridor near the kitchens, on the absence of the usual mid-day activity. All was quiet, prompting us, against all reason, to go almost on tiptoe, like intruders. The marked contrast between the villages and hills we had visited—so fresh and open—and this silent grey interior, struck me with force. Despite my having been content here, enjoying my education, especially since Miss P.'s malevolence has been curtailed, now The Academy seemed constricted and stifling to the spirit. Physically, too, the atmosphere was unpleasant: an even stronger odour than usual was emanating from the direction of the drains, and we made haste towards the more rarefied air above stairs.

On the morrow we would be leaving for Talbot Castle for the festive days. I unpacked my bag to prepare it anew for that reluctant sojourn. I was quite alone as I did so; few pupils remain during the Christmas vacation. Solitude suited my reflective mood; I felt myself to be not quite the same girl who had left this place mere days before. It seemed that I viewed my surroundings with newly-opened, more independent eyes. I believed that henceforth I would look less fearfully upon certain aspects of the world since learning more of my Mama, her character as both child and adult, and the impression she had made on others. Now I knew where Mama used to live and play, to ride her pony and take her walks; where she had met my then happy, affectionate Papa, who so ardently had wooed her. My Mama was no longer a shadowy dream. More than that, I had been convinced by old Mrs Macgregor's assurance that my Mama's death was no fault of my own. And, most extraordinary of all had been the revelation that I was not born alone! Fleetingly, I had had a twin sister—and now I, *myself*, inexplicably, was more solid and real. I could not *wait* to tell my story to Emmie. As I reflected thus I turned my mind resolutely away from Papa, for I feared that a deep current of anger, born of injustice, would surge to the surface and intrude upon my new-found strength.

But there, in any case, my reflections were interrupted by the hasty arrival of Dora, who sleeps on Emmie's other side.

She was greatly startled to see me, crying: "O! I believed the dormitory empty. I wanted to hide from—" The poor girl then sat upon her bed and burst into tears. "I am so very unwell and afraid!" Dora's complexion was shockingly pale; and inky shadows encircled her eyes.

Sitting beside her, I put my arm about Dora's shoulders. "If you are unwell we must tell Matron," I said. "But why are you not at home?"

"No, no!" here cried Dora in passion. "I beg you, please do not tell Matron. She will cancel my coach tomorrow and keep me here."

I asked what had happened, what had distressed her so.

"Have you heard nothing?" Dora wept. "It is disaster! And poor Emmie—! I would be at home but Mama and Papa were delayed in London. Now I am afraid I may die and never see them again."

Alarmed, I asked: "What has happened to Emmie? Tell me plainly."

It was beyond poor Dora's powers to relate anything plainly, but tell the story she did, aided by Harriet hastening in to relay the bad news the moment she had learned it.

The day after our departure, a terrible fever had broken out among girls and teachers. All those unaffected went as planned to their homes for the vacation, but ten pupils and two mistresses were severely unwell and unable to be moved. These occupied the beds of the largest dormitory, hurriedly converted to a sickroom, under the care of Matron and her assistant, with twice-daily visits from the Doctor.

Emmie had been the first to fall ill, and it was at once clear that hers was an exceedingly serious case. "When I woke," Dora said, "she was lying deathly still, with such a white, agonised face! She whispered to me to help her, she said her head would split in two and she was burning and icy in turn." Dora added to herself: "Alas, I know now how she was feeling."

Miss MacIntosh had sent word to Emmie's parents, but her Mama was herself indisposed and had been forbidden by her doctor to travel. Her Papa had hastened to Edinburgh, to be told by the Academy's Doctor that Emmie was too sick for any journey and would furthermore endanger her entire family.

I had leapt up at this dreadful news. "Is she improved at all?" I demanded, trembling in fright, for I could not help but recall the little boy on Papa's estate who had died of fever. All my peaceful reflections about myself and my Mama had flown as if they had never existed.

"Emmie knows no-one," came the low reply. Dora was now shivering as if in a snowstorm, yet her forehead was fiery.

"Dora is not well," I explained to Harriet.

"I am very well!" cried poor Dora, jumping up. "I am going home!" With these words, she fainted on to her bed. Leaving Harriet to attend to her, I ran from the dormitory and down the corridor towards the sickroom, my only thought being for Emmie.

As I arrived Matron and the Doctor were emerging from the sickroom with troubled expressions. I drew back into an alcove to await the gentleman's departure, straining to hear his words—instructions for all patients to drink *thoroughly boiled* water constantly, and, should abdominal pain develop, Matron must send for him. Meantime, nursing assistance must be sought among Mistresses dwelling nearby, and—with the permission of their parents—any willing older girls still unafflicted who remained at the Academy. He then bleakly departed. At once I sprang forward in Matron's path and begged to help in nursing the sick.

"My child," cried that startled lady, "it is too dangerous!"

"O please Matron, I beg you. You need help—the Doctor said as much. I cannot *bear* to be idle while my friends are ill. And I may be ill no matter what, for Emmie's bed is next to mine, and I would far rather be of use and know how she is faring! I beg you, dear kind Matron, I beg you!"

Matron relented, seeing my sincerity and, indeed, knowing that assistance was vital. "I will allow it, if Miss MacIntosh agrees," she said.

Thus, from this evening, I have become a nurse in the Academy sickroom. I am desperately fearful for Emmie, who is dreadfully thin and tosses in her bed in fever, alternating between delirium and pain. I bathed her face and body with cool water and whispered words of comfort, but I do not believe she realised I was present. Matron insisted that I leave the sickroom for supper (of which I could eat no more than a mouthful) and go to bed. She expects me at eight o'clock in the morning. "If you are to help, then you must guard your own health," she told me sternly.

23rd December, 10 p.m.

This morning Harriet was herself admitted to the sickroom with fever and a headache she declared could burst her skull. O, I am so afraid for my two dearest friends!

Despite her suffering, Harriet urged me to keep my Christmas plans—for the hazards of Talbot Castle were surely preferable to this fearful disease.

"I prefer to stay," I told her resolutely. "Even if I die."

As matters have turned out, Harriet's hopes for my escape could not have been realised. This afternoon I learned that Sir John and Lady Talbot, protecting their son and heir, have resisted the Headmistress' suggestion that I seek quarantine in their Castle. For myself, since I have no wish to endanger my little cousin, I declared this most reasonable.

Despite being deeply exhausted I sleep restlessly, picturing poor dear Emmie in her distress. I pray that Harriet does not worsen.

24th December: Christmas Eve.

The number in the sickroom has reduced; four girls have recovered sufficiently to be nursed at home—one of these fortunates being Dora. Less happily, one of the Mistresses lost her life in the early hours of this day and my fears for Emmie grow. Her belly has swollen and she cries out in agony, sometimes vomiting, sometimes sinking into a stupor. I worked from early morning until late evening, refusing to acknowledge my fatigue. What else could I do—I could not leave these suffering friends! However, it was some relief to find that Harriet's fever abated a little. Eventually Matron chased me away by saying that I must eat and sleep—or I would not be permitted to return. I left, but am in too much anguish to do either adequately.

December 25th, Christmas Day.

What a festive season is this! Miss MacIntosh herself has been taken ill. Rather than further burden the sickroom she has remained in her own bedroom and her only sister is journeying across Scotland to nurse her. Almost worse than this was news of the imminent return of the Detestable Miss P. to act as Headmistress during her superior's indisposition. Now dread has joined my other emotions.

Late today Harriet's illness worsened—a cruel blow, for yesterday evening we were optimistic. Now she has succumbed to the malaise, flux and wrenching pains that many others have endured. All day I have been in despair. Only one other child had been as badly afflicted as Emmie—a child but ten years of age—and to my horror this poor little creature sank today into a wide-eyed coma and died, after suffering terrible pain. The Doctor was present, and I heard him murmur of failed kidneys and interior bleeding, filling me with new terror—terror that grows with the Doctor's daily anxious questions, before all others, as to Emmie's welfare.

December 27th.

I could write nothing yesterday, shaking as I was with fear. Emmie's symptoms had begun accurately to mimic those of the recently-dead child. Her body was a mass of inflamed weals and her undernourished abdomen swelled. The slightest touch caused screams of agony, from which her only release was restless sleep. When awake she fought for breath and muttered disjointedly, tossing from side to side.

Today, however, anger has joined my fear and stilled my trembling. Emmie's distress continues, and this evening during one of her brief stupors I begged Matron through my tears to tell me what else I could do. That good woman sadly shook her head and told me frankly that I could do nothing but wait. Shortly after this, Matron bent to whisper that she was going to see Miss MacIntosh and would not be long, and then I must go for supper.

Perhaps two minutes later I sensed that another person had entered and was standing behind me. I had heard no sound, but knew from the altered atmosphere exactly who was present, and as I drew upright on my chair my nightmare was complete.

"What is this? Why are you here?" Miss Pottinger snapped, with no attempt to lower her voice for those patients fortunate enough to be sleeping.

"I am assisting Matron," I replied plainly but softly. "With Miss MacIntosh's permission."

"Stand when you speak to me."

I stood, while dizziness made me clutch my chair.

"Miss MacIntosh is unwell," said the Detestable. "*I* am now in the role of Headmistress of the Academy. You are dismissed. You are not suitable to the task. Do you understand?"

I looked my foe in the eye. "I am sorry to say I do *not* understand, Miss Pottinger," I replied. "Matron is pleased with my efforts, as is the Doctor."

"You will not be insolent!" The woman's voice rose, and with it my loathing. "Nor will you tell such shameful, boastful lies. It is *my* observation that you are sentimentally involved, and that is no basis for proper medical care."

A feeble voice called my name from across the room. I saw Harriet's pale face turned towards me, and hurried to her side to help her drink a little water.

"Be careful," she whispered.

"Do not concern yourself," I quietly replied, "She cannot harm me." I hardly knew my own meaning, save that my fears for my beloved friends had made me fearless of my enemy.

I then returned to Emmie's bedside where Miss Pottinger waited quivering. "How *dare* you walk away while I am speaking!" she all but screeched.

"I apologise," said I without emotion. "One of the patients needed help—and I followed Matron's instructions." Again I looked directly at Miss P. and said: "If Matron confirms that my work is acceptable, may I then continue?"

"It is *my* word that carries authority!" the hateful woman spat. "Not Matron's. *I* am in charge. You will leave—*now*. Your insolence is insufferable." Fiercely seizing my upper arm, she forced me to the door and thrust me from the room.

I enter herein my deep abhorrence of that woman, and my vow that I will not be defeated by her. I shall speak privately tomorrow to Matron and beg her support and that of the Doctor. I intend to continue my work. She *shall* not keep me from helping to nurse my friends as best I can—nurse them, I pray, back to health.

Chapter Twenty

Edinburgh, February 1848.

For innumerable weeks I have been too enfeebled to lift a pen. My hands are thin and ugly, transparent, with veins and sinews visible. My face is pale and bony, my eyes even more protuberant. I have scant energy and less resolve, and cannot imagine recovering either.

My memories are hateful and haunt me like nightmares. They *are* my nightmares.

I am determined, little by little despite my weakness, to write them down, to continue from my last entry.

Of events immediately following my expulsion from the sickroom, I recall little. Dimly I remember writing of it in my journal, and I was evidently sufficiently alert to put this away safely in my trunk. I was to learn that Matron, wondering where I had gone, had found me on the floor beside my bed, barely conscious and feverish. Not until dawn did I come to myself again, clad in a nightgown, shivering and with a throbbing head, and greatly frightened to be lying in a sickroom bed. Each movement was a torment, yet I turned my head to seek out Emmie—and saw her bed empty. I believe I cried out, but nobody approached me.

It has not proved possible to obtain a full account of that terrible night, for likely witnesses were too unwell to observe all events. Harriet, swooning in fever, had heard voices—one, that of Emmie's Papa, greatly distressed—agitated movements, whispered instructions, also muffled weeping from Matron's young assistant who was fond of Emmie. The next morning this witness was gone, sent home by Miss P. who judged her weak and unsuitable. She was not seen again. Matron too was absent; she was tending Miss MacIntosh, whose sister was now also unwell.

Desperately I questioned other sickroom occupants but none could report more than a few words overheard, sorrowful exclamations and muted tears. The truth could no longer be avoided, and my nausea and fever were now joined by immeasurable grief: my dearest friend Emmie had departed this life and her Papa had taken away her poor wasted body.

Had I wished to delude myself with some kinder explanation for Emmie's disappearance, I was not to be so comforted. The facts were stated frankly by none other than Miss Pottinger. She had not been in the sickroom that morning while I was awake, but when I awoke from a feverish doze as dusk was falling, the loathsome woman was standing over me with a lit candle, waiting for the smallest flicker of wakefulness.

"Punishment is visited upon the sinful," she pronounced, "by powers higher than our own."

For a second I fancied that this was an hallucination, but Miss P. bent to speak into my face and her rank breath made me jerk my head painfully aside. "Your friend is *dead*," came the terrible words. "Dead and gone. You and she will never be able to make your mischief again. Right has triumphed." I closed my eyes against her, and soon heard my enemy's dress rustle and the faint crack of a bone as she straightened and strode away.

I think of my dear friend Emmie, and pain wracks me—it is as if I am drowning in waves of grief. During my fever I prayed for a mistake—that Emmie had been believed dead but in truth survived; or even that Miss P. had lied. My hopes were proved foolish when Matron reappeared in the sickroom and came straight to me, saying: "My child, I was so sorry that your dear friend was taken. Draw comfort from knowing that she is now released from all suffering." I was unable to speak for weeping, for I am far too selfish to find comfort in her kind words. Matron then announced further sorrowful news to all present: that morning, the fever had robbed us of our Headmistress, Miss MacIntosh. Harriet let out a cry of anguish, while I was stunned almost senseless. What God allows such terrible things to happen? What is His purpose in removing two such admirable people from the world? And how could He allow the Detestable now to be Headmistress? This blow makes all others yet more cruel.

At least He was so good (or absent-minded) as to permit Harriet to recover. Had she also died I would have found a way to embrace Death myself. Harriet says we must not be defeated, or we should betray the things our dear departed represented—goodness, courage, integrity, and love. Harriet gives me what little strength I have. Yet, my heart dies within me of grief. I have lost Emmie, and this I know: never in my life shall I draw as close to another person.

During the worst of my fever I experienced a kind of vision. I saw *her*—the one who awaits, although I do not recall her face. I held out my hand to her, but sensed she could not grasp it for we can never meet in this life. Then I knew—I *felt*—she is more than one. She is *all* my lost ones: my mother, my twin sister, my friend.

30th April 1848.

A further long interval since my last entry. My lack of strength has caused all my old joys and desires to diminish, and seldom do I have an appetite for writing.

Harriet and I are just returned from Easter week at Talbot Castle. The Academy closed for repairs to the drains, and pupils had perforce to make other arrangements.

I despise my Uncle. There, I have written this sin! I also have a strong aversion to a number of his friends, particularly Lord and Lady G.—dullards convinced of their superiority. The corpulent Lord G. and my Uncle, while cramming their mouths with roast beef, touched upon the famine in Ireland. Harriet and I have often discussed the tragedy of the many thousands of innocent poor who have died.

My Uncle said: "They continue to flee the country—boarding ships for America and Australia, and good riddance. Such are vermin, a burden to our economy."

Lord G. replied: "Aye, no denying the potato famine has been a Godsend. Small wonder the government encourages those breeding masses of idle poor in our cities to take the same route—although, I declare, if the wretches are so keen to depart, the country should not pay out. Why should we be taxed to assist their like? Many are diseased and die on the journey—although, certainly, this must be considered good fortune for America and Australia!" The two men laughed in comfortable agreement.

Since Emmie died I find it impossible to be tolerant of their kind. Harriet's horrified gaze reflected my own feelings.

The following afternoon, Harriet and I were seated in the drawing-room alone, welcoming a quiet time for reading—other ladies having left for a carriage-ride. Harriet chose her favourite secluded window seat while I selected a comfortable chair near the fire, with my back to the door.

After perhaps half an hour, I heard the door open, whereupon my Uncle's voice rang out: "Why, it is my dear niece, all alone and hoping for company!"

Before I could move, his hands were upon my shoulders and sliding lower—and I shuddered as he bent over me to kiss my neck. In recent years I have become nimble at escaping my Uncle's grasp when I have been unavoidably alone with him. I sprang up, and at the edge of my vision I saw Harriet also rise swiftly. Attempting a merry laugh, I cried: "O, I am not lonesome I assure you! Miss Avery and I are reading together."

How he blustered at the sight of Harriet, who retained the coldest expression. My Uncle declared he was looking for his wife, the ladies should surely be back, but never mind, he was delighted that I was suitably occupied. He scurried away, banging the door.

Trembling in embarrassment I sat, unable to speak. Harriet came to me and knelt, took my hand and said calmly: "Do not be ashamed of your Uncle. It is impolite to say so of your family, but in truth *he* should be ashamed." Taking a nearby chair, she opened her book and read me a long, lovely poem. I did not so much listen as allow her beautiful voice to flow over me like healing water, bringing me solace.

As we drove back today Harriet referred obliquely to my Uncle, saying: "On future visits, I suggest you request of your Aunt that we *share* a bed-chamber. Perhaps you might claim to be suffering nightmares, screaming loudly enough to waken the household. Also sleep-walking—a danger to yourself and others. These should warrant a night-time protector."

Without Harriet's quiet understanding I could not have survived these months. She is indeed my protector—at the Academy also, where she defends me from Miss P. whenever possible.

Each night I hide beneath my covers and weep. My body must be filled with tears, so many spill from me.

15th September 1848.

These pages remained closed throughout an unhappy summer at the Hall.

After but two weeks at home, Harriet and I were summoned to Papa's library—a surprise, for until then he had been neither seen nor heard—and he brusquely ordered us to return at once to Scotland. At Harriet's astonished reply, he shouted furiously that she could not take his charity for granted. Exceedingly wounded, she flushed and was silent.

Papa no longer looked as handsome and elegant. His shirt was rumpled and stained, his hair awry. The house, he declared, was to be closed for repairs, and we women with our frivolous pursuits would be an impediment. Harriet turned without a word and left the room, with me close behind; we departed within forty-eight hours. Harriet would not discuss this injustice, despite my frank indignation. I am deeply ashamed of my Papa.

Nevertheless, I was not sorry to leave, for almost all that was good at home has altered. Only Mrs Williams the Cook and one little maid remain as servants, neither cheerful. Several times I came upon Cook muttering ill-temperedly, but she would not explain. Nor was her cooking of its usual standard—for which she apologised, claiming a local difficulty in obtaining ingredients. Neither Tommy nor Dottie was there. I learned from the one remaining groom that they had married in the spring, but almost immediately afterwards Papa had dismissed Tommy, accusing him of shoddy work *and* dishonesty. The groom told me: "The Master, beg pardon Miss, was in error, for Tommy was a good, reliable worker." I said I knew this—but what had provoked Papa? The man replied awkwardly: "He has not been himself, is all I can say, and has treated many of us thus. I am sorry to speak so."

I had so looked forward to seeing my friends—for I swear I have not laughed since December last. But they have moved far away to the south-west, no farm work being available for miles around. I wept for the loss of dear Tommy, my ally since childhood. I hope he and Dottie are happy and will remain so.

Life was made still lonelier by Harriet's frequent sojourns in the village because her mother is ailing. Listless days were spent reading, embroidering, and watercolour-painting. Or I walked and dreamed, barely knowing where I was, weeping for no reason and scolding myself for the indulgence of self-pity. So weak is my character, my scolding had no effect.

Edinburgh, 10th December 1848.

Today I am seventeen years of age: almost a year has passed since Emmie died. For my last birthday she presented me with my portrait, in delicate miniature. "To prove to you," she teased me gaily, "how very *interesting* you are!"

This morning my gift was a note from Aunt Clarissa, with birthday wishes and an invitation to join the company at Talbot Castle for the Christmas vacation. (Miss Avery was included, if I so desired.) At that time, continued my Aunt, she and my Uncle would inform me of their plans for my future. Aunt Clarissa is sure I shall be pleased and grateful. I do not care for the word "inform".

22nd December, Talbot Castle.

Most unhappily, a letter was delivered to Harriet here at the Castle this morning bidding her hasten home. Her mother is close to death, and she took the first stage-coach south. I am sad for her and for myself—for I am without my protector and supporter.

Yesterday evening at dinner—while Harriet was still present—one of the ladies asked me about my education. I described it, but at the end was sufficiently naïve to opine that it was only a matter of time before women were permitted places at Universities and would enter the professions.

Here my Uncle (impolitely) guffawed. "The *professions?*" came his incredulous cry, echoed on all sides. I stubbornly held my ground (encouraged by a tiny nod from Harriet) continuing that were it possible today, my own wish would be to study medicine, having become interested by several conversations with the Academy Doctor. He, I added impertinently, was *enlightened*, believing that a feminine approach would be a healthy addition to his profession. Cries of dismay arose deafeningly, the most strident from the females, one of whom, looking fit to swoon, quavered: "Disgraceful!"

Lord G. was typically condescending. "It is a well-established fact, child, that the female's brain is smaller than the male's. Even if one could tolerate the impropriety of a lady being involved in the sordid intimacies of doctoring, she would not be capable of the rigorous study entailed."

My self-satisfied Uncle agreed. "Men are stronger both physically and mentally, with superior reasoning powers. That is why the male is the female's *protector*." Oblivious to my stony stare and unable to hear my heart beating fast with fury, he continued: "Ladies' weakness makes them timid, while their smaller brains make them virtually incapable of logic." His good wife smiled her approval—demonstrating to my satisfaction that *her* brain must be smaller than a sparrow's.

Harriet spoke quietly. "I believe that Miss Moore's powers of reasoning are a match for those of any male I have encountered."

"O!" bridled Lady G. on my left, "I fear for Miss Moore's feminine modesty!"

All applauded this sentiment save Harriet and I, while Lady G. then hissed into my ear: "A lady's greatest intelligence is to conceal cleverness. The powers of the female brain fluctuate with our other tides, waxing and waning. We are but weak vessels."

Her eyes were fixed meaningfully upon me while her lace-frilled head nodded so irritatingly that I was seized by a desire to pick up my fork and plunge it into her fat hand, or even her heart. I wonder if I have become a little mad.

How I miss Harriet's calm intelligence.

My door is locked and bolted, a heavy chair against it.

30th December 1848, The Academy.

An entire week has passed since my Aunt ordered me from Talbot Castle. Since then I have been unable to eat or sleep. My body has suffered seizures of trembling and vomiting. Matron, who is staying at the Academy throughout Christmas, has insisted I remain in bed in case of infection. I begged her, against her better judgement, not to summon the Doctor. I fear his perception and wisdom.

Rest was no remedy: my thoughts whirled ever faster and my body was further wracked. Matron has informed me that tomorrow the Doctor *will* be called, therefore I have forced myself to rise, assuring her I am much improved and telling my*self* that improve I must. To this end, I took up my pen and replied to Harriet's letter that told me of her Mama's sad demise. For a while I thought of her pain and not my own and sternly lectured myself. As a result of *one loathsome person's* actions, I had permitted myself to succumb to selfish self-pity, and this must cease.

After this, I ate a little breakfast and for the first time did not vomit. Perhaps the nourishment gave me strength to instruct myself to live my life again no matter what the effort—or I would no longer be the person Emmie had loved and would also be a disappointment to Harriet. Evil must not defeat me; and despite my turbulence and anguish I must attempt to write down what occurred, in the hope of understanding how it came about, lest I be at fault.

After sunset on December 23rd, Aunt Clarissa bade me go to my Uncle's library. I was to be told about my future. I suggested it would be agreeable if she were to accompany me and they tell me together, but she declared herself too much occupied with little Lossie.

My Uncle, seated at his lamp-lit desk in swirls of cigar smoke, smiled, enquired after my health, and announced that in the Spring I would attend a Finishing School in Paris, residing there for one year. Thence, I would return to Talbot Castle and, under the patronage of my Uncle and Aunt, come out in Society and be married to an eligible young man. They had in mind two or three candidates. My father had agreed to this plan.

"There!" my Uncle concluded. "That is my Christmas gift to you—a privileged, secure future in the best possible Society!"

After thanking my Uncle for his generosity, I asked if I might express a preference regarding my future. Having expected, I surmise, nought but delighted acquiescence, he mumbled his surprised permission and I explained my hopes for a more independent life than is afforded in the kind of marriage they planned for me. I preferred to work—perhaps to teach, or help heal the sick. If I married—and I was in no haste to do so—I would not wish to be totally dependent upon my husband.

My Uncle was in swift succession astonished and indignant. "Work!" he cried. "What a reflection *that* would be upon your family! A lady of breeding *teaching?* Healing the *sick?* What foolishness!"

Gesticulating as he spoke, he rose and strode around his desk. I also stood, to be less vulnerable—but alas, I had not foreseen his forcibly returning me to my chair and holding me there. His tone became wheedling. "Dear girl, do not displease your loving Uncle. Consider. A wonderful life in Paris, where I shall visit you often. The best of everything—gowns, hats, cloaks and jewels, all you desire. You and I shall become closer and ever closer friends. Won't you like that? Say that you would." Filled with dismay, I realised that on the many occasions when I have been obliged to escape my Uncle's attempts to fondle or kiss me, he had never fully believed my repulses—even when I raised my voice, risking discovery. Always he had protested his "adoration" while declaring I was "coquettishly tormenting" him. He had convinced himself I was playing a game and in good time would submit to my own true feelings—*and to him.*

Somehow I slid from beneath his hands and scrambled up, backing away, protesting *No*, I would *not* like that, I *hated* his touching me, hated his plans, I hated *him*. Next, I was knocked to the floor—my Uncle's weight was upon me, his hand pressing my throat. The words "ungrateful", "cold" and "cruel" were spat into my face. If I would not express my gratitude to him willingly, well—he had been patient enough. Tommy's advice, alas, was impossible to effect under the vile burden of this despicable man.

O, I *cannot* write of the horror that ensued. At last his violation ended and I struggled free of his weight, retching, hearing my own incoherent cries. I escaped the room, staggering with shock and pain.

It was my further misfortune to encounter my Aunt as I started up the staircase. She exclaimed at my dishevelment and demanded the cause of my weeping. Deranged, I gasped involuntarily: "He— Uncle John—"

Here I was stopped, both by my own sobs and my Aunt's fury. She slapped my face and stamped her foot, shrieking: "What are you saying, wicked girl? How *dare* you?"

I fell back half-fainting, then stumbled up the stairs, twice being obliged to pause and vomit.

After locking my bed-chamber door I undressed and washed in cold water from the ewer, hiding my stained garments in my reticule so no maid should see them. I donned clean clothes, selecting a lace collar to conceal my bruises. All was done with great difficulty, for I was shaking and weeping all the while.

My Aunt came to find me towards supper-time. I admitted her, turning my swollen eyes away and remaining in the shadows. She informed me coldly that she had learned from her husband of my shocking incivility in refusing their patronage. His unavoidable conclusion was that I was an ungrateful, foolish girl without a brain in my head. Did I not realise that he had been paying my Academy fees for over a year, helping my Papa out of difficulties? She herself was utterly appalled at my graceless rejection of opportunities that any normal young lady would seize with joy. What intolerable meanness of spirit! I could pack my bags and return to the Academy; she would inform whomever was in authority that indisposition had obliged her to cancel her social programme. Supper would be sent to my room, where I should remain until my departure. A carriage would be ready at ten o'clock next morning. Finally, I would speak of today to nobody.

Despite my tumult of emotion I was relieved. I prepared my bags at once, and neither ate nor slept that night.

After writing, these few things are now clearer:

I cannot hope to *forget* what has happened, and I shall never *never* forgive. I believe that no action of mine provoked or earned that which happened. I hate my Uncle still more, and despise my Aunt for her weakness and cruelty. I cannot tell Harriet—or anyone—what has happened.

However—*a plan is forming* that will obviate the need for further fees for my education, bed or board. To depend on my Uncle for even one penny would be repugnant; nor need Papa provide for me. I will be free of them *all*. I shall be poor, but not destitute. With experience I shall improve my lot and become independent *for ever*, without need of any male, suitable or otherwise, to 'protect' me.

As I reach this decision, I am a little stronger.

3rd January 1849.

Today I am far from strong. I am truly frightened.

From time to time I reflect upon the badness in me. Today, I fear my wickedness may be able to escape *outside* me without my knowledge. Am I, indeed, *deeply* wicked? More wicked than I dreamed? There is nobody I can ask.

I have long believed that most human beings have no real understanding of their fellows. So, if others cannot be trusted to understand, nor can they be trusted to help. Could I but speak to that shadowy one who waits on the edge of my imagination! Perhaps this amorphous presence is my own inward invention, devised to counter the bleakness of my untrusting nature. She will occasionally come into my mind like a stray vision when I am writing my journal, and, inexplicably, I feel I am writing for her. I have wondered if she is connected to my 'absences'—interruptions in my mind, when I am nowhere, no person, in no time. Once in a while during these interruptions, I have had the strongest impression that she stands nearby.

There were many such episodes in my childhood. Often I have been asked—angrily, curiously, or suspiciously: "Where have you been?" Frequently I have not known, and been obliged to invent. I have told no person of this strangeness (save Harriet) for fear that I would be judged a lunatic. Today, I ask myself: *am I?*

Now I must attempt to recall every detail since bed-time yesterday.

I was seated in my dormitory bed, my lamp upon the sill and my bed-curtain closed. Since returning from the Castle I have been the dormitory's sole occupant, most girls being expected to return today. Solitude has been most welcome to me, as has been the freedom to write or read until late and delay the onset of my violent dreams.

Mistakenly, I had taken the wrong journal from my trunk, but was settled warmly before realising it. Loath to climb out of bed again, I decided to cheer myself by reading my earlier words, those of the summer of 1847, a far far happier summer than last year's.

During that summer of '47, I had glimpsed my Papa but once at home. His appearance was gaunt and unwell—and perhaps he was then experiencing the "difficulties" mentioned by my Aunt—but I refused to reflect upon him. I did however observe that the house itself had seemed a little shabby, its windows less than sparkling. Papa had already begun to reduce the number of servants, and when I asked Mrs Williams why Elsie had left and Dottie was not in the dairy, she shrugged and looked away, saying it was not for her to query the Master's decisions. Subsequently, Tommy informed me that Dottie had been dismissed wihout explanation and was seeking other employment. I apologised for my Papa's behaviour, but Tommy was too courteous to comment.

Most of my attention, however, was upon my happiest hours—those spent with Tommy when he was free of work. Tommy had recently passed his eighteenth birthday—indeed, was now truly a man—deep-spoken and with bristles upon his chin! He is very handsome, and far taller than I. I thought how elegant he would look in gentlemen's clothes driving his own carriage. (Yet the 'gentlemen' of Talbot Castle would sneer at Tommy as a creature beneath their notice.)

What a foolish thing I was that summer! Sometimes as Tommy and I sat together in the garden or pony-trap, I longed to touch and kiss him. On long light evenings lying in bed, making believe Tommy was my husband, I caressed my own body to delight myself. Now, when I recall my girlish, tender love for Tommy and my yearnings for his proximity, I see how *utterly unrelated* is the selfish violence recently encountered.

I have briefly recalled in this journal these aspects of that summer for one reason alone: *the journal I was reading has gone.*

The Detestable Miss P. returned early, and came prowling. My curtain was wrenched open and my journal scythed from my grasp in one movement. I have neither will nor energy to write all that she screamed on the subject of disobedience and wickedness; suffice to say that her 'speech' ended with instructions to see her in her room before breakfast. She left with my journal clasped to her chest.

After a restless night I went to her room (once Miss MacIntosh's cosy place, now an unsavoury lair) where she sat in the pink chair, quivering from head to foot. I was exhausted rather than fearful, for what further harm could any person do me?

She surprised me by not referring to my journal—instead informing me a letter had just arrived from my Uncle. It stated, without providing reason, that he would henceforth not be paying my Academy fees, nor providing further allowance to Miss Avery. Both I and Miss Avery, declared Miss P. savagely, could depart. Sir John evidently had reason to regret his kindness—a fact that did not surprise her.

My Uncle had acted ahead of my own plan for independence. I was somewhat taken aback to learn that he had assumed *all* my Papa's financial responsibilities, even including Harriet. Concealing my surprise, I replied:

"It happens that I wished to discuss the matter of fees with you, for I had already decided to accept no further charity from my Uncle—charity of which I have but recently learned. I intend to apply to the Governors for a teaching post here."

As Miss P. leapt up and I saw her suffused face and heard her shriek, I confess to these pages that I wished fervently for her to suffer an apoplexy and die at my feet.

"The impertinence! How dare *you* presume? How dare *you* imagine you could have a responsible position here, in charge of young girls?"

I remained silent—eloquently, I trusted.

She continued: "The Governors shall learn of your disgraceful character and misbehaviour. When they are apprised of your Uncle's disowning you—and your unhealthy, evil writings—they will see that you are a blot upon the Academy's name."

Hers was the upper hand, and struggle was pointless. But I saw that she had pointed me towards greater freedom. I could apply to other schools. Harriet and I might even work together! Or I could become a governess to a family. *Either* was preferable to remaining here with Miss P.! Why had I not thought of this earlier?

For a moment I was tempted to tell this odious woman that *I* could reveal facts about *her* that might engender considerable doubts about her own suitability as Headmistress. But I resisted. Instead I asked with deliberate insolence: "This, then, is my punishment?"

Enraged, Miss P. struck my face; one of her claws burned my cheek and the force of her blow made me stumble. Righting myself, I saw her bend to seize a fire-iron from the hearth, and I made ready to flee further assault. But she gave an ugly laugh, pointing the fire-iron at the fireplace and screeching victoriously: "*Here* is your punishment for your degenerate behaviour!"

As she rushed to jab the fire I gasped to see the still-smouldering remains of my stolen journal atop the coals, while black flakes floated towards the chimney. "It is destroyed," I heard her gloat, "and you will bring me all other disgusting writings in your possession to meet the same fate."

Here my memory is broken. My mind, like the charred paper, floated away—while my head filled with a roaring, rushing avalanche, through whose darkness came my thin voice: "I have no others." I remember the hearth, and Miss P.'s distorted mouth. But around the edges of my vision were deep shadows and my skin chilled as if I would faint. I knew only that she must not find my journals in my locked trunk, and determined to declare the key lost—and, before the lock could be broken, I would hide my journals elsewhere, *somewhere*.

Then, my hatred for Miss P. and for my Uncle merged and tangled: both had robbed and bruised me, both had violated what was mine. The roaring avalanche swamped my brain.

This is the last thing I remember in that room. She was standing near me, hissing: "You are lying." The fire-iron was close to my face.

Next, I was back in the dormitory. She had not struck me: I felt my head for bruises and stared at my face in my hand-mirror. The only signs were a reddened weal made by her claws on my white cheek, and a feeling of immeasurable fatigue.

Eventually, since I had no duties until the younger pupils' arrival and no appetite for breakfast, I decided to pen a letter to Harriet about my Uncle's decision and my thoughts concerning our futures. While thus engaged, I distantly heard a maid call for Matron. Indistinctly I knew there was a commotion that I supposed connected with the new term's arrivals. But little entered my dazed consciousness beyond my letter, my hatred, and the future.

Not until I took the letter downstairs to arrange for its posting did I learn the sensational news of the morning. I received it silently, without sorrow but, when I was alone, terror followed. Has my memory rejected something too abominable to contemplate? Am I in possession of some particular knowledge—yet unaware of it?

I have told Matron that I am not entirely well and wish to rest before the duties of the afternoon. My weariness is overwhelming, my brain in turmoil: heated, swirling in shadow. My soul is in fragments. Above all, I am frightened of myself.

6th *January 1849.*

I attach this letter within my journal, to complete my account of three days ago.

5th January 1849

Dearest friend,

Thank you for your most interesting letter, which evidently was sent before you learned of Miss P.'s sudden death. My dear, what a frightful shock it must have been to all! As you will have been told by our Deputy Head Miss Hamilton (now presumably acting as Headmistress), I was apprised of it this morning in a kind letter from her. She gave a brief account, as explained to her by the Doctor, of what must have been a fall against the mantelshelf, resulting in fatal injury to the temple. Who could imagine such an accident within our own familiar walls? I know that Miss P. was never your friend nor mine and, poor woman, was not blessed with a charitable nature, but none of us could wish such a cruel end to anyone's life. May she rest in peace.

Miss Hamilton also informed me of Sir John's unexplained cessation of funds. It was disquieting to learn that he had assumed your Papa's financial duties without our being informed. I thought to ascertain further facts, but a walk to Mudstone Hall this noon-time revealed that your Papa has been absent for over two months.

As you might expect, I applaud your wish for independence. It is my view that your first idea, which you discounted because of Miss P.'s opposition—an application to the Governors for a teaching post—would be well received. It may seem heartless so to express it, but your main obstacle has been removed. I intend to consult Miss Hamilton about my own ambitions. I hope to obtain her support in applying for Deputy Headship if she is to be Headmistress. This would increase my income sufficiently for me to subsist reasonably, I believe. Let us discuss it upon my return, in approximately four days' time.

Forgive me, I have overlooked thanking you for your kind condolences as regards my dear mother; her end, at least, was calm and painless. She was a good woman and I shall sadly miss her.

Yours affectionately, Harriet Avery.

The Academy, Edinburgh. I do not know the date, nor does it interest me.

Harriet tells me it is still January and she returned to the Academy two weeks past. I know my name, and that I am 17 years of age. Harriet has been appointed Deputy Headmistress.

Time has lost its shape, and comes in fragments. Sometimes it is long ago, sometimes it is now, and all events merge. One recent day I found myself bleeding and was greatly afraid. A suppressed scream squeezed from behind my hands. What could account for this? Had I been wounded by my uncle's savagery? What could I do? To whom dared I speak? But then, with painful slowness, I learned again what I had already known. I am no longer a child; this was a natural, female bleeding. Now profound relief replaced my terrors. Without my awareness, a frightful dread had been buried deep within me. One horror, at least, has been spared me.

The Doctor gives me laudanum. Cushioned by cloud, my strength has vanished. Ink spills on the page and my hands. Laudanum dulls my nightmares; soft dreams of foreign places melt and flicker, sleeping and waking are close cousins. At times the birds sing with the voice of my dear dead friend, for she is sending these songs to comfort me, to help me forget violence and evil.

People at my bedside; I do not need to open my eyes. Fractured words. The Doctor: "Neurasthenia, madam... aftermath of fever... shock of deaths... losses. Other distress, perhaps... a sensitive child..."

"*Sensitive?*" My good Aunt Clarissa. She is afraid: she loathes me. "She should be locked in an asylum."

The words explode in my ears—their truth terrifies me. I hear a frightened cry—from myself! And Harriet: "No no no!"

"...My little boy to protect. Look at her... deranged... tells lies... is wicked... should be restrained." I would never harm Lossie. Why does she say this? "She is mad... tore her clothes, broke the window, cut her arms."

My nightmare. How does she know my dreams? What more have they discovered?

"She is ill, *I* will look after her."

"*We* are her guardians, *you* are a servant."

"You are *hateful*." I speak this fact aloud, but realise it only as my Aunt shrieks.

"The wickedness! The ingratitude!" She weeps noisily. My mouth smiles.

Harriet, so dry: "Her illness makes her less able to conceal her feelings."

"How *dare* you!"

"Ladies." The Doctor draws the voices away. "As regards health at the Academy, the decision is mine."

Splinters of sentences scatter against the door.

Locked up. For her own safety. You! Her Aunt! Her father's own sister... *Ladies, I beg you.* Sir, your professional opinion— *Rest and sleep... People she knows and trusts—*

I shall nurse her, with Matron's help...

And fees? My husband will not countenance— The Academy cannot be expected—

She has taught unpaid for a year. The Academy is in debt to her. Our Headmistress is in agreement. Charity is quite unnecessary. From any quarter.

5th June, 1849.

Scarcely can I believe that so many months have passed, and O such a sorry, blotted sight is my last entry!

I am undertaking light duties. Time is gradually taking shape again. The laudanum has been reduced to the minimum, only to help me sleep. The Doctor says I will regain my physical strength in time, I should not be impatient.

Do not, he advises, *dwell upon past events.* I do not intend to, I attempt to explain to him, but in the night the events, uninvited, come to dwell on *me* until I scream and struggle awake. They will eventually fade, he assures me, and suggests that I describe them to him with the aim of understanding them better and speeding their departure.

"I understand them too well," I tell him.

He is considerate, a man who does not dictate or demand explanation. He pats my hand as a gentle father might.

"Then you will progress," he says.

Chapter Twenty One

I begin a new volume of my Journal.

My previous journal is not full—I made my last entry over a year ago—but I wish to set aside its miserable events, in the hope of a fresh beginning.

30th June, 1850. The Academy.

Following my previous entry concerning my conversation with the Doctor last summer, I resolved to write no more in my journal until my nightmares had ceased, along with the need for narcotics, and my life as an invalid was over.

Thanks to the Doctor's belief in me, and his wisdom, I was persuaded that I could make a full recovery from my nervous exhaustion and be a useful member of staff. Were it not for his kindness and perception, and his diplomacy with others, I would have been committed to an asylum one and a half years ago, and would be there yet, strait-jacketed and indistinguishable from the rest of the raving mad. This upon the kindly instructions of my Aunt and Uncle, such was their concerned wish that I be locked in a safe place.

Soon after the turn of the year I resumed teaching duties at the Academy, increasing them as the months passed. It is both challenge and pleasure to guide younger minds towards learning—and *enjoyment* of learning—passing on the valuable lessons received from Harriet, encouraging my pupils to have faith in their intelligence.

The Academy's atmosphere is changed, thanks to the combined efforts of the Headmistress Miss Hamilton (a quiet-spoken though firm woman) and her Deputy, my dear Harriet Avery. Children are seen to smile; fear has departed. Unnecessary chatter is discouraged but discreet conversation is permitted. Many pointless rules have been discarded. The result is a freer, warmer atmosphere wherein the young mind flowers more readily. How Miss P. would disapprove of this grievous situation!

The memory of that woman is seldom permitted to trouble me now. For the most part, she and other inhabitants of my nightmares are shadows in the past: unreal, unlovable, unlamented. Mourning for Emmie remains, lying below all my feelings, deeper than a well. It will be so forever.

I am changed—physically stronger and with greater resolve. In December I shall be nineteen years of age, but I feel older. Certain aspects of life no longer daunt me. Certain persons can no longer wound me.

I know too well that the majority of mankind, even those with exceptionally tolerant and forgiving natures, if they could observe the interior workings of my mind, would be bound to say that its store of wickedness is frightful. At one time the thought of such a judgement would have filled me with guilt. No longer.

Now—I look into the future with hope, and have but one wish. It is time I wrote out the truth of it.

I was twelve years old when I first acknowledged the feelings that were the source of my subsequent secret wish. How clearly I recall it. I was seated on my bedroom chair next to the tall window, the velvet drape floating a soft, dusty perfume past my nostrils, watching my Papa (whom I loved and respected as a daughter should) on the drive below while Harriet laced my new boots.

He awaited his carriage, which would carry him from the Hall to his Rugby legal practice. A second carriage would appear fifteen minutes later to take me and Harriet—whom I addressed as Miss Avery then—to the railway station for our journey to Scotland. The thought would not usually have crossed my mind that Papa might delay his own journey in order to say farewell. Papa never said farewell, and this, like his rarely speaking to me, was something to which I had grown accustomed. But this was to be my longest journey ever, and I would be absent from home for months, and so a little dream of him behaving differently took hold in my imagination.

Harriet had told me, on occasions when I was downhearted at Papa's coldness, that like all gentlemen he preferred to conceal his softer emotions, and that he carried a huge burden of sorrow for my mother's death. Watching him, I pitied him in his grief, but at the same time I yearned for something that I did not then understand.

It is nearly seven years since that day, yet I still smell the sombreness of old velvet and the freshness of Harriet's lavender perfume. I feel my sadness and my shuddering dread at being on the point of travelling to an alien place so far from home—a home I would miss painfully: its rambling stairways and lofty rooms; high windows and broad fireplaces; the haven of the library; the friendly kitchen of Mrs Williams and Elsie and Mavis; the stables and grooms and horses and dogs and cats and rabbits. Most of all I would miss my friend Tommy, the white owls shimmering over the meadows and the flickering, diving swallows in the barns, the stream with frogs' spawn and sticklebacked fish. They were all that made me safe—but Papa was indifferent to my feelings. The sole, important comfort was that Miss Harriet Avery would be accompanying me.

I watched my handsome father on the drive, frowning, knocking his cane against his glossy boot, impatient. Perhaps he would look up, smile and wave. He did not—of *course* he did not; how very foolish I was to imagine it!

Harriet inhaled deeply as she rose to her feet after her dextrous work on my boots, which boasted many tiny black lacing-hooks, gleaming like little tear-filled eyes. "There, my dear," she said smiling, "How elegant! You are quite a stylish young lady." I looked away from my Papa and up at her. She was kind to call me elegant, a word that suited herself far more aptly in her new dress of dark blue brocade, its skirt plumped by petticoats and almost reaching the floor, a pretty lace collar the perfect frame for her long neck.

Harriet stretched her arms and looked out of the window. She saw Papa and her face changed, flushing slightly, but at once she turned briskly back to me, saying: "I shall go downstairs and have your new cloak and bonnet ready in the hall. Be sure to visit the water-closet. Your gloves and handkerchief are on the table. Now don't delay my dear." Her words were fading even before she left the room, for my mind was drifting away.

Staring from the window I was emptied. I had no understanding of why I sat in that chair, wearing those boots and stiff new petticoats and pinafore, looking at nothing. My father was gone and I had not seen his carriage. The sky had clouded. Little drops of water sprang on to the panes. I cannot guess how long I sat there, but suddenly Harriet returned gasping, rosy from the exertion of the stairs: "Why, you have not moved! Pray stir yourself. The carriage is here!"

Her exasperation shook me back into myself. Our chaise was rolling into position below. I apologised, saying I had felt faint, and Miss Avery pulled me into a rare embrace. Do not be apprehensive, she murmured, I shall be there to help you, while you shall learn far more than I can teach you. You are to be educated as a young woman *should* be educated.

My face was scraped by her new woollen cloak, and my eyes closed fiercely to hold in my tears, but I could not prevent my trembling. My returned mind was saying to me with frightening clarity: *Papa hates me, and what is more—I hate him.*

With the admission came calm. I leaned away from Harriet and breathed deeply, thanking her for her kindness. I could not explain that from this moment I was resolved to be a different, stronger person.

Realisation of my loss of love for my father brought me no pleasure—rather, it filled me with guilt at my own evil. Today I accept the truth of my wickedness without any such guilt, having lost what little faith I had in mankind's virtue. More than one person has fully earned my dislike, and I have no remorse.

Now to the truth of my wickedest wish. At first it was so secret that I hid it even from myself, but for many years now I have acknowledged it—and have clothed it in words, not spoken aloud but with great clarity in my thoughts. Simply, I have wished my father was dead. Dead, dead, *dead*.

The wish began in my wounds. He should have loved me a little. I had never harmed him, yet he detested me. Unjustly, he blamed me for my Mama's death—and all the evil things that have befallen me sprang from his hostility. I did not wish him to suffer for causing my sufferings—I simply wanted him to *be no more*. If he had only died and my Mama had lived! *She* would not have sent me unloved away from home. I would not have suffered at the hands of Miss Pottinger and my vile Uncle, and come near to madness.

Now I add a *practical* motive for my wish. I have long known that one day I, as my father's sole heir, would inherit a sizeable fortune and a fine house and be *independent, without need of male protection*. Therefore, as cold-heartedly as he has treated me, I wish for his death *and my inheritance*. Wickedness! I am at heart a murderess—and I care not one jot. I make my wish in pagan and superstitious ways whenever the opportunity arises. On the first occasion long ago I chose to wish upon the breast-bone of a roasted Christmas fowl, a moment of secret but considerable triumph at Talbot Castle, but thereafter I have wished many times on wishing-wells and wishing-gates, the evening star, four-leafed clovers, and rainbows—and O, countless silly things that I decided might bring me good fortune. At one time I prayed for forgiveness for my corrupt thoughts, until I saw that God too discounts the suffering of a young female. Therefore I do not *pray* for the granting of my wish. *If* God exists, a matter for some doubt, He is exceedingly cruel and I care nothing for Him. With these observations I add heresy to my sins.

31st December 1850.
This evening it is as though I stand alone upon a bridge, straining to see down the river of time that flows from tomorrow's New Year, but everything is obscured by an unexpected fog. Perhaps the Deity I denied has seen fit to strike at my hubris.

I was summoned to the Headmistress' room at tea-time. I supposed I was to be asked to undertake some of Harriet's duties, for she has fallen ill with influenza. Miss Hamilton stood looking out at the smoky dusk, not turning as I entered but addressing the trees that bowed against the moaning winds. "Do be seated, Miss Moore."

I waited. Miss Hamilton at last turned, as if resolved, and came to sit opposite me, quite grave. "My dear," she began, "I have sad news. It is my sorry duty to inform you that your dear father has been taken from you by the Lord."

By lowering my head rapidly I concealed my feelings. My hands clutched each other in disbelief—which doubtless would be taken as a sign of grief—while I struggled to control my features. She murmured softly of the tragedy, a fine gentleman only forty-five years of age, passing so suddenly.

I thought: I believe I am expected to weep. But I did not weep. Through my head there repeated the ecstatic words: *It has happened, it has happened!*

Finally I raised my head and, with appropriate gravity, asked Miss Hamilton how this sorrowful event had occurred. Perhaps she expected no display of emotion from me, for she well knows how little attention my Papa has paid to me. At any rate, her face betrayed no surprise. Rather, she appeared embarrassed by my question.

I said firmly: "Please tell me."

Being an honest woman, she did so. "I fear that your Papa was found early yesterday in a collapsed state, in an—I am so sorry—in an *inn*. In Rugby." (Miss Hamilton blushed.) "A doctor was summoned, but your father's heart had failed and he was beyond saving. He passed away shortly afterwards." (Passed away? He *died.*)

Miss Hamilton's own eyes were now lowered. I saw that she either knew, or guessed at, details unsuitable for a young lady's ears.

"I see," I said. I was ashamed of my father and filled with contempt for him, recalling his harshness and pious remonstrations as to family honour, and I at once determined to learn the truth. "Have my Aunt and Uncle been informed?" I enquired.

"Indeed yes my dear. It was Lady Talbot who asked if I would break the unhappy news. She will be sending details of the funeral arrangements."

I was silent, my mind too full for speech; and I could not stop thinking: *I am a woman of means!*

Miss Hamilton then added: "Lady Talbot requested also that I explain one or two further circumstances, lest you labour under any misapprehensions."

A chill entered me; and now she told me, haltingly, that my Papa had died in considerable debt, a virtual pauper, having lost the fortune he had been known to possess, although she could not say how this unfortunate situation came about.

Miss Hamilton was obliged to reveal my financial situation. My father, four years previously, had ceased payment of fees and other expenses including Harriet's vacational duties. Thereafter all accounts had been settled by my 'good' Uncle, until approximately two years ago, when the arrangement had ended without explanation.

"This I have known—" I interjected, to save her further awkwardness, "for my Aunt informed me those two years ago, although I was left in ignorance as to my Papa's difficulties. My *good* Uncle ceased payments as punishment for my perceived discourtesy and ingratitude."

The Headmistress regarded me with new interest.

I explained briefly: "I had no wish to be married to a *suitable* gentleman only to be a dissatisfied lady of leisure."

Miss Hamilton said: "My dear—that was most courageous."

"No," I told her truthfully. "I felt obliged to save my own life."

She silently observed me while the facts sank coldly into my mind. But even then I had not fully grasped my predicament, for when Miss Hamilton voiced her hope of my continuing at the Academy as a "valued teacher", I replied: "Why, I might simply return to my own dear home. Surely I might still be somewhat independent, living frugally—perhaps teaching in the local day school?"

Alas, Miss Hamilton now revealed that that beautiful, beloved house had long been relinquished to pay my father's debts. Strangers dwelt there now. I was truly destitute.

And so I stand on the bridge between last year and next. The fog has lifted a little. I see that my only choice is to make certain decisions in order to move forward.

I must accomplish the following swiftly:
    1. Send a request to my Aunt to visit me here (*not* at the Castle) and for my own satisfaction ascertain the truth about my father's death and reasons for his debts.
    2. Resist (*if offered*) the Talbots' help.

3. Decide how I shall support myself. Here or elsewhere? Academy income: £12 per year plus bed and board. As governess to a good family, 30 to 50 guineas.

4. Investigate the advertising bill that drew my eye recently in town. The bold name of a ship, the *James Chisholm*, was followed by an invitation to "Females between the ages of 16 and 30" (among others) to sail to Australia and New Zealand, with the Government's financial support. Opportunities existed for employment for "ladies of breeding and education"—as governesses for genteel families. Close by was posted a small bill, a cautionary message, headed: *The British Ladies' Female Emigrant Society*. It exhorted that no wise woman sail from this land without taking up the Society's offer of advice, practical assistance and "invaluable information".

Suddenly I feel hope, even excitement. Is *this* the doorway to true independence? I cannot wait to speak to Harriet! Would she come with me, if I decided to emigrate? Perhaps I am too hastily enthusiastic, made irrational by shock. Nevertheless, today the prospect of leaving my past life and being a new person in a new world holds considerable attraction.

4th January 1851.
All doubt is gone. I shall sever every connection with my past, especially that with my father—of whose character I trust I have inherited no part.

My Aunt Clarissa, who has a preference for ignorance, hypocrisy and obfuscation over unsavoury truths, was reluctant to part with her knowledge. Thanks to Harriet, I have read of many disreputable human activities, and was able to deduce much from my empty-headed Aunt's blushing prevarications, and spoke frankly. How shocked was she to discover I knew the words 'common prostitute'—and, worse, what they meant! Finally I extracted the facts—although my success may have owed more to her wish to wound me than to any dawning of *intelligence* on her part.

My father, insensible after imbibing a quantity of claret, died in a harlot's bed in a Rugby tavern of ill fame. In this establishment he had spent most of the previous few years in gaming, drinking and debauchery, and here gambled away my inheritance, my home *and* his legal practice. Sizeable debts are outstanding in Rugby and London, and my Uncle will *most generously* settle them—"to protect the family's reputation".

Renewed anger fills my heart at my father's hypocrisy in scolding me on the matter of guarding the family's honour!

My Aunt, doubtless taking my disgust for dismay, now exhibited a degree of satisfaction.

"There, Aunt," said I with a dryness she did not comprehend, "you are less agitated. In telling me facts instead of evasions, you have freed your mind."

She almost smiled at me, saying: "Dear child, can we not be friendly, as we were? We are sorrowful that your dear Papa has passed away in unfortunate circumstances.

But fear not, they shall be concealed—the family name shall not be tarnished. You remain a young lady from good background, able to marry well. Would you not prefer, *dearest* niece, to remain part of your loving Aunt's family? Pray reconsider our offer—a future befitting your station in life."

I replied: "I have given it close consideration, but cannot change my mind."

Her manner became petulant. "I believe you have *not* considered it from *all* aspects," she declared, tugging at her gloves and bonnet ribbons. "Perhaps you have thoughtlessly overlooked *our* position. Your Uncle tells me you wish to *work*, like a common woman. Have you thought of *Society's* view? Of how we will be regarded? The speculation? The gossip? What, pray, shall we say to the world in our humiliation?"

Steadily and silently I gazed at her. Flushing, she cried: "But my chief concern, dear child, is for *you*. Why suffer such degradation? You could live a lady's life—with all you could possibly wish for."

Observing her flustered face I pitied her briefly, for had it not been for my despised Uncle, at this moment I could have wearily weakened and chosen a life of ease. But I replied: "I find nothing demeaning in honest work. I prefer independence to being an eligible husband's property. I am sorry, Aunt, if my preference offends you."

"Foolish child!" she cried, jumping up. "Women have subtle ways of dealing with such matters. You have been influenced by the shocking modern attitudes of your former governess—that woman so bold, so *disregarding* of her proper station. *She* has put these coarse ideas into your mind."

I retorted: "Harriet harbours not a single coarse thought! She is the most refined, intelligent woman—*human being*—I know. Her influence has been only for good. She has helped and protected me through many unhappy times. She has shown me support that I have received from *no other person*."

"O!" My Aunt, with some melodrama, flung her hands over her face. "Cruel, ungrateful girl! We have loved you and opened our home to you, providing for you as if you were our own daughter."

Dropping her hands, she looked at me wildly. "Tell me! So that I may understand, tell me the truth. *Why* do you refuse us, when we want what is best for you?"

I answered her truthfully, if not as fully as I would have liked: "Aunt Clarissa, my reasons are those I have given. If you seek any additional reason, then—forgive me—I believe you know it already."

One kid-gloved hand rose, as if she would strike me as on that past evil day. Instead she rushed from the room. Her boots clattered upon the hall flagstones, and I knew I would not see my Aunt Clarissa again.

Tomorrow I shall with pleasure compose a letter to her describing my plan to become a governess in the Antipodes. It is probably as well that I did not reveal my intentions today, for she would surely have swooned, from the shock of a shame greater than her restricted mind could endure.

15th March, 1851. The Academy.

For the past two months I have been too greatly occupied to keep my journal.

In but a fortnight, I sail from the port of Liverpool! After much enquiry, New Zealand is my choice. The advantages of N.Z. outweigh the disadvantages of the longer voyage. I have read a great amount about the enterprises (conducted on behalf of the better-educated emigrants) of the radical Imperialist, Mr Gibbon Wakefield, and his views attract me. Notwithstanding that gentleman's obsessions with class and gentility, I feel one might find in N.Z. a broader and gentler civilisation than is the case in Australia. The reason for this, it is said, is that no convicts were transported to New Zealand. Furthermore, there are fewer families in Australia likely to hire a governess, since rumours of gold have caused a huge influx of poverty-stricken unmarried males.

My Aunt has not replied to my letter. I was sufficiently courteous to thank her for all past kindness and material support—but she may have been made too distraught by the news of my plans to read as far as these gracious details. My Uncle, however, sent a note wherein he declared I had put myself on the same footing as common criminals, and would come to a bad end (like my Papa, I infer). If I changed my mind and stayed, he and my Aunt would forgive me and the matter would be forgotten. (Forgive *me*!) If I persisted and his dire forecasts proved correct, I need not imagine he would rescue me. This last is a great relief.

There is no shortage of such advice. Yesterday came a note from Lady G. Evidently news of my departure has been broadcast, doubtless with explanations of my uncontrollably wayward nature. Lady G. warns me that my reputation in Society will be ruined, that I will be coarsened by the company of orphaned Irish females who are (rightly) being shipped out by the government from the workhouses; if miraculously I am not thus debased, my chief danger will be the "drunken crew", members of whom will assault female emigrants. I have refrained from replying that drunken assaults by *gentlemen* may be encountered nearer home.

How I look forward to leaving *forever* my previous life and all who have inflicted misery upon me.

As a result of the kind influence of the Governors of the Academy I have secured a government-assisted passage—rarely granted to a lady of my background. If I had not, I should have been obliged to part with ten or fifteen pounds. Fellow-teachers urged me to spend *fifty or more guineas* for a "respectable" cabin—but this represents too great a proportion of my savings (and more than a year's income as a governess). I am already obliged to spend a sizeable sum on supplies for the voyage, and I must retain some savings lest I do not secure immediate employment in N.Z. It is of no consequence if I travel with crowds of emigrants in 'steerage'. Those who have lived in such as the Academy are accustomed to discomfort and little privacy. As for 'respectability', I have mixed with people who think themselves superior and have found them corrupt; I have known those who are unfamiliar with the manners of the drawing-room, yet who are by nature *truly* honourable and genteel.

24th March 1851.

Thanks to excellent advice in *The Emigrant Voyager's Manual*, I have a fine hoard of supplies—including jam, tea, coffee, oatmeal, treacle, dried milk, nuts and fruit, tins of fish, butter and cheese, a ham, preserved eggs and pickles. Upon all this I have spent more than *twenty pounds*, and trust it will suffice to supplement the ship's rations for a possible four or five months. I am also equipped with 2 each of my own knives, forks, spoons, drinking cups and plates, as well as a simple mattress (which rolls up neatly), sheets, blanket and copious 'marine soap'—a miracle which functions in salt water.

All are packed in a sturdy tin box that I am assured will not corrode in the sea air. In a bag are personal possessions and clothes (for both warm and cold climes) required on the voyage; also my current journal, writing and drawing paper, ink, pens and pencils. My leather trunk will be stowed in the ship's hold; it holds my best clothes, not to be worn before N.Z., my earlier journals, other books, a few watercolours, letters, childhood mementoes, the miniature portrait painted by Emmie and my favourite doll, given to me before memory by Harriet. In addition there is my reticule, to carry necessities for my journey to Liverpool.

I survey my luggage with considerable disbelief. In five days' time I begin an exceedingly long voyage across vast oceans. To think I once considered the journey from Rugby to Edinburgh to be interminable!

All being well, I should arrive in my new land, New Zealand, in July or August—when, a further astonishment, it will be wintertime. I wonder if I am dreaming.

Chapter Twenty Two

I attach two letters hereto for the sake of chronology; they describe events occurring shortly before my voyage to New Zealand. It is now December 1851 and I have been living in New Zealand near to three months.

The First letter is from dear Harriet, received nearly nine months ago—mere hours before I left Scotland. It contains what have proved to be her last words to me, for news has come from her sister Jane of Harriet's death from consumption—within a month of my departure from England. Alas, she was not given time to read any of my letters written during my voyage nor subsequently: they arrived too late. Jane has returned them to me, unopened. I have lost yet another friend, the most valued and faithful of all. I must find the strength to continue. I am glad that dear Harriet was with her own beloved family when she died.

The Second letter is my reply to hers, written from Liverpool, England, just prior to embarkation on the James Chisholm.

Little Mudstone, near Rugby
25th March 1851

Dearest,

The accompanying package is my modest gift to you as you set off on your great voyage. My heart is heavy as I wish you farewell, but I am proud of your courage, and happy to have seen your eyes so bright at the prospect of this renewal of your life. You have grasped independence with enthusiastic hands, and I am certain you will find what you seek and be an excellent example to any in your charge or liable to your influence.

I have not always felt able to express, as openly as I would have wished, my thoughts and feelings, such were our positions in relation to one another. Now that you are fully independent of me and all others, I feel I may confess that since your infancy I have held for you the deep affection that I feel towards my own family, as if you had been a little sister or even my very own daughter. Yet, as your nurse and governess I was obliged to be somewhat distant, being an employee who, while given a certain parental authority, was not permitted by my position the degree of frankly expressed attachment that would have been natural between family members. This has saddened me, but society's barriers are robust edifices, whether we consider them Divinely ordained or born of human limitations and prejudice.

In the world to which you are voyaging, I understand that the social barriers are less rigid, and members of the so-called gentler sex (while welcomed, it is said, for their refining influence upon the opposite sex in that newly-forming society!) are less likely to be patronised as inferior beings. I feel sure that this *must* improve relations among all concerned. I do not doubt you will find new liberty in such an invigorating atmosphere. I was exceedingly impressed by your stand against those who protested that emigration to the Antipodes implies an unsavoury reputation because of its connection with convicted felons, and also that one might be seen to be escaping from pauperism—though, indeed, I can see no shame in the latter!

Rather, there is cause for applauding such excellent intelligence.

I understand, perhaps better than you have known, your refusal of protection and security offered by your Uncle and Aunt. By this I mean reasons that exist *in addition* to your reluctance to be confined to a life of comfort and leisure where subservience to some 'suitable' husband would be expected by all. I have perceived much in unwilling silence during our years in Scotland, admiring your courage, restraint, and resolve.

How kind you were to invite me to accompany you on this momentous voyage. I was touched, knowing your invitation sprang from the wish to give me, also, a new beginning with fewer prospects of poverty, and not from fear of travelling without a chaperone. How I wish I could have accepted, but my constitution, alas, is not sufficiently strong, and I should be more burden than companion.

In this package I send you a different kind of companion, one that I trust will afford you distraction and comfort. Here are contained five new journals for your own writing. These sturdy books should survive your voyage and indeed last for many years thereafter.

You will recall my own ambitions to write. Ah! I would never have been a Miss Austen or Mr Thackeray—but now that my health fails and I reach the extraordinarily advanced age of seven and forty years, I cannot pretend I shall ever realise even far more modest ambitions. Perhaps you will write the books I dreamed of writing, who shall say? But I do know that should you decide to write, you will strive for honesty, setting aside the difficulty that—as we have often discussed—the majority of publishers and readers do not deem acceptable, or even believable, certain aspects of human nature, such is the propensity of the human mind to refuse to acknowledge mankind's more offensive characteristics. Concealment is preferred to honesty, as we know too well.

No matter what direction you take in your new life—go well, dearly-beloved. I shall think of you every hour and long to hear of that day when you step safely upon dry land once more. I wait with great impatience for your promised letters.

Yours with the greatest affection,
Harriet Avery.

Liverpool, 28th March 1851.

Dearest Harriet,

I am waiting with a crowd of hundreds—emigrants like myself, and many families and friends bidding them farewell—in the Emigration Depot on the Mersey River.

We may have to wait one night or three for the ship's readiness to depart.

O! It is a cold, clamorous scene. In comparison with this vast, cheerless warehouse the Academy was luxurious seclusion! I say 'warehouse' for it is clear that we emigrants are viewed by the Captain as *merchandise*—like sacks of beans or bundles of timber, good only for profit. We are addressed 'en masse' without a shred of politeness, and it is *most* provoking.

Row upon row of beds, harder than board, are placed barely two feet apart. We are all single females. Single males and Married Quarters are separate, as will be the case on board. The government rigorously guards against 'indelicate' sleeping arrangements, and strict watch is kept on potentially licentious behaviour! (In *these* unappealing conditions?)

My own blanket is some protection from the bedding provided. My eyes and nose tell me that my bed has been oft-occupied without any fresh 'linen' (far too fine a word!). Several complain of bed bugs. A dreary beginning—but once we are on our way matters will surely improve.

A young Irishwoman with a baby tells me she is both orphan and widow, yet only twenty years of age. Destitute, she wishes to join her brother and his wife in Australia. I fear she may not be permitted to embark; the poor little babe is feverish and I saw a rash upon her chest that her mother hastily tried to cover. If infectious, she will not deceive the ship's doctor. Poor creature! What can she do if turned away? All her family died in the potato famine. Do you recall those 'gentlefolk' who described such unfortunates as 'vermin'? Most here are very poor, thin, wretched and in rags. But I will not be downhearted: soon we shall sail away. *Sail!* I, who had not even set eyes upon the sea before today! (This is true of most of us here.)

I thank you, dear Harriet, for your affectionate letter and touching gift. It arrived on the day I left Scotland, and no time to send a note. Such a generous supply of journals! I shall certainly try to keep good account of all events and, in addition, shall write letters to you recounting them. I must say to you, Harriet, that in one great respect I do consider myself a most fortunate woman. Without you, I believe my optimism would have been crushed, my outlook embittered, and my character weakened; your strength was always my example and support. I miss you deeply and shall always do so. Writing to you will be my mainstay (to borrow a nautical expression!).

It was no surprise that you had deduced what lay behind my refusal of the Talbots' 'protection'. Doubtless you also understood my not confiding in you, and were not wounded. I would tell all now, but hesitate to put it in writing lest it fall into other hands; I suspect you guessed, besides, at the crisis that precipitated my collapse. Now, I have left behind those unspeakable individuals and need never think of them again—and it is largely thanks to your belief in me that I emerged stronger, looking to the future with hope.

It is dusk; the lamps are few and feeble. My letter shall remain unsealed, lest I have the opportunity to add more on the morrow.

The following morning.—I cannot describe to you my excitement and joy! Forgive my handwriting, but the post leaves shortly and, besides, I tremble! O, Harriet—I have found my darling friend again—can you imagine!—my beloved *Emmie! She did not die!* She is one of the hundreds here. To *think* that had I not embarked on this adventure, I would have mourned her always. Emmie arrived last evening; she spied me and came running betwixt the beds, crying out my name. I thought I should faint—the entire world had turned on its head! We embraced, weeping and laughing, deprived of speech for some time. At last, however, we discovered how horribly each had been deceived. Here is the story, in short.

Emmie was taken home on the point of death—but her devoted Mama nursed her back to health over several months. Emmie then wrote to me, two or three times. Undoubtedly Miss P. intercepted her letters, for that hateful woman had lied to me and all others (including poor Matron, who was not in the sickroom that night) in declaring Emmie dead. When Emmie received no reply, she feared that *I* had succumbed to the fever, and wrote to The Headmistress—unaware that by then this was Miss P.—and received a terse note stating that I had departed and my whereabouts were unknown. O, my loathing for that evil, gloating woman! For the first time I wish she lived—so that I might convey it to her. Out of wicked spite she caused Emmie and me terrible grief.

After Emmie's recovery, her Mama herself fell ill—and was to die within a year. Emmie was greatly occupied in nursing her and—after her demise—caring for her brothers, her Papa and the household, but found time at last to send a note to my home address. This was returned with information that the Hall was vacant, the family moved to an unknown address. Emmie, at a loss to understand my silence, considered me gone for ever.

Soon afterwards her Papa remarried. His bride had no interest in her step-children, veering between hostility and indifference. This woman succeeded in turning her husband against his own daughter. Emmie was miserably forced to consider how she might support herself. Her brothers decided to seek their fortunes in America and suggested Emmie follow them but, reluctant to be dependent upon them, she found employment as nursemaid and governess to the children of a farmer and his wife; they could pay her little but at least she had shelter and food, and refuge from her stepmother's antagonism. Her Papa made no offer of additional support.

Here the story grows stranger. Emmie is travelling to N.Z. under the protection of this very family—Mr and Mrs McIvor with three small children and a fourth expected. Emmie is 'engaged' to Mr McIvor's brother Henry... *although she has never met him!* Henry McI. went to N.Z. two years ago. Both brothers are Scottish farmers who enjoyed mixed success in the west; Henry (the elder) has prospered in N.Z., and so the younger (Keith) decided to join him there and invited Emmie to accompany the family. Henry seeks, but has not found, a bride. The plan is for Emmie to be introduced to him in the hope that this may lead to marriage. The 'engagement' is in truth an agreement that neither considers any other partner before they meet. Should they decide against a future together, neither is under any obligation. A singular arrangement! Whatever the outcome, Emmie intends, like myself, to work as a governess or teacher.

Alas, she does not look well, having become exceedingly thin, mourning her Mama and deeply wounded by her Papa's coldness. Perhaps these losses led to her strong attachment to the McIvor family. (*They* sail in Married Quarters, and must do without Emmie until disembarkation, single women not being permitted therein.)

Now hasten I must, or miss the post. Dear Harriet, I shall think of you every day with more affection and gratitude than I can describe.

Your loving friend—

GEE SAID: "I absolutely *must* interrupt before we go on. On two points. First of all—look at the top of Harriet's letter: *Little Mudstone, near Rugby*, it says."

"So it does. Then Grandma McIvor's childhood home must be have been very near. So you'll know which parish registers to look in, won't you? There! We always thought—"

"Yes, but what I mean is—Margaret Esther refers to her home as 'the Hall', doesn't she, and *I* happen to know that there is, or was, a *Mudstone Hall*, a real country pile. Millie—*I've been there*. I think I've stayed in Grandma McIvor's actual childhood *house!*" She and Millie gawped at each other.

"Ooh," said Millie, her eyes wide. "*Tell* me. Tell me *all* about it."

"It's a hotel now. Five-star stuff. At any rate, it was then—must be twenty years ago or more." She could hear Sebastian's voice: *The Conference is being held at Mudstone Hall. Rather luxurious country hotel, old manor house just outside Rugby.*

"Seb had to go to a conference there. I was told to take walking shoes because there were some outings for wives I might diplomatically join. And there were going to be some formal evenings, so I should take some long dresses, ladylike ones." *Nothing too off the shoulder, if you don't mind, this is country.* "I thought it was going to be dead stuffy, boring business talk and conventional wives, but as soon as we arrived I reckoned I could bear it, because Mudstone Hall was just beautiful." Gee was quite breathless, getting to her feet and walking about the room.

"Go on. This is *so* fascinating!"

"It was late afternoon. I remember, the sun was low and red. The house was weathered red brick, mostly Tudor, with those huge soaring chimneys and ornate brickwork, a glorious heavy wood door and leaded windows all twinkling in the late sun. Huge house. But comfortable and friendly. Our room was enormous, with crooked beams and a vast fireplace, and there was a high diamondy window looking out on to the front drive and lawns. You know—the sort of place you could just *imagine* carriages drawing up, footmen, maids in caps."

"Oh my," Millie said softly, "and now you can imagine Margaret Esther's father, standing on that driveway waiting for *his* carriage, and his young daughter looking sadly down at him from her bedroom window. To think—you might have been in her own room!"

"I might. And I'll tell you something else that I haven't thought about for years and years. Something odd happened there, that I've never *really* been able to explain to myself."

"Don't tell me you saw a ghost."

"Not quite. But now I'm beginning to wonder if I *heard* one. Or two."

Millie squeaked: "I can't *wait*."

"Well, after I'd unpacked, Seb wanted to make some phone-calls, so I thought I'd go and explore the grounds for a bit."

Watch the time. Seb pointed warnings at his watch. *We don't want to be late for the reception.*

"There was a grassy walk and I felt drawn along it towards the old stable block. It had been converted—quite nicely—to a gymnasium and a swimming pool. I reached the main entrance, which was a lovely old, divided door—the original stable door, I'd say—and something made me stop. It was that feeling I'd often had when I was a kid—a sudden feeling of being utterly alone—"

"*There. Just* like her!—"

"—and it was the sheer *aloneness* that held me there, stock still, unable to put a foot in any direction. This time, though, it was a bit different, because I wasn't just alone, I felt—well—*alien*. I mean, I was detached—from Seb, from all the people indoors that I'd soon be mingling with, from my purpose in being there."

"You mean this was *different* from the childhood feeling?"

Gee returned to her chair, thinking, dragging up the memory. "It was similiar, but it was more intense—and obscure. It was a kind of *otherness*. Oh, I can't explain. But I had the sense that the sky was darkening, though *rationally* I knew perfectly well that the evening was bright. And somehow, like out of the corner of my ear, I could hear young voices. You know how it is when you're half awake, half in a dream? In my mind, quite clearly, was a picture of the original stables, and not far off was a rose-garden and an old bench where before I'd been looking at tennis-courts. And there were flagstones where I was standing instead of gravel and grass. And, I *swear*, Millie, I was breathing in the unmistakable smells of straw and horses."

"Oh *my*. *How* extraordinary. *Then* what?"

"Nothing. There was a blank. I don't remember leaving that spot, but then there I was walking back into the great wide foyer of Mudstone Hall, and there was Seb marching briskly towards me, all toffed up in his dinner jacket, none too pleased."

Where on earth have you been? The Reception starts in fifteen minutes!

Millie giggled. "Was he very cross? Did you explain?"

"I couldn't. I didn't know what had happened myself. I just apologised for forgetting the time, and got ready in a record fifteen minutes, so everything was fine."

"Did anything else strange happen while you were there?"

"Not a thing. I decided to put my odd experience down to tiredness, or an over-lively imagination."

Gee did not say: years later, she had wondered if it had been an early, unconscious signal that her marriage was going off track.

"But now, one wonders," Millie murmured. "Though I've never really believed in all that paranormal stuff."

"Nor me. Maybe it was just an hallucination. A dream? Time-warp?"

"Jolly strange, whatever it was. When you go back you can find out if it really was the Moore family home. But what was the second thing you wanted to talk about?"

"Oh yes, look. The signature's been torn off the bottom of Margaret Esther's letter. Why's that, then?"

Millie took the letter. "That's odd. Hardly to conceal her identity, since the writing's so obviously hers. Ha. Maybe she tore off a strip for a shopping list."

Taking pains to read none of the content, they peeked at all the later letters written in Margaret Esther's hand. Every one had been truncated in the same way.

Millie said: "Maybe she hated her own name, like you hate 'Georgina'."

"Doubt it. She would've adopted a nickname long since, or used initials."

"Never mind," Millie smiled, "I expect she'll tell us in the end."

Gee laughed. "Don't tell me you reckon Margaret Esther is talking specifically to *us*?"

"And don't you pretend you haven't thought of it. You said yourself that it felt as if she was expecting someone to come looking. And *she* said she felt she was writing for the mysterious woman of her imagination."

"I know," Gee admitted on a sigh. "But I don't always trust *my* wilful imagination."

This journal was much damaged by sea-water. How this occurred is related in one of my letters to Harriet.

4th April 1851. *At sea aboard the* James Chisholm.

Our fourth day under sail; departure was delayed by more than forty-eight hours for reasons not revealed to this lowly cargo of emigrants.

Such a departure! Three sturdy tug-boats hauled us seawards—like a trio of ants dragging the body of a fly—and an enormous cheer arose from the crowd ashore. How they waved, shouted and sang, while guns were fired and bands played. When the gaiety had grown too distant for eyes or ears, there appeared a Parson upon the poop deck, calling upon the passengers and conducting a Divine Service. Such a marked contrast: the merry horde ashore and the pious man of the Church! In lugubrious tones he uttered dire warnings to us sinners and entreaties to God to keep us virtuous on our journey; reminders of Hell-fire and repentence followed, and several pertinent Commandments. One gloomy hymn was sung. I saw no-one comforted or uplifted by all this. Later this joyless gentleman went aboard one of the tugs, and I was happy to see him returned to shore.

The following day the English coast had vanished! Some, not all, sails were 'set', as it is said, and with so slight a breeze, progress was slow. But when we arose yesterday, the remaining tugs had departed, and today *all* sails are now set: how lovely, high and huge! We billow and swoop.

By far the most important occurrence has been my reunion with dearest Emmie. I remain in constant disbelief, anxious if she is not in view for fear that I merely dreamt of her return—or, rebirth. My bitterness towards Miss P. is beyond measure. I recall my fear that I had been the instrument of her demise; now my murderous heart regrets that I cannot remember it, if I was. I would now *relish* making her suffer an agonising death. I say nothing of these wicked thoughts to Emmie. Sweet Emmie! How we rejoice—and I believe this has helped us face shipboard conditions more light-heartedly than we otherwise might.

The scenes as we embarked were fearful. Upon the crowded main deck was a Babel of men shouting, women shrieking, distraught farewells, children hither and thither and spanked for mischief, babies screaming, bundles and luggage everywhere, the crew bellowing, and countless ropes for one and all to trip upon. We the 'Emigrants'—those with assisted passages or having paid a few pounds for the cheapest accommodation—were brought aboard first. The Cabin Passengers, Second or First Class, remained on shore until departure was imminent: *they* were staying in inns, *not* herded into the Depots.

These exalted beings came to the ship (by then anchored offshore) in boats. Many of the females were dressed in their finest clothes and laciest bonnets as if to make an entrance before us lesser mortals! They succeeded in making themselves vulgar and ridiculous. Worse, they also wore insufferably smug expressions, looking along their noses at us 'steerage' passengers with disdain. Their claim to superiority is to have paid fifty to eighty guineas out of their own purses. Persons *truly* refined would not conduct themselves so vulgarly. I was thankful (despite our discomforts) to have resisted purchasing a First Class cabin beneath the poop deck, thus saving myself from the need to consort with these persons in velvets and taffetas!

Emmie and I succeeded in securing a bed-space (thus it is called) together, in our Unmarried Women's Quarters. What a sight greeted us when first we went below-decks to view our home for the next months! At first it seemed as dark as night: few lamps were lit, and the windows (port-holes) of this long, narrow 'room' are small. Our eyes learned to see through the gloom, and focused upon Matron. She, after 'welcoming' us with a list of shrill instructions and rules, shouted out names and allocated numbered bed-spaces, all amid much chaos—young women laughing, weeping, all uproarious.

O, the bed-spaces! These are best described as boxes, arranged row upon row exactly next to each other and one above the other in two tiers, most being arranged across the ship, with only a few running 'fore' and 'aft'. A central long 'corridor' contains a line of oblong tables and seats fixed on either side. Each bed-space measures 6 feet by 3 feet. This seemed adequate—until we learned that two ladies were expected to sleep therein, and many of us would thus sleep in great proximity with a stranger! I learned from the ship's Surgeon that bed-spaces follow the pattern of those on slave and convict ships—the Owners having learned how most profitably to pack human bodies into the available space. However, we modern fortunates are allotted 2 *whole inches more* than convicts! (We have approximately fifty bed-spaces, similarly the Unmarried Gentlemen's Quarters—at the other end of the ship; twice as many are in the Married Quarters. Almost 600 souls are travelling steerage, 75 in Cabin accommodation.)

Emmie and I were allotted bed-spaces far from each other. We quickly conferred, and soon succeeded in bribing our intended bed-partners—with packets of tea and a tin of jam—to share one space while Emmie and I took the other. Our space is on the upper tier, and we are obliged to clamber into it. Beneath the lower berth is a tiny storage area, while within our bed-space are fixed pegs for hanging personal items. Matron advised that these be tied securely in case of rough weather. Emmie deduced that rough weather must account for the raised edges along the tables—to prevent cups and plates from sliding to the floor!—and for the tables and seats being fixed to the floor. Despite some misgiving, we agreed it would be unrealistic to hope that our entire voyage could be as smooth as our departure from the Mersey.

We can *just* sit up in our 'bed'. A thin wooden partition, 2 feet high, separates us from the girls on either side. Farewell to privacy! At least we are all females, and poor light allows us to dress and undress without undue exposure! What *can* it be like in the Married Quarters, the couples close upon each other, and children heaped in the bunks below?

However, it seems that for some our situation is no hardship. Two young Irish sisters declare this vessel to be far better than home. Home was a hut of mud and straw, one earthen-floored room. They and seven brothers and sisters shared one hay-filled 'mattress', their parents another. Water was fetched from a communal well, a good walk away. As for water-closets (for we have some, of a sort—no more than cupboards with plank seats and a chute to the sea!), why, they had never heard of them, far less seen one. In their community all had shared a pit with a board over it.

The family's diet was chiefly potatoes, cooked over a fire, and many of their friends and relatives perished in the famine. To these young women and many others, the rations on our ship are unimagined luxury—and, in truth, they compare well with our Young Ladies' fare at the Academy! Our rations, weekly *per capita*, are: A half-pound of salt beef, one-and-a-half of salt pork, one pound of preserved meat (dubious, nameless—in tins). A quarter-pound of suet, likewise of butter; one pound of hard 'biscuit'; one pound of flour; a half-pound each of oatmeal, rice, preserved potatoes, carrots, onions, raisins, sugar and molasses; half a pint of peas; 3 ounces of lime-juice (against scurvy). Children receive half-rations. A small daily quantity of drinking-water is held in casks beneath our tables; this, we learn, will become stale and we shall drink it as tea or with other flavouring.

The Cook, we are told, is a Black man, more than six feet in height! He prepares porridge, stews, soups and vegetables, but we may prepare our own pies, puddings and cakes. *Only* the Baker may enter the Bakehouse; he will bake our prepared dishes, as will the Cook—or we may ourselves cook during special hours allocated to females in the galley. Emmie and I belong to a group, or 'mess', of ten females. Thus has our throng been divided up by Matron. Everyone has brought on board provisions according to each person's means, and we shall exchange and share to make the best of them.

For washing one's person, there are few handbasins; more than 20 women share each. To be *entirely* clean will prove difficult for the very modest. It is fortunate that Emmie and I are accustomed to wash in full view of other females. Prudish modesty has no place here, unless one wishes to be malodorous or lice-ridden!

11th April 1851. Off the coast of Spain.
Who could have dreamed I would ever be in this foreign sea?

We head South. I am anxious that Emmie is too easily sea-sick on a mere swell; what will she suffer on wilder seas? She feels better walking on deck, although there is meagre space on the main deck for a true promenade. First and Second Classes may use the poop deck for exercise: their privilege is greater space for fewer persons. However, on certain days, part of the poop deck is available to us lower orders; Emmie then likes to walk with the McIvor family, the children of which plainly adore her. They are two boys and a girl, of seven, six and four years of age, who have inherited their Papa's looks: dark-haired and twinkling-eyed. He is, one must acknowledge, a handsome man—if roguish, looking at one appraisingly in a manner *not* gentlemanly, and yet he is amusing in conversation. Mrs McIvor compares colourlessly and has little to say; but perhaps she is exhausted by her children—*and* the prospect of another! Emmie treats her solicitously and relieves her of her boisterous brood whenever she encounters the family on deck.

18th April 1851.
Flat calm, warm sunshine, and no sight of land. It is as if we were lost. The ship is motionless. How strange and dream-like, this world that is nought but water, so vast that we seem to be nowhere definable. I stand at the rail gazing out until I become dazed by infinity. It would be understandable if people became a little mad if left too long upon the endless ocean.

Below deck the atmosphere is too warm and the lack of breeze means the air is stale. Emmie and I find a shaded corner on deck and watch the crew's endlessly interesting activities, amazed by the countless ropes, lines, masts and spars and wondering how the sailors know them all. (One of our unmarried women found one young man *so* interesting she addressed a few friendly words to him: she has been confined below for a week! She weeps that she "never meant no harm" and indeed her punishment seems harsh.)

19th April 1851.

A strange occurrence yesterday afternoon. Emmie and I waited for the day to cool before going below decks to take our turn in preparing food for the evening meal. Few others were present. We had been working for barely ten minutes when we heard Matron approaching in a series of immense thumps down the hatchway steps. She is an exceptionally muscular woman, more like a man (including hair upon the chin!)—yet her voice is paradoxically shrill. This was an unusual hour for her—and our surprise was doubled by the sight of Matron's superior, the Surgeon, close behind her.

Matron began to shriek my name. "The Surgeon wishes to speak with you! Stand, young woman!"

I almost obeyed, but Emmie laid a hand upon my arm and whispered: "She *ought* to be more courteous."

The Surgeon, Mr Young, forestalled Matron's further cries. "Pray excuse our intrusion," said he, "but we have to inform you of an administrative error. You should not be in these quarters."

I stared, possibly open-mouthed.

"I do not understand you," I replied, choosing on my own account to stand. "Are these not the Unmarried Women's Quarters?"

"You are in the wrong class," he smiled.

"Sir," replied I, "I elected to travel steerage on an assisted passage. I have the papers in my bag——"

He declared: "A First Class Cabin was reserved in your name." Here he consulted the paper in his hand. "Your—Aunt?—Lady Talbot, made the reservation. The cabin remains unoccupied. Your own steerage booking was not cancelled and the coincidence of name was not observed. You did not come aboard as a First Class passenger, and it was assumed you had not embarked. Only now has it come to light that you are here, all the while."

He smiled again. Several of the other women had drawn closer to listen.

"Well, girl?" shrilled Matron most rudely.

I addressed the Surgeon. "Sir—I chose to refuse my Aunt's financial aid, for good reason."

"What *can* you mean?" came Matron's cry.

"Are you saying that you do not wish to change your accommodation?" Mr Young asked, his face comical with disbelief.

"I am."

Matron snorted. Aside from this inelegant sound, both were silent, staring at me. A general intake of breath was audible from my female audience.

The Surgeon then said: "Perhaps this will change your mind?" He held out a sealed letter. "Lady Talbot sent it. It has lain in your Cabin these many days."

I took the letter but did not open it. The Surgeon watched me almost pleadingly, as if my assent would restore his belief in human sanity, saying: "Pray read your letter and reconsider. At least come and view the Cabin—it is one of the best in the stern, with the choice of two comfortable beds, supplied by Lady Talbot. As soon as you see it you will understand how much more congenial it would be. And furthermore——" he bent his head and added in a whisper, "——you will be better fed, without need of extra provisions."

"I cannot imagine, Sir," said I, "anything that would alter my decision."

The poor man was at a loss. At last he said: "I shall wait three days. Thereafter I am bound to allot the Cabin to another. Two Second Class passengers are interested."

"Do please give it to them," I replied carelessly.

He ended earnestly: "I shall not regard this as final. Pray inform Matron if you wish further discussion with me at any time." Thereupon he led Matron away before she could make loud her disapproval; I saw him glance back at me in mystification.

There followed from my audience a chorus of comment upon my assured lunacy in turning down such a gift, with questions as to my Aunt being a titled Lady. Some were impressed and a few hostile, shouting that doubtless I thought myself better than they. Emmie answered the latter: "She is *fortunate* in having received an education and certain privileges, but she does not confuse this with superiority. When has she acted so? It was her own choice to travel in your company." Silenced, they gradually dispersed.

Emmie then asked me: "Is it because of me that you refuse?"

I embraced her. "Possibly I would refuse on that account—but in truth I have no wish to accept my Aunt's charity." At her puzzlement I continued: "I shall explain some day, but not now. It is a matter that wearies me dreadfully." At this the dear girl declared I need explain nothing whatsoever, and I was most noble and self-sacrificing. I retorted that I was no such thing, merely filled with the wicked sin of pride!

Chapter Twenty Three

21st April 1851.
Ending our 3rd week aboard the James Chisholm.

Dearest Harriet,

Such terrifying adventures we have had! The worst is over—or so we trust—but those of us travelling 'steerage' have experienced more than two days of horror, with the weather our raging enemy. Gigantic waves, *cliffs* of water, washed over the ship day and night. Had anyone described to me previously, no matter how meticulously, the power and size of the ocean, I could not have imagined it! It is more than frightening—it induces a terrible panic, as if a demented monster had come upon us intending to swallow all alive.

On the first night of gales, the lower beds near the hatchways were swamped with cold sea-water rushing down upon them. (What good fortune we are on the upper level!) There was much screaming—out of a justifiable terror that we were sinking. Many poor souls' clothes and bedding were utterly soaked, tins of food and iron utensils were tossed hither and thither as the ship was thrown up and down on the waves with frightful rending sounds. Several were struck by flying objects (a tin of molasses, I assure you, is an exceedingly painful missile!). The entire floor of our quarters was awash, with all manner of possessions floating about in the dark, beyond rescue, while luggage beneath the beds was saturated. Included in the drowned was my bag containing my current journal, horribly damaged. All the other journals you gave me are safe in my trunk in the hold. Fortunately I had wedged a bundle of notepaper on the shelf in our bed-space, and have the comfort of writing to you.

I have fixed myself in the corner of our bed. The ferocity of wind and waves has subsided a little, but from time to time another upheaval makes me seize hold of my surroundings to keep from falling. You will excuse the deterioration of my writing!

The worst occurrence, at the storm's height, was when the Captain, or Master of the Ship, ordered the hatches of all steerage quarters to be battened down—*for our own safety*. We remain trapped, without fresh air! It is almost unendurable, to be treated worse than cattle. There is widespread terror lest the ship go down and take us with it. Fear, I have realised, spreads faster than flames. I try hard to control my own, for what can we do but wait and hope? (Or pray, as many do.) We hear shouting and the crew running on deck, as if all are in panic. Unable to see what is happening, we find every noise more terrifying. The ship creaks and pitches frightfully as if it would turn somersaults, and loud crashes convince us it is being torn asunder. Gloom by day, darkness by night: lamps are forbidden for fear of fire—the greatest of all hazards. I write by the grey light from a little port-hole.

Many are in great distress from sea-sickness. I am thankful not to be a victim, but Emmie suffers greatly. As the third night of being battened-down approaches, the stench is intolerable, not only from epidemic vomiting (and no possibility of cleaning) but also general reluctance to attempt reaching the water-closets in the rearing ship. All manner of receptacles are used for personal relief (even drinking vessels) and many spilled. This is a truly odious situation, worse than anything I could have supposed.

The following afternoon.—The waves have appreciably subsided; the Master has ordered the hatches open to allow air to enter. At last freshness enters this noisesome place! We are not yet permitted on deck for the ship still rolls dangerously. At dawn, we learn, one young crew member was washed overboard, never to be seen again. Emmie fainted at this tragic news. I have told Matron she is sick and she will ask the Cook for some mild soup. (Matron has organised us into teams with the aim of returning our quarters to cleanliness. An obnoxious task, but essential.)

Another day has passed. The weather is so benign one cannot believe its previous ferocity. Our quarters are cleansed, with wet items hung in bed-spaces and on deck—where I sit in the sunshine with my journal spread to dry beside me. A serene day—but alas, dear Harriet, I myself am in turmoil.

Emmie spent this morning green of countenance and vomiting—despite the calm. I pressed her unrelentingly to consult the Doctor, and at last she burst into tears and told me her story, crying that she could keep the truth from me no longer. O, poor dear girl, what a sorry tale! As a result of it, my resolve as regards the First Class Cabin has vanished and I have asked Matron to inform the Surgeon of my change of mind. I may say it was a trial to witness that lady's triumphant smirk!

It pains me to tell you that Emmie is with child, and has been so for nigh on four months. In anguish she explained she had been sufficiently foolish to fall in love with none other than her married employer Mr Keith McIvor, and he with her. Keith McIvor—the father of three legitimate children! What could I say? It could not benefit Emmie to see my shock and dismay. She declares herself ashamed, dishonoured and a sinner.

"I make no justification for my actions," she wept. "It was as if I could not help myself."

My surmise is that after her mother's death and father's rejection, she was in need of affection and mistook Mr McIvor's flirtatious charm. I thought him entertaining; now I see him shallow and despicable.

I did not contradict Emmie's belief that Mr McIvor fell in love with her, nor did I reveal my condemnation of his having shown no responsibility towards Emmie or his wife. Both with child! What 'gentleman' is this? What 'love' has he demonstrated?

When Emmie realised her condition she told Mr McIvor, who had already begun preparations for emigration, and assured him she would do nothing to bring unhappiness upon his family. He declared (belatedly) he wished to act decently, and so was born the scheme involving his brother Henry in New Zealand. Should they marry, her infant would be legally a McIvor, with Mr Keith McIvor helping his brother to support the child. At first Emmie resisted but her quandary was great. How could she gain employment in her condition? She could not go to her father and step-mother. At a Lying-In Hospital she would be treated as a sinner and her baby would be snatched from her and sent into an orphanage. At last, for the sake of her child, she accepted Mr McIvor's suggestion—but insisted he write to his brother with the truth; thus Henry McIvor would know of the situation before her arrival and if he disapproved of such a bride he need not even suffer an introduction. Emmie would then forge her own path, inventing a recently-dead young husband to explain her baby—for no family would accept her as governess were the truth known.

I suggested she invent the dead husband at once, for the facts cannot be hidden indefinitely. The story, we trust, will also convince Mrs McIvor. From her simple demeanour I deduce she will accept a story of widowhood, Emmie's grief having kept her from mentioning it earlier. Emmie is assured of my affection and support. This afternoon I see the Surgeon to confirm my acceptance of the Cabin reserved by my Aunt, and shall insist on Emmie joining me, at *my* expense. Later I shall summon Mr Keith McIvor and inform him that he must finance her accommodation. (Writing this account reminded me of my Aunt's letter, unopened in my purse! I have just unsealed it.)

"Dearest niece," she has written, "I beg you to accept my own personal gift, a comfortable passage more fitting to your background as a young lady. I wish you happiness in your new life. Pray let me know of your whereabouts upon arrival. Your affectionate Aunt, Clarissa."

In the *smallest* of writing beneath, she has added: "I am sorry."

25th April 1851.

The deed is done—Emmie and I are installed in our First Class Cabin. Already there is more colour in her face and she appears less apprehensive now that she has told me her story rather than endure her misery alone.

Our cabin is one of those known as the 'great' cabins. There are two such, at the stern, each with a good-sized window. The cabin measures approximately 9 feet square. Enormous! *And* with our own little water-closet! Also two *real* beds with thick mattresses and linen sheets, a chest of drawers, several strong shelves, pegs and hooks, and two chairs.

There are a further six First Class cabins. Also upon this deck are the Captain's, the Surgeon's and the Purser's Cabins—and The First Class Pantry. The solid maple-wood doors of the passenger cabins open directly on to each side of a wide corridor, which leads into the Saloon, whose centrepiece is a long, polished dining-table. One might be in Talbot Castle—for this Saloon reaches from one side of the ship to the other, surely 30 feet, and is most ornate, with inlaid wooden panels, gilded pilasters, flower-decorated cornices, soft carpeting and damask-covered chairs. What contrast to our previous quarters! (I have resolved to reimburse my Aunt when I am able. I cannot accept her charity, although I concede that her gesture was an apology.)

At the dining-table, Captain Wilson (a grave Glaswegian) presides over all the First Class passengers, as well as the Surgeon, Purser and one other Officer. The passengers number fifteen (excluding a baby, Percival aged 1 year, who does not dine with us); therefore we are 19 at table. Stewards and stewardesses wait upon us. "It is exactly like being at home with one's own servants," sighed one satin-clad lady yesterday with a satisfied wriggle.

We have established the deceit of Emmie's own background and, I confess, I shall willingly perpetrate as many untruths as are needed to protect her. I told Mr Young, the Surgeon, that Emmie was tragically both orphan and widow, and had decided to emigrate with the McIvor family before realising her condition. Mr Young believed every word, swearing that he would do all in his power to guard Emmie's health and (with genuine emotion) agreeing to inform the Captain of the situation on our behalf—thus discreetly allowing the information to reach the other passengers and sparing Emmie from the embarrassment of speculation and gossip as her condition progresses. Mr Young appears a kindly man.

His forecast of an improved diet was correct. Indeed, we are *too* well fed! Copious meats are served at dinner—and some at table have *astonishing* appetites, eating almost everything available rather than choosing one sufficient dish. One gentleman, exceedingly large of girth, today at dinner devoured a dish of roast pork, followed by one of boiled fowl (a mountain of currant jelly atop!) and then a plate of duck, boiled ham and pickles! Many vegetables were also consumed. I supposed him then to want only to lie in his cabin, but he had *no* difficulty in eating fruit pudding *and* bread and cheese! No wonder he is so huge. Emmie and I, more than satisfied by roast duck followed by almond tart, were occupied with avoiding an exchange of astonished glances lest we laugh aloud. No-one else appeared to think him remarkable, but everyone's appetite seems far greater than our own. The wife of the fat gentleman (you will not believe that they are Mr and Mrs William Chew!) also eats copiously, a different cause for wonder as *she* has an exceedingly *lean* frame! Most of our companions consume a hearty breakfast at nine in the morning—ham or salmon, eggs, bread rolls, boiled rice with marmalade, coffee—followed at noon by a mere snack of bread and cheese with Port wine or porter. Were I inclined to follow their example, it would be impossible to fasten any dress by the end of this voyage!

Emmie and I were introduced to our fellow Cabin passengers; I do not recall all their names, but gradually we shall learn more of them. My impression is of assorted characters from several walks of life. All treat our Captain with deference, although I cannot imagine the more prosperous among them regarding him so highly if they encountered him on land. Perhaps he earns particular respect because our lives are in his hands!

The explanation for fresh meat and eggs on board (of which we saw none in steerage) lies on deck: on either side of the poop, two rows of hencoops, occupied by squawking fowls; on the main deck, ten or so sheep and the same of young pigs. (I had assumed them emigrants for farms, not for our consumption!) The pigs are fed on refuse from our table, so in eating them we finish our own recent repasts—a nice economy.

27th April 1851.

My interview with Mr Keith McIvor was conducted this morning—with the co-operation of the Surgeon. Unmarried females may not be alone in a male's company—but I could not speak my mind in any other person's presence. I told the Surgeon that Mr McIvor is an Executor of Emmie's late husband's Will, and Emmie had prevailed upon me to discuss with him aspects of the Estate, she herself being too distressed. This shameful invention and deceit achieved my object: Mr Young remained with us in the Saloon—but sufficiently distant to be out of earshot, and he encouraged other Cabin passengers to take the air on deck for a half-hour.

O, I do *not* like Mr Keith McIvor! He has no shame or remorse. He is *insufferably* pleased with himself and his charms, has no respect for Emmie or understanding of her sufferings (which she "brought upon herself"!), and appears careless of morality. Had he not "behaved decently" in arranging for a possible match with his own brother, virtually ensuring her respectability where another man would have abandoned the foolish girl? Somewhat sullenly, he agreed to pay for her First Class passage, perhaps fearing I might otherwise expose the truth to his wife. (This I would not threaten lightly.) Most outrageous, and despite my open contempt, he behaved throughout in a manner more fitting to a *flirtation* than to a discussion of responsibilities—even paying compliments upon my bonnet and eyes! Only unwillingness to alert our chaperon to the true nature of our subject kept my anger under control. Had the Surgeon not been present, I am certain Mr McIvor would have attempted to touch my hand or arm; often he leaned forward as if to do so, until I deliberately rose and moved my chair out of reach. Was he abashed? Not Mr Keith McIvor: *he* laughed mockingly, staring most insolently! How can Emmie have been so deceived by this person? My conviction grew that the less she sees of her erstwhile lover, the better; therefore I insisted that he came nowhere near her until the time came for her introduction to his brother. With a further, lingering, and impertinent contemplation of my person, he agreed.

Emmie's rejoinder, when I reported that he would finance her accommodation, was that she had known he would be kind! Sorely was I tempted to describe his indifference to her plight and his manner towards me, but could not. In time she will learn his true nature.

7th May 1851. These things have occurred since my last writing.

We have seen Land. On the first occasion we were to the north of Porto Seguro in Brazil, or so the First Mate was heard to say. South America! So far from home! On the second occasion, the same Officer boldly declared to the Captain (who blustered) that we were *excessively* near Land. We could see surf breaking upon the shore of some islands off the coast. Could our Captain have misjudged our position? The men murmur that our Captain has little experience of the new, faster "Southern route" (now the choice of most Shipowners) which will carry us towards Antarctica before traversing the huge Indian Ocean. There are alarming tales of ships going down on these voyages. I shamelessly eavesdrop on the men's conversations, in which they prefer not to include us fragile females!

Last week we endured days of breathless heat in the strange calm of the Doldrums, but now we are exceedingly *cold*, colder than I could ever have imagined, and the weather grows savage. Those of us fortunate enough to possess warmer clothing have gladly donned it. Icy winds rage, *sleet* falls! Waves crash over us again, and now darkness comes early. The men tell one another dreadful stories of the danger of unseen icebergs and broken ships.

On the old "Admiralty" route, I have learned by my assiduous listening, ships travelled by way of the optimistically named Cape of Good Hope—whereas now, alas, we shall pass that balmy place some seventy nautical miles further south, where winter prevails. I confess my thankfulness for our Cabin: we have heard tell of freezing water pouring down into steerage and many unwell. Mr Young told us that the unfortunate Mrs McIvor suffered a miscarriage (relieving her husband of *one* responsibility!). She is confined to the female hospital between decks; her children are in the care of another mother. Emmie wept piteously over the event, declaring that the wrong woman had been punished. There is no news of Mr McIvor's reaction.

8th May 1851.

I am obliged to finish this letter for the best of reasons. A 'brig' has come alongside. Everyone is excitedly finishing letters, for this vessel will carry them to England. I had not thought to post you a letter for many weeks—but now I shall!

How I miss you dear Harriet. With the greatest affection—

2nd June 1851. The James Chisholm.

At last I am able to write again in my journal. Its pages are now fully dry—although sadly stiffened, buckled and discoloured. But no matter, now I have the opportunity of relieving my mind of the tormenting emotions I could not allow myself to include in my letter to Harriet.

Over a month has elapsed since I talked with Mr Keith McIvor, but my subsequent mood of anger and confusion has remained with me. The shameful truth is that he had a regrettable effect upon me, and that despite my *despising* his contemptuous disregard for morality and for Emmie—I understand *far too well* how Emmie fell under his spell! I am shocked still to say that even as I drew coldly away from him, I *wanted* his touch! Worse, I believe *he* knew it—hence his mockery. How I loathe myself—and him. Dottie's words come back to me: how men and women may be drawn like magnets, even without love. *It's wanting somebody, wanting your bodies as near together as they can be.* Mr McIvor has obeyed my instruction not to approach us. I could never have imagined it, but the hateful truth is that I have yearned for a sight of this man whom I utterly dislike! I have even dreamt of him—and *detest* myself for my helpless disgraceful dreams, and for my betrayal of Emmie. She has been foolish and gullible—but I am the sinner, far worse than she could *ever* be.

Fierce squalls have arisen this evening; they match the raging within my head. The mainsail has been lowered, the sea is all white foam. I wish for the greatest, most raging storm in the world—one that would wash that unspeakable man from this ship.

"Hey, I'm confused," Gee said. "It was *Henry* McIvor that Margaret Esther married, wasn't it?"

"It was indeed. He was always our 'late Grandpapa, Henry McIvor, a fine man'. But of course I never knew him. I suppose, then, the plan for *Emmie* to marry Henry didn't work out. So what happened to her and her baby, I wonder?"

"And what happened to the wicked Keith?" Gee wanted to know. "He would've been your great-uncle, right?"

"Yes. I met him only once. He and Great-Auntie Lily lived far off in South Island. We children were taken on a visit once, when Daddy wanted to paint there. I was about nine or ten, and Great-Uncle Keith was over eighty then—*ancient* to me, but handsome, with a devilish grin, and always joking. He nicknamed Mother 'Jack-in-the-Box-Jemima' because she was always jumping up, busy with something for Daddy or us. Compared with him Great-Auntie Lily was wan and wrinkled. Not surprising, poor woman—she'd had nine children altogether! One does wonder how many *other* little illegitimate McIvors were begotten, besides Emmie's. He must have had a way with him if even Grandma McIvor wasn't immune. I remember Auntie Mollie—she was one of my mother's sisters—saying *That Uncle Keith, what a rascal he was!* She never said *how* exactly. She'd purse her lips and close her eyelids, slowly. Disapproval—but relishing it just the same. *Rascal.* It's like *naughty boy.* Doesn't exactly condemn him, does it?"

"Did your mother like her Uncle Keith?"

"I think so. Not that she saw much of him of course. I think everyone liked him."

"Except Grandma McIvor."

"You know, I never once remember her mentioning him."

6th July 1851.

We are more than three months at sea. The ocean continues to fascinate me— ever-changing, beautiful, terrifying. Our ship, at first so huge and towering, is now tiny under a vast sky, upon an ocean that encompasses the entire world. When its mood is benign, I fancy I could throw myself into the waters and float sublimely into nowhere; its calm lures me like sirens lured ancient mariners. But when mountainous waves loom and spill crashing avalanches upon us, I am stricken by fear and awe, utterly powerless.

My intention was to write a brief description of our First Class companions, but they irritate more than interest me: possibly this indicates my intolerance rather than their failings. Nevertheless, conversation is narrow. The ladies speak only of children, food or clothes; a preoccupation is whether their dresses will be out of fashion when we arrive in N.Z.! The gentlemen's discussions are limited to money and trade—made tedious because of their braggartly air. Occasionally they find a more interesting subject—politics, perhaps, or navigation—but they patronisingly discourage any woman from contributing. Does it embarrass or alarm them, the society of a rational, enquiring female? For Emmie and myself, the best conversations are held in our own cabin, away from these often pretentious people. (I except the Surgeon from such judgements, his manner being more paternal than lofty, while his interests extend to poetry, history and astronomy.)

Emmie and I are employing ourselves usefully at sea! This came about because young Megan, one of our steerage friends, walking with us one day on the poop deck, observed the book in my hand and asked me bashfully if I would teach her to read. From this sprang (with the Captain's permission) a rota of classes in our cabin, women between 18 and 30, all concerned to improve their prospects in the Antipodes. We have formed small groups of 4 to 6 persons, depending on ability—as many as will fit into our cabin. It is encouraging to see the seeds we plant sprout and flourish, and useful experience for us both. We ask no payment: none of our pupils has sufficient funds. Several, however, are sewing for Emmie's baby, and one (Maureen) has displayed some skill with scissors and is the first person ever to impose order on my odious hair! At last, I am not altogether displeased with my appearance. Emmie remarks that I look "even more interesting"!

12th July 1851.

Well South, exceedingly cold. Last evening, gales snatched away one of the booms and the wheel was damaged; several crew were injured. We travel rapidly under little sail, but powerful waves strike the ship and it shudders alarmingly from stem to stern. The deck remains at a fearsomely steep angle: impossible to walk out of doors, and our little school is closed. Our Surgeon Mr Young has patients in hospital quarters, and reported recently that while "doing his rounds" he found the deck one inch deep in hailstones! Once he was almost swept away by colossal seas, only saving himself by clinging to the sailors' deck-house. Steerage and Second Class hatches are battened down.

14th July 1851.

Winds remain fearsome. The ship is tossed like a mere cork. At mealtimes, each person must cling to plates and vessels. Appetites have subsided—even those of Mr and Mrs Chew! The weather provoked a certain fearful (and in some respects shameful) conversation at dinner last night, beginning with one of the ladies, Mrs Robinson, nervously enquiring of our Captain: "Sir, what if we should go down?" All regarded her with some dismay.

Captain Wilson replied firmly that we would *not* do so, and that he had taken ships through far worse than this. Mrs Robinson was not so easily reassured. "But—*what if?*" she persisted, adding: "I do not imply any failing on *your* part, Sir."

Here our gourmand Mr Chew interjected with some impatience: "Confound it, madam—we should have to take to the boats, that is all." (Here I was greatly alarmed at the vision of the enormous Mr Chew sinking a small boat single-handed.)

As if she had had the same thought, Mrs Robinson then asked our Captain: "Sir, forgive me but—could *everyone* take to the boats? Are we not too many?"

Captain Wilson replied without a trace of emotion: "In such an *unlikely* event, Madam, *Cabin* passengers would take to the boats. Do not fear."

Emmie and I, the Surgeon, and one or two others, stared incredulously at the Captain, but around us were heard several exclamations of relief.

Emmie said: "Sir—is your meaning that those in steerage would be left behind?"

To our horror he confirmed it. "That is indeed my meaning, Madam."

Emmie cried: "But they, too, are human souls!"

We were shocked to hear Mrs Robinson interject: "Do you not mean human *rabble?*"

Emmie and I steadfastly ignored this 'gentlewoman', although I was sorely tempted to respond with outright disapproval. Only Mrs Chew and Mr Young had the grace to show embarrassment, recalling that Emmie and I were lately of that *rabble*.

Our Captain said, somewhat wearily, that it was a "matter of what is practicable, not of preference."

The well-fed Mr Chew here gave a large shrug and pronounced that it was "well known" that these ships "seldom carry sufficient boats for the numbers of passengers".

Emmie and I exchanged disbelieving glances, and I was unable to resist a sharp rejoinder to Mr Chew: "And does this not trouble you?"

The 'gentleman' chose to laugh comfortably at this, saying, "Why else do you imagine I elected to travel in First Class?"

By this time the Captain appeared uneasy. "It is a matter for the ship-owners. It is not in my hands."

"Our *lives* are in your hands, Sir! *All* our lives!" cried Emmie.

Now Captain Wilson grew heated, and raised his voice. "Do you question my integrity or dedication to duty, Madam?"

Emmie was not afraid of him, I am proud to say. She replied: "I do not, Sir. But I do wonder whether, were Captains to refuse to sail any ship *unless* it carried sufficient boats, the owners would be obliged to act more responsibly."

Many must have seen the truth and justice of this, for a brief silence fell, to be followed by an explosive order from our good Captain Mr Wilson to end this discussion forthwith—the subject was not our concern. An astonishing response. Neither Emmie nor I said one word further until it was time to bid everyone goodnight.

20th July 1851.

Further contrast: we have been becalmed 5 days. It remains cold. The Captain says that if we continue thus, our voyage to Australia will be nearer to 5 months than 4. How much longer to N.Z.? My greatest fear is that Emmie's confinement may occur at sea. There have been several births on voyage; three resulted in deaths—two mothers and one infant. Their shrouded bodies were tipped into the ocean, even as the ship continued its journey. It is impossible not to be frightened (although I conceal my fear), but Emmie is tranquil and determined to make the best of her mistakes and to be philosophical and practical. I am glad her spirits are so improved. Her condition is now obvious, but thanks to the Surgeon our First Class companions have curbed their curiosity.

As for Mr McIvor, I am relieved to find that his prolonged absence from our sight has brought me detachment—and embarrassment at my earlier preposterous feelings. I believe Emmie too has her emotions in better perspective. There, then, is the cure for his power—simply to banish him!

30th July 1851.

The calm was short-lived, soon shattered by storms. We passed a hilly island in the midst of nowhere, whose snowy rocks and fierce surf we could plainly see. Snow—and this to us is a summer month. Children play snowballs on deck! In England, they will be paddling at the sea-side. The world is upside-down.

15th August 1851.

The entire deck is frozen, a sheet of ice, and all ropes coated with it. It is difficult to keep warm. We sail at moderate speed; if we continue thus we may reach Australia in a fortnight. It will have been (some gentlemen say, *sotto voce*) a far longer voyage than it should upon the Southern route. They are critical of our Captain behind his back, all deference to his face.

Beautiful lights in the sky—an 'aurora' of the Southern Pole. The sea rolling and high: albatrosses follow our ship! Such noble birds, graceful and strange, fully deserving their myths. We have seen whales also—what colossal creatures. But all these things are distractions. I am fearful for Emmie, although the Surgeon declares my anxiety unnecessary.

Chapter Twenty Four

WALKING ONE AFTERNOON along the endless, empty beach, its serenity seeped under Gee's skin: and she lay flat on the sand, eyes shut, letting the sun sink warmly into her face and arms, picturing albatrosses over an icy August ocean, and the courage of two women far younger than herself.

Perhaps she had drifted near to sleep, or the hiss of frothy waves stroking the sand had woken a dream. Gee was back in Dorset, on the beach, with Sam. Sam, digging a moat around the castle of sand she had helped him build. Gee had told him that if he did it right, the sea would fill it. She lay there, leaning on one elbow, watching his industry, giving guidance if asked. Sam, in his little blue trunks and the smooth skin on his back tanned the colour of strong coffee stirred with cream. Salt and sand grains sparkled on his forearms. He said: *When it's got a moat, the enemies can't get in, can they?*

Gee's throat tightened at the memory, and she wondered if Sam, so small, knew about enemies. If he pictured himself inside a castle of damp sand, protected by a moat, in the way that she used to feel safe up her tree, surrounded by rippling leaves.

When she was about five, the family moved from a sooty Midlands town to the house in Dorset. She had immediately fallen in love with the sycamore beside it, with the house too, and, in an all-embracing way, with the countryside around.

Nearly there, her father had said. And she had been thrilled, gawping out of the car's window, at the lane. A *real* lane, a picture-book lane, grass and dandelions sprouting down the centre and sides, dirt ruts and potholes all over. It was summer and the lane was baked dry and rutted; the car bumped along. In the following years she would get to know that lane in all its seasons: squelchy with mud, shimmering with frozen puddles, cracked by heat, or full of the green spears of spring. The lane was narrow, and in the height of summer it was a shadowy green tunnel, with clustering wild flowers rarely seen nowadays. She loved it best then, when the crowds of elder bushes, hawthorns, wild roses and sloe trees seemed to lean in, jostling to see whoever passed by. Two hundred yards' worth of mixed hedgerow, all now vanished, along with the row of lime trees down the other side. In flower, their perfume was wonderful, but then in summer they would drop sticky dew on passers-by.

The lane was a *cul-de-sac*, and their house stood at the closed end in its own leafy corner. It had a high, none too neat, privet hedge and an iron gate. The only other dwellings in the lane were two cottages near the open end, standing like sentries. Opposite their house was a meadow with a distant spinney, and a half-hidden farmhouse. Next door to the house, behind the limes, lay another meadow of rough grass, with buttercups and cowslips in springtime, and usually a couple of harrumphing ponies cantering about. A barred gate guarded the meadow, and here Gee remembered seeing half a dozen fledgling swallows lined up, gossiping. They'd been so unschooled in the danger of humans that she could stand right next to them, entranced by every creamy feather on their breasts. She could have picked one up, but didn't.

It had seemed to Gee, when the family clambered out of the car outside the shaggy hedge, and the iron gate announced them with a squeal, the mellow, maternal house opened its arms in welcome. And now, she thought, it was empty. Selfishly, she knew, and childishly, even though she knew Miriam was happier in her town-house, Gee still wished her mother lived in the old place. It was big, lovably battered, mostly red brick, full of character, poking out in all directions. In there somewhere it was possible just to make out its original oblong, but generations long before theirs had added to it spontaneously, if haphazardly.

Warmth was the over-all impression: the brickwork was topped by terracotta-red roof-tiles and the softening effect of moss. Gee came to think of it as possessing a curiously *settled* look, as if it had not been built but had grown out of the ground.

Then, the house was suffering from years of neglect: otherwise, Miriam and Frank could not possibly have afforded it. They worked hard together to turn it into a decent home, mending, painting, papering, and somehow creating order out of its rambling lump of land—but nothing formal or manicured. There emerged a mixture of wild parts, flowery parts, vegetable parts; a paddock for the goats and rabbits; a yard for chickens; and at the very end of the quarter-acre property, they planted a little orchard. Gee had seen the apples and plums grow from saplings to mature trees. And back then, there was harmony.

There was a memory that always returned. The first day of school summer holidays, before breakfast. A sunny, fresh morning. Gee ran right down the garden towards the young fruit trees—running and leaping for the joy of it—and saying to herself *I'm happy I'm happy—don't let anyone call me back and say tidy your room or anything to spoil this morning.* And nobody had. She hadn't known quite what was causing her happiness, and she sat down beside an apple tree, looking back at the house and trying to work it out. In the end she told herself: *It must be the whole place.* It was the way the house sat there so comfortably with its warm face looking out, as if it smiled at her and understood what she felt, out there in the sunshine.

Its gaze, she felt, had somehow followed her as she delighted to find fruit plumping on the currant bushes; it marvelled with her when she stroked the silky fur of the rabbits; it chuckled as she relished the wicked humour in a goat's eyes. The house surveyed its property, holding it together, guarding it. And it beamed in satisfaction.

One summer, she had put that beloved house in danger.

Just to see what would happen, she set fire to a bramble bush down the lane. Looking back, she saw the strangeness and thoughtlessness—as if there could be no consequences. It happened during the disturbing period after Sam had died, when she'd developed a frightening urge to destroy.

That foolish, dreaming match, the terrifying ease of destruction. A second here, a second there, one tiny move and utter wreckage could result, twisting the future.

The weather had been dry and hot, and the wind seized the flames and swept them up the lane towards the house. Even now she could hear the greedy, crackling sound, the speed of its gobbling. And in a second she came to her senses and ran and ran to overtake the monster, screaming, shrieking: *There's a fire, there's a fire!*

The two goats were tethered in the lane, peacefully munching as the flames raced towards them. Gee grabbed their ropes and hauled them inside the gate, ignoring their indignation. Her parents came tearing out of the house with buckets of water, and Gee helped her father get a hose going. Suddenly other people galloped up to help, probably from the cottages in the lane. It was over in minutes.

Nobody said anything about how it might have started. After two or three agonising days, Gee had confessed to Miriam. *It was my fault, Mum. I just didn't realise how bad it would be.*

Miriam had answered: *I knew that, dope.* She wasn't angry.

Had she known, really? Perhaps she guessed. Gee's face had probably been bright white. Either way, Gee was grateful.

But the worst thing was, she might have killed the goats. Gee climbed to the top of her sycamore and wept tears of shame and remorse. The tree seemed to embrace and rock her gently, even though she hardly deserved its kindness.

Gee had recognised the tree as a friend, in some unknown layer of her mind, from the beginning. Stretching its arms up and out, tapping its twigs on an upper window, it was benign and welcoming. She made the tree her own. *It's a sycamore,* her father told her. And when she was big enough, around seven or eight perhaps, he had taught her the safest way to climb a tree. *And this is especially important with a sycamore, which has brittle wood. Keep your feet close to the trunk. Always hold on with at least one hand. Do not hurry. And look where you're going. Those are the golden rules.*

Way up in her tree, Gee could sit on her favourite, slightly flattened 'sitting branch' and stay there for hours, doing drawings, writings, staring at the sea a couple of miles distant, or watching the sun set. Other people couldn't tell her to make her bed or peel some potatoes. Jo couldn't torment her. Couldn't lie in wait for her and pounce, pin her in a corner, push her face up to Gee's so that Jo's ferocious, popping eyes were so close that Gee could smell her skin, while Jo's mouth made terrible threats that turned Gee's dreams into nightmares and frightened her half to death.

Gee was at peace in her tree, unseen from the ground. Nobody could be sure she was there. She would keep silent, even if they yelled her name. There on her hospitable branch, leaning her head against the trunk and breathing green air, she could work out her moods and thoughts. Could think more clearly, it seemed, high in her eyrie. Miriam called it day-dreaming. It used to drive Jo mad.

Poor Jo. Gee had gradually seen, as she'd grown up, what the bullying was about.

Their father and Gee went biking or sailing together—things that didn't appeal to Jo. Gee got praise, and more of his attention. The *right kind* of attention. As well as that, Jo had needed a more demonstrative, *huggy-kissy* mother. Jo clearly had been an unhappy child, but Gee couldn't see that then. She'd merely thought Jo was being beastly. But maybe she herself had been beastly to Jo. *You really should listen to your own voice sometimes.*

Sebastian's voice crept unbidden into her ear. *You could learn from your sister. She's a very warm, caring person.*

GEE SAT UP SHARPLY, brushing sand from her hands, looking at her watch. Time to start back for lunch with Millie.

As she walked back towards the house, Sebastian hovered with her in a jumble of random, drifting, often accusing images, just as he did in the small hours, dragging insomnia in his wake.

Often and warily nowadays, she tried to approach the tangles in her head. But as always, she was confronted by a thicket of thorns, and the realisation that the only way through it would tear her flesh. So she baulked and turned away. Her cowardice disgusted her; yet she knew she couldn't continue like this.

After coming out with the truth to Sebastian, she'd at first felt some resolution, or even purpose, return to her life. But now, every time he came to mind, her spirits sank. On rare days, Gee could talk herself into truly believing that leaving him had been the only possible step. And then, almost invariably, her bad dreams caught her out. And Mildred, seemingly with the power to absorb Gee's actual thoughts, caught her out.

A question waited, there on the verandah, as they settled down for their pâté and salad. Gee felt Millie's keen green gaze upon her, and knew the time had come—as it was bound to do—when Millie could say:

"Will you tell me about you and Sebastian, Gee?"

The marvellous thing about Millie, Gee thought, was that she could ask this without a hint of prurience. From anyone else's mouth it would sound damned nosey. But today Gee actually welcomed the question—had, even, hoped for it. She nodded, but was silent, uncertain of where to start. Millie, dependably, delivered a gentle push:

"Did you want children, Gee?"

"At one time, yes I did."

Mildred read her pensive face and hastily added: "You don't have to talk about it if you don't want to."

Gee smiled. "I never do, but it's really okay. Somehow or other, with you, Millie, I can." She sighed, looking out at the garden, the sunshine turning the flickering leaves to silver.

"Funny isn't it, how women take it for granted they'll get pregnant—until they don't. I didn't. When Seb and I had been three years married and no sign of offspring, I saw a doctor. He asked to see Sebastian too, said both of us should be tested. But—" she shrugged wryly "—Seb wouldn't go."

"Oh *dear*. What was that, manly pride?"

"Well, it's true he was aghast at what I might have said to this *total stranger* about our sex-life. Sebastian told me: '*I'm* not going to some quack who'll say drop your pants and make me do some disgusting tests, or dose me with hormones!'" Gee laughed, then added soberly: "It wasn't funny at the time."

"How *did* you cope?" Millie wondered sadly.

"Essentially by not acknowledging how much his refusal mattered. Or not for ages. I persuaded myself that wanting children was a biological trick played by Mother Nature, a profligate old bag if ever there was."

"Mother Nature's a pretty *mean* old bag, too, if you ask me."

"Too right. But I knew, as well, there was social pressure. In those days, you got married, you had kids. There were delicate hints. Jo gave me useful booklets about conception, that sort of tiresome stuff."

"I hope you told yourself to ignore that!" Millie was all indignation.

"In a way. After all, I thought, I might still get pregnant—what was the rush? Why embarrass Seb if he hated the whole idea. And to be truthful, I'd never been particularly maternal. Unlike Jo. So I said to myself, *she* could produce the babies—*messy* babies, were my exact words—and I would be a saintly aunt while concentrating on my painting."

"Buried yourself in work. But still, that's another form of creation. And you made a success of it."

"Oh, I don't regret any of *that*. It saved my sanity. And if I'm *scrupulously* honest, I know I wouldn't have been a very good mother."

"I can't believe that!"

"Believe me. Too much of a know-all, as my sister would rightly say. I *am* a fairly good aunt, but that's altogether easier." Gee grinned at Millie.

Mildred nodded. "Must admit though, I regret not having children. I always thought the mixture of William and me would've been a good one." She laughed slightly. "Coo, what a big-head!" She added more seriously: "Probably we should never have listened to that doctor."

"What doctor?"

"Some gynie man. Said I was too old. Did I tell you I was thirty-eight when we married? *Very* late for those days, on the shelf—but I wasn't going to marry any old body." She chuckled. "I turned down *lots* of likely lads. Mother was in despair! Well, the specialist said it was risky at my age—and also something might turn out wrong with the baby. Doctors sound so *certain*, don't they? And nobody argued with them in those days." She sighed.

"Still, childbirth was much more dangerous then," Gee tried to reassure. "And no tests for the baby."

"Even so. I've often wished we'd ignored him. Should have been inspired by my mother's example. I mean, for heavensake, she was thirty-eight herself when she had Frankie, and forty when she had me. No problems with any of her pregnancies. And we all popped out as quick as greased piglets, apparently."

Mildred smiled, then added wistfully: "William would've been a good daddy. But there I was, five years after my wedding, no babies and then out of the blue, no husband either. I tell you Gee, the memory can still give me a shock. He was so well one minute, it seemed, and then sick with that horrible cancer the next. He was gone within three months. There weren't the treatments then that they have nowadays, so nobody could buy him any time."

"Cruel bloody disease." *It's cancer,* Sebastian had said.

"I'd still have a part of William, that's the thing. Selfish, I know. My child wouldn't have had a father. So perhaps it was just as well I wasn't a Mum." She looked at Gee. "D'you think Sebastian would have been a good father?"

Oddly, Gee realised, she had never consciously thought about that, and yet she knew the answer.

"Not really. Another good reason for not having had kids, hm? Together we might have proved Mr Larkin to be painfully accurate."

Though sometimes, Gee inwardly confessed, she did think of what it might have been like to have a son or daughter. But she also knew it for a sentimental thought, sprung from the biological clock, not *real*.

"No regrets then?"

"It's not a serious regret, not now."

"*Some*thing is," said Mildred.

"Oh yes," Gee said. "Something is. Quite a lot is."

Millie asked softly: "Have you *left* Sebastian?"

Gee stretched out on her verandah chair, drew in a huge breath and braced herself. Millie, evidently, wanted to try to help her through the thorns.

"That's what I told him. Yes. And do you know how long it took me? About twelve years, and I've been married for twenty-two. Tough part is, I know it was the right thing to do. And yet it haunts me."

"It *is* a walloping great step. For anyone who takes marriage seriously, anyway."

"You hit it on the head. I'm too old-fashioned for words. It's my own fault for reading my mother's weekly magazines when I was a kid."

"Oh, go on!" Millie scoffed.

"Really. There was a particularly prim, moralising agony aunt. Stuff about preserving your virginity—for godsake, it might have been bottled fruit!—and the sanctity of marriage vows. And the *woman* was supposed to *work* at the marriage. No mention of fun. You'd think it was a hundred years ago. Fact is, I got indoctrinated."

Millie nodded, smiling wryly. "Mm. Know what you mean. *Our* sex education was nil, really—Mother never told us a *thing*. I only knew what a man *looked* like from art and sculpture. Still, instinct is amazing. When I met William I fell for him totally, *passionately*, and I wanted him, even if I didn't know quite what to do!" Millie giggled. "Well! I didn't want to be too much of a blushing bride, so I got the goods from Alice. She also told me not to worry, just enjoy it. Indeed, I needn't have worried—William was a truly loving lover."

She smiled, rather dreamily. "But go on. Your brain-washing."

"The propaganda worked, that's all. Very effectively. Until my twenties, I simply didn't *question* adult wisdom in the form of the agony aunt, or from anyone else, come to that. And it was obvious my parents shared the same values—and they weren't even married!"

"And there I was, thinking you young folk were all at it like rabbits after the war," Mildred grinned happily.

"No such luck. Not for anyone, really. Days of rationing, freezing, and floods, is how I remember it. Ghastly. But along came the Fifties and rock'n'roll, and I did eventually get modern enough to have some kind of a sex-life before I met Sebastian. Which was when I was twenty-five. But I always felt guilty and furtive about it."

"Did you fall in love with him?"

"I suppose I did. Sort of. I didn't feel *passion*. It was comfortable, we got on. He seemed to be all I needed. A good bit older than me. I think, subconsciously, I was attracted to a mature, guiding hand."

"D'you mean something you hadn't had as a child?"

"I had, originally. But later— Well, it got lost. I'd say that both Jo and I sought out a father. In our different, immature ways. She picked Eric, taking his domineering nature for strength—he's a bit of a weirdo, candidly—and I chose security and what I *thought* was maturity."

"Did you feel you'd been duped, you mean?"

"Only by myself." Gee snorted. "Pathetic. I chose not to see Seb's own *naïveté* for a long time."

The older man, Gee had learned, was not always the wiser. Sebastian had appeared self-possessed, solid, yet he'd proved to be anything but.

"I saw what I wanted to see, I guess," she sighed. "The way people do when being romantically wooed—and Seb certainly was adoring."

Gee made a little grimace, not quite a smile. The rock-like Seb had, in fact, been fashioned by herself. And when the light at last dawned, she had received a severe shock.

"Was it when he wouldn't see the doctor that it started going wrong?"

"Not at once, no. It *was* the first blow—but as I said, I turned a blind eye to what it meant. My marriage *had* to go on appearing a success. Feeble, I know, but I was the daughter who was seen as smart, top of the class, decisive, doing well in college and at work. I couldn't be seen to fail, you might say. What a fraud, with my fake façade!"

"Poor Gee. Then what?"

"Oh, we were quite a pair. We both worked hard. My paintings were selling quite well, and Seb went up his own business ladders and began making serious money. I respected his success, and he was *so* proud of me: he'd always been inclined to put me on a pedestal, and make lavish declarations of worship to anyone who'd listen."

"Oh my—all *very* flattering."

"Yeah, but not what you'd call real life. Rather later on it struck me that sex and worship don't make good bed-partners: it's pretty difficult to romp with someone on a pedestal. Our love-life vanished. Just the same, we maintained the edifice. Of the marriage, that is. I supported his career, he supported mine. We were friends—conspirators even—and I kidded myself that was enough. And, pure naïveté here, the notion of other women simply *didn't cross my mind*."

"Aha! But then——"

"Then, after *ten years* of marriage, I found out."

Gee had often wondered if she would ever have known a thing if it hadn't been for that one odd-woman-out who, evidently, had deluded herself that *she* would be the one to win Sebastian away from his wife. So when he sorrowfully jilted her in his customary way, regretting that he could never hurt the wonderful Gee, the lady scorned was angry and cynical.

This woman, it had soon become clear, had been a willing subject of Sebastian's secret hobby. Which was erotic photography. And, suspecting she might not have been his only model, she raided his files. Soon afterwards the post had brought Gee a heap of photographs depicting Sebastian and several partners in various *in flagrante* poses, some quite startling.

"Accompanying these," Gee told Millie, "was a letter giving the history, right up to date, of his adulteries. There were a lot."

"Oh!" cried Millie. "What a *beastly* thing to do!"

"Pretty spiteful, but it was just as well to know. And I shouldn't have been surprised, should I? I must have known, really, underneath."

"And you told Sebastian?"

"After a few days of being rather ill, I did. He was shaken at first, and embarrassed."

"I should jolly well think so."

"But in no time, he recovered. Quite composed. Amazing. He denied nothing, just stated that his 'wanderings' were unimportant. He actually spoke the classic words: 'They meant nothing to me, they don't affect our marriage.'"

"But they had!"

"He couldn't see that. Seb sincerely expected me to grasp his viewpoint—which, to him, was that the marriage was separate. He made it sound like a valuable commodity, a show-piece behind glass, and—though he didn't put it this crudely—indispensable to his ambitions in business and the social ladder. The rest was discreet recreation, indulgence, like an urge to eat a chocolate bar, an appetite soon sated. Men did such things."

"For heaven's *sake*." Millie sounded quite impatient. "Did he apologise?"

"He was sorry he'd hurt me. But he said he adored me, I was the one who mattered. It sounds ridiculous, but his whole attitude made me feel at fault—narrow, for not understanding."

"*That* wasn't fair."

"No. But it did force me to acknowledge—at last—that when he'd refused to see the doc, he'd really, *selfishly*, rejected *me*. For all this so-called adoration, he hadn't cared enough to try and give me a child. I guess that hurt."

Gee remembered her humiliation, so intense that it was physically painful. And she'd never understood how he could so convincingly say she was beautiful and special, when all the time she wasn't satisfactory. Sebastian's explanation was: *It's not like that. You think too much.*

Mildred was frowning. "Didn't he at least say it wouldn't happen again?"

"Nope. Honestly, I used to wonder why on Earth he'd married me. I was *nothing* like any of the others in the photographs. They all had long fair hair, pouting lips and lavish bosoms—in fact, a mixture of matron and tart. Voluptuous. My absolute opposite."

Gee would stand miserably looking in the mirror at her straight dark hair and off-beat face and that long, lean, body. She hated her reflection.

"I felt like a sexless loser, an inadequate female."

"But, darling Gee, the truth was—*Sebastian* was inadequate. You were selected as a good wife. Admirable in all respects. But too good for sex. Hence the tarty types."

Gee remembered Caro saying: *You're probably like his mother, who I expect was a saint. Taboo territory for sex, what? I expect he needed some tart he didn't respect just to get it up.*

"Well, when I thought about it," Gee told Millie. "I began to be haunted by aspects of our married life that I'd chosen not to notice. A certain detachment about Seb. I'd never felt truly *desired*."

"Did you feel like leaving at that time?"

"I did, yes, but only briefly. Maybe I felt so much a failure, I couldn't face it. I was already hiding inside what I thought of as the walls of my marriage. After the photographs, I slammed up the shutters too. I felt ashamed. I wanted nobody to know. Except Caro, who'd guessed anyway. I couldn't sleep in the same room as him any more, but I lived with his so-called 'wanderings'. I even covered his tracks when necessary. For most of the time I refused to look further than work, while—in public—for another seven years, I suppose, I played my part of good wife. I'd *married* him, you see."

"Yes, I do see. But something pushed you over the edge eventually."

"I went off on a painting trip to Sicily, and I was gazing at those barren Mediterranean hillsides, and I suddenly thought: *My life's like that.* There and then I admitted I was miserable. And I knew something had to happen."

"And?" Millie smiled as if she had guessed.

"Less than a year later—about five years ago—I met the man I wish I'd met long before Sebastian. It'd never occurred to me that *I* would ever have an *affair!* Appalling! But rather late in life, I discovered passion. I couldn't, I really couldn't, resist."

Chapter Twenty Five

BEN HAD BLOWN IN from New York one summer's day. One of the secretaries alerted Gee as she arrived for work: an American, Ben something, had called. Claiming to be a film-maker, documentaries to be precise. He wanted to interview her that very morning. The secretary had told him she didn't know Gee's schedule, and besides she wasn't in yet.

"Hey," she said to Gee, luridly rolling her eyes. "He might be Hollywood!"

"Yeah, right," Gee snorted. "And I'm Audrey Hepburn. So did you say he could have my autograph?"

"He said he'd come back later, on the off-chance you'd have a free hour."

Quite soon, in fact, Reception informed her there was a gentleman asking to see her, from a film production company apparently.

And then he was in her office, grinning, with his short American haircut and Brookes Brothers button-down shirt, a navy linen jacket and pressed khakis on long legs. His loafers were shinier than new conkers. Scrubbed clean, this man, the way only Americans could be.

He strode towards her, hand held out. Gee stood up; her heart jumped at the extraordinary vigour of him; his height, his shoulders, seemed to fill the room. And he smelled delicious. A soft draught from the window sent a waft of expensive shaving soap and vanilla towards her.

He wasn't conventionally handsome, but he was, most certainly, startlingly attractive. For a few moments she stood staring at him, stupefied by a wave of desire for the man. Then she was woken up by his hand gripping hers. Just the right degree of strength, the skin cool—smooth without being soft, and inexplicably thrilling. He said his name. Gee confirmed hers.

Thinking about it afterwards, she could remember very little of their conversation. But he did sit down at her bidding, and at the same time placed a little recording machine on the edge of her desk. She took the chance of looking at his hands. Beautiful hands; broad across the palm, with long fingers. The words grace and strength flicked disturbingly into her mind.

But she did remember the information that he was in London to research a television film he intended to shoot the following year. It had been commissioned by an independent channel back home in New York. Someone had had the interesting idea of a programme on artists who were also teachers—from the studio system of the Old Masters, to modern painters teaching in colleges.

"Not all our TV channels are crap," he'd declared disarmingly.

She vaguely remembered asking: "What made you decide to talk to *me*?" There were, after all, hordes of artists out there who also taught. She could think of several far more distinguished (or expensive) than herself.

It turned out he had spotted some of Gee's paintings in Manhattan, in a SoHo gallery. He'd liked them and had asked about her. They gave him an art magazine with an article about Gee and the college's teaching methods.

"It was very interesting." He grinned at her. "*And* there was a shot of you, and I said to myself, hmmm, *inter-*resting, I guess the camera likes *her*." And here he looked at her quite unnervingly, objectively, as if appraising her for camera angle or lighting. "You're even *more* interesting in the flesh."

Flesh! The word went straight through her body. Her breath stopped. Gee feared she had blushed. Soon after that, she seemed to remember agreeing to be part of the film, if the tests worked out.

They fixed a meeting for the following week. Much of the script would spring from this interview. Somehow she had become part of the team: she would be called an executive producer. And would have a contract to read and sign. Ben would explain when they met how he saw the filming schedule working out.

As he rose to leave, he asked: "Fancy some lunch?"

She did not dare, could not trust herself. And, in spite of another unsettling hand-clasp, she managed to say *No, thank you, too much work.*

"Okay." He waved a cheerful hand. "Next time? I hope you realise we're going to have a *lot* to talk about."

Gee couldn't tell if he was being mischievous, or merely good-humoured. She sat looking at the door for some time, wishing she had run after him.

A MONTH LATER THEY were lovers. Gee spent her days and nights in high tension, a conflict of reckless delight and guilty disbelief. Her body revelled in her womanhood, aroused as never before, and her physical confidence bloomed anew. But inside her skull she was stunned by the shock, the sheer undreamt-of thing she was doing. Every morning she was awoken by her scandalous secret, trembling electrically through her, and would be torn between laughter and alarm.

She lost all faith in her own judgement. One part of her longed to be with Ben all the time; another could still grieve—*like some gormless adolescent*, she berated herself—for dead hopes and dreams. And she had vowed. This was her soft, weak centre. On which Sebastian's manipulations would so easily go to work.

Gee decided early on to tell Sebastian, loathing the way she was sneaking about, telling lies—even if he himself was hardly in a position to complain. And he actually smiled slightly, tolerantly, as she straightforwardly confessed.

"You're free to do as you please," he said. "Just keep it under wraps, right? I can't afford any scandal, thanks. I don't want anyone else knowing about your affair. We continue as before. After all, you *are* still my wife." Gee stared at him. This was extraordinary. Sebastian hadn't even hinted at finding causes or solutions. She could do what she liked, bar leave. And she agreed to his terms.

Affair. Gee would not use that word. It was too trivial, too ephemeral for what she was feeling, and for what she and Ben shared.

Sebastian wasn't curious about who the man might be, beyond his name and his occupation. Perhaps, she thought, he merely wanted to know if there was any risk of their paths crossing.

"Not tired of that fellow yet, then?" Sebastian asked her once, a mocking note in his voice, when she had told him she would not be home one evening. "Or is it a new one?"

CARO WAS THE ONLY OTHER PERSON who knew. Not because Gee broke her promise to Sebastian. Caro worked it out for herself.

"Listen, old pal," she said to Gee over a sandwich one lunchtime. "May as well tell you. After all, it might help. I *do know* what's going on—or at any rate I'm taking a very shrewd guess. Let's say, I know the signs."

She laughed, though kindly, when Gee made a flustered attempt to feign innocence.

"Ha. Caught the first clue when you were looking altogether too bright-eyed after one of your meetings with the filming man. You were just a bit too casual, but dying to talk about him. Then I *really* smelled a rat—in more ways than one—when Seb made some excuse for you when I rang the other evening. Said you were having a production meeting on the documentary. Bit bloody unlikely, thought I. You'd told me you were having one in the morning. He sounded shifty, besides." Caro smiled. "I can tell when a feller's trying to save his own face. And I know enough about tom-cat Seb to realise he must have his own motive for giving you an alibi."

Gee said weakly: "I promised Seb I wouldn't tell anyone." She snorted, faintly. "He doesn't want any scandal."

Caro had hooted. "That's rich! Well, you're *not* telling me. I'm telling *you*—that I'm hoping you've found a life of your own."

Gee said, relieved: "Dammit, I don't see why I *shouldn't* tell you. You're hardly going to hatch a scandal and wreck Seb's reputation are you?"

"Not unless severely provoked."

So Gee told. She needed to say very little to paint the picture, since Caro already knew much about her life with Sebastian. And only she had heard about the photographs. Caro knew too about what she, sometimes exasperatedly, called Gee's over-developed sense of loyalty to the undeserving. And, in the circumstances, she couldn't quite get her head round the way Gee was so tyrannised by her marriage vows.

"But now," she urged Gee, "you've met the right one. Haven't you?"

"I'm crazy about him. I've never felt like this about anyone. And yet. I don't know. I deluded myself over Seb. What if I'm doing the same thing all over again?"

"That way madness lies," Caro said. "And staying stuck in that hole you're in." She smiled, but was serious. "I speak from experience. Sometimes, Gee, it's more cruel to stay than to leave."

ONE EVENING IN A LITTLE BISTRO, Gee told Ben as much and as honestly as she could of her ingrained feelings—hang-ups, she called them—about matrimony, and some of the background to her life with Sebastian. Not all. She would not be entirely disloyal. Besides, she and Sebastian had agreed not to spill any of each other's beans.

To Ben she said: "I want Seb and me to stay friends. To understand each other. I don't want bitterness and quarrelling. I'd like us to part amicably."

Ben listened, his face unreadable.

"I do care about him, you see. It's not as if I *hate* him."

"I must admit," Ben said frankly, "if a wife left me, I wouldn't be that keen on remaining friends. I've never been quite convinced by the amicable divorce." He had put his hand over Gee's, on the table. "But that's just me and my ego. It's okay, sweetie. You've got to do it your own way, in your own time. I know, I've been there. I can wait. *You're* what I've been waiting *for*, for godsakes. You're the best thing that happened to me in my whole goddam life."

Ben told her then more about himself. His unwise marriage when too young, long in the past, that had made him swear never to marry again. His gradual, clumsily-managed withdrawal from it and the slightly wild 'bachelor days' that followed in reaction to it. Other mistakes he'd made. *All the crap and stupidity*, as he put it.

"I can hardly believe now, that that was me back there. So dumb. So immature. It's like looking back at a completely different person. A stranger." He laughed, a little embarrassed. "See the effect you have on me? I never tell *anybody* about my life like that. It isn't something to brag about, is it? All the garbage, that came before you."

LONDON BECAME BEN'S BASE for the duration of the shoot—and beyond. From here he could easily get to most continental capitals as well as to New York. His plan, after the documentary was done, was to set up a European branch of his production company. Not only good economic sense, this would provide every reason to spend long periods with Gee. With this scheme in mind, soon after meeting her, he found and rented a small, decently-furnished flat overlooking the Thames.

In this hideaway he and Gee spent many evenings and every available weekend— as long as Gee was free. She continued to co-operate with Sebastian. She played the dutiful company wife whenever Sebastian wanted. But she refused to entertain, or be entertained by, their personal social circle, beyond what was absolutely unavoidable. The television documentary turned out to be a useful alibi at times, and Sebastian had become adept at lying about her movements. And Gee, indeed, did the same for him. Beyond Caro and Ben himself, none of her friends or family knew about her double life.

Ben went along with the secrecy, avoiding the restaurants or theatres where there was any risk of being spotted by someone who knew either of them. He revealed nothing to his own friends. Sometimes they vanished into the countryside for an anonymous weekend.

In the little flat or out among fields and woods, Gee felt safe. No glancing over her shoulder, no tension or fear. They were free.

They created their own world with its own traditions. Among the best of them were the Sunday breakfasts. Ben had introduced her to the American way of bacon. The smell of grilling rashers would, all her life, conjure up the first of those morning feasts.

Ben, laying strips of streaky side by side on the grill-pan: "The stuff you serve up in this country!" One hand held his wrinkling nose, the other pulled an invisible chain. "Not, of *course*, that I want to be rude about your local customs. But you Brits have *no idea* how to cook bacon. *Jeez*!"

"It's designed to go with the cold toast and hard butter," Gee teased.

He shook his head in horrified wonder.

"This is a serious matter." Wagging a fork, just managing to remain dead-pan. "I bring the one true gospel of bacon to Britain. Without *crisp*iness there can be no salvation! That means a good hot grill. Not a frying pan in sight. Okay? I will now demonstrate how the real thing is done. Take notes!"

"Yes*sir*!" she snorted. They were in their bath-robes after showering, and Gee had thrown her arms round his middle as he worked, glueing himself to his side. She breathed in the cleanliness of his skin, the soap and after-shave, and watched his hands gracefully, meticulously, arranging the rashers. Never, ever, had she felt so physically and mentally at ease with a man.

Ben pretended to shake her off. "Let go. I'm working. Outa my way. Are you doing the eggs, or what?"

"Not yet," she answered, and turned him round for a kiss.

"But on the other hand," he grinned, "you taste so much better than bacon." He reached past her to turn off the grill, and gathered her into his arms. To Gee, his hug would always, in some way, be magical. Breakfast was served at lunchtime.

THE PHYSICAL ELECTRICITY never went away. And they had realised from the time of their second meeting (and first lunch) that their minds and tastes sparked each other off too.

On that occasion Ben, at Gee's prompting, was having a stab at describing how he approached the translation of an idea and a script into film. She was caught up as much in his enthusiasm as his words.

"It's complex, but it has to appear simple," he began. "I'm not sure I can explain. But—for instance—even with documentary film, where you need to get across hard facts," he'd said, "you can convey a hell of a lot without words. Atmosphere, place, history, even a person's character and emotions. It's marvellous, what you can put across *just* visually. It can be in the way you use the light, or colour—or lack of it—or where the camera's eye is in relation to its subject. Some of it happens, I guess, on an unconscious level. You kind of feel your way, wait for things to happen. Happy accidents, almost. But that's just part of it." He smiled ruefully. "Am I making *any* sense?"

"You are." She felt something extraordinary had happened. "You know, it sounds remarkably like painting. At any rate, the way *I* approach painting."

Gee knew then that she was falling in love with him. And intuition told her he was falling for her, even if he didn't yet know it. Through production meetings, a few working lunches, occasional pub drinks, coffee conversations, each time they met they fell a little further. Each waited impatiently for the next encounter. They seldom stopped talking, as if they had been waiting with pent-up bundles of information to exchange, like little stacks of gifts.

But Ben was hesitant: she was married, after all. Gee waited, barely believing what she knew was happening. They began to see each other without waiting for the excuse of business.

Ben introduced her to jazz, something she'd often enjoyed but never particularly examined. He, on the other hand, was a buff, and—from years of visits to London— knew every smoky dive or pub where the best might be found. She got hooked.

Gee introduced him to European fiction. Up until then, he had been a non-fiction man with occasional forays into American literature. It was a revelation. He got hooked.

He discovered, when Gee produced binoculars on a walk through Richmond Park, that she liked to spy on birds. And knew quite a lot about them. At first he teased her: *Look—it's a bird! It's brown!* In fact his innate curiosity was piqued. He bought a pair of binoculars for himself.

They discussed everything they saw, heard and read. And they made each other laugh. Gee told Ben she hadn't laughed so much, so easily, ever. He felt the same. Neither had felt so unwary with the opposite sex. They could say what they thought without preliminary mental editing, confident of being listened to, not judged. With each other, as they put it, they were actually them*selves*.

Their opinions matched on politics; on classical music as well as jazz; on Woody Allen for wit and laughter and Ingmar Bergman for *angst*; on dancing, at which Ben proved to be a natural, self-taught; on Mediterranean people, food and wine; on the superiority of certain malt whiskies; and on the pointlessness of mosquitoes.

This harmony reached its zenith one evening over dinner when they each decided there seemed no point in not admitting they were head-over-heels in love. Afterwards they couldn't remember how the conversation had begun: it was as if they had spoken in the same instant. And they celebrated with a weekend in New York, making love, at last, in a huge, welcoming bed in a hotel beside Central Park.

Showing New York to Gee, Ben rediscovered his own city. They walked, clasping hands, across the Brooklyn Bridge on a bright frosty morning, to eat *pastrami* on rye (Gee's first) in a favourite old deli of Ben's boyhood, beside the East River, with the Manhattan skyline glittering across the water. Kids again, they dared to skate on the ice-rink at the Lincoln Center. Gathering dust and second-hand books, they rummaged through the Village shops of his student days. And they were free.

THEY BOTH KNEW it was a fairytale, a fantasy life, a let's-pretend—a dream.

Gee's double life continued, but now it was even more painful. And every now and then, inevitably, the fragility of their situation would show. Ben had accepted the rule of secrecy, but fundamentally he wanted none of it. Every so often his resentment and frustration would surface.

"How long," he demanded angrily one day, "are you going to keep up this dumb charade?" She had arrived late at the flat: Sebastian had held her up, wanted her to do something. "You tend to his needs, you do his housework, you cook his meals—you play the *wife*. And I'm waiting here wondering what the hell's happened to you and are you okay, and not a goddam word from you." Ben was actually shouting. "And I can't call *you*, can I? *Jesus*."

Gee stood trembling, apologising. Distraught. In fact, she had been too busy hurrying to him to think of calling ahead to explain the delay. She went to the bedroom and wept. Ben stayed coldly away for an hour before he relented, apologised and drew her close to him.

"It's just I want you here," he said, his voice muffled against her hair. "With me. We're *right* together. I know you have to do this your way, but sometimes it gets to me. The secrecy, the hiding."

"I know. It gets to me too." She added: "Though at the beginning you said the secrecy made it all the more exciting. Being illicit." She knew, really, she was clutching at a straw.

"Yeah, well. I don't think that now. It's been well over *two years*, sweetie. I want us out in the open."

"I know," she said again, almost in a whisper. "But I promised, you see. I promised I wouldn't tell anyone."

She just needed, she told herself, to learn how to *un*promise.

ONE DAY SHE GOT TO THE FLAT and he wasn't there. There were some flowers, and on the table a note saying he'd be back in half an hour, he'd gone to buy steaks. The card on the flowers said: *Marry me.*

Gee panicked. He had said he wouldn't pressure her.

"You told me," she said later, cautiously, "you never wanted to get married again."

"I know. But that was before you. Never say never, right?"

She thought: *Why can't we go on as we were?* But she knew that was unfair. And that was Sebastian's way. She also knew she didn't want that either.

Sometimes she felt herself ripped through, down the middle. But always powerless. She knew that what she really wanted was someone—*Sebastian*—to make the decision for her. Avidly, she watched for signs that he might be genuinely, emotionally involved with one of his women. If he were to choose to leave Gee for one of them, the problem would be solved. She and Sebastian might even part without animosity.

She knew it would never happen. Yet she clung to the hope.

SEBASTIAN, TOO, had been hiding his impatience.

One week, Ben was away in New York on business. So, one evening, unusually, Gee came home straight from college. To find that Sebastian, no less unusually, had arrived there before her.

"Well, well! So Georgina is deigning to spend some quality time with her husband. Not seeing your stud tonight?"

He was standing over the drinks table, a large tumbler of whisky in his hand. By the sound of him it wasn't his first. His entire face was tense with hostility.

Ever after, the memory of that scene would punch home to Gee how quickly a life can change.

Gee turned away from him and picked up the portfolio and briefcase she had dumped in the hall.

"Let me know when you're in a better temper."

She heard her cool, not to say frosty, voice; but she felt slightly sick. "And you can tell me what you'd like for dinner."

Gee headed for the stairs and her studio. She stayed there for half an hour. She knew he'd be too proud to call her back. After ten more minutes she went down to the sitting-room again.

"I don't want anything to eat," he said, faintly martyred, as she reappeared. "You don't have to bother preparing anything for *me*. I suppose I should be flattered that you're here at all." His glass had been refilled and his voice had thickened.

"For god*sake*, Seb. It's no bother. Cooking for one, cooking for two, not much difference."

"Plenty of in*difference*, though. Plenty of *that*. So caught up with that fucking American—literally! You barely give me a thought. Oh, you do *practical* things. You shop, you clean, you launder, you iron. You even cook once in a while. But that's not *caring* for someone!"

As if he cared for her.

"What d'you want, Seb?" she asked. "I've obeyed your rules for three years now, nearly. You've had *your* own life. As always. What's this about?"

Sebastian took an enormous mouthful of his drink.

"I think," Gee observed, "you'd *better* have something to eat."

"Oh that's what *you think*, is it?" And now he was yelling. "Well save your stupid thinking for that hanger-on, that fucking bastard. You think he doesn't have other women? Don't kid yourself Georgina."

And then she was shouting back.

"*You* thought it would be all over by now, didn't you? *That's* what this is about. You reckoned it'd all fizzle out in a month or two—like *your* dreary little affairs! No wonder you were so tolerant. Ha. And I thought you were being *fair*, given the way *you'd* behaved."

"At least I don't behave like some bloody schoolgirl, mooning about. At least I'm realistic. I suppose," Sebastian sneered, "you think you've found true *lurve?*" He laughed harshly. "For godsake grow up, Georgina." He downed the rest of his drink as if it were lemonade, then looked straight at her.

"So you're not giving him up, then? Is that it? You won't give him up for *me*?"

"No. I'm not giving him up. I'm not."

Once, she had tried to, once when she feared her riven mind might not stay sane. But the very thought of pushing Ben out of her life had been unbearable. She had fallen ill. Her body refused to do the deed.

"Well, fuck you then," said Sebastian, almost neutrally. "I'm going out. I don't want your smug bloody company. Or your cooking. Frankly."

"Fine," Gee said tightly. Trembling, she walked down the hall towards the kitchen, trying to shift her mind to something harmless, like her own supper. Thank God he *wasn't* staying in. An omelette or a sandwich would be fine for her. She'd watch some mindless thing on television, and have an early night.

It didn't occur to her that he might take the car. She took it for granted he'd call a taxi. Only when the front door slammed, and she realised she hadn't heard him on the phone, did she wonder. But she didn't move to stop him. The car's engine started, the tyres squealed away.

The telephone rang two hours later. Sebastian was in hospital with several broken bones. There was spinal damage: they were doing scans.

He was in a specialist unit for weeks. They mended him as best they could. But for the rest of his life, they explained kindly, gently, Sebastian would be in a wheelchair.

Gee would tell herself: *He did it to himself. He went out of that door bent on punishing me. He wasn't going to kill himself.*

But then: *No. It was my fault. If it hadn't been for me, he wouldn't have been drinking. He would've reacted faster. Wouldn't have hit the bridge. He did it because of what he'd asked and what I'd answered.*

Either way, I'm to blame.

"I can't leave now. How can I?" Gee, weeping, said to Ben.

Unlike Caro, Ben said nothing.

THEIR SECRET LIFE CONTINUED for another two years. In that time they almost never talked about Gee's marriage, or their future. Then Ben's business in Europe was drawing to a close. He needed to be back in his own country.

"Come to New York with me," he said. "Now's your chance."

How she longed to. To *run away*. Yet, at once, she conjured up some ambiguous, equivocal answer. Ever after, she was unable to recall what exactly she had said.

For inside, she still hesitated, suspended by hope for the impossible. Why couldn't Sebastian admit their marriage had failed? Why couldn't he be honest, and say *Okay, we got it wrong, let's split and be civilised about it?* She paralysed herself.

And in the end Ben was defeated.

"I'm sorry," he said wretchedly. "Gee, I love you more than anything. But I've given up hope."

In despair, she was silent.

They agreed that she wouldn't see him off at the airport. It would be too cruel. They said their goodbyes at the flat. Gee walked home in a trance of grief.

LOOKING BACK to the day of his departure, it was clear that she must have been out of her mind. Or an utter fool. Both.

She couldn't stay away from the airport. Keeping her distance, she watched him go, her spirit dying.

She saw him stuff a newspaper into his luggage. Watched his hands and all their familiar movements: graceful hands for such a masculine man. She knew their sensuousness and warm scent. He should have felt the heat of her gaze and turned, should have seen her, should have changed his mind. But no: it was up to her. And she did not cry out—*Ben, Ben, wait, wait*—missed her last chance. He didn't look back. She saw him show his boarding pass and disappear down a blank passageway.

She told Caro: "I watched him, and did bugger all. And now it's as if he had died."

Painter's Block kicked in the same day.

Chapter Twenty Six

How UNFINISHED THE WORLD IS, Gee said to herself. She'd never been so close to the Earth in evolution before, unsteady and unpredictable. The planet was heaving under a thin skin. Here she was, standing on a volcanic fault-line—so the guide-book said, disconcertingly mentioning "unstable mountains". And she had always taken for granted that the Earth was solid beneath her feet.

"What you will do," Mildred had commanded, "is take a break for three or four days. Time you saw more of this remarkable land. Go and empty your head of bad dreams and dilemmas. Head for Rotorua and the boiling mud and steaming pools. Sulphur City! Take my old banger and head for the geysers. Spectacular. Much more interesting than this old geezer—who will be perfectly all right in the care of my good girls and doctor. What you need is a complete change of scene."

"I'm absolutely fine here," Gee protested. But her aunt held up a hand for silence.

"No arguments. I've got a visitors' guide and a good map in my bureau somewhere. There's masses to see, and don't miss the museum either—packed full of Maori history, well worth adding to your education. There's even a place to get a close-up of kiwis. It's the devil's own job to see them in the wild. Believe me, that place will make you think. Grandma McIvor used to say, when she first saw the geysers it made her wonder if Heaven and Hell might be the same place."

THIS ALIEN GROUND was hot, beating through her sandals. The bowels of the Earth, she thought. That's what the stink made you think of: that you were right beside the planet's intestines bubbling and gurgling on a colicky day, ready for evacuation or regurgitation. Heaving mud, streams on the boil, steaming pools, craters, vents, incontinent geysers, volcanoes building up for a belch, a pool signed 'Champagne' bubbling with turquoise and ochre. Each of the places she visited was steaming, pulsating: a world alive and kicking violently, yet within an area serene and breathtaking—the latter quite literally, with this pong. Once past the car parks, highways and shops, separated from the crowd and positioned for the view, you saw, beyond the exquisite colours of the silicate lake-terraces, how the countryside spread on and on, an infinity of mountains, lakes, trees, blooms of exaggerated shape and intensity—and the sky's vastness. She was unnerved, overwhelmed, and a stranger.

Try painting that little lot. Her grandfather Frederick, Grandma McIvor's son-in-law, had done not a bad job of the extraordinary landscapes, judging by the work Gee had seen in both Mildred's and Pamela's houses. His cherished canvasses crowded the walls, mainly landscapes and seascapes and an occasional portrait. He had captured and contrasted lush and barren, ocean and mountain, with some of the most exciting painted skies ever; but as far as she knew he'd never tried to depict this particular boiling, mobile scene. Perhaps too unsettling.

Unfinished world. She and Mildred had talked about how most people viewed life's unfinished business or unrealised dreams with regret and unease. The human craving for things to go right: with a beginning, a middle, an end. Unrealistic, Millie briskly said. Plans get thwarted, relationships spoil. Loose ends usually don't get tied.

"Why is it," Millie had asked, "that it bothers us so much? What's the matter with the odd loose end?"

Staring into simmering mud, Gee felt the same childhood fascination she'd found in a pot of porridge on the stove. Blip, blip, soft craters forming and falling, as if some primeval creature slithered beneath, breathing or farting. How near, our molten centre. Ferociously-heated rocks lay not so very far down, transforming gentle rainwater into steaming surges, actual hazard just under the shell. In this place, there was no escaping the fluidity of our Earth.

She had overheard a tour guide stating, with startling frankness, how many tourists were killed on average each year. Gee forgot the number, but wondered about the spontaneous "natural" explosions casually mentioned. What happened? You got blown up? Tossed in the air, splatted into the molten ground? Scalded to death? Nobody in the group had been brave enough to enquire. In one place she had found a white cross: it marked the spot where four tourists had been blown away in 1903.

Here indeed was chaos amid order: a boiling, belching place set in a tranquil landscape. Chaos and beauty. Chaos and danger. Look at it either way—and no signposts, no beginning, middle and end. Heaven and Hell the same place. It was no surprise, then, to come upon a place that had been dubbed Hell's Gate. An enormous hot waterfall plunged and crashed in wreaths of infernal steam. More heavenly were brilliant gems of peacocks, stepping daintily around smoking vents. Visiting angels. Bizarre.

Finding a shaded bench and sitting to rest her overheated feet, Gee felt for the first time since she had been in New Zealand that Sebastian was truly a vast distance away, not only in miles but in her mind. And that mind was detached at last from her old shores. She might never have lived and worked in London. While seated prosaically, undeniably, upon this bench, she was bodiless, drifting, dreaming. Perhaps the sulphur was addling her brain, like the fumes from smouldering laurel leaves breathed by ancient Delphic priestesses. For a marvellous moment she thought she might rise in a trance and come forth soothsaying, startling the tourists.

STOP OFF ON YOUR WAY BACK from the hot-spots, Pamela had invited. Stay the night. It's ages since we saw you, and Daniel will barbie some lamb.

But within an hour of her arrival, as she and her cousin sat in deck-chairs on Pamela's lawn, Gee saw she had blundered.

"*What* are you getting at?"

In a breath Pamela's tone had cooled to iced steel, freezing her guest. Her arms had folded tightly across her chest as if she would push her own backbone through the chair canvas.

"Um," Gee felt carefully. "I, um, don't know. I suppose that's why I asked."

Pamela did not speak. The evening sun continued to shine upon the exuberance of flower and leaf, but warmth had vanished. Daniel might have jollied things through, but he was elsewhere, laying charcoal and skewering meat.

There was nothing to do but plunge on good-humouredly. "Maybe I put it badly. I just wondered what you knew about their relationship. All *I* know is that my mother told me, and Millie said so too in a letter ages ago, that when my father's first wife wrote to his sisters back here in New Zealand, reporting his wicked sins, Alice was the one sister who was particularly upset, you see. Millie said everyone was shocked to hear he'd run off with some, quote unquote, *floozy*, who'd also had his baby, but your mother took it specially hard. Dad himself once said that he and Alice were close when they were growing up. He used to say very little about his family so I particularly remember it."

Pamela's face had not thawed. Fixing a reasonable smile on her face, Gee went on: "It's just wanting to know more about my father, I guess." Encouragingly, interest appeared subtly in Pamela's watchful eyes. "So I wondered if your mother ever told you any anecdotal stuff."

"If you believe *Auntie Mildred's* gossip, you'll believe anything," Pamela said stonily. "She is a very sweet lady, but she has always dramatised."

"I swear she hasn't gossiped," Gee said cheerfully. "Mind you, I haven't asked her yet." She couldn't resist adding: "*Is* there gossip, then?"

"I didn't say that."

Pamela rose in one tall movement and walked to a flowering bush to snap off dead heads. Watching her strong hands, evidently thorn-proof, Gee waited. In a few minutes Pamela spoke, her back still turned. "I believe my mother and Uncle Frankie did get on well through childhood and their teens, the way some siblings do. Uncle Frankie was the only boy, and I dare say Mother was good company, being a bit of a tomboy. I remember Grandma Jemima saying how when Mother was a girl they were always discouraging her from tree-climbing and fishing with Frankie. Not ladylike. Naturally Auntie Mildred—who to the other two was the baby and far too girlish—felt left out."

"Sounds straightforward enough."

"So she told stories about them, to get them into trouble."

"Oh, I see. What sort of stories?"

Pamela carried her handfuls of garden debris away, tossed them into a corner, and returned. She sat down looking more relaxed. A spot of beheading had apparently soothed her.

"Lord, how would I know? That's all my mother told me. Childish mischief, I s'pose, blaming mishaps on them so they'd get punished. You know how kids are. '*I* didn't break it, *they* did! *They* started it!'"

"Nothing out of the ordinary about that, either."

"So what on earth are you looking for?" Pamela was impatient, but less icy.

"Clues," said Gee, "as to what made my father what he was." She decided to go for a degree of frankness. "In some ways," she said warily, "he was not a nice man." Gee saw a flicker, perhaps of disapproval. "You may think I shouldn't say that. Disloyalty. But it's true, and I'll never learn more by pretending otherwise, will I?"

Pamela nodded, evidently accepting that. "Did you love him?"

"When I was little. Before I knew him better, let's say."

Her cousin sighed and leaned back in her chair, eyes closed. Her face looked suddenly drawn. "And then came disillusionment."

Gee said: "That's the word."

"What about Jo?"

"Difficult to say what she feels. I mean, it's difficult for *her* to say, let alone me."

"Would you say she's confused, then?"

"Maybe."

"I think my mother might've been confused." Pamela's admission took Gee by surprise. "By her own emotions, I mean." Her look was guarded but hostility had gone. "I knew nothing about the Uncle-Frankie-did-bad story until I was grown and married myself. When I was a child, all I was told was how he'd left his boring job in the Wellington bank and romantically gone off to sea in a square-rigged ship. Then he married in England, and was hardly ever in touch. That must have upset my mother. I guess it didn't occur to her that his marriage might've turned out badly and he didn't want to admit to failure. When eventually Mother did talk about the scandal I could feel how dreadful it had been for her. But she couldn't explain why. Things can't always be explained, all neat and tidy, especially when you can't understand your own feelings. My guess is she'd adored him, hero-worshipped him even though he was a year younger than she was, and he'd let down her idea of him. They'd been best friends and he'd done all these immoral things that she would never have believed—and without any word of explanation to her. Naturally she was hurt. That's how I see it. Whatever Auntie Mildred likes to think."

Pamela lay back in her chair, eyes shut again. Gee watched her face; it was relaxed, but somewhere sad.

"Anyway," Pamela added, "I haven't got any anecdotes. That's all I know." She sighed. "You know, the trouble is that nowadays nobody believes in innocent love. People always look for something suspect."

"True," said Gee.

Indeed, Pamela's account was utterly plausible—and for Pamela, the only one. *This*, Gee told herself, *is where you stop.*

"I'm sorry your Dad wasn't altogether a nice man," Pamela said, startling her. "But I'm afraid I can't point you to any causes."

And clearly was going to ask no questions.

"Still," she went on more cheerfully, sitting up and stretching, "not being nice is true of lots of men, isn't it? Except for *that* one over there, of course. He doesn't have a bad bone in his body."

If Pamela hadn't been so clearly aware of her good fortune, she might have sounded smug.

Daniel appeared around the side of the house, wrapped in a striped apron, a pair of barbecue tongs in his hand. "Dinner in an hour, give or take. Who's for a G and T? Or shall I crack open some champers? No, don't get up," he gestured at his wife, "nothing for you to do. Made the salad dressing. You girls continue with your nice chat. Not often you get the chance, eh. Doesn't bear thinking about, all the family stories there must be to tell."

MILDRED DEMANDED, clearly affronted: "Did Pammy think I'd been gossiping to you?"

They were sitting on the verandah, finishing lunch, enjoying the sunshine. Edging warily up to a question she wasn't sure she should ask, Gee had told Millie how Pamela had reacted when Gee asked about her father and Alice.

"Well?" Mildred said. "Did she?"

Gee shrugged. "I said you hadn't. Honest!"

"But I bet she didn't believe it. Cheek!"

Gee grinned at her indignation. "Well? *Is* there any gossip?"

Mildred was silent for some time, looking out at her garden.

She was decisive at last: "There was never any *gossip*."

After another silence, she spoke at a tangent.

"There were some things that Frankie didn't quite *grasp*, if you know what I mean. I remember, one summer day long ago when I was quite little, maybe eleven, Frankie and Daddy were closeted together in the sitting-room, for hours. Daddy was upset afterwards, and I heard him saying to Mother: 'I couldn't make Frank understand the difference between right and wrong.' Mother was looking so worried, and later on I heard Grandma McIvor talking to her, soothing her, saying they were just growing up, it would all pass. But I thought maybe she was playing matters down for Mother's sake, because afterwards Grandma told Daddy she would have a word with Frankie."

"'*They* were just growing up'? Did you know who she meant?"

Mildred looked out at the garden again, and up at the curtain of roses hanging from the top of the verandah.

"Oh dear," she murmured.

"Dear Millie," Gee took her hand. "You've guessed, haven't you, why I asked? You may as well tell me."

Millie said: "I'm going to. Yes, I guessed why you asked. I saw your face when you looked at the photos. It's Jo, isn't it? Oh my dear. I'm so sorry."

She gathered herself. "Well. Now, I think, it'll be a relief for me to tell the tale at last. I've never told. That's what I mean about there being no—that's why there wasn't any—*gossip*."

And so Mildred told.

SHE COULDN'T REMEMBER why she had been on the landing that summer afternoon; perhaps she was fetching something from her room.

"I heard Alice laugh. It sounded as if she was in the bathroom. And the door was open, just a bit. I heard her say: Go *on*, go *on*. Well, I pushed the door, *ever* so slowly, to peek in. I *was* a horrid little spy! I was always trying to eavesdrop on Frankie and Alice because they didn't want me around. Too young and silly, *they* said. I guess they were right! What did I understand of what I saw that day? Bah, nothing. I was barely eleven years old.

"Frankie would have been thirteen, Alice a year older. And there she was, lying in the bath, with her lovely fair hair hanging over the end of the bathtub. I thought: she looks like a mermaid. And I was astonished to see that Alice had real grown-up breasts, and what's more she didn't seem to mind being naked in front of Frankie! As for Frankie——" Millie sighed, "Frankie was on his knees beside the bath, his back to me, and he was wearing just his tennis shorts. Stupidly, I was thinking how peculiar it was that they weren't outdoors in the sunshine. But I was uneasy too. I knew not to make a sound."

Mildred had watched, rigid, as Alice had taken hold of Frankie's hands and drawn them slowly, slowly over her breasts and smiled straight at him, but Mildred couldn't see Frankie's face. Her own body had felt strange, warm and shivery, and Frankie was leaning towards Alice as she took one of his hands and drew it down inside the bath. Mildred thought how strange that was: it must have gone right under the water. Alice was saying softly, 'Come on, Frankie, come on, do it,' at the same time pulling his face to her breast then moving her hand to his shoulder, stroking, then his back, and then round to his front where Mildred couldn't see, and they were both murmuring.

"But I couldn't catch any words, couldn't even tell which voice was which, and then something about it all really frightened me—the sounds and the way they were moving, and I ran away. I ran to the kitchen and my mother.

"Mother said: 'Whatever is it, Millie?' But I didn't say—didn't and couldn't.

"It was years of course before I really understood. But Mother must have found out, if not that day then soon afterwards. I was sure that was why Frankie and Daddy were in the sitting-room for hours. Later, I found Frankie and Alice laughing softly together, like conspirators, turning their backs on me. I heard Frankie say to Alice, 'I told Dad I don't see what's so wrong if you're not doing anyone any harm, and Dad didn't have an answer to *that*, so there you are.' And Alice said: 'Good, that's good. I'll say the same if he asks me, but he won't of course.' And she laughed, bold as brass.

"After that I followed them like a shadow. They turned on me in a fury one day, calling me a stupid brainless baby, and I was so indignant I shouted back at Alice: 'I know what you do, you and Frankie!' A complete lie, and a fat lot of good it did me! Alice hit me, really hard around the head, telling me to keep quiet or they'd knock my silly head *right off*. I completely believed her. But I knew they were still playing their mysterious game. Alice used to take his arm and whisper in his ear, and they would go away and hide.

"Grandma McIvor did speak to Frankie. His face was one big scowl afterwards and he told Alice in a fury that Grandma was a horrible old woman and he hated her. I *suppose* Grandma McIvor was right, and I hope, I imagine, they did grow out of it. But Frankie was always cold towards Grandma McIvor after that, never had a nice thing to say to her or about her."

OK, DAD, I'VE GOT all the poop now on you and Alice.
> A few loose ends tied, for a change. So you may as well come clean, if that's the word. Millie told me.

Pah. Mildred was always making up stories to get attention. Stupid child.
> Millie was hardly old enough to make up stories like *that*, who are you kidding?

I haven't the faintest idea what you're talking about.
> Do let me enlighten you.
> [And here I would give Millie's account, in graphic detail. Somewhere along the way I'd mention that Alice had a very grown-up body at the age of fourteen, and did it remind him of anyone? This would bring on his most pompous voice.]

Have you quite finished?
> Far from it. I imagine you told Grandma McIvor what you told your father—that you didn't see what was so wrong, if nobody was harmed.

And I was right, wasn't I? [Shouting a bit now.] *Who was harmed? For godsake, it was just a game.*
> Ah, the *harm*. That came later. The lines blurred a bit when you clapped your greedy eyes on Jo's beautiful body, so *very* like your more-than-willing sister's. *That* was no game. But we've gone over that before. I just want to tell you that I *get* it now. I don't *forgive* what you did to Jo, but at least I better understand what was done to *you*. But you see, Dad, you should've listened to Grandma McIvor's wise words about growing out of it. That *might* have helped you grasp the difference—between a seductive sister, and a helpless daughter. But no.

She was an infuriating old woman. And oh-so-tolerant. But I could see through her smug little smile.
> Ah. Not... quite... taking you... seriously. Unforgivable.

I've had enough of this nonsense.
> I haven't. I'd like to set the record straight on your grandmother

McIvor. She was not self-righteous and po-faced, the way you invariably presented her to us. She was a quite remarkable woman. Courageous, resourceful and strong.

You know nothing.

Give me a break. I *know* all right. And, you know what else, you really don't deserve such a forebear. And now, something I've been longing to say to you all my life: I don't wish to pursue this matter a moment longer.

"I'VE BEEN MEANING TO ASK," Millie said next morning when they met for breakfast. "What became of James? Speaking of loose ends, as we do. Your father never really did tie them up."

"Didn't Dad tell you *anything?*"

"Barely. Once he was in England we'd get one letter a year, at Christmas, if we were lucky. He did write when James was born, but no details. Well, now we know why! We had no *idea* of the dramas going on. It was Anita who told us what had happened. She *certainly* dished the dirt. This long, furious, rambling letter! All about how Frankie had got some 'floozy' pregnant at the same time as herself, and she'd left him 'to his tart and his bastard daughter'. It was all rather savage, I'm afraid."

"Fairly accurate, though, aside from the 'floozy' and 'tart' bits."

"Mother and I both said there had to be another side to the story. But Alice and Rose were disgusted. I heard Alice crying, for ages. She wrote an angry letter, but Frankie never answered. Too hurt, maybe? Or proud. If Frankie's name ever came up after that her mouth closed like a clam."

"But your mother kept writing, I think? Dad said."

"She did. Until he moved and a letter got returned—and no forwarding address. It was years and *years* before I decided to trace him, through the Salvation Army."

"Ho, I remember their letter coming. First time I knew the Sally Army did anything beyond bash tambourines. And that was when *we*, Jo and I, started writing to you," Gee remembered. "I was about fifteen. It was rather exciting, that you'd tracked us down from the other side of the globe."

Gee and Jo knew, by then, that their parents were not married. They had also known for some time that they had a half-brother. Their parents had been strangely vague about the age-difference between James and Jo, until Jo, hunting for her own birth certificate, found his. She had gone weeping to Miriam. *Three weeks! How could he? How could he?* Miriam had no reply.

Frank hadn't seen his first son for many years. He explained this to his daughters by saying Anita made it unbearable. *She always was unbalanced.* Gee wondered about that; maybe he had unbalanced her.

Always, on his fortnightly paternal visits, there had been a scene. Too often the little boy stood between them, sobbing, afraid, and ignored. Anita screamed, delivering familiar accusations. Frank shouted. One day he stormed out within ten minutes of arriving. Back home, he told Miriam he was never going back. *That damned bitch makes it impossible.* Miriam said: *But what about James?* Frank hadn't answered.

James grew up convinced that it was something he had done that drove his father away. When he asked when Daddy was coming back, Anita said: *You don't need him. He's not a good Daddy.*

Jo and Gee were both married, living in London, before James actually materialised in their lives. Probably he would never have appeared during his father's lifetime, if Anita hadn't died. James felt he should be the one to give the news. His plan had been to deliver the message, tell his father that the funeral arrangements were under control, and vanish into a longed-for peaceful life of his own.

But Frank was persistent. He wanted to meet him. And James must get to know his sisters. Frank sent James a photograph taken at Jo's wedding. A big crowd of grinning people on registry office steps. James was alarmed: the picture made him feel suffocated. But out of politeness, he gave in.

"He found it utterly beyond him to be part of this newly-discovered family," Gee told Millie, "no matter how Mum and Dad tried to welcome him. He didn't really know what family life was like. From what he said, his mother's relationship with him had been pretty unhealthy. I think Anita really was a bit bonkers: violent, obsessive, erratic. And James looked like Dad, too. In her later years Anita was getting confused, and sometimes she'd mistake James for Dad when young. Got all loving and sentimental. *Deeply* embarrassing. Poor James. He had some hilariously awful stories—but really his mother's death had been a release from jail. Then he met us lot *en masse*, including husbands and Jo's kids, and—he admitted years later—he found us noisy and terrifying. So he chose to disappear. Can't say I blamed him."

At least Anita had left him everything: the house, the bank balance, some shares. James sold up, cashed in, and made off to Portugal, where he had many friends and spoke the language.

Frank and Miriam were outraged. They had always felt that Anita had prospered while—*because*—they had made all the sacrifices. In their view, that money belonged to Jo and Gee.

Frank said: *James wouldn't have all that money to fritter away if that woman hadn't fleeced me.*

His words appalled Jo and Gee. They reckoned James had earned it, and it was nobody else's business what he did with it. Their parents never quite got the point.

It had taken James three years of travel and blessed freedom to run out of money, and he returned to London to earn his living. He stayed in touch with his half-sisters, but visited his father's home only when courtesy demanded it.

"Do you like him?"

"Very much. He's interesting, knowledgeable, intelligent, and writes poetry, among other things. But when we first knew him, by his own admission he was a psychological mess. Thirty-five going on seventeen, as he put it. He could be unpredictable—promising to turn up for something, but instead vanishing for a month, and not a word. A sort of stage fright, I think. It took time, but he's more settled nowadays. Found his *niche*—in Brazil. He's with a charity set-up, teaching kids from poor backgrounds. Loves it. He visits London once a year. But he'd never come back to live."

"And meanwhile, Frankie and Miriam got married."

"Mm. Sad thing was, it was too late. All that love—well, it had faded. Been damaged by events. Sam. Jo. What a shame."

"Yes." Millie drew the word out. "So why did they *bother*, d'you think?"

"Oddly enough, I think they wanted to do the *right thing*. Maybe for what *had* been, what they wished it still was. And they were very conventional in some ways, in spite of their situation. He could be so pompous, you know, moralistic. And Mum'd had a strict upbringing, as you might've gathered, from when she got pregnant. *I* think she needed to show her father, before he died, that everything had come out all right: she was an *honest woman* at last. Dad actually used that very expression himself." Gee snorted. "So sensitive."

Millie nodded wryly. "All too often. But neither of them was actually being *honest*, were they? Still, if it made them feel better... And are you still angry with him, Gee?"

"Not any more." And, at last, she meant it. "Finally got him sorted and filed away." After a pause, she added: "I suppose I mostly pity him."

"Yes, poor Frankie. He did manage to get an awful lot *wrong*."

"On the other hand," Gee grinned. "He did go out on a lighter note."

SHE AND JO AND MIRIAM had gone out in a sailing boat on to the Blackwater Estuary in Essex. The boat was a converted fishing smack, gaff-rigged, broad and comfortably scruffy. It belonged to Mike, one of Frank's old sailing pals. He'd been delighted to take them out to scatter Frank's ashes upon the face of the deep.

It seemed appropriate. The two men had had many a companionable time sailing these waters together. Jo and Gee prepared a simple picnic, including a bottle of chilled wine in a cooler-bag. In a plastic Sainsbury's carrier bag, Miriam carried the urn containing her husband's ashes.

It was a beautiful sunny Spring day, and the water was merely ruffled by a perfect breeze for the relaxed, smooth sailing they'd hoped for.

Mike was heading for a spot near an island, where he and Frank used to drop anchor and fish. Once there, he brought the boat about skilfully and emptied the sails. Gee helped him with the anchor, suddenly a little girl again, pulling in the slack, securing it in a cleat.

The urn was brought forth, the lid unscrewed. Miriam invited Mike to do the honours, and pour the ashes on to the water. Careful to choose the lee of his ship, Mike, rather touchingly moved, spoke a few lines of a seafaring poem in honour of his old friend. And then he tipped the urn.

At that moment, the breeze lifted and changed direction, swirling sharply around the boat. A cloud of what had been Frank swept over everyone.

Mike was abjectly apologising, Jo was yelping in dismay and disbelief, frantically brushing at her clothes; Miriam said *Oh my godfathers*, choking on the edge of a laugh. And Gee just had time to lean over and murmur to her mother—"As in life, so in death. Up our noses"—before being shaken by an enormous sneeze.

Chapter Twenty Seven

GEE RAN IN FLAPPING AN ENVELOPE. "Just look what came! Finally, we heard from Internal Affairs. Remember—I sent them details of when your mother died? *They* took their time! Shall I read it to you?" Without waiting for a reply, Gee began.

Dear Madam,
Thank you for your letter providing us with information about your paternal grandmother, Jemima C. Brookes. We sincerely apologise for the delay in replying, which has been due to pressure of work.

In accordance with our proposals, we searched for her Death Certificate in 1929. This was readily found and a copy of her certificate was provided. We enclose a photocopy of this document.

Jemima Brookes (née McIvor), widow of Frederick Brookes, was 79 years old at the time of death, and apart from medical and locative information, the most important genealogical detail was the name of her parents. These were Henry McIvor and *Charlotte Elizabeth* McIvor, formerly Moore. This was of the greatest interest since it suggested that the name given to you of *Margaret Esther* Moore was incorrect and that the person's name was in fact Charlotte Elizabeth Moore.

Given this information we were able, in accordance with your instructions, to return to the General Registration for the Death Certificate of Charlotte Elizabeth Moore with the aim of discovering more about her origins. The certificate states that she was 73 years old when she died on 9 June 1905 and additional information was that she was born in Scotland. This confirmed your own recent findings in family papers, along with your estimated year of her birth as 1831. At death, therefore, she would have been approximately half-way through her seventy-fourth year. Her father's name was Charles Maximilian Moore and her mother was Elizabeth Sarah Moore, née Eddington. A search in the parish registers in Scotland of that time would probably yield further details.

Mildred was sitting open-mouthed. "*Charlotte?*" she gasped. "How can *that* be true? Grandma McIvor?"

"*Charlotte,*" Gee said. "*Charlotte Elizabeth.* Can they be right? You *couldn't* have got your own grandmother's name wrong, could you?"

"I'm not that ga-ga. Margaret Esther, we were told. The only Charlotte I know of was Mother—her middle name. Jemima Charlotte, she was."

"But what about her death certificate?" Gee waved the letter exasperatedly. "How come no-one noticed her real name on it, when she died?"

"Well I certainly never saw it. No reason to. *Presumably* none of her children did either. Doctors and lawyers took care of that sort of thing in those days, didn't they?"

"I suppose," said Gee, with doubt still lingering. "But it must *be* Grandma McIvor, mustn't it? Her parents' names are right. He was Charles Maximilian. And Eddington was definitely the maiden-name of Grandma McIvor's mother. It's in her journal, where she went to her mother's home town."

"And the dates are right. It *must* be her. Who else could it be? Grandma McIvor had no sisters. And, oh my, what about her missing signature? *She* must have torn off the Charlotte. She changed her name!"

Gee did not know whether something had clicked into place, or had become more elusive.

"*Charlotte*. Of all the names. D'you remember, Millie? That was the name Mum had chosen for my twin."

SEBASTIAN LOOKED EXACTLY AS HE HAD before the accident; younger, healthier, undamaged. In dreams, he always did. He was riding a horse, a situation that even her dream-self found astonishing. The clothes suited him in a squirely way: jodhpurs, shiny boots, a tweed jacket. He rode down a green hill directly towards where she sat on a stone wall, holding a sketch-pad and pencil, wearing a cream linen dress bought early in their marriage. He reined in the horse and glared at her.

"That's typical," he declared in a temper, and she knew he was continuing an earlier quarrel, "just sitting there doing nothing useful. As if you didn't know what you ought to do. You promised, Georgina, you *promised*." She woke, her throat thick and painful.

MILDRED SAID: "You'll be going home soon."

"Ten days yet."

"Wish you could stay for Christmas. The pohutukawa trees will be in bloom, all aflame, *such* a red. They're our Christmas trees. Will there be time to finish all the reading?"

"There isn't a lot to go. No proper journals for some reason. There must be at least one more missing, besides the journal the Detestable Miss P. burned. But we've got notebooks, diaries of a sort, dated from after her arrival here. But we want to know what else happened on the ship. And what about her *name?*"

"This might be one answer," Millie offered, holding up the last journal they'd read. "I was re-reading a bit at the end, where she was worrying about Emmie, and I realised there's a good-sized chunk gone at the back. Look, there's an actual gap. Do you think some pages could've fallen out?"

"It looks as if they've been deliberately removed," Gee said, and they both laughed at her Sherlock Holmes tone. "That's weird. Maybe she didn't want anyone to know, ever, the end of the story. Damn. What a disappointment."

She felt oddly hurt, as if a close friend—*Charlotte*—had invited her near and then pushed her away.

Millie said, quite crossly: "As you say. We end up with more questions than when we started."

"Maybe we'll find out more from her notebooks." Gee's hope revived. "It seems she always did need to write down what mattered most."

Millie sighed. "I'm going to miss you, Gee."

And, neither said, they might never see each other again.

Millie rocked her chair. "Why don't *you* write a book about it all?"

"Who, me? You're crazier than I am."

"You can laugh."

Suddenly Gee's eyes zeroed in on tiny, faded, almost invisible words pencilled at the bottom of the final page.

"Hey," she said. "Look at this: '*Henry will keep the secret until the time is right.*'"

"*Henry?*" Millie squeaked. "Well, *that's* a fat lot of use, isn't it?"

What game was this new Grandma Charlotte Elizabeth McIvor playing?

WHILE MILDRED WAS EXERCISING with the physio, Gee took a couple of Grandma McIvor's notebooks at random, along with mail just in from London, and climbed the hills to lie under the pohutukawa trees that she would not see bloom.

A letter from Jo began decisively: "Dear Georgina—*not* Gee". Then a parenthesis: "(I've decided—yes, without consulting you—to go back to calling you Georgina. I've always basically agreed with Daddy—and Sebastian—about nicknames and abbreviations, and Gee *is* a bit childish—you did invent it when you were really little. And *I'd* like to be Josephine again, please.)"

Gee rolled on to her back, sighing. How did Jo do it—make their nicknames so weighty that deciding to drop them deserved the next best thing to a bloody press release? If Jo had just gone and done it, Gee probably wouldn't even have noticed. Wearily, she read on.

> By the time this reaches you, you'll be planning your return. I thought I'd just prepare you for something, before you speak to Mummy. I saw her last weekend—I hadn't been down for about three weeks. On each of my previous visits she's been much the same—forgetful, vague, losing things—but this time she was *really* different. Bright as a button and talking non-stop (wait for it)— about The Man Next Door!! *He* is a widower, ten years younger than Mummy. She met him because she was trying to prune her pear tree, struggling with the stepladder (at *her* age!) and he (I mean, *Doug!* She *could* call him Douglas) popped up across the fence and offered to help. Next thing is she's invited him in for coffee, and *next* he's offering help with all kinds of things—shelves

in the shed, mend a trellis, clean out a gutter, you name it. A proper little handyman, is Doug. In the space of a fortnight, he's done all that *and come in* to put new sealant round the bath and fix a washer. And *she's* cooked dinner for him at least twice, to say 'thank you'. This is all very fine and jolly, but (and I admit I haven't met him yet, he was in Bournemouth visiting his daughter) I can't help feeling uneasy. For one thing the way she goes *on*—all starry-eyed like a teenager, Doug says this and Doug thinks that. She *is* a bit elderly for this sort of thing. I couldn't ask if there'd been anything *between* them, but suppose there has? I can't explain but it feels faintly indecent to me. But actually, that isn't my main concern. I'm afraid he might be after her money. Old ladies get exploited all the time. The thought obviously hasn't crossed *her* mind, because she tells him everything, including how much she expects to get for the old house—*a lot*, and since Daddy left enough for her to buy the new house outright, her expenses are minimal, so she'll have a *whopping* sum to spare. She claims she's taking 'investment advice'—but I wonder who from! She was *very* cagey, clearly thinking it was none of my business. Well, it isn't in one way, but I can't help worrying. Equally, I admit she's in good spirits and 'with it'. But suppose he winkles her money out of her? And what if he's one of those who con old ladies into changing their Wills?

Anyway, I wanted you to know what to expect. I hope that next time I'm down I'll get to meet this Doug. Maybe I'll be reassured—or have my worst fears confirmed!

Won't stay for more. Hope everything's gone well.

Lots of love, Josephine.

P.S. You said you might stay with Caro while you looked for a new place. Is that still on?

P.P.S. Nearly forgot! Sebastian said to tell you he's dismissed your housekeeper and gardener couple, the Parkers, a fortnight ago because he couldn't stand the way Mr Parker whistled in the garden. Said they'd receive a month's pay. Point is, you need to cancel your Standing Order so's they don't get overpaid. Sebastian's made other arrangements for himself.

Other arrangements.

For Christ's sake. *Let him.* If it made him happy. It was his life.

And then, finally, she was sure. *She had really left him.* Not only had she told him so, but she had said so out loud to Millie. And now the waking words she'd spoken to the ghostly Ben, visiting the edge of her dreams, were solid words: *I'm leaving him, I am, I really am.* Not a wobble left. She was free of the tyranny.

And *hoo-bloody-ray* if her mother was getting her leg over. The physical exercise was being a lot more effective than the doctor's pills, obviously.

But Jo? Gee couldn't unlatch her sister's tone, and was left again with a sense that something was eluding her.

"How did you and Jo get on after that?" Millie asked, after listening in unhappy silence to the story of Jo and her father—the story Gee had never told before.

"Unpredictably," answered Gee. "We can be fine one minute, and the next she'll be flying off the handle at me. She might imagine I was getting at her, or being condescending, or taking my fortunate life for granted. Bit of a minefield. So I stayed scared of her, very wary, right through my teens to adulthood. But, don't let me give the impression it's been like that all the time. In many ways we've often been okay, quite harmonious. If it hadn't been for our father, we might have been close friends now."

"I'm so ashamed of my brother. I suppose he's what Jo's rage is about. But why does she get so angry with *you*?"

"We're angry with each other, really. And with ourselves. I was a cowardly witness, wasn't I? I let her down."

"It wasn't the *children's* responsibility to stop him, Gee. You were powerless."

"I know. But that was how it felt. Feels."

"And do her explosions still happen?"

"Sometimes. But our relationship changed once we were both married. Eric's a total bastard. Vicious and violent. I hadn't guessed even half of it till she began to confide in me and ask for advice. She thought I had the answers. Didn't I have the most successful marriage in the world? Naturally, I didn't disabuse her. She would come over, new bruises on her neck or arms, and tell me his latest exploits. Then Jo would be weeping and I'd be comforting. But I was no more than a sort of receptacle. She was—is—confused about the ghastly man. *And*," Gee sighed ruefully, "about the duties of matrimony. Jo would tell me: 'I love him, you see, I must do, even though I'm afraid of him—otherwise why would I stay?'"

"And there were the children," Millie said.

"That's right. And poor Jo deluded herself that she hid everything from them."

It was as if Jo had built a barbed-wire fence round herself, and all Gee could do was stand outside and beckon. Jo was the only one who could cut the wire. At the time Gee hadn't seen the parallels in their lives. Jo would always end up saying she didn't know what she'd do without Gee. *Such a good listener.* Then Jo would feel things were more in perspective.

"What this *really* meant," Gee said, "was that Jo had renewed strength to go back home to Eric and be a wretched wife. Ha. *I* should talk."

"But you and Jo are pretty well okay now?"

"More or less," Gee grinned wryly. "But there'll always be times when we speak different languages."

And here was one of those times. Gee folded Jo's letter and pushed it aside. Jo could wait.

Better by far to pull one of Margaret Esther's notebooks from her bag. No, Charlotte Elizabeth, not Margaret Esther at all. But still her great-grandmother, who had seemed to speak directly into her ear, and come startlingly closer still with her real name. And then had vanished with her secrets.

She opened the notebook, and looked fondly at Grandma McIvor's now familiar writing. Then she realised, with a small shock, that the date of the first entry was the same date as today, 121 years ago.

10th November, 1859.

It is midnight, sleep is impossible. I sit beside my slumbering children's beds. Jemima, eight years old; Duncan, named for Henry's father, seven; Constance, almost five; Mollie, three. So young to be robbed of their loving father.

They brought Henry back from the hunt on a pallet. His head was terribly damaged and bloody, his back broken. He had been thrown upon a rock. In an instant, so they told me, his life left him. His horse died shortly afterwards from a bullet, having fractured two legs. Henry's favourite horse had been a steady beast, yet had shied at something unknown; a simple enough jump had gone awry.

Possibly I had a premonition—or perhaps it was coincidence. One of my 'episodes', rare nowadays, occurred shortly before they brought him. I had been sitting outdoors on a chair near the garden door, watching the children play, making pencil sketches of them. Something happened. The children's voices faded and vanished; they themselves were gone, and their playthings. I was alone; the colour of my dress had altered as had its style and fabric, and now I was perched upon the low stone wall along the side of the garden, facing the steep green hillside, holding my sketchbook and pencil as if I would draw the landscape. Then came a shout: *Mrs McIvor!* Reality returned, the children played. I leapt from my chair and saw the men coming down the hill, I saw the pallet they carried, I ran towards it, calling to the children to stay where they were, dreading but knowing what I would find.

GEE WAS ON HER FEET hurling books and papers in her bag. Gasping for breath before she even started, she ran half-falling down the hill knowing what she would find.

"There was a call for you from Scotland," announced Jean, running downstairs, "I was just coming to find you. A doctor Kennedy. He left an Edinburgh number, it's a hotel, said to call as soon as possible, don't worry about the time difference."

Sebastian had given a terrific talk at the conference, he'd been having a wonderful time, top form, great audience. He'd complained of a bit of indigestion, that was all. He was chatting with friends afterwards and suddenly he cried out, collapsed in his chair. A heart attack. Everything possible was done. There were plenty of doctors on the spot, no delay. They did everything they could.

Gee heard their old friend's controlled distress, and was grateful for his frankness and professional calm. They would all have agreed that he was the obvious one to tell her. The telephone was clutched in her hand as if it were the only thing holding her up. She had no idea how long she was silent. And after she had at last spoken, she had no memory of the words.

Chapter Twenty Eight

EVERYONE SAID she shouldn't feel guilty; it followed, to Gee, that they believed she was. In the front pew, her back turned to her accusers, she waited for the words that signalled the coffin's glide towards the hidden flames.

A woodlouse hurried along the shelf in front of her, sneaking behind the hymn-book, and Gee wondered what it lived on in a crematorium and where it was heading. Her ear tips felt hot and red, all eyes were upon her tensed, sinner's shoulders. Sebastian had predicted it would be like this.

Within three weeks she would hit her forty-ninth birthday. Or it would hit her. Not so old, these days, but she felt ancient, the oldest crone in the world.

"Was there any history of heart trouble?" the once-libidinous neighbour-widow had asked, her brows corrugated with concern. She leaned too close; Gee could feel her body heat and smell her nauseating talcum powder.

Well, there must have been, mustn't there? she didn't say, though the words yearned on the sharp end of her tongue. Your heart doesn't seize up if it hasn't been planning to. You may not know that atherosclerosis is a gradual process. *And it was probably his mother's fault, since you ask, not mine, feeding him out of the frying pan all his childhood.*

"If you mean, did he complain of any symptoms," she had replied coolly, "no, he didn't." But of course what the woman meant, and what everyone was thinking, was that Sebastian had died of a broken heart.

It was her heart that was breaking. Her worst nightmare had crashed through into daytime.

He'd invented the cancer. *Bastard.* She'd known really. Still, she'd made a point of asking their doctor: *Did they find any other problems? Cancer for instance?*

Good god no whatever gave you that idea, he'd said, handing her the post-mortem report. *No disease at all besides the arteries, astonishing he'd had no warning signs—or if he had, knowing your husband, I'd say he probably ignored it, put it down to dyspepsia. Common enough mistake.*

No symptoms, no scans, no tests. All lies. But Sebastian had been right about the death. *I'm doing my best for you, it'll be better if you wait a few months. You'll only feel worse if.* In the past five years there'd been too much drinking, too much rich food for anyone sedentary. *I'm doing my best.* Like a campaign. A suicide. A punishment. All his underlying misery, that was what got her, what pointed the finger. He'd known it would.

He was in there now, in that box, laid out, dead. Unbearable.

The parson droned on about Sebastian's selfless works. Miriam sat on Gee's left, very still, as if concentrating on every word. Jo, on her right, felt curiously apart. There was something about Jo since Gee's return to London. A distance, even when Jo hugged her, weeping, saying *How sorry, how dreadfully sorry.* She had judged Gee guilty.

Oh, she said, *you must feel so terrible.*

Yes, Gee had replied, and Jo had added no comfort.

The murderer.

I do not believe, Grandma McIvor had written, *one fully recovers, ever, from losses such as these. But one cannot, either, stand still.*

But being still, for ever, curled up in a hidden place, was all Gee wanted now.

Millie had said that she'd been told in childhood how, within a year of Henry McIvor's death, Grandma McIvor had hired a farm-manager and started up her own school at the house. The McIvor School for Girls. All her own children attended, for the school included boys below ten years of age. She must have been businesslike, for she drummed up capital and started with just three teachers; the school grew and flourished, with a reputation for enlightenment and high academic standards, paving the way for girls to enter universities. She'd even written her own text books: in one of her later notebooks was a draft of one of a series on New Zealand history, about the Maori land wars that had happened in her own lifetime.

So, despite everything, she had done what she'd wanted to do, inspired by Harriet and Miss MacIntosh—teach, and teach well. *And* achieved her independence. When she retired the school merged with a larger Academy, fully co-educational—and it was still going strong in Auckland. Mildred said: *She did it again. Lifted up her chin and went right on.*

Mildred, putting her gentle arms round Gee on the day she left, said: *You'll do it too, Gee, I know you will.* But Gee's chin was weightier than a boulder.

As THE CROWD GATHERED in the hotel afterwards, Caro handed her a strong drink. It muffled her misery enough for her to perform, forcing her feet from group to group. So many eyes watching her face, waiting. For remorse to show, perhaps. Or simply tears. Impossible to weep here, where it would satisfy. A bosomy fair-haired woman clung to her and sobbed. Gee recognised her from her photograph, although now she was better covered. Perhaps this was an apology? A mad thought came to her to thank the woman for giving Sebastian a good time. Maybe his physiotherapist was here too. Maybe all of them.

Caro came and held her elbow. "Doing all right?" Gee nodded. "Don't let them shit on you, baby. Shout if you need me. I'll be over there tormenting Jo's nasty husband."

A waiter deftly swapped her empty glass for a full one. She swallowed deeply. There was Miriam in an armchair next to Jo's daughter, who had sobbed violently when the coffin had finally rumbled away. She looked calm but sad now, listening to her grandmother. Naturally she'd been fond of Sebastian. *Why not, he'd been a kind uncle.* Everybody had been fond of Sebastian.

Gee was almost knocked from her feet, then, by utter incredulity that she was here at all—wrenched cruelly from a sunny hillside to a drizzly November day, with these people, at a *wake*, and Sebastian now a heap of ashes. There was a scream of strung-out wires inside her head, her skin chilled and sweated. Perhaps she would satisfy everyone by passing out cold, smack on the carpet.

Through the dissipating mist she saw Jo signalling and mouthing: they must speak. *Oh God.* For a moment Gee thought her sister looked insane, manically earnest, her hair sticking up in front. A few gins and tonics must be skidding round the bloodstream. Jo was filled with some information that must burst forth and, recognising the unstoppability, Gee let herself be guided into a corner.

"Georgina, I must tell you," Jo breathed, turning her own back on the room as if afraid someone might read her lips. Trapped, Gee shifted to make more space, but Jo stuck close and urgent, speaking quickly.

"I hope you won't mind me telling you here but you absolutely *have* to be first to know, and tomorrow I tell the kids. I'm leaving Eric. I am, really. And I am so *relieved*. You don't know this but I almost, *almost* left a year ago, but at the last minute I just couldn't, he was crying, lying on the floor in the foetal position—well, *naturally*, he *would* be—screaming he'd kill himself. And I stayed. I think I didn't tell you because I knew, deep down, that you'd say he was manipulating me. Which he was. After all, it was threatening to kill himself that made me give in to his demands in the first place. God, I was so young and at the time I really did think I *had* to get married—but of course I don't regret my children—oh but you know all that."

The avalanche of words had made them both breathless. Gee said: "That's great. Well done." And she was genuinely glad. "Seizing the nettle at last."

Across the room she saw Eric, tall and mesmerised, unreadable, while Caro undulated wickedly under his nose—flirting with him for the satisfaction of seeing a sadist look terrified, as she put it. Gee watched her affectionately. Caro seemed the one safe spot here, the only person to say absolutely the right things after hearing about Sebastian, probably the only one who didn't have the word *Guilty* flick into her mind, even for a second.

When someone dies, Grandma McIvor had written, *people's condolences are frequently couched in stupid and insensitive ways. It is possible that no person truly appreciates how the bereaved feels at such a time, such are the limits of human imagination. Further, most people cannot believe that silence would be preferable to the sound of their opinions and advice.*

The exception was Caro who, understanding at once that Gee would be getting too many telephone calls of dubious helpfulness, had chosen to write.

> I was shocked and grieved, of course, but after that's lessened my feelings are all for you. Oh, this is hard Gee. And yet you know we all choose our own time to go and Seb was a wise enough man. I'm so sorry you have to

go through this now, and it will take time to move back from it and see it clearly. You did too much, never not enough, to make things easier, and have nothing to reproach yourself for. It's the burden and detail of all you have to cope with now that so cracks the spirit. So hold on. Remember too, as you often forget, that it's your life that comes first, it's that life that must be lived. I've said this before, but the past is a tenacious brute—and must be cut back sharply. And you, Gee, are a woman of great perception, so please use that clear and balanced eye on yourself and remember, too, how many of us love you and are thinking of you through this lousy time. Call me when you are ready.

So hold on. Gee took a deep breath and forced her eyes back to Jo, who was saying: "I don't want any drama this time. I'm telling him after I've gone."

"Which is when?"

Jo's eyes wriggled; she whispered, spy-like: "Waiting. For a definite date. To sign. This place I'm buying. Won't say more, superstitious." She leaned towards Gee. "I'll be entitled to half the value of the matrimonial. Got a bridging loan." Now she looked shifty, as if she'd stolen something. Money had always made her nervous. "Fingers crossed."

"Great," Gee said, barely following. "Where——?"

But Jo rushed on. "It's thanks to you, Georgina—*and* Sebastian—that I've managed this. I haven't stopped thinking about you both for weeks—all the things you've ever said to try and help me and all the time you had your own troubles and never said and you must've had very little emotional energy to spare. But then, I wasn't to know, was I? It was your choice not to tell me or anyone." Jo paused for an intake of breath, almost a sniff. "It made me determined to be more objective, the way *you'd* be, d'you see? And I thought—if Gee can leave someone like Sebastian, then *I* can leave fucking Eric!"

Jo gulped at her glass and laughed angrily. Gee had never heard her swear before, let alone put such an epithet on Eric, however apt.

"Oh—I'm sorry!" Jo cried, "I didn't mean— You leaving Sebastian— I didn't mean—"

"It's all right." Except *No, it bloody wasn't.* "Look, I'd better get back to the throng. Do have something to eat, won't you? We'll talk again soon, Jo."

"Josephine."

"Josephine. Anyway—I'm very pleased for you."

"Did I ever tell you——?" Jo held her by the forearm and put her face close, eyes popping, too reminiscent of how Jo had intimidated her as a small child. Gee recoiled involuntarily, bumping into the wall. "When I told Mummy and Daddy I was expecting a baby and Eric and I were getting married, did you know that Daddy put his head in his hands and *wept?*"

For a moment Gee thought she might not be at Sebastian's funeral after all. She had wandered among lunatics. Jo's eyes were shiny with intensity.

"Yes," she replied. "You did tell me. What a bastard."
Not waiting for Jo's reaction, she slid away and headed for Miriam.

"So how's the Painter's Block?" Caro asked.

Sitting with Gee on the floor of the studio amid a disorder of partially-packed boxes, Caro poured champagne.

"Not many glimmers of hope," Gee answered listlessly. "Yeah, I know I was doing a bit in New Zealand—but I was pushing myself. Still, I did start a painting of Millie that might be decent. Sometimes on good days I fancy things stir in my head. But only a titchy bit."

"I'll call that potential good news," Caro said, raising her glass. "Happy Birthday."

"Shit. Do you realise that next year I'll be *fifty?*"

"Big deal. Me too. My next question is, *where* will you paint when you get round to it? Do you intend to sell this house, or just keep farting around for ever?"

"I'm selling. It's on the market. No more farting around. Time to get along. *Where*, I'm not sure. Lost my sense of direction. Only thing certain is I'm taking a quick trip back to New Zealand. For Christmas, to see the pohutukawa trees in flower. Among other things. Millie and I have a puzzle to solve and a painting to finish—and I didn't say a proper goodbye. And then—oh, heaven knows..."

"How would you like to come with me to New York and share my loft?"

"*What?*"

"I've landed this contract—Manhattan theatre group wants a British stage designer, and they picked me. Heaps of gold. Three-year contract. Then they decide whether they still adore me enough to go on. If *I* want to, of course."

"Caro! Fantastic! Why didn't you say? You just let me wallow on, and all the time——"

"I only knew for certain yesterday. Anyway, you needed to wallow, as long as it took. It's only a month since Seb died. But now I see signs of you peeking above the brim."

"Have you really got a loft?"

"I have. Well, it's the theatre group's. I'm getting a bargain rent. Jesus, it's a dream. Space! You'll love it. We can have half each and still have room to swing several tiger-sized cats. I start in March. What d'you say?"

"I really don't know. Knocked me for six. I've got to think."

"Think on. You're a bit wobbly at the knees yet."

"How long do I get to decide?"

"As long as you like. I wouldn't share it with anyone else. If you're not ready by March, it'll wait."

"You know what? I think you're my best friend," Gee said, for the first time in her life.

Chapter Twenty Nine

Warm and wined in the shade of Pamela's verandah, they digested the kind of Christmas lunch that goes better with a cold climate, and gazed up the hill where the pohutukawa trees were aflame with flower.

"Glad you saw them," Mildred said.

On such a verandah as this, dreamed Gee, *somewhere not far from here, Charlotte Elizabeth would also have sat at Christmas. Looking at blazing trees. And being Margaret Esther McIvor.*

"Everything smells so good in this country," she said dozily. "Leaves and flowers and grass and hills and sea, all mixed up."

"Not to mention cattle and sheep," Daniel laughed.

Pamela remembered: "Grandpa Frederick once said that Great-Grandma McIvor told him—when her ship was approaching Australia but was still much too far away to sight land—some passengers claimed they could smell mimosa in bloom and hay in the fields and fruit ripening."

"Marvellous." Mildred said. "D'you think it was a sort of mirage of the nose?"

"Why not? Or there really was pollen on the breeze," Gee said, losing focus, adrift, from long-haul travel and gluttony.

Perhaps, she half-thought, half-saw, it was down such a hill as the one facing them, that Henry McIvor had been carried down on a pallet. And somehow, mysteriously, it was the same hill Sebastian had ridden down, squirely-smart in unlikely riding clothes. As Gee watched, the vivid pohutukawa flowers faded, the air grew cooler, and she was not in her deck-chair but was sitting again on the low wall, wearing the linen dress, pencil ready to sketch. Or it was Charlotte Elizabeth sitting there, or it was both of them. The men shouted, bearing the pallet. He lay there, his head terribly damaged, his clothes and boots covered in blood. And she—they—Gee, Charlotte—were on their feet, running, knowing what they would find.

Henry will keep the secret until the time is right.

Awake in shock, Gee sat up straight in her chair and knew exactly what she was meant to find. "Millie—"

But Millie was snoozing with her own dreams.

An impatient twenty-four hours later, back at Pohutukawa Farm, Gee stood in the Blue Room with Henry McIvor's boots before her on the table, their stuffing of hard-packed newspaper carefully removed. The objects that had been concealed below this unremarkable filling now rested in her hands. Two wax-paper cylindrical parcels tied with kitchen string, and a small cardboard box secured with tape. There was something unreal about them—yet she was as excited as a child on a treasure-hunt, and a giggle rose at the sheer playfulness of Grandma McIvor's choice of hiding-place.

The first parcel contained the rolled, missing chunk of journal; a notebook and some letters were tipped from the second.

Millie said: "What's in the box?"

On its lid was one handwritten word.

"*Merrythought*," Gee read. "What does it mean?"

"Merrythought? That's the old word for a wishbone."

On a neatly folded lawn handkerchief lay the larger portion of a broken wishbone from a sizeable fowl.

"Ah, the pagan wish she described," Millie nodded. "And eventually, what she wanted came about, didn't it?"

"*Merrythought*," said Gee again. What a word for the means of making a wicked wish.

October 1851. New Zealand.

I write this account of our voyage and my arrival in New Zealand several weeks after events.

On the 30th of August, but two days from Melbourne, I awoke before dawn. The severe pitch and fall of the ship, and the too-familiar crash of the sea on the deck above, had disturbed me: yet another storm. Then I heard from Emmie's bed stifled cries of pain, and was at her side in a moment. "It has begun," I heard Emmie whisper. "It is too soon."

Flinging a blanket over my nightgown I ran along the lurching corridor to beat upon the Surgeon's door.

The ferocity of the storm prevented Mr Young from taking Emmie to the hospital quarters; the decks were awash, and besides in bad weather the floor of the lying-in chamber was frequently under-water. He sent for a young stewardess with midwifery experience who had helped him at several accouchements. "And I shall assist," said I, knowing this to be against Ship's Rules, but he did not attempt to dissuade me.

Poor Emmie's travail was prolonged, and no relief was available for her pain. By late afternoon, with little progress apparent, I asked the Surgeon's opinion. He murmured: "It is piteously slow, as often with a first confinement. Do not be anxious." But I sensed his own concern. Still later, during one of the Surgeon's absences to attend other patients, his assistant Jenny—a sensible girl—drew me aside and whispered that the Surgeon might be obliged to deliver with forceps, to save both mother and infant. This indeed proved to be Mr Young's decision upon his return. He drew forth from his Surgeon's Box a frightful set of instruments, saying to me swiftly: "Remain beside your friend and avert your eyes. Do not fear, this is the best possible action for her and her child."

Never shall I forget Emmie's screams during the eternity of that operation. My tears flowed upon her hands as she clutched mine in paroxysms of agony, while I told her over and again that all was well and would soon be ended. And then—I heard the Surgeon say: "There!" and in the same second, a croaking little cry. I turned my head and saw a bloody little body, O so tiny, in Mr Young's hands. "You have a little daughter," he smiled at Emmie, "and she is perfect." He handed the baby to Jenny, that she might clean the mite before placing her in Emmie's arms. As for Emmie herself, she drew a deep breath and smiled at me; and now my tears sprang from happiness and relief.

Evening was well advanced by the time Emmie was in fresh bed-linen and night-gown, holding her little infant to her breast—a beautiful baby despite her bruises, with thick dark hair and the daintiest of fingers, but exhausted and sucking little. Sleep would help her as it would Emmie, and I was not concerned. Only after our late supper, when Emmie was again assailed by pain, was I made sufficiently anxious to go in search of Mr Young.

He was seated in the Saloon, his face drawn, but upon seeing me he immediately rose. "Is anything amiss?"

"I do not know. Her pains have returned intensely."

Mr Young suppressed a yawn, but followed me. After his examination of both mother and infant, he declared all was normal. Some pain was inevitable after lengthy labour and the intrusion of instrumental delivery. He urged us to avail ourselves of a good night's rest—as he himself hoped to do.

Before obeying him I made Emmie promise to call me, at any hour, if she required anything. She smiled, kissed me goodnight, and vowed thus to humour me. I looked upon her darling little slumbering daughter and was reassured.

Moments before I fell asleep, Emmie's voice floated through the darkness: "I shall name my daughter after my own dear mother. But her second name shall be yours, because you are my dearest friend."

Dawn was breaking and the sea was calm when I was woken by the short, urgent cries of the baby. For a few moments I could not imagine what they might be. I lit a lamp and carried it to Emmie's bedside. Drawing near, I was shocked by her pallor and extreme stillness. Not knowing why I did so, but calling her name in dread, I drew back the bedclothes. Her night-gown, the sheets, the blanket—all were gleaming wet and dark. A warm drop fell upon my bare foot: a pool of blood was forming upon the floor.

MR YOUNG'S ANGUISH WAS PLAIN but I was too possessed by grief and anger to feel compassion. Raging, hating, I accused him cruelly. He attempted to explain that tragically, occasionally, a complication may be undetectable, a tiny rupture can enlarge. (*Something broke and all the blood ran out. It was naebody's fault.*) He had been meticulous. Nothing had appeared untoward. I shrieked at him, beyond reason, he had killed her with his terrible instruments, I would report his incompetence to the Authorities. White-faced, he told me soberly that had he not used the forceps both mother *and* child would have died. I refused to listen, screaming through the storm in my head.

Emmie, Emmie! I had lost her twice—and this time with no hope of her return.

W<small>E HAD BEEN SENT OFF-COURSE</small> by the gale, and remained two to three days' sail from Melbourne. The Captain insisted that Emmie's funeral be conducted at sea: arrival time at port was uncertain and the crew was superstitious about a corpse on board. Unable to endure Emmie being sewn into a rough canvas shroud, I persuaded the Captain to allow me to order a more appropriate coffin to be made by the ship's Carpenter.

Having also gained permission to retrieve some possessions from my trunk in the ship's hold, into Emmie's cold hands I tucked the miniature portrait of myself that she had done for my sixteenth birthday, and close by her side I placed two of my journals written at the Academy. In these were my accounts of some of our happiest times together, during the two years before the fever struck Emmie down. Irrational though it was, I wanted my fondest memories of our friendship to go with her. The coffin was then sealed. At daybreak, with only myself, Mr Young, the Captain and Purser present (for I wanted no pious hymn-singers), the Captain conducted a brief, simple ceremony of prayer. The Purser and Surgeon lowered her coffin gently into the sea. Mr Young had requested this method for my sake, in preference to the usual tipping over the rail, and I was grateful. Nevertheless, to see her consigned to the deep was an agony I shall never forget, and, had it not been for her orphaned baby, I would have cast myself in with her.

O<small>UR SHIP DOCKED AT</small> M<small>ELBOURNE</small> on the 4th day of September and most passengers disembarked. The town was singularly unappealing: flat and swampy, with felled trees, temporary buildings, half-finished houses, dirt tracks and widespread dreariness—all reflecting my state of mind. I gazed through and beyond the commotion on ship and shore; time had ceased to exist and nothing was real. I recognised these signs and knew I must beware.

To save myself I concentrated on Emmie's daughter—for who else could care for her? My first task had been to find a wet-nurse, and I was fortunate in Mrs O'Brien—a strong and warm-hearted woman who had produced her sixth child on the voyage, without any difficulty whatsoever, and who was conveniently headed for Auckland where she and her family would reside some months. She was greatly pleased to earn a few shillings to nourish my infant charge, and even offered to adopt her as sister to her brood—a generosity I refused.

The threat gradually passed of my mind spinning loose and wild—and I was surprised one day to find myself in possession of a plan that had been forming without my awareness.

All that remained of beloved Emmie was her child—her little face frowning in new-born perplexity, but in good health despite her harsh beginnings. Behind the crumpled grimaces I saw the prettiness of Emmie, the same delicacy of feature. I saw, also, myself—as an infant whose mother died giving me life; an infant held culpable for that loss. Holding her, I knew I could love no child of my own more than this, and that no-one should be blamed for Emmie's death.

As we sailed from Melbourne I sought out the Surgeon and apologised to him for the disapprobation I had heaped upon him, explaining my distress and near-insanity. He was gracious and understanding. Upon receiving his assurance that everything I told him would be in total confidence, I decided to reveal my plan to him—for his knowledge of officialdom might help to avoid possible pitfalls. Emmie had no family, I told him, and I intended to adopt her daughter as my own and rear her with all the love her true mother would have given.

He tried to dissuade me, citing Society's prejudices against an unmarried woman with child. I explained my intention of taking Emmie's name—untruthfully reminding him that she was a respectable *widow*. (I did not say: I want to *be* Emmie, to be this infant's mother—*and* to cast off *fully* my past miserable life and hateful self. *I* shall have died, Emmie shall live.)

Taken aback, he pointed out: "Your friend's name will be on the ship's Record of Deaths, while your own is on the Passenger List. You will not get past the Immigration Authorities."

"Ah," said I, thankful I had consulted him, "then I shall change my name *after* entry."

He admitted that in law I might call myself what I wished. "But," he added, "what of Mr McIvor, who is handling your late friend's affairs?"

I had not forgotten him, but did not intend to reveal my entire plan. "I shall be explaining matters frankly," I replied.

The Surgeon saw my determination. "Your surname will change little, Moore and Muir being versions of the same."

"I shall keep to Moore—it is marked on so many possessions, including my luggage."

"And Emmie is for Emily? I have not yet checked the Passenger List and completed the record of her demise."

"The list will say Margaret Esther. Emmie was my nickname for her since schooldays. A childish word-play, from her initials. M.E.—Emmie."

"She addressed you as Lottie. Is this another nickname?"

"My full name is Charlotte. Charlotte Elizabeth. I despised Charlotte because I was named for my Papa, Charles, who despised *me* from birth. But since Emmie chose Charlotte as her little daughter's second name, I look upon it more kindly. For myself, I am happy to lose it."

After parting from Mr Young, I hastened to arrange a meeting with an apprehensive Mr Keith McIvor. He had learned of Emmie's demise, and I loathed him anew for having sent no message of sympathy or remorse. It took mere minutes, with *his daughter* Jemima Charlotte in my arms, to 'persuade' him of the wisdom of introducing *me* to his brother Henry McIvor, as if I were the Margaret Esther that he was expecting to meet. This for the sake of the innocent child and with a possible view to marriage were we to find ourselves compatible (unless Henry, having by now received the letter telling him of the pregnancy and its origins, had not already rejected the arrangement). I would not, I assured Mr Keith McIvor, compromise him or distress his wife—unless he refused my wishes or failed to keep them secret. Pale-faced, he agreed.

I could do no more until we arrived in New Zealand, beyond hope that Henry McIvor was possessed of finer qualities than his brother, and found me acceptable as a wife—and *vice versa*. Then Jemima would gain a better 'father' than her own and we would both be protected. Were this ideal not realised, I resolved to make my way in the world by some other means. Whatever happened I would give little Jemima the loving upbringing she deserved.

From that day, in my mind, I *became* Margaret Esther Moore. In a short time Margaret Esther would be my name publicly, to remain so for the rest of my days.

"WELL!" MILLIE KEPT SAYING. "*Well!*" Her eyes were like marbles, threatening to plop right out of her head. "I think I've lost the power of speech."

Did one laugh, or feel a fool? Gee felt as if she had been running at speed—in the wrong direction, and was suddenly lost and out of breath.

"So Grandma McIvor wasn't..." Millie couldn't quite say it.

No more could Gee. She had felt so unlonely in her presence; the gap had been filled.

Millie was definitely babbling: "To think Great Uncle Keith—*he* was our grandfather, and our real Grandma was Emmie, the *real* Margaret Esther. And she never even *reached* New Zealand. Grandpa Henry McIvor wasn't our real Grandpa! And—heavens!—*that* means Mother's brother and sisters were really her *cousins*! And none of us had any idea. No wonder Grandma McIvor hid away her trunk. No *wonder* she hardly mentioned her past."

Wonder was all Gee could do. Could she still allow herself the fantasy of being the woman half-seen on the edge of things, waiting? The explanatory notes Grandma McIvor had written—they were for *somebody's* eyes. Not Jemima's. Clearly she hadn't wanted anyone to know as long as Jemima lived.

"So much for either of us being lucky enough to inherit her good qualities," Gee said. But at least she now knew where she might locate genetic markers to a corrupt, corrupting blindness to others' feelings. Great-grandfather Keith had been a bad lad living far off, as Millie had put it, in the South Island. Banished there, perhaps.

Millie murmured: "To think I never knew my *real* Grandma. Emmie seems to have been so lovely, and she's always been lost and gone. All we know of her are through Charlotte Elizabeth's eyes, the writings, and the little sketches."

Gee offered to do a search if Millie liked, back home. The real Margaret Esther, *née* Muir, was bound to be in some Scottish parish register. But Millie said no, those were only statistics. All Gee might uncover was a cartload of cousins in America.

To Gee, Emmie seemed a phantom. She said: "Charlotte Elizabeth, the Grandma McIvor you knew, feels to me like a far more solid Great-grandma."

"To me too. After all, she was part of my upbringing. I like to think that some of her good qualities rubbed off on me—even if I can't claim any of her genes. And say what you like, the fact is dear Gee that there *is* a link between you and her. How did you put it? Echoes and parallels, or some kind of thread. There are mysteries in this life we'll never solve."

Chapter Thirty

1st December 1851.

Much has happened, more than I can believe, since the September springtime day when, unbelievably, we entered the huge harbour of Auckland after so many turbulent weeks at sea. Standing at the rail and looking down at Jemima's little face, her fine-fingered hands clenching and opening, I was both afraid and excited. Despite grievous loss, I saw that with her birth might have come a kind of rebirth, for myself. Our two new, unknown futures were bound together. But what if my plan failed? What if Henry McIvor rejected me? What, indeed, if he was as offensive as his brother, and I could not possibly contemplate a future with him? My fears rose again, seeing Jemima's helplessness, her life dependent on my decisions. Shock, grief and fatigue had weakened me and I had no confidence in my ability to be the tender loving mother that Emmie would have been.

Reminding myself that I could not turn back, I vowed I *would* not fail her. I must prepare my mind for the lonely path and not depend on one slender hope of support. I must remember what Harriet had said—that this was a new land, with fewer prejudices and established *mores*, greater opportunities for all. And O!—I could not but be affected by the colour and activity that awaited on shore as I watched the tugs draw us past a thick forest of anchored sailing ships, some even larger than our own, in this apparently endless harbour. It was impossible not to feel wonderment at the scene.

The town of Auckland is not large, but that is to be expected for it is very young compared with the cities I have seen in England and Scotland. A seemingly haphazard crowd of low-lying dwellings follow the harbour shoreline and occasionally push inland along some of the dirt roads. As the ship drew nearer, I could see the vivid colours of flowers growing around some of the houses and clambering on to their very rooftops. How foreign and exuberant they seemed to me! Horses and carriages moved briskly to and fro, people walked and ran, carrying baskets and bundles, and as we drew nearer to our mooring-place, voices reached us—calling out from fishing boats and from vendors ashore—and there was a general clatter and hum of early-morning activity. I could not help but feel excited and alarmed at one and the same time.

Once ashore the noise greatly increased, and I was obliged to use all my powers of concentration not to be caught up in the confusion and panic—shouting, pointing, commanding, running. We were directed to a wooden building with a painted sign announcing it as Immigration Depot, and here after a tiresome wait I gave my name as Charlotte Elizabeth Moore for, I trusted, the last time. An official took my signature, questioned me as to my plans, prospects and connections, and (evidently satisfied) provided details of a respectable inn a mere five minutes' walk from the address of Jemima's wet-nurse, Mrs O'Brien.

Farewell, Charlotte Elizabeth, I said inwardly as I walked away from the Immigration officers. Goodbye for ever. Goodbye, Papa who hated her; and Aunt and Uncle who ill-used her. Now I am *Margaret Esther*. With these declarations I was stronger and braver—freer, perhaps—pushing through crowds and clamour, ignoring the blandishments of daguerrotypists who promised "a fine likeness of a fine lady" for a few shillings "to send home to your loved ones". Then I was lifting Jemima from Mrs O'Brien's arms and confirming our arrangements before hurrying to the porter waiting beside the hackney carriages with my trunk and other luggage.

The Olde Englande is a pleasant wood-and-brick inn set among trees: clean, simple and hospitable. Once settled, as agreed I sent a note of my whereabouts to Mr Keith McIvor at his brother's residence.

I waited. Did Henry McIvor still wish to meet Margaret Esther? What story had Keith McIvor told his wife? She must know of Emmie's demise. Very likely, certain of her unquestioning docility and obedient silence, he had revealed that he would now introduce her friend to his brother—one young woman being much like another.

Two days later, at the end of September, Mr Henry McIvor and I were introduced in the public sitting-room of my inn. Mr Keith McIvor immediately absented himself, and this was a relief—as was the discovery that Henry McIvor proved to be far more a gentleman than his brother.

I now transfer to my journal the notes I made of my first impressions.

1. Compassionate, regarding my—Margaret Esther's—plight.

2. Disapproving—of his brother's irresponsibility. (Excellent!)

3. Plain-spoken. His disapproval has not been recently acquired: Mr Keith McIvor's *history* is of philandering. (Unsurprising.)

4. Uncommon: Henry McIvor does not automatically classify a 'wronged female' as immoral and disgraced. (Observing him through Emmie's eyes, I am grateful.)

Impressions of his person: Largely favourable. Taller, broader than brother. Less handsome at initial glance, being more rugged of feature. But this, combined with an awkward, modest demeanour provides more subtle appeal. None of K. McI's insensitivity and arrogance. Rather, gentle courtesy. Robust physical strength, yet diffident glance. Voice: deep and resonant, while Highland inflections invest a softer timbre. Interesting contrast of strength and mildness.

Chief reaction: Moderate Hope. Did not dislike him. Received no impression of adverse opinion of *me*. Am heartened by his suggestion that we meet daily for a week in a nearby respectable tea-room to converse discreetly. After one week, we shall exchange frank opinions as to the future. (He requested that Jemima be present at our second meeting.)

My notes of the ensuing days.

Meeting 2. Henry McIvor did not fear to show how taken he was with Jemima's diminutive charm, saying: "A bonnie wee lass. And not unlike her mother." He could not realise how accurate he was! (Was he pleased to find no resemblance to K. McI.?)

Exchanged accounts of our origins: upbringings exceedingly different. He, raised in poverty, Western Isles, crofter parents. Brothers taught by father to read, with Bible their primer. From 4 until 10 years, village 'dame' school. Henry developed passion for books—continued to educate self when obliged to cease lessons and work land with parents. (Am here much reminded of Harriet.) Perforce, I related my *own* childhood—that of Charlotte Elizabeth Moore (omitting odious details), for it was impossible to invent minutiae of Emmie's background. My earlier life became hers, her recent life mine. H. McI. remained silent on his brother's unfortunate role. For this I respected him, and took pains to counter his possible misgivings, revealing my now *low* regard for K. McI.—and disbelief that I had been so beguiled, having allowed personal sorrows to undermine me. *But* I made no excuses for my folly. He received my abject reflections in what I believe was a kindly silence.

Meeting 3. Despite our different backgrounds we find much to agree upon. Am ever grateful to Harriet for helping me towards a broader, less complacent view of society than might have been mine.

Meeting 4. No small admiration is due Mr Henry McI. At 15, he left home for the mainland of Scotland to seek farming work. By frugal living over a dozen years, he was able to invest as a farmer in N.Z. (I deduce: a determined, courageous man.)

Meeting 5. I cannot continue my deception! Each day I have looked forward with greater pleasure to seeing him. Now—in direct proportion to this pleasure—my conscience grows less easy. How can I dupe so admirable a character? I hold him in esteem and, dare I say, growing affection. I should tell him the truth. I believe he has some regard for me, but cannot tell if it be sufficient for him to want me and Jemima as wife and daughter. I must properly confess *before any proposal be made*, even at risk of his rejection—for Mr Henry McIvor has no tolerance for deceit or dishonesty, nor does he deserve them. Confess I must.

Meeting 6. Confess I did. Tremulously and under his unreadable scrutiny, I revealed my true name, how and why I had spurned it, told of Emmie and the Academy, our mutual loss and rediscovery, *everything*; also how I had threatened his brother with exposure to gain his co-operation, and concluded: "Now you see me as I am: a calculating woman prepared to deceive you for the sake of my adopted daughter, child of the true Margaret Esther. You do not deserve such deceit. I shall not protest if you wish to end our friendship forthwith."

Henry McIvor laughed. Others in the tea-room turned and smiled as he slapped his great hand upon the table and cups leapt in their saucers. He declared that if I wished to name myself Margaret Esther, it was of no import—he had met me as Margaret, and so I *was* Margaret—and laughed at my "callous and clever" treatment of his brother. As I gasped my disbelief, he declared: "Margaret, I say this a day early, but I knew I might come to love you from the moment I first set eyes upon your beauty—not that *that* asset alone makes you the woman I have long awaited. You please me in every respect. If you will not wed me, I shall be forlorn the rest of my days."

Beauty! Had he but seen Emmie! Relief, astonishment and happiness joined with sorrowful memory, and provoked my tears. These at once prompted his cheerful proffering of a kerchief—*and* a further rustle of curiosity throughout the room.

Later I reflected that his response need not have surprised me. Surely he had been gladdened to learn that the woman he had decided he loved had *not* been seduced by the brother whose morals he despised. I vowed then and there that *never* would I cause this good man Henry McIvor the slightest unhappiness.

Meeting 7. I gave Henry McIvor my answer. He had insisted that I delay my reply since my emotions were "a wee bit upset". We are engaged to be married, and shall wed as soon as Jemima is weaned. This means our wedding may be in January, in the summer. I am in a turmoil of emotion! But, though I mourn Emmie, I am happy that she would be satisfied with Mr Henry McIvor as her daughter's Papa, not only from the viewpoint of his excellent character but also for the sake of little Jemima's security.

Henry has described his farm to me and one day soon we shall be taking an excursion there so that I may see my future home. My impression is that he has established himself well upon a good-sized holding, with several hundred sheep. He employs a foreman and half a dozen workers, and two house-servants. Three farmworkers and a housemaid are Maoris, a people, Henry tells me, with a fascinating history and culture and—in his experience—of amiable character.

Most importantly, Henry is to prevail upon his brother to move far away for the sake of Jemima's future; he says his brother needs his financial assistance and will have little choice but to submit. Jemima will be reared as our own, without risk of her ever discovering the truth. I am relieved that we shall set eyes upon *that man* rarely if at all. I prefer to forget his very existence.

4th December 1851.

A cruel blow this day: Harriet has died. I cannot bear nor believe it. My two dearest friends lost, within weeks of each other. Why are the most beloved people taken from me?

A letter came from her sister Jane by way of the Immigration Authorities. At the same time, a package containing many of the letters (alas, unopened and unread) written during and after the voyage. All signed with my old name, for I had yet to write to her of my betrothal and future name and address.

31st December 1851.

I have stumbled through this month, but Henry has guided me. His own parents died, drowned in a fishing-boat on a squally loch when he was but 13, his brother

10. For weeks he was in a despair of grief, and without purpose. At last the good neighbour who had taken the boys in declared brusquely that Henry's duty was to confront life with greater courage. His responsibility was towards both his younger brother and his parents' hopes of his ambitions to better himself. His guardian's harsh admonition shook Henry to his senses and, although his sorrow did not leave him, he saw that he must learn to accept it and to find a way forward.

Both Henry and I have lost much, but he has shown me that we are also blessed with good fortune. We have a child to rear, and neither of us is alone.

7th February 1852.

A few minutes ago, looking from the window above my writing-table, I observed Mr Henry McIvor—*my husband*—dismounting from his horse and leading it towards the stable. To one side of the doorway, one of the stablemen, a Maori named Rangi, rose from his squatting position where he had been busying himself with one of his intricate wood carvings while waiting for Henry's return. Earlier today I myself admired Rangi's exquisitely detailed craftsmanship; his current work is a tiny box covered in a design of whorls and symbols. Henry greeted him, and the young man made to take the horse's reins, but Henry shook his head and indicated that he would first like to see the artifact. I watched him take the carving in his hands and examine it closely. He nodded and smiled, perhaps questioning Rangi about its design. Finally Henry relinquished the object, but then indicated that he would take care of his own horse and proceeded into the stable. Evidently he had given Rangi permission to continue with his art, for the man settled down again and was soon engrossed.

What a good, gentle man dear Henry is. When I look upon him at such moments my heart fills with gratitude and astonishment.

Our wedding took place quietly in mid-January in this beautiful house, Henry's—*our*—farmhouse, set among magnificent hills and within walking distance of the sea. For my wedding-gown, a new ivory muslin dress brought from England served the purpose well, and I carried a posy of white roses from the garden. The local Scottish church minister officiated and our sole witnesses were Mrs O'Brien and her husband, who knew me by my former name.

Upon the advice of the minister, in whom we confided my change of name lest we endanger the legitimacy of our marriage, my true identity was not only spoken aloud at the service, but entered upon the certificate; he suggested that we would be wise to do the same for any future registration certificates. (I had explained to him that I did not welcome changing my name by legal—and therefore public—means.)

"AH," SAID GEE, on reading this out to Mildred. "If the minister was in the know—"

"Then the doctor and the lawyer were probably in on it too. In *cahoots* with Grandma McIvor!"

"Exactly what I was thinking."

"And so, no doubt," Millie smiled faintly, "those confidential gentlemen would take good care to keep things like her death certificate away from her family's prying eyes."

"What about her children's birth certificates, though? Her real name would have been on those."

"Good Lord, when would they ever need to see them? None of them ever had a passport or anything, as far as I know. I'm not sure I've ever clapped eyes on my own, even, though I suppose it must be stuffed away somewhere in this house."

"And what a house full of secrets *that's* turned out to be."

30th April 1852.

Jemima is eight months old. I have no difficulty in regarding her as my own daughter. This is not gainsaid by her being, also, the embodiment of my memories of her beloved Mama, for I feel we are *both* her Mama. I forget that Henry is not her true Papa, such is his affection for her. All these feelings are reinforced by the happiness of my now carrying a new life in my womb, a brother or sister for Jemima.

From time to time I pause in my busy new role as mother and farmer's wife, and consider how completely my life has changed. Never could I have dreamed that I would one day be carrying out the heavy and menial tasks that are now my habit—hauling pails of water and baskets of wood, cleaning windows, scrubbing stone steps and flags, blacking stoves, and many more—and relishing it all! From the outset I determined to convince Henry—lest he have the slightest doubt, given my background as a *gentlewoman*—that I was not one who expected to be waited on by servants, but would be a true farmer's wife, taking a full and active part in the running of our home rather than be content to remain in a supervisory role. In the same way Henry himself works alongside his farm-workers and stablemen. Our lives have no similarity whatsoever to that of the aloof and privileged 'landed gentlemen' of my experience, such as my father and uncle. Of this I am exceedingly proud.

Henry's two house servants thus far have been Grace, a married Yorkshire-woman a few years older than myself and a good-hearted soul, acting as both housekeeper and Cook; the other, Marama, a charming Maori girl of barely thirteen, as general cleaner and maid. These two have been my willing teachers in housecraft. It happens that Grace plans to leave Henry's full employ in a few months, since she expects her first child. She has promised, however, to be available when we need extra help in the kitchen. Therefore I suggested to Henry that my first sensible action must be to learn all I could from her of the culinary arts before she departs, for my sole knowledge to date is some basic, though useful, experience of food-preparation acquired when travelling in steerage. As to our little Marama, she will continue in her general duties but will in addition, when necessary, help me in caring for Jemima and my expected new baby.

From Grace and Marama, I have I learned: how to launder, starch and iron; to polish a floor; to beat a rug efficiently; to burnish a pan until it is like a mirror; and even to make scouring powder and household soap. O, and other tasks beyond number! Thanks to Grace in particular I can now bake bread, boil puddings, and make pastry; I can skin a rabbit and pluck a fowl and butcher a lamb—and, indeed, cook them properly, whether by roasting, baking or stewing. I know how to select the best fruit and vegetables, how to tell if an egg be good or bad, and how to avoid curdling a sauce. All this brings me a happy satisfaction: we live, it seems, closer to the earth here, closer to the seasons and nature's many faces.

Nature, indeed, has in this land presented me with sheer wonder, beauty and wildness—well beyond my imagination. What contrast with the bleaker or more formal aspects of my surroundings in Scotland and England! In this land there is space beyond anything I could have expected, and a freedom to roam and explore that could never have been countenanced as part of ladylike behaviour in my former life. Henry is teaching me to ride a horse, and although he urges me to go gently because of my condition, I am now sufficiently competent to ride out on my own. In this country, it is acceptable for a woman to ride astride—a far more practical and comfortable method than the side-saddle fashion demanded in my more genteel past! Harriet was right, there is greater tolerance and less snobbery, pretentiousness and prudishness in society here, and it is not deemed shocking if women show an independent spirit or engage in serious conversation with either sex. For the first time in my life, I feel *free*.

Little by little I am learning about the glorious flowers and trees that grow here. On occasion I feel I have been transported to Eden. Near to us are herbal fields, covered by a mass of different flowers through the whole of summer. (It is still a little strange, to be encountering summer at the 'wrong' end of the year.) I often wander there and marvel, relishing the fresh and perfumed air and intoxicated by colour. Less than an hour's ride away is luxuriant forest-land where Henry has taken me to see trees I could never have imagined and, all about and in between, lush, giant ferns. There is a tree called 'rimu' that utterly amazed me, for it grows as high as 150 feet! Different species of palm, of great beauty, grow here also. Another tree impressed me greatly—its name being 'totara' if I remember aright— which Henry told me lives for 1000 years or more! Traditionally, its wood has been the Maori choice when carving their remarkable war canoes. However, in the farm's immediate vicinity is the most 'English-seeming' tree I have encountered: an old friend, the beech, although in this land it exists as several different kinds. Contrasting with it and covering many of our hillsides is the exotic, exquisite pohutukawa. These glorious trees presented an astonishing display of vibrant red flowers during December. On occasion, I feel my breath snatched away by wonder at my surroundings.

Many of the trees in the forests and on the farmland hold an additional attraction: they are hosts to flocks of feeding birds. Some shine like jewels, with vividly flashing blue and green wings, while others have bright yellow heads like bursts of sunshine; there are many more of all sizes and colour and voice, and I know none of their names as yet—save the easiest name of all, the black robin, a most appealing little bright-eyed bird. I asked Henry, one day in the forest, whether I would see kiwis, the country's most famous bird. He smiled and said: "You may do so, either in the forest or at the farm, but it would entail sitting up through the hours of darkness and moving not one muscle, for they are nocturnal creatures and—wisely—wary of mankind." Perhaps, I said to myself, we shall do it sometime.

It seems that almost all the flora and fauna possess Maori names, many of which I can barely pronounce. I have *much* to learn—but learn I shall. (I am collecting names in a notebook and am determined to master at least the rudiments of the Maori language: young Marama, plainly an intelligent child, has promised that she will help me.)

In the midst of all this newness and discovery, I frequently consider my love for my husband. It is a solid yet living entity: like one of the sturdy trees, perhaps, constantly sprouting new growth and deepening its roots. Mine is not that passion which can be close to madness; our profound affinity has certainly grown from attraction, but also from friendship, affection, respect and esteem. My husband professes to find beauty in me, and for my part I consider him to be most prepossessing. Our married proximity brings me pleasure and comfort; how fortunate I am to have been led to a husband whose kindness and consideration have healed the scars of my memories.

Sometimes, lying beside him in our marriage bed while he sleeps, I watch his face, strong and benign, and ponder that Emmie was sacrificed for my contentment, and I wonder: Why should *I* be advantaged by her suffering? I know not whether to believe in Fate, or in mere Chance. From whichever viewpoint I regard it, even were I to allow the possibility of a Deity, there appears to be scant justice involved.

"I'VE LOOKED AT THE LETTERS she hid," Mildred reported. "They're from solicitors in Scotland—dated 1875, Grandma McIvor would've been in her forties—and copies of her replies. What's fascinating is that they confirm the whispers I remember from childhood, and they certainly say a lot about her character. Evidently her Aunt Clarissa had died, wicked Uncle Sir John having expired a while before, *and* it seems the boy must've died young too, as they refer to Grandma McIvor as Lady Talbot's sole heir. Well, guess what! Aunt Clarissa had left *virtually all her estate* to Grandma McIvor. No actual sums are mentioned but the word 'substantial' comes up a few times. And bless me, she wrote back turning the whole lot down! She said she'd brought up her family to have different values from those of her late Uncle and Aunt and wanted no part of their wealth. Bless my cotton socks! Just think. We could all have been filthy rich lolling on velvet cushions in a castle in Edinburgh, if Grandma McIvor hadn't been so principled."

Gee laughed. "Think of the draughts! The heating bills! I'm just grateful for her strength of character."

"Daddy used to joke that she was the strongest woman he ever met, and it was an enormous relief when she approved of him."

"Speaking of *that*," Gee said, "you'll like this bit I found in a notebook this morning. Grandma McIvor wrote it on the eve of your parents' wedding. Listen."

> My beloved Jemima will marry her artist Frederick tomorrow and I believe she will be happy. He is a good man and clearly loves her. I doubt if they will ever be well-to-do, but neither is troubled by this. If only Emmie could have seen her baby grown to a lovely young woman so like herself in appearance and good nature, and if only Henry could have been here to give away as graceful bride the child he so cherished.
>
> I have loved Jemima best of all my children. Like so many things, this I can admit only to my private pages. The strength of my bond with Emmie was such that my love for Jemima transcended the ties of blood. I wished to appear equally-loving towards all my children, therefore Jemima may never have realised the depth of my feeling. I hope some instinct informed her, despite my strictness as she approached womanhood—strictness born of fear lest she had inherited waywardness from that other quarter. Foolish fears! Dearest Jemima, my daughter, Emmie's daughter. May she and her artist enjoy a happy, fruitful marriage.

Millie smiled. "*Waywardness?* My mother? Not a chance."

Gee turned the page and felt a pang at the stern opening words.

> Marriage vows should not be taken lightly—by male or female. I acknowledge that I was prepared, for Jemima's sake, to marry for security. I was fortunate in Henry, with whom I found respect and love, but can I be sure I would have kept my vows in a merely convenient marriage? I have known the force of unwise passion, and therefore whenever I have heard of infidelity in others, I cannot condemn—for although I believe in duty and even sacrifice in marriage, especially where children might be affected, I observe that each marriage is different. Many are entered honestly but mistakenly. The human being is many-faceted and mysterious, confused by self-delusion and buried longings; these cannot always—and, perhaps, *should* not always—be resisted.

"Goodness," said Millie, "She was ahead of her time."

Gee thought: *Thank you, Charlotte Elizabeth.*

ON GEE'S LAST EVENING, Millie said: "I'm so happy you came back. It was a proper ending. Life doesn't supply too many of those, as you've said."

"I'm going to miss you, Millie," said Gee, with a smile. "Haven't we had this conversation before?"

"Don't miss me. We did what we wanted to do. It's been important—though don't ask *me* to explain quite why. And didn't somebody once say that endings are also beginnings? I'm sure they didn't put it as cornily as that."

"'To make an end is to make a beginning,'" Gee provided. "That one? It was T.S. Eliot, but it might just as well have been Grandma McIvor."

Chapter Thirty One

OUT OF SUMMER INTO WINTER. A grey start to this year. Dreary sodden London. In New York it would be shining, crisp, the buildings like diamonds. Gee weighed possibilities, driving towards the western suburbs and the motorway to Dorset, scowling through the misted windscreen. Often now she felt sick of London, a city of ill-lit corners where lurked memories of grief, or guilt.

Perhaps, she told herself, the clouds would lift in the West Country. But they persisted the entire way, and by the time she reached the old Dorset by-roads she was grumbling aloud at the ceaseless rain, wishing she hadn't embarked on this disagreeable journey. If Jo hadn't been so adamant that no other day would do, she would have put this visit to her mother off, for a brighter day. And how stupid, not to ask why Jo had wanted to meet her *here* in particular.

Her tyres squelched on the verge as she swung the car bad-temperedly into their old lane; gardens cowered behind their hedges, dripping gloomily.

THE GLARING STICKER was visible fifty yards away, startling her. Yet she should have expected it. Her mother had said before Christmas, good offer at last, just under the asking price despite the back roof. Nothing more had been said; Gee assumed a hitch. But SOLD, it shouted, in fluorescent red. Other people's hopes and dreams were moving in, and all who'd gone before would become ghosts.

So that was Jo's plan—that they say fond farewells to their childhood home. *Oh god*, she thought. *Some ghastly kitsch nostalgic ceremony.*

But that wouldn't account entirely for Jo's most recent letter. Jo surely didn't need this setting for the "Important matters of Destiny" that "absolutely must be discussed with you, Georgina." And furthermore, "Significant Dreams might be Shared". Gee had felt slightly rattled. But, what the hell, Jo had probably just read a new self-help book or visited a clairvoyant and was itching to spread her new-found understanding. Besides, her final sentence had been straightforward enough: "I hear you're visiting Mummy next Monday, but before you go there please meet me at our old house at noon. This day is the very best for me, so please don't say no."

Stopping outside the gate, she realised Jo hadn't said where exactly they were to meet. Now that somebody else owned the place, they could hardly wander around as if they still had rights. The new people might've moved in. But there was Jo's car tucked in by the side hedge. She must be in the garden, and with any luck she had an umbrella. Yanking her coat belt tighter Gee pushed open the gate. It wore new black paint and no longer squeaked. No sign of Jo. Hovering, Gee was struck by the sheen of the front door, more new paint. Window-frames and sills too. Big improvement. Maybe somebody nice was going to cherish the old place.

"I'm indoors!" Jo's voice startled Gee from above her head. The window of their parents' old bedroom was part-open. A small wave of lace frothed outwards.

"Where are you?" she called.

"Come on in," answered Jo, disembodied. "You're invited! It's all right—really."

Had the new owners asked her in, invited them both? Guest or intruder, Gee turned the door-knob and stepped out of the rain. A draught snatched and slammed the door. She whispered, "Ooh, sorry!" to nobody.

The hall had new rugs on a polished floor, a small table orderly and gleaming. The sitting-room door stood open: black magic-marker words on packing cases. Gee stared at the thick black letters in disbelief. *Jo's writing.* Her skin froze and her heart began to bang behind her ribs as if she'd been running. It couldn't be true. It mustn't be true. But it bloody well was, and she should have known. Why on earth had her mother not told her?

Gee hurled herself up the stairs.

At the landing she paused, taking deep breaths, getting under control. Then she walked, slow and careful as a burglar, tiptoeing over new carpet towards the master bedroom, to be jolted to a halt outside the partly-open door.

This was where she had stood, outside her parents' bedroom, frozen by the reflection in her mother's dressing-table mirrors. Her father lying on the bed, careless of the neat quilt, fully-dressed, smoking, smiling. *Don't be silly, fuss about nothing, it was like stroking a kitten.*

Her mother leaning there, looking so old and only thirty-something.

The dressing-table looked the same, and in its mirrors was a bed identical to their parents' old-fashioned, dark oak bedstead. But it was Jo who lay there now, crushing the covers, ankles crossed, her smile dreaming at the ceiling, her light curls against the deeper gold of the duvet. Lace in the windows, a vase of yellow flowers, the ones Miriam used to buy.

He never bought me flowers, Miriam said, *waste of money.*

Gee shoved the door fully open. "*You* bloody bought the place!" she shouted.

Jo sat up slowly and swung her legs over the edge of the bed. For a second or two they stared at each other. Jo's smile was victorious.

"Yes," she said. "I did. *And* I organised it all by my*self*. From deciding to leave Eric right through to the painters and decorators. Proving I could manage every detail without consulting you *at all*. Oh I know I said *you'd* inspired me to go. But I was exaggerating. You were upset. But I didn't need you. *And* I am very proud of myself."

Gee had no reply, fixed there on the threshold. Jo looked young, even girlish, in a full-skirted blue wool dress and matching Alice-band. Sweet Little Alice Blue Gown.

Smiling still, Jo stroked the duvet. The smile did not hide her enmity. "It's *their* bed, you know. Mummy's and Daddy's. Mummy had found a man who bought practically the whole houseful, and he still hadn't sold lots of things. People don't buy this sort of bed any more, he said. Got the wardrobe and dressing-table too. Lovely, aren't they?"

Jo stood languidly and strolled to the window to pull down the sash. "There's something I have to tell you. Do sit down."

"In here? Can't we go downstairs?"

"No. We can't." Jo returned to the bed and sat there. The hostile words were gently delivered. "*I'm* in charge here now. *You* will take the back seat for once. Yes, Georgina. It is *your* turn to kneel to *me*."

Do as you are told, Gee said to herself. *Do not provoke*. Thrusting her hands into her pockets to conceal their trembling, she chose the seat nearest the door, a hideous brocade-covered bedroom chair, pink and green, but did not remove her coat.

Jo lay down again. As if on a psychiatrist's couch, she gazed upwards and not at Gee. "I wish to tell you this," she said almost formally, "for reasons of frankness and honesty. When I visited Sebastian, the evening I cooked dinner, while you were visiting Mummy, we made love."

Gee had known, really. Hadn't wanted to know.

"And while you were away, we did so again. Often. Sebastian said he had always wanted to, he'd always loved me, and now he felt free to say. He wanted to be with me for always, and he said he was happier with me than he'd been in his entire life."

Why don't you just stick a knife in me and turn it? Gee didn't say.

"Actually, a few years ago at one of your parties, I did *sort* of realise he might have strong feelings for me. We were dancing on the patio, and I suddenly realised he had a hard on."

Gee gaped. Jo never said things like that. She'd labelled Gee crude for far less.

"Then later he tried to kiss me, in the hall by the kitchen. Anyone could have seen!" Jo actually giggled. "I thought he was tiddly and made a joke of it. But I have learned that he was sincere. You see Georgina, he stayed with you out of duty, but really he wanted to be with me."

Her sigh was deep and satisfied. Gee fought an urge to walk across and slap her sister's sunny face.

"I want to thank you," Jo surprised her softly, "for leaving him, for giving us the freedom to realise our feelings. Fate gave us only a short time, but you would want to know that he died happy."

She continued to address the ceiling. "Our plan was to live together. Marriage itself wasn't important—besides, we thought the law wouldn't allow it. Brother-and-sister-in-law. Well, not unless you were *dead*." She laughed softly, hugging a secret joke. "Sebastian was so helpful over this house. Got me a bridging loan at a *really* good rate, and was *extremely* generous all round."

Jo's eyes flicked briefly to and from Gee, like a snake's tongue.

"So *that's* what finally pushed you to leave Eric," Gee said, unable to hide her contempt entirely.

Jo's voice developed an aggressive edge. "It usually takes a catalyst, doesn't it? Sebastian was *my* catalyst."

"Yeah, mine too," Gee said.

"No need to be sarcastic, Georgina. You can be quite a bitch."

"I suppose *you* were living in the basement after he fired the Parkers," it dawned on Gee. "*You* were Seb's 'other arrangements'."

Jo ignored this, but now turned her head to look directly at Gee. "I loved Sebastian *deeply* and was *devastated* by his death. I still am. I shall never, *ever* get over him." Her voice shook. "And you! You're not just a bitch. You're a hypocrite. Sebastian told me about *your* lover. *Benjamin.* You left plenty out, didn't you, that day at lunch? Fucking off to New Zealand to see old auntie, 'got to think things out', but you couldn't come right out and say you were *leaving* him, never coming back, not a word about the *other man* you were running off with. Ha! You were quick to tell me about Sebastian's physiotherapist and your dirty painting, which I learned was a *gross* exaggeration, but nothing about *you*. Why not? I'm your sister, aren't I? You have a very deceitful nature, Georgina. You made out that everything was Sebastian's fault, but *you* were unfaithful. *You.* And Sebastian was so good and patient, covering up for you."

Gee could have laughed or screamed or punched her. Or could have dished the real dirt on Sebastian, photos and all. But something about Jo lying on their parents' bed, her blue skirts spread around her, told Gee not to. Besides, she didn't know what to believe. Had Sebastian really wanted to spend the rest of his days with Jo? It would make her a first out of all the extra-marital women. But if he believed Gee wouldn't come back, or really had sensed his own death approaching, maybe. She could believe he'd fancied Jo for years. Would they have lived in this house, sleeping in the parental bed? It was too bizarre.

But Jo was right in guessing Gee would be glad if Seb had died happy: it lifted some of the guilt.

"IT IS MY BELIEF," Jo said, mildly conversational again, "that Sebastian was a reincarnation of *Saint* Sebastian."

Are you mad? Gee managed to stop herself screeching, but her stomach lurched.

"The martyr," Jo was saying. "Suffering the slings and arrows of this life, sorely wounded. Sebastian had a quality that I can only call... otherness. Even *holiness*."

"Holiness." Gee squashed hysterical laughter.

"*Yes*, Georgina. Holiness. It's a pity you couldn't have perceived it, and made that into a painting, instead of your actual filth."

Gee snorted: "Does the world *need* another Saint Sebastian painting? I reckon he's been done to death. So to speak." She laughed rudely.

Jo seemed not to have heard. "I've learned a lot about reincarnation. Sebastian and I knew each other in previous lives. And I was one of Christ's disciples when *you* were a Roman soldier. Persecuting me, of course."

"Really. How did you discover that?"

Leaving her ugly chair, Gee walked the length of the room to the end window, as far from Jo as she could get. The bedroom stretched the full depth of the house, overlooking both front and rear. Gee had always liked this vantage point, where you could see each section of the garden, especially in leafless months: flower-beds, lawn, paddock, shrubs, orchard, poplars and meadows beyond. The wintry fruit trees, planted in her childhood, now leaned knobbily, maturely towards each other. And it all belonged to Jo.

"These are things one *knows*," Jo answered impatiently, "if one is given the gift of knowing—of sight—and one is helped by the right guides."

"Did you mention to Sebastian that he used to be a halo-wearing saint?"

"Please don't be flippant, Georgina. I have come to understand these things more clearly since he died. Often *he* guides me. Had he lived he would certainly have understood."

"Yeah, right." More likely would have sent for the white coats.

"I have been a little Chinese girl with bound feet. And an Egyptian princess, wed to my brother prince. And *you* were always my cruel and murderous enemy."

"I see." Gee looked out at the heavy cloud hanging above the poplars. Still raining. A breeze tossed the overgrown privet.

Behind her Jo said: "Another thing I realised. About Destiny. *You* would not have been born in *this* life had it not been for me. Your very existence depended on *me*."

Gee didn't turn. She felt slightly sick. And something was different in the garden.

"How come? You advised Mum and Dad from the cradle?"

"My birth *paved the way* for yours. I don't suppose you understand."

"Er, no. I don't, actually."

"They wanted *me*, and as a *direct result*, they wanted you and then Sam."

"Crap," Gee snapped, turning at last. Jo was sitting up in the centre of the bed staring intensely beyond her. Gee went on: "We were *all* total accidents. You're hardly suggesting that Dad *wanted* Mum to get pregnant at the same time as his wife?"

"Unconsciously, oh yes." Calm and sure.

"They went into the woods and had it off, simple as that." A little brutality might shake Jo. "Couldn't wait. That's what it was about. Oh, they *were* mad about each other. Call it love if you like. But the last thing they wanted was a *baby*."

Jo sneered: "You know *everything*, don't you?"

"I do know—*you* know too, for godsake—that Dad suggested half a bottle of gin and a hot bath when Mum told him she was pregnant. Hardly sounds like he was longing for your arrival. *Or* for mine. His idea that time was a metal coat-hanger, sterilised of course. He was prepared to do the bloody deed himself."

"*I* don't remember anything about gin."

"Oh, Jesus."

Jo began to shout: "You're making it all up. *Coat*-hanger! Typical. Anything to make Daddy look bad. You went to New Zealand to find some dirt, didn't you? And did you find any? Ha. I *bet* you didn't. Nor anything worthwhile about that old granny whatsit either. And most of all I bet you didn't find out anything about your*self*."

Gee briefly considered telling what she had found out. But Jo's expression, the tremors crossing her flushed face, stopped her. This was not one of Jo's routine explosions. What did one do?

She turned back to the window again, hearing her own shaky breathing.

"There—*see!*" Jo cried. "You haven't got an answer, *have* you?"

"Not really."

Behind her, Jo sighed; springs twanged as she flopped back on to the bed.

Gee thought: *I'd better leave. I'd better phone her doctor.*

But something about the garden held her gaze. Her painter's eye: the light was altered. Something missing. A gap where there had been no gap. Peering obliquely she saw a heap of branches, a vast mess of twiggy garden refuse. Soil, a huge uprooting.

"My tree! What's happened to my sycamore?"

A soft laugh from Jo. "*Your* tree?"

"What have you done to it?"

"Obviously, I had it cut down. *Chopped up.* Dug out. It was too near to the windows. It hit the panes and made the house too dark."

The pale springtime leaves opening sunnily at the windows, its autumn keys rattling before they were whirled away. Gee felt tears fill her eyes for the first time in weeks, at this new death.

"Oh, Jo."

"*Josephine*, if you please. I never liked it, frankly. *Your* tree. Honestly! Nor the way you used to scurry away and skulk in it and do your stupid secret drawings."

Gee turned her back on the garden and leaned against the sill, feeling out of place, out of time, in one of her odd limbos. The soles of Jo's stockinged feet faced her. She could see the curve of her stomach and breasts, the bulges of chin and cheeks that meant Jo was smiling. She could kill her. Right now. Easily. Pick up that poker by the fireplace and go over and hit Jo until she was dead.

Jo leaned up on one elbow and stared at her. "You'd like to kill me," she said. She sat up straight, clenching her fists passionately. "*Just* as you wanted to kill me before—when I was an apostle and when I was a little Chinese girl."

She sprang off the bed and ran a few steps towards Gee, awkwardly, as if her own speed had knocked her off-balance; and stopped, swaying like a toddler, fists up. Gee walked carefully past her.

"Mum's expecting me for lunch in twenty minutes," she lied. "I'd better go now. I guess you've said all you wanted to say."

Shakily she bent to pick up her shoulder bag, dropped beside the chair. But before she could straighten, her back was assaulted by blows, ferocious fist-hammers, and Jo was screaming, yelling: "How would *you* know what I want to say? Bloody know-all! You're trying to kill me *again*, trying to *kill* me, like you killed your twin, *and* Sebastian!"

Gee twisted away. Jo's screams became sobs. She staggered to the bed and fell on it, putting her hands over her face. For a few minutes she wept quietly. Gee stood still: she could offer no comfort. Quite soon, Jo was calm. She lay as before, with her ankles crossed, arms by her sides.

Warily, Gee watched her sister. In the grey daylight she did look extraordinarily like Aunt Alice as a girl. And lay here on her father's bed.

Turning her head to smile ingratiatingly, as if the previous violence had meant nothing, or hadn't even occurred, Jo stroked and patted the bed. "You do agree, don't you? It's a lovely bed."

"I don't know how you can bear to sleep in it," Gee said tightly.

"Why ever not?" Jo's eyes were wide and childlike. "It's *so* comfortable, *so* welcoming. A truly beautiful bed."

"Perhaps I mean, *I* couldn't."

"Why ever *not?*"

Gee considered how to put it. "Physical repulsion, I suppose." Her voice was harsh.

Jo moved pillows, propped herself against them, and gazed fully at Gee. "You don't understand, do you? You just don't get it. You never did get it."

"Don't get what?" Gee was jittery again. Her sister lounged in her Alice-blue gown, in her parents' bed. In her mother's womb, or her father's arms. Or both.

"I don't feel like that at *all*. I feel as if—as if I have at last *come home*."

"I'm going," Gee said, "goodbye."

"And *you*——" Jo shrieked as Gee ran downstairs, "you're jealous, you were *always* jealous. It was me he loved, not you, it was me, me, me, me, *me*——"

Gee's heart was choking her as she fought to open the front door. Something had stuck—the handle wouldn't turn. Reeling away, she ran through the house to the kitchen, past shining new machines, out through the back door, slam, down the path where columbines had once leaned and her mother had waited to tell them about Sam, towards the gap where used to be her tree. There she was halted. A great hole gaped, a heap of dirt waited: it was exactly like a grave.

Chapter Thirty Two

GEE WATCHED HER MOTHER and was mesmerised and soothed. Miriam sat on her sofa, a pot-plant on her knee, patiently picking out shrivelled leaves and dropping them into a wastepaper basket. Inch by inch she turned the pot, inspecting, selecting.

"So," she said, "*are* you going to New York?"

"Depends."

"On what?" Miriam shot her a hard glance. "You don't have to worry about *me*."

"I'm not worried about you. Anyway, I would nip back on regular visits. You'd probably get sick of the sight of me. And they do have telephones in New York."

"All right smarty-pants. I mean, don't hesitate on my account. I'm fine, fit as a flea. Being in your seventies isn't so very old these days, is it? Used to think it was, but I felt older a year ago than I do now. Nothing to do with years." Miriam snorted. "My new G.P., nice young bloke, says I could make it to a hundred. God forbid, I said."

"There you are then. No need to worry about you."

"So what else is there to stop you? Not Josephine? She'll be all right. Goes a bit doolally sometimes, like I said, but—— I suppose Simon told you about the dramas? He is *so* good to her, a lot of sons wouldn't have the patience. But she'll be fine once over the shock."

"What shock? I haven't spoken to Simon since the funeral. In fact both my nephew and niece have been pretty bloody elusive lately, though now I think I understand why."

"Ah." Miriam looked gratifyingly guilty. "The house."

"What shock?" Gee said again. Had her mother known about Jo and Sebastian?

"The shock of leaving Eric. At last. Being on her own for the first time. Two different things—thinking about it, *doing* it. *You* know. But you're more independent, you could handle it."

Gee thought: *Oh, sure.* But she said: "So tell me about these dramas."

"It was right after Sebastian died, before you got back from New Zealand. Jo was staying with Simon and his family for a few days. He thought she was behaving weirdly—*erratically*, was his word. Playing music until after midnight—loud, same song again and again, dancing and singing, driving Simon and his wife nuts and waking the baby."

"The perfect house-guest, then."

"I'll say. And then one night in the small hours, Josephine went out and floated about London in her nightie. No kidding. They hadn't even heard her leave. She was after revenge—so she told Simon later. Shoving something disgusting, as she put it, through certain people's letterboxes, including Eric's. *She* thought it was hilarious." Miriam rolled her eyes.

Gee shivered. "I wonder she wasn't arrested."

"Luckily for her, a cab driver spotted her running down the middle of the road. Like some sort of wraith, I should imagine. Anyway, he did the decent thing and brought her home. Simon took her to her therapist. *She* gave Josephine some new pills and they settled her down. I suppose she still takes them. Simon's keeping an eye on her. They called it nervous reaction to upheaval and stress. It's true to say, on top of everything, she *was* terribly upset about Sebastian. How did she seem to you, anyway?"

Carefully, Gee said: "A bit—um, odd. Aggressive. Maybe *not* taking the pills. I'll ring Simon later and suggest he talks to her shrink. I'd keep your distance for a bit. You and I can't help her. Let's leave it to the experts."

"Pah, I'm not going back *there*. If she wants, she can visit me here." Miriam added apologetically: "She swore me to secrecy about the house. Wanted to surprise you."

"She did." Gee paused. "She always has."

"D'you know what? Before she signed on the dotted line, she had the cheek to ask me to promise that Doug wouldn't get any of the money! I ask you." Miriam's laughter rang with scorn. "She must take me for a complete moron. As if Doug would be interested! He's *very* well off, I can tell you—though I didn't tell *Josephine* that. Told her I'd spend my money on toy-boys and cannabis and gambling if I wanted, and if *she* didn't buy the house somebody else would." Miriam laughed again. "So she signed. She *wanted* the place, *fixed* on it. Well. You know Josephine."

Exhausted, Gee changed the subject. "How is Doug?"

"He's a damn good friend, is Doug. Good *to* me, good *for* me. Heavens, I never thought I'd say that about any man, let alone at my time of life."

"Let's drink to that," said Gee. "That's the best news I've had all day."

"There's ice in the freezer. I'll have a whisky."

Doug might be a magician, never mind friend. Gee watched Miriam inspecting her refreshed plant with satisfaction. Never in her life had she seen her mother so relaxed.

During dinner, Miriam grinned at her and said: "Shall I come?"

"Where?"

"New York. I don't mean to live, soppy. You should see your face, I suppose you thought I'd gone senile after all. I mean to *visit*, when you're settled in Caro's loft thingy. I've never been to New York. Doug says it's exciting. I think I'd like it."

"I dare say you would. Mind, there's nothing to stop you visiting New York whether I go there or not."

"That's true. But it wouldn't be the same without you to show me the sights."

"When I've sold the house I'll decide."

Miriam looked at her. "Is *he* in New York? The one you told me about?"

"Ben. I'm not sure. Probably."

"Hm. Well," Miriam said, "if you don't go, you'll never know. But you'll always regret not finding out. Believe me. Remember I told you how I nearly left? What I didn't tell you was that a few years later I nearly left again. I'd heard he'd been divorced. Free at last. But I was scared stiff he'd lost interest. I used to imagine myself finding him—and he was in some other woman's arms. I said to myself, if he wanted to, *he'd* get in touch with *me*. But he wouldn't, actually; I'd told him first time around I couldn't leave and that was that. So I was just making excuses to myself. Cowardice, actually. See?"

Gee saw. Had lived a similar imaginary scene: walking down Fifth Avenue, seeing Ben from the back, knowing his head, his walk, his shoulders—and he was hand in hand with someone fair and beautiful, quite unlike herself, and they looked at each other with that intimate smile. And she too had made cowardly excuses. Seb's work had been international enough to earn him a *New York Times* obituary: Ben would have seen. *He* could've got in touch with *her*. But really, she knew he wouldn't. It was her move.

"What I want most," she saw suddenly, "is for Ben to know that I really did leave. Before."

BREAKING THE SPEED LIMIT before dawn, Gee felt as if power streamed from her body through her leather soles directly into the engine. Supercharged, lightweight, she might easily fly, so acute was her sense of liberation. No unwanted passengers now, in her vehicle or in her life. The nearly deserted motorway was smooth and straight. The streak of dawn light in the sky ahead might have happened in her brain.

Lying awake in Miriam's spare bedroom, her mind humming, she'd heard her mother filling a kettle and caught the creeping smell of her first cigarette. Once fortified by nicotine and tea, Miriam did not sleep. It was all the permission Gee needed.

"Beating the traffic?" Her unsurprised mother dropped bread into the toaster. "I expect you've got a lot to do in London."

Visible in the light from the kitchen window, a robin was singing outside as Gee wolfed her breakfast.

"Listen to that," Miriam said, "silly ass thinks it's daytime, just like us." And when Gee kissed her goodbye, she said: "I can see by your face something's cooking. I won't ask. I 'spect you'll tell me when you're ready."

"I'll let you know I'm back safely. Then I'll be busy—so don't expect to hear for a while." On impulse, she put her arms around her mother in a brief, strong hug.

Miriam called after her: "Good luck!"

One particular, sharp memory in the dark early hours had done it. Ben's voice,

Ben's look, Ben's hands, Ben's soft cotton shirt—the very smell of him, crisp and fresh. Every detail. She was with him again on one of their earliest evenings together, when they'd sat in that bistro and he'd told her about his youthful mistakes. How clearly she could hear his voice: *If you painted a picture of my life up to now, before you, that would be it: a gigantic mountain of goddam garbage.*

It would be the very last thing she did in her studio. She would open her brain and yank the garbage out, every accumulated scrap, and throw it on to canvas. And, however painful, she wouldn't stop until she was emptied.

NEVER HAD SHE PAINTED with such energy and concentration. The answering machine stacked up messages. Food was irregular and straight from tins, cutlery tossed in the dishwasher. For over two weeks she slept on top of her bed, still dressed; without showering, changing, cooking, or any ordinary routine. To prevent neighbours raising an alarm, she retrieved mail and papers from the front door.

When the last stroke was complete, she sat opposite the canvas and stared at it dazed, drunkenly. For perhaps an hour she was paralysed; then, creepingly, she knew her body smelled and her eyes were hot lead.

And it was time to talk to him.

HI, SHE SAID MILDLY. It's me, Gee.

> *Georgina? Well, this is a surprise. I didn't expect to hear from you again.*

I wanted to tell you I've finished what might be the best painting I've ever done. It may also mean I've finished with you at last. It seemed only right to tell you.

> *Finished with me? That's not very kind.*

I don't mean to be kind or unkind. I mean to be indifferent. Dispassionate. Simple fact is, I'm free of you. You remember I said that understanding wasn't forgiveness—*à propos* Jo—because, for godsake, where's your bloody self-control? But I do pity you—and now, none of it has to bung up my mind any more. I've thrown it all out on my wonderfully horrible garbage heap and burst through my Painter's Block.

> *I have no idea what you're talking about.*

You can say that again. But it doesn't matter now. I don't even feel, in any *real* way, as if you're related to me. I feel more related to your Grandma McIvor. And you know what? I'm *not* related to her—and nor were *you*, it turns out. Not by blood. She wasn't your real grandma and Grandpa McIvor wasn't your real grandpa. Your *real* Grandpa was his brother Keith—a charmer and fornicator, which might explain a lot. Your mother Jemima was Grandma McIvor's adopted daughter. How about that?

> *My, you are inventive, Georgina.*

I know. How d'you like my painting?

It's a bit, well, chaotic, isn't it?

That's the word.

You always were one for disobeying the rules.

Hmm, you should know. Which rules, exactly, Dad?

The rules of composition, of course, and what things really look like. Heaven knows, you're the one who had the art education. You're like those people who refuse to write poetry that rhymes, just to be different. Showing off. I never did understand why you didn't want to paint beautiful landscapes and proper portraits, like my father used to do. It's not as if you don't have the talent.

Wow, thanks, Dad. Look, this is you, here. And here, and here. This is you acting like a good Daddy when you weren't, and this is out-and-out *bad* Daddy. The *sincere* bits of good Daddy didn't get painted: I decided not to chuck them out as they weren't garbage—and I guess that's as near as I'll ever get to forgiveness. And look, this is Alice, this is Jo. A good likeness, I think you must agree? Over here is Jo *now*, in case you need proof that you screwed her life up. This is me here—and here. Here's Mum—before, after, and now. This is Sam, and this is my dead twin, Charlotte, and the grave of two innocent slain caterpillars and a robin, and someone I could have harmed, the little boy down the lane. Here's Jo on the beach and a man I would've liked to kill. He looks rather like you, hm? I also wanted you dead, and this is the wishbone—the *merrythought*—upon which I wished for your demise. It's the real thing, the actual one, I glued it on.

Here's Seb, as he was and as he became. Speaking of death, I assume you'd heard? Maybe you've bumped into him in the saloon bar at the Holy Martyrs. And speaking of fornicators, this is Seb having it off with Jo—no, I'm not making it up—and with various other blondes. It's a shame, isn't it, because Seb could be so nice, and I did love him at the start—so that's not on the garbage heap. But he fucked things up and I didn't help, didn't seem to know how to. Pathetic.

This is me pathetic. Here's Miss Pullinger of the hamster jaws, a sneaky would-be child-molester, you might've got on well with her. Oh, and lots more people, but I can't give you the full guided tour.

Certain people are *not* included simply because no aspect of them belongs on a garbage heap. Your sister Mildred, for one, and my good friend Caro who used to make you nervous and you had the cheek to call her a show-off, like Jo did, but she's nothing of the kind, and Ben isn't here either, because he's the best man that ever happened to me, and none of your damn business so don't even ask—and oh, a crowd of people who've walked in and out of my life but are not forgotten, none of them goes in the garbage. Significant loose ends, I call them, and some might get tied one day, who knows.

Remember my sycamore tree? You, as good Daddy, taught me the best way to climb a tree and to come down. You taught me a lot, I hand you that. Then you spoiled it all, you fool. I've painted my beautiful tree as it is now—murdered. It's garbage. As is the weight of sheer fucking rage that you put on me. I've put it all into paint at last. And I'm not angry any more.

Nobody would buy that painting. It's obscene.

They can't have it. It's for the artist's collection.

Well, that's something. At least nobody else will have to look at it.

Worried what people might think of you?

You're being ridiculous. You can't seriously imagine anyone would recognise me, or anyone else for that matter, from that mess?

We shall see. I didn't say it wouldn't be *shown*. It will some day. But marked Not For Sale.

I sincerely hope you will do something a lot better than that.

My next painting, since you ask, will be about Grandma McIvor's trunk, and all the tragic and wonderful things that emerged from it. But I mustn't confuse you with things you wouldn't understand. The truth is, if I hadn't opened that trunk I wouldn't have been able to paint this heap of garbage that you so pleasingly dislike. Or be able to have this little chat. And d'you know what's so good about our conversation?

I can't say I do. Nor do I see any purpose in going on with it.

Excellent. But just let me tell you that the best thing about this conversation is the very last word—which, believe it or not Dad, I say kindly. And that's Goodbye.

IN THE YEAR OF HER DEATH, Grandma McIvor wrote: *In the course of life, we encounter people to whom we feel more closely bound than to any blood relation (to whom we may feel quite unrelated). There is a kinship, a harmony, within the soul—if souls exist.*

Harriet, Emmie, Jemima and Henry were more truly my family than any tied by blood, with the exception of the children of my marriage who occupy a unique place. As does she, the woman who waits in the shadows.

"TELL ME AT ONCE," Caro commanded, as they settled into bistro chairs. "You look great," she added.

"I'm out of the shadows."

Gee led up to her moment.

"I heard a woman on the radio the other day. A physicist or astronomer—talking about the size of the universe. Did you hear it?"

Caro laughed. "Not quite my thing."

"She said there are one hundred thousand *million* stars in our own galaxy alone."

"That's impressive," Caro said. "Pass the bottle."

"But she also said, we know there are at *least* ten thousand million *other galaxies* in space. You can't possibly imagine it. My mind, as they say, boggled. And *then*, get this, she said all the stars and planets and stuff, all those billions of heavenly bodies and all those galaxies we actually *know* about, are just a drop in the ocean of the Universe as a whole. Literally. She reckoned they take up about as much room in the *whole* of space, probably, as a *mere spoonful* of water in the Pacific Ocean. How about that?"

"Aha! But how does she know how big space is?"

"Heaven knows, so to speak. I suspect that's her point. Infinity."

Caro snorted. "Well it's no wonder a person can feel puny."

"I reckon you can look at it two ways," said Gee. "You can think: How can there be any purpose in all this? Or you can think: There *must* be a purpose."

"But how can we know?"

"Exactly. So, I decided the way to cope is to create one's own purpose." Gee made a self-mocking face.

"And is that what got you out of the shadows? A few billion heavenly bodies?"

"I was out by then. This is merely an illustration of my new optimism."

"*Do* get on with it."

"I *did* it Caro—broke through the block, busted out, painted my head off—and I've got this stack of exciting paintings jostling for room in my mind—"

"Wonderful! This is the best news since—"

"And I'm off for a weekend in New York. On a fishing trip."

"*Ben?*"

"Got a buyer for the house. Probate's pretty well sorted. So I decided—*purpose*. Do it. Oh God—don't know what I'll say or if he'll listen and I'm scared shitless but I've found out his number and I've got to *know*, haven't I, or spend my life loathing myself. I'd like a spell in New York anyway, Ben or no Ben. Might be for a few months, might be indefinitely. But I do want—I *need*—a whole new world—"

"But you want to go it alone. I know. No crutches. No kindly Caro-shoulder to cry on. Not even in a flash loft in SoHo."

"You don't sound too surprised. Do you mind?"

"Mind? I'm delighted old pal. I had a bet with myself you'd get to this point in the end. I was merely dangling a carrot."

"LISTEN," GEE SAID to her mother when she telephoned to say goodbye. "I want to read you something I read yesterday."

> I look back on my life now, on my seventieth birthday, and wonder about whether it has had any purpose, or whether purpose is a human delusion and we are quite meaningless despite our little achievements. Nobody on earth knows the *point* of our existence, though many claim to do so. Where, for example, is the *point* of a young life cut short? But all our lives are brief, even when we survive to my age.
>
> It is argued we cannot understand 'God's' mysteries, and that 'His' purpose

will be revealed. But that is a *non*-argument concocted for comfort, to fill an otherwise frightening void. Why should a void be frightening? It is of infinity, not in itself harmful. Why should it not be filled by our own determination? If we so choose we can rid ourselves of the detritus of the past, retain those things that fortify us, and *use* our time. We cannot know what is in store, yet we cocoon ourselves from this fact by wrapping ourselves in plans, as if tomorrow's arrival were inevitable. It is not. It was not for my good husband nor for poor Margaret Esther. My losses were brutal shocks, forcing a complete change of direction. At such times we are certain we cannot continue; but eventually we say to ourselves that we *must*. The alternative would be to remain shivering in dread of the possible future—dread of life itself. It is *we* who must decide our purpose, even if we fail to decide on a greater meaning.

Miriam asked: "Is that your old Grandma McIvor talking, or you?"
"Both," Gee answered.

IT TOOK AN HOUR of seizing and dropping the receiver before she could complete his number. And then it was ringing, oh God it was ringing. Don't let him be there. Let there be a machine. Shaking all over, she had no idea what to say. Wouldn't be able to speak anyway.

That was his voice. Not a machine. His own voice, saying his whole name and number. Not many Americans did that. She might choke on her own silence.

Ben said: "Hello? Anyone out there?"

"Did you know," she said faintly, "there are more than a hundred thousand million stars in our galaxy, and besides that there are at least ten thousand million other galaxies in the Universe? It's a lot, isn't it?"

She heard a shock in his breathing, and a soft laugh.

"It's no wonder," she added, silently thanking Caro, "that a person can feel puny."

"I didn't know that," Ben said, and she could tell he was grinning. "But it's the news I've been waiting for all my life. Where the hell are you?"

Inevitably, she was going to cry. "Ben. This puny person is really sorry. I'm sorry to be so late."

"The hell with that. Where are you?"

"But I want you to know that I really did—"

"—I know you did. You wouldn't have called otherwise. Gee! Are you actually *here*, for Chrissakes?"

"I'm six blocks away." She hadn't meant to ask, but couldn't help it: "Am I *too* late?"

"Just get in a cab. Get your sweet puny self over here. Who cares what time it is?"

Thanks and Acknowledgements

I MUST GIVE heartfelt thanks to several people who patiently allowed me to pick their brains or bookshelves on the subject of the mid 19th century.

They are:

Philip Atkins, Librarian (now retired) at the National Railway Museum in York, who guided me through complicated railway timetables and routes, and generally cast light on the many hardships and mixed pleasures of travelling by train in Britain over 150 years ago.

The Headmistress of St George's School for Girls, Dr Judith McClure, and the now-retired Secretary to the Principal of the Mary Erskine School, Mrs Dorothy Silver, both of whom added to my own education by pointing me in the direction of many sources of information on the schooling of girls in the Victorian era, including:

Anne Morrison and Anna Pearse of the Central Library, Edinburgh, who both very helpfully supplied me with book recommendations and miscellaneous advertisements and newspaper cuttings in my search for close-up accounts of the personal experiences of those who were sent off to Schools for Young Ladies in Edinburgh in the 1840s.

I am also indebted to Don Charlwood, author of *The Long Farewell*, and Helen R. Woolcock, author of *Rights of Passage*, who in different ways opened my eyes to the adventures, dangers and horrors of being an emigrant in wooden, overcrowded sailing ships taking months to reach Australia or New Zealand in the 1850s—if indeed they reached their destination at all.

Particular gratitude goes to Mary Sandys and Broo Doherty, who were the first to spot potential in this novel and to nudge me forward encouragingly; also to Peter Brookesmith, who wielded his editor's pen (mightier than any sword) with gimlet-eyed zeal, to the considerable benefit of the book.

FIRECREST
FICTION

WWW.FIRECREST-FICTION.COM

PUBLISHERS AND REPUBLISHERS
OF REMARKABLE ORIGINAL FICTION

Facts About Our Fiction

FireCrest Fiction is an independent imprint dedicated to publishing genuinely creative novels, old and new. Books like ours are now rarely issued (or re-issued) by the big conglomerates, because they're not deemed to be immediately profitable. Our books resist easy definition, don't fit any preconceived genre, and don't mix easily with a mass-marketing mentality.

FireCrest Fiction was founded to create an outlet for authors who are striving to keep the art of the novel alive, and to put some neglected twentieth-century masterworks back in print where they belong.

If you have a favourite out-of-print masterpiece that you'd like republished, get in touch with us through our website, and we'll see what we can do. If you believe you're a misunderstood genius with a modern masterpiece on your hands that's going to waste, read our Notes for Authors on our website, and go from there.

Real Novels

Our authors address the human condition. They write quirky, enjoyable, innovative, ingenious and provocative novels that will leave you pondering them, and their implications, long after you've read the last page.
Some of them will also make you laugh out loud.

How to Find our Books

FireCrest titles are available to the book trade through major distributors – Bertram's and Gardner's in the UK; Ingram, Barnes & Noble, and Baker & Taylor in the USA; and worldwide through Amazon.com or Amazon.co.uk.
This means you can order FireCrest books online, at your local library, or *through your local bookshop.*

Republished by FireCrest as a companion volume to *The Merrythought*

No End to Yesterday
SHELAGH MACDONALD

A Whitbread prizewinner in 1977, this beautifully poised novel chronicles the extraordinary upbringing and early adulthood of Marjory Bell in the 1920s and '30s, in a rambling South London house teeming with eccentric uncles and aunts and their hangers-on. By turns harsh, kind, immoral, hypocritical, hilarious and spiteful, they are dominated by Marjory's unrepentantly Victorian grandmother.

Marjory is motherless, her father a remote, weekend visitor to 'Gran's house', where Marjory belongs, but is isolated. She soon learns to hide her sensitivity as she masters how to withstand her grandmother's cruelties. Gran would crush her individuality, or crush her entirely: Marjory has to bring all her intelligence, tenacity and humour into play to survive. But she does survive. Glimpses of her adult life tell us the price she pays – but how she also never loses her wit, integrity and spark for life.

No End to Yesterday won the Whitbread as a book for teenagers, but it's an adult story. Reviewing the paperback edition in 1980, Yvonne White wrote: 'The injustices and mental cruelties suffered by Marjory during her childhood are conveyed in some of the best writing for teenagers there is available. They should pass it on to their mothers who will find it just as powerful.'.
Amazon currently gives it four stars with this comment:
'A fascinating book worthy of both children's and adult attention – thought provoking – a fine novel [that] deserves a wider audience.'

At the Whitbread awards ceremony, Lynne Reid Banks said: 'Out of the scores of books which were submitted, one… was entirely different in style, texture and approach from any of the others. The writing showed signs of a literary gift far beyond what one normally expects in children's books or *finds* in adult novels. … But the characters are not the only factors in the book which leap from the page into the reader's imagination and embed themselves there. The whole environment and the period are imparted… . The imagination is engaged, pricked awake by the author's skill … and finds itself capable of evoking settings, smells, textures and even the strongly "other" emotions of that earlier time.'

ISBN 978-1-906174-04-0
204 PAGES – £9.50/$18.95

Printed in the United Kingdom
by Lightning Source UK Ltd.
133446UK00001B/360/P